THE LAST TEST OF COURAGE

CHRIS GLATTE

SEVERN RIVER
PUBLISHING

Severn River Publishing
www.SevernRiverBooks.com

This is a work of fiction. Names, characters, businesses, places, events and incidents are either the products of the author's imagination or used in a fictitious manner. Any resemblance to actual persons, living or dead, or actual events is purely coincidental.

ISBN: 978-1-64875-405-0 (Paperback)

ALSO BY CHRIS GLATTE

A Time to Serve Series

A Time to Serve

The Gathering Storm

The Scars of Battle

The Last Test of Courage

The Light After the Storm

Tark's Ticks Series

Tark's Ticks

Valor's Ghost

Gauntlet

Valor Bound

Dark Valley

War Point

164th Regiment Series

The Long Patrol

Bloody Bougainville

Bleeding the Sun

Operation Cakewalk (Novella)

Standalone Novel

Across the Channel

To find out more about Chris Glatte and his books, visit

severnriverbooks.com/authors/chris-glatte

1

Norfolk, Virginia
February 21, 1944

Abby Cooper's mind drifted as she turned slow circles over the Atlantic off the Virginia coast, awaiting instructions from the navy boys onshore. The T-6 Texan's flight stick felt good in her gloved hands. Even in late February, the cockpit warmed as the sun's heat passed through the plexiglass. Any warmer and she'd need to pull the gloves off. She hated flying with sweaty hands.

Since becoming a WASP flyer, she'd moved from Sweetwater, Texas, to Norfolk, Virginia, for her new job towing targets for the U.S. Navy. She enjoyed it, but she'd already put her transfer request in for the ferry pilot program. She'd always intended to be a ferry pilot, but had signed up for the towing gig because of the reliable schedule. Her priority had been to be there when her best friend, Beatrice Malinsky, gave birth to her first child.

She thought back to that happy day as she slowly orbited. She'd gotten a call, not from Beatrice, but from Sal. He told her that the doctor expected her to go into labor any day over the next week. She still didn't know how she felt about Sal and would rather have heard from Beatrice, but Bea had been bedridden over the past week and Sal had been there to take care of her, so she couldn't complain.

Sal had come from her past life in Seattle and into her new life in Sweetwater, completely out of the blue. At first, she'd resented him being there. She still hated him for his involvement in her father's illegal and immoral business dealings. She thought he'd be better than that—expected it, actually. But her attitude softened as she saw how he and Beatrice got along together. There was an undeniable spark between them and it wasn't just because Beatrice was in such a vulnerable position. They couldn't take their eyes off one another. It reminded her of her own relationship with Clyde.

After Sal's call, she asked for a few days off. Since the weather had been awful and would be for the foreseeable future, her commanding officer reluctantly agreed. Sweetwater was some 1,500 miles away. She'd hopped a train and started the long rail ride spanning nearly half the country.

Miraculously, she arrived in Sweetwater on the very day Beatrice went into labor. When she'd burst into Beatrice's rented house, and saw the note telling her they'd gone to the hospital, she'd nearly cried in frustration. All that way, and she might've already missed it? She hopped on the rusty bicycle she found in the garage and pedaled as fast as she could to the hospital.

She burst in and saw Sal pacing in the waiting room of the tiny hospital. Nurses rushed back and forth from a room. When the door opened, she could hear her friend's grunts and groans. She rushed to Sal and gasped, "Am I too late?"

Sal never let anything bother him, but Abby saw his pale, sweaty face and wondered if something terrible had happened. But he gave her a tight smile and pointed at the door where a nurse had just entered. "I don't think so. She's in there. They won't let me in."

"Well, of course not. It wouldn't be appropriate," she said in exasperation.

She burst into the room. Two harried nurses looked up from their tasks and glared. A young doctor sat on a wooden stool propped firmly in front of Beatrice's propped up legs. He never looked away from the task at hand.

Beatrice's red, sweat-streaked face changed from pain to joy for just a fraction of an instant when she saw her best friend. "You made it," she gasped, then was interrupted with a long, painful contraction.

The baby, a beautiful little girl with a full mop of hair, came only an hour later. Abby thought it had to be the most beautiful moment of her young life. The shriveled little being squawked, lodging a formal complaint about her new accommodations, but quickly quieted when she latched onto Beatrice's breast and enjoyed her first meal.

Abby snapped from the happy memory when the radio squelched in her ear. A tinny voice said, "Red One, this is Zeke Four. Do you copy? Over."

She'd missed the first call. "This is Red One. Please repeat last. Over."

"Red One, you asleep up there? Over."

"Negative Zeke Four. You broke up. Over."

"Red One, the shooters are ready for you. Unfurl the target and start your pass when ready. Over."

"Zeke Four, starting my turn now. Unfurling the target in three minutes. Over."

"Roger. Proceed. Over."

Abby found the ship that would shoot at her. She chuckled. That's what it always felt like. She imagined the young sailors down there on their guns, licking their lips in anticipation. She hoped they weren't complete novices this time. She'd had plenty of those already and sometimes she wondered if they really *were* shooting at her. At least the gunners with more experience actually could hit the target, but sometimes she wondered how they'd ever hit a maneuvering aircraft with ill intent.

She leveled off, checked her speed and altitude, then unfurled the target. The lines unwound behind her, then the target snapped into place with a whip-crack sound. She felt the slight tug of resistance and adjusted her throttle and RPMs accordingly.

She radioed. "Zeke Four, this is Red One passing through the target zone in thirty seconds. Over."

"Red One, roger. The cannon cockers are standing by. Over."

"Remind 'em to aim for the target, not me . . . over," she said only half-jokingly. Zeke Four didn't respond, and she wondered if the entire ship's crew listened in on the frequency. Most likely, but she didn't regret giving them a subtle reminder.

She kept the T-6 on a steady course. She glanced at the ship, sitting broadside so all the gunners would have a chance. The trainers told her not to look. She'd have the urge to evade instinctively, but she couldn't help herself. She always looked.

Tracers suddenly streamed up at her. She ducked, even though it wouldn't save her if the gunners hit her fuselage with their big 20mm cannons and .50-caliber machine gun rounds. She heard the roar of multiple weapons firing all at once. Even from this distance, it sounded terrifying. What would it sound like if those rounds struck her aircraft? So far, that hadn't happened. None of the WASP flyers had experienced such incidents yet. A few close calls, but no friendly ordnance had struck an airframe.

As she finished her first pass and flew out of range, she looked back at the target. It was still completely intact. *Nice shooting, boys*, she mocked to herself.

She made a wide turn and approached the shooting gallery from the opposite direction this time. The image of the captain who'd given her final check ride came to mind. He'd been very upfront about his combat missions in Europe. He knew what those rounds hitting his aircraft felt like. She wished she'd quizzed him more about it. He must be back overseas by now. Was he still alive?

Her thoughts shifted to her husband, Clyde. His letters came with regularity now that they had taken him off the line and he was back in Australia with the rest of his paratrooper unit. His letters had taken on their regular upbeat tone, a far cry from the one he'd written her from the front lines. That one had chilled her to the bone and made her worry not only about his physical safety but also about his mental well-being. He'd obviously experienced things he didn't talk about in his letters. She hoped one day he'd be able to open up to her, but for now, she was happy to know he was safely out of the crosshairs.

She settled against the parachute she sat on. She set her speed and altitude for another pass through the shooting range. "Zeke Four, this is Red One, making another pass. Over."

"Roger Red One, they're ready for you. Over."

She settled into the cockpit as low as she could manage. She peeked over the fuselage at the exact moment every gun opened fire. The tracers seemed much closer this time. She clutched the stick and fought the urge to push her throttle. With more experienced gun crews, they sometimes varied the speed, but it could be dangerous to the pilots because the gunners might overcompensate their leads.

She tore her eyes away from the blinking muzzle flashes and concentrated on flying. Suddenly she felt and heard a sound she'd feared hearing since starting this job—heavy bullets hitting metal.

The stick shook in her hand and the left rudder pedal slammed into the sole of her foot. She sat upright and looked out the back. A large-caliber bullet or cannon shell had passed through her rudder, shredding the bottom half.

She instinctively cut the line towing the target and sped up out of the gunnery range. The radio squawked, but she ignored it while she fought to control the aircraft. She tested the elevator by pulling back on the stick. It felt a little heavier, but her nose lifted with the input.

She finally answered the desperate calls from Zeke Four. "Zeke Four, I'm okay. Some dummy took out half my rudder, but I won't have a problem making it back to the airfield. Over."

"Thank God, Red One. Turn on heading of one eight seven. The Tower's been notified and you're cleared to land. Emergency vehicles are standing by. Contact the tower as you approach. Over."

"Roger Zeke Four. I hope that sailor gets what's coming to him. Over."

"Just get her down safely, Red One. Over and out."

Abby flew the heading, keeping tabs on the aircraft all the way. They trained to expect the unexpected while flying, but nothing else went wrong. The rudder felt odd, but there was enough of it left to maintain good flight characteristics. It just wasn't as responsive and had a little stiffness and shudder to it now.

She landed without incident. Firetrucks and ambulances screeched out to where she parked and men dressed in fire suits surrounded the T-6 holding water hoses. A mechanic hustled up the wing and assisted her with the harness. She stepped out of the fuselage and onto the wing, then waved at all the rescue crew personnel. "I'm fine. I'm fine."

Once clear of the airplane, crews descended on it as though it would burst into flames at any moment. She said to the mechanic who led her toward the hangar, "They're overreacting, don't you think?"

"They haven't had an emergency in months. They're itching for some action."

The mechanic passed her off to Glenda Ronnistat, her commanding officer. She watched the emergency crews poring over the T-6. She shifted her gaze to Abby. "You okay, Abby?"

"Of course. It's just a ding out of the rudder. No problem at all."

"Captain Raleigh, the ship's CO, called to ask about you. He also apologized for his gunner's shooting skills, or lack thereof."

"Well, I'm fine. I suppose the T-6 is out of commission for a few days, though."

"Yes, well, that won't matter. You feel up to flying tonight?"

Abby hadn't been slated to fly that night, Agatha Bailey had been slotted to fly spotlight practice.

"Sure thing. Something happen to Agatha?"

"She's sick. She can't keep anything down. The doctor grounded her, fearing she's too dehydrated to fly. You haven't flown spotlights, have you?"

"Not yet, no."

"Well, they're a hoot and no one's shooting anything except bright lights at you. Plus, you'll be flying the P-40."

Abby's eyes lit up. She'd flown the P-40 a few hours and loved it. It was a true warbird, a real pursuit aircraft. "That sounds a whole lot better at the moment." She laughed and followed Glenda into the office.

"You've got a few hours to get some food and a shower if you want it. You go up at 2200 hours."

"So late?"

"The moon sets about that time. The CO wants complete darkness for this one. His boys are heading overseas soon and he wants to make the exercise as hard as possible for them. Briefing's at 2130 hours."

"Okay, see you then." Abby hustled to the barracks. She wanted to read up on the P-40 as much as possible before the flight. She felt comfortable in any aircraft, but being prepared was a hallmark of safety and a basic tenet of aviation.

Once in the barracks, she held out her hand. It shook slightly, and she formed a fist and squeezed. On the surface, the incident hadn't really affected her, but perhaps her subconscious had something more to say about that.

~

ABBY HAD TIME FOR A MEAL, so she joined other WASP flyers in the mess hall. She sat among them and the questions about being hit came quickly. She answered them as best she could. Chandra Moore asked, "Does it bother you?"

"What? Being shot at? It's part of the job."

"I mean, how close you came to buying the farm. If that cannon round hit even a foot further up, it would've torn the T-6 in half. At that elevation, you'd barely have time to get out, let alone pull your parachute."

Abby gulped. She hadn't thought about just how close she'd come to disaster. Up till now, it almost seemed like a lark, but Chandra's question hit her hard. She'd literally dodged a bullet.

"I guess I hadn't really thought about it that much, but you're right, it was close." She pictured what would've happened: the tail would've ripped off, sending the front-heavy fuselage end over end. Most likely, she wouldn't have had a chance to unhook her harness. She would've certainly died on impact or drowned soon after hitting the ocean.

Chandra placed a hand gently on her shoulder. "Sorry, I didn't mean to spook you. Just kinda makes you think."

Abby forced a smile. "It's okay. I guess I haven't really had time to fully process things."

"You're going up again tonight?"

"Yes, but no one will shoot anything at me this time . . . well, except light beams, I guess."

Chandra slurped beef stew, minus the beef. Between bites she said, "Have you done that yet? The night attacks, I mean?"

"Not yet. Sounds fun and I'm thrilled to be flying a real pursuit again. The P-40's a gem of an airplane."

"Just watch your speed. They get fast, quickly, especially in a dive."

"I'll be careful," Abby assured her.

She finished the rest of her meal in silence. The other flyers left by ones and twos until she found herself alone with just her thoughts. She shivered, thinking how close she'd come to dying. Clyde would never forgive her. The irony hit her. He was overseas fighting a stalwart enemy, yet she'd been the one that nearly died on the very coast he struggled to defend. Would they send him home if she died? She thought so and it just added to the irony—by dying, she might save her own husband from the same fate.

She stood abruptly. This kind of thinking did no good and probably made things worse. She vowed not to think about the incident for another moment. She had a mission to prepare for.

A few hours later, she sat in the cockpit of the P-40 and marveled at the lit-up instrument panel. It wasn't too different from the Texan, just more knobs and gizmos. The seat didn't feel as comfortable as the plush Texan, but she'd get used to it. The only padding came from the heavy parachute she sat upon.

The night air blew through the open canopy as she painstakingly went through the engine start-up sequence. The engine sparked to life and smoke billowed into the cockpit. Abby loved the smell, and the power she felt at her fingertips was intoxicating. Every light at the airfield glowed, illuminating her immediate surroundings. Beyond the lighted area, darkness prevailed. She couldn't see much beyond the pool of light, but she'd soon be flying through the inky blackness. Night flying came with its own level of terror, but at least it wasn't a cross-country flight.

The tower controller cleared her to taxi, and she weaved the high-nosed Warhawk side-to-side in order to see the taxi-way. The controls felt solid in her hands and beneath the soles of her feet.

Once on the runway, she lined up on the centerline and smoothly pushed the throttle forward. She pressed the rudder pedals to counteract the torque of the large spinning propeller blades as the aircraft picked up speed. The faster the aircraft traveled, the less input she needed to give.

The tail wheel lifted and the P-40 eased off the tarmac when her speed hit 150 mph.

In an instant, she left the comforting glow of the airfield lights and entered the darkness. The transition left her slightly breathless and she felt a momentary spike of panic deep in her guts, but it quickly vanished. She'd trained for this, and exhilaration quickly overcame any fear.

She felt the cool breeze and reluctantly closed the cockpit glass, shutting out the wind noise. She climbed away from the glowing airfield and quickly glanced over her gauges. The engine purred like a content alley cat after a meal of stinky fish.

She set her heading and continued climbing until she reached ten thousand feet. She marveled how quickly she'd gained the altitude. The Warhawk had plenty of power.

She imagined what it would be like for the pilots overseas. P-40s had seen a lot of combat so far. Combat pilots had stacked an impressive tally of kills using the P-40 both in the Pacific Theater and the European Theater, but they still complained that the Axis aircraft were superior in many ways.

She glanced at the glowing gauge telling her the gun ports held zero ammo. What would it be like flying into combat with fully loaded gun ports? Flying mock attacks as she'd do tonight would be the closest thing to combat she'd ever see.

She heard the radio crackle in her headset, then heard the laconic voice from the ship she'd be attacking. She radioed back, telling the young man to light up the target.

Even though she couldn't see it, she knew she flew over the ocean some four miles out from shore. Her target would be a floating dock that they'd set on fire only a quarter mile off the port side of the destroyer, which would try to pinpoint her with spotlights.

Even though she flew only a few miles off the East Coast of the United States, she saw no lights. People took light-discipline seriously here. They had spotted more than a few Nazi submarines in the waters beneath her wings. Some merchant marines had given their lives not far from this very spot.

The thought chilled her to the bone. Being blown to smithereens was one thing, but dying of exposure in a cold, relentless sea only miles from home was a different matter. She'd heard stories of bloated bodies washing up on shore—found by ordinary folks out for a morning beach walk.

Suddenly, a flare of light sparked, and she spotted the flames marking the target. She keyed her radio. "Target in sight. Attacking in one minute." Her adrenaline spiked, and she barely heard the acknowledgment reply over the pounding in her ears. She felt like a hunter. She remembered her mother telling her to be a lioness. Well, this was as close as she'd likely ever get.

She lined up on the glowing target and pushed the stick forward, pushing the Warhawk into a dive. She adjusted her position until her eye looked through the gunsight. Her finger went to the trigger even though she knew it would only activate the camera and not the six deadly .50-caliber wing-mounted machine guns.

Beams of light suddenly sliced through the darkness. She ignored them, keeping her dive speed in check and her gunsight centered on the glowing target. The beams of light swung from side to side. From the corner of her eye, it was difficult to tell how far or close the sailors were to spotting her.

With the target filling her gunsight, she depressed the trigger and imagined what it would feel like to unleash such a deadly stream of lead. She kept the trigger mashed for ten seconds, doing the loose math in her head —six hundred index finger–sized bullets would've torn the tiny floating platform apart.

She pulled up only a few yards over the top of the target. Her body weight increased to three times normal as her butt pushed into the seat. She darted into the night and none of the beams of light found her. She couldn't contain the yell, "Yeehaw!" She laughed as she climbed away. She couldn't resist a snappy barrel roll. At night, no one would see.

She calmed herself before calling into the controller. "Spike One, this is Candy Two. I've completed my first pass, preparing for pass number two. Over."

"Roger Candy Two. Proceed with your mission."

She thought she heard disappointment in his voice. She'd completed her attack and hadn't been spotted. She glanced behind and saw the spotlights darting her way, knowing she'd be climbing away from the target, but no light beams came close. Perhaps she'd slow her dive this time to give them a better chance.

She lined up for the attack again. The target still burned, but the flames weren't as robust. She decided to help the navy boys out a little. "Starting my attack, now."

She didn't get a response, but the beams of light pulsed toward her position a moment later. She pulled the throttle back and pushed the nose over until the target centered in her gunsight again. Her finger hovered over the trigger and she split her time between monitoring her speed, the target, and the light beams.

She was just about to pull the trigger when her world turned bright white. She shielded her eyes, but it was too late. All she could see were colorful dots. She pulled on the stick, knowing she might be too late.

She shut her eyes tight as the g-forces built and waited for the crash that would end her young life, but it never came. She opened her eyes to slits and saw the spotlights still illuminated the P-40, but now it came from behind and wasn't as blindingly bright. She blinked away the spots and leveled off, then checked her gauges.

The radio blared in her ears and she noticed the concern in the sailor's voice. "Candy Two, are you okay? Over."

She rubbed her eyes before replying. "Roger Spike One. I'm fine. Your boys got me good, though. Congratulations. Over."

"You got pretty low, Candy Two. Over."

She bit her lower lip but didn't respond. The lights still illuminated her and it annoyed her. She yanked the stick left, then pulled back, reversing her course. The beams of light couldn't keep up and frantically tried to reacquire her but couldn't.

She cursed herself. She wasn't supposed to fly as low as she did, and now she understood the reasoning. Would Glenda find out? Surely the gun cameras would give it away, but they only reviewed them if there was an incident they needed to investigate. She hadn't pressed the trigger on the last pass, so there'd be nothing to see.

She keyed the mic. "You ready for another attack, Spike One? Over."

"Roger Candy Two. Ready when you are. They're raring to go now. Over."

"I won't make it easy on you this time. Over."

She could hear the laughter in his voice. "Give it your best shot, Candy Two. Over."

She climbed to attack altitude and found the target far below. The slices of light searched, but they weren't close. She smiled and realized she loved this job more than anything she'd ever done. She pulled the Warhawk into a loop, then leveled her wings and dove on the target. *I'm a lioness.*

2

East China Sea
Unknown Island, northern Philippines

Frank Cooper sat on the beach and watched the gentle waves of the East China Sea lap against the sand. The rhythmic in and out hiss made his eyes droop. A month had passed since the bizarre game, which had ended the lives of the Japanese sailors and that of Private Glenn Madison. He closed his eyes and thought he could still hear Glenn's pleading calls for his mother as he took his last few breaths.

One of the young native boys suddenly plunged his pointed stick into the depths and soon held up a good-sized flailing fish, skewered just behind the gills. He held it up for Frank to see. Frank's eyes were slits, but he smiled and nodded to the boy.

He'd seen the same scene played out countless times, but the children always looked for his approval. When did youthful joy finally turn to jaded adulthood? Was there a certain age, or did it just happen randomly for each person? He hadn't smiled like that in ages. Such simple lives they lived. Happy lives.

Grinning Bear snorted beside him and woke himself. He startled and sat up abruptly, but quickly relaxed. He rubbed his hair, which had grown much longer than any good marine would find acceptable.

"Dreams?" Frank asked his friend.

"Yeah. I was back on Corregidor."

"Seems like another century."

"Remember the tunnel? Remember how the dust and concrete fell from the ceiling during all those bombardments?" Frank nodded and Grinning Bear continued. "I was suffocating. In the dream, I mean."

Frank gazed out over the empty ocean. "So many men didn't make it out of there. Seems impossible that we're still alive."

"Don't get all introspective on me again. We've got it good, that's all that matters."

"We can't stay here forever, Larry."

Larry Grinning Bear squinted up at him. They'd had this conversation countless times. "We can, actually. But the question is: should we?"

"You having second thoughts again? You know how I feel. We need to get back into the war."

"For all we know, it might already be over and done with."

"That's bullshit and you know it. I thought we agreed on this."

"Yeah, I know. Just easy to talk big when we've got full bellies and plenty of water. Might wish we'd never left if we have to dodge bullets and bombs again. Not to mention sharks and the open ocean."

"You just don't wanna leave your new squaw," Frank said with a leering smile.

Grinning Bear said, "And you're just jealous."

Frank laughed and threw a small, perfectly smooth stone at him. "I must say I get sick of hearing your damned war whoop whenever you finish your business. It's embarrassing."

Grinning Bear laughed with him. "You're one to talk."

Frank thought about the woman he'd bedded a few times. The touch of her soft brown skin and her loving manner had increased his health as much or more than the daily food and water, but she wasn't exclusive to him—not like Grinning Bear's girl. He didn't hold it against her. She was young and beautiful and the men outnumbered the women on this small island.

Frank turned serious. "I wouldn't blame you if you changed your mind. Leaving paradise—well, it might be a stupid decision—but I just have to get back into it. I don't know why, but I feel I just have to."

"The full moon's just two days away."

Frank nodded. The headman, who they called the Shaman, had used his hands and sand drawings to lay it all out for them. From what they gathered, the water lanes, which acted like invisible highways, shifted closer this time of year and they could paddle their dugout canoes out to them and ride the current toward bigger islands to the south. The Shaman made it sound as though the opportunity was finite, but Frank wondered if he simply wanted to be rid of them. After all, they were eating their food and screwing their women. They helped as much as they could with the day-to-day business of survival, but they mostly just got in the way.

"I'm going with or without you, Larry. I'll send someone your way once I hit friendly lines."

Grinning Bear tossed a stone into the tidal pool. It splashed the boy's back, and he turned and grinned awkwardly. "No need. I'm going with you. All this peace and quiet will likely drive me crazy eventually."

Relief flooded Frank, but he didn't let on. He couldn't imagine being apart from his friend. "Gale's still planning on staying here."

Grinning Bear's jaw rippled. "Good. We've seen his true colors."

Gale had tried to keep Grinning Bear and himself off the piece of floating jetsam after their transport ship sank off the coast. Frank had been unconscious at the time, but Grinning Bear told him the tale and never forgave him.

"Micah and Neil were in on it too," Frank stated.

"Yeah, but Gale was the ringleader. He'd sooner cut our throats than let us tell that story. Probably why he isn't coming—figures we'll die out there before we find any friends. Then he can tell whatever story suits him if he's ever rescued."

The young boy speared another fish and held it up jubilantly before plopping it onto the growing pile of fat, colorful fish.

"Should be enough fish to last us a while," Frank said.

"If I never eat another fish for as long as I live, it won't be long enough." Grinning Bear hefted himself to his feet.

He looked nothing like he'd looked only a month before. They'd all filled out—gaining ropy, powerful muscles attributed to their daily swims, walks, and even a few sedate games of Brain Ball, as they came to call it.

They didn't play as aggressively since that fateful match against the Japanese, but they still came away with nasty cuts and scrapes. The natives loved playing them and usually beat them handily, but the Americans surprised them a few times. The women were especially susceptible to their charms after the matches and Frank wondered if all the blood secretly revved their engines, or perhaps it was just all the scantily clad, sweaty men running around like lunatics trying to beat each other to pulp.

~

THE WARM EVENING breeze blew in their faces as they stood beside the two outrigger canoes the natives had given them for their journey. Grinning Bear stood beside the woman he'd been bedding with. She hugged him fiercely, and he kissed the top of her head. Frank wondered if he really had feelings for her, or if he it was simply a relationship of convenience. Neither spoke the other's language, but he supposed that didn't really matter.

The Shaman stood with his arms raised, holding his ever-present staff. He spoke loud and deep, and everyone turned to listen. He droned on for nearly five minutes. None of the Americans had a clue what he said, but he sounded sincere.

With the speech finished, the natives hefted the canoes and pulled them the rest of the way into the sea. The canoes bobbed at the lapping waves. They'd practiced paddling the canoes around the island a few times, using the heavy paddles the natives had carved for them. Despite the outriggers, they still managed to tip once or twice before figuring out their balance. The last time they'd circumnavigated the island, they'd done it in record time and hadn't come close to capsizing. But no one doubted they'd have a hard time if the seas turned rough.

Stacked in the center of each canoe was extra food and water. Dried fish mostly, but also fruits and even mashed fruit paste mixed with coconuts and spread into halved coconut shells. A delicacy that they were thankful for.

Through hand signals and drawings, the Shaman told them they'd reach land in three days if they stayed in the current and did nothing. Less time if they paddled. They'd conferred and decided they'd paddle most of the time to keep their daylight exposure to a minimum. They had seen little shipping traffic since landing on the island, but a few times they'd seen smoke on the horizon. It would be terrible luck to be spotted by a passing Japanese ship, but they wanted to keep the possibility to the minimum.

The amount of dried fish seemed more than they needed even if they took the full three days, and the pile of fresh fish was an even deeper mystery. They had no way to cook the fish. When they tried to ask about it, the Shaman made many emphatic gestures until they finally nodded their agreement, although they had no idea what he meant.

Frank hopped into the back of a canoe and steadied the rails as Grinning Bear entered and stepped to the front. Grinning Bear sat down heavily and turned back to his woman, staring at him forlornly from the beach. He waved, and she flashed him a smile, then ran up the beach and out of sight.

Frank gave him a sideways grin. He felt bad taking him from a woman who obviously felt some love for him. "You sure about this?" he asked lamely.

"Course I am. Let's go."

Neil and Micah sat in the other canoe beside theirs, waving at the natives. Both of them had also been with native women, but nothing past carnal desires formed. The native men pushed them off, and the canoes sliced easily through the tidewaters.

Frank hefted the paddle and stroked steadily. Grinning Bear gave one last wave and took up his paddle. The Shaman yelled something indecipherable and Frank held up his paddle and waved, but didn't turn around. Both canoes soon slid through the narrow inlet leading out to the open ocean.

The evening air felt magical. The swell was nearly nonexistent, and the water felt warm and inviting. The western horizon shone with an intricate and varied color show as the sun set behind a few scattered clouds. Twilight seemed to last a long time, but soon darkness enveloped them. Frank gazed behind, and the island that had saved their lives reduced to just a faint outline of blackness. No lights from the village shone. It looked truly deserted. *Was it even on a map?*

He wondered what it would be like for Gale now that they were gone. He hadn't bothered coming out to say goodbye. Perhaps he'd feel compelled to join them. It would be lonely unless he could learn to communicate better. Would they ever meet again?

They paddled steadily until they figured they were at least a mile out. The wind ceased, and the canoes drifted side by side. They threw woven vines to each other and latched the canoes together.

The Shaman indicated that they'd feel the current beneath them. The canoes slowly turned south as they stopped paddling, but it was a slight change. Frank wondered if they'd come out far enough.

"Perhaps a bit farther. I don't think we're in it yet."

With the canoes tethered and the outriggers facing away, they could only paddle on one side. The rails clunked into each other, but the canoes were stoutly made and glided through the placid waters with ease.

The tip of the moon showed itself on the horizon. It looked immense, as it seemed to rise straight out of the water only a few miles away. It looked as though they could paddle right up to it and touch it if they so desired. None of them spoke as they watched the breathtaking spectacle.

The canoes abruptly turned south and the acceleration, although slight, was noticeable. They turned to one another and grinned like crazy people. They'd found the current.

They let the canoes travel, helping them along with the occasional paddle stroke. The moon lit up the world to near-daylight brightness. Nothing but the glowing ocean water and a few brighter stars overhead could be seen. Occasionally, they heard a great crash as some aquatic beast broached the surface. Once, they saw the great splash of churned white-water in the distance, but couldn't see what had caused it. It made Frank feel small and inadequate. Those beasts didn't give a single shit about the war going on all around them. It made him wonder if they should've stayed on the island.

He looked back, but couldn't see even an outline of land. He wondered how far they'd traveled. With the moon blazing bright, they couldn't use the stars for navigation, even if they knew how.

Hours passed. They stopped paddling, letting the current pull them along. They lay in the bottom of the canoes and watched the sky pass. Despite the bright moon, they could still see stars. The canoes rocked side to side, the clunking of the wood sounded satisfying and reassuring. Frank closed his eyes. He hadn't wanted to, but he couldn't help himself. The rocking of the boats and the rhythmic sound acted like a sleep drug.

He jolted awake and sat upright. He heard soft snores all around him. He hadn't been the only one to succumb to the gentle lapping and swaying. Judging by the moon and his grogginess, he figured he'd slept at least a few hours.

He hefted himself to his knees and pissed into the half coconut placed there for that purpose. He tossed the pee overboard and washed it out haphazardly. He pulled back quickly when something big and dark moved just beneath the surface. His guts tightened as fear swept through him. He knew immediately it had to be a shark.

He leaned forward and slugged Grinning Bear's shoulder. "Shark! There's a shark circling us. Wake up!"

Grinning Bear sat up in groggy confusion. When he got his bearings, he leaned over the rail, searching the water. Skittering clouds obscured the moon, occasionally plunging the world into utter darkness. It felt as though they'd fallen asleep in one world and awoken in a darker, more sinister one.

"I don't see it," Grinning Bear said, then spit a wad of snot into the choppy waves. "The wind's picked up."

Neil and Micah sat in the other canoe, gazing over the side, too. Frank asked, "See anything over there?"

Neil, sitting in front, shook his head. "Nothing. But it's a lot darker right now."

Micah suddenly reeled back from the rail. "Jesus Christ!" Something massive broke the surface, hit the canoes, and moved them sideways. "Sh—shark!" He yelled.

Frank clutched his paddle and waited to see it emerge on his side, but nothing happened. "Let's paddle. Let's put distance between us and them."

"You think you can outrun a shark?" Grinning Bear asked.

"It's better than drifting like sitting ducks."

They all took up their paddles and started stroking. Nothing happened for a few minutes.

"Think we lost 'em?" Micah asked.

Frank shrugged. "Doubt it, but we can probably slow down."

They slowed their strokes, but they kept sharp eyes out. Frank placed his paddle in the water and pulled, but he felt it hit something just beneath the surface. He nearly lost his grip, but recovered and pulled the paddle out of the water as though it were hot lava.

"Shit! I just hit one with my paddle."

"Is it better to paddle or keep still? Maybe the paddling agitates them more." Neil suggested.

Grinning Bear said, "Keep paddling, but don't splash too much. They might think it's a struggling fish or something. Slow and smooth."

It sounded reasonable, and they smoothed their strokes, splashing as little as possible. But soon the canoes jolted as a large dorsal fin slammed into Micah and Neil's canoe.

Neil held onto the sides, but Micah had been mid-stroke and couldn't keep from toppling into the water. He went headfirst and deep. He was there, then he wasn't.

He broke the surface and spluttered, "I—I fell out! Wait!"

The canoes had already drifted past him and were stretching the distance every second. Micah flailed as he frantically swam to catch up.

Frank pushed his paddle in, trying to stop their forward momentum. "We've gotta back paddle." The others dug in and the canoes slowed dramatically and finally reversed direction, but Micah was still a few yards out. Micah's panicked, thrashing swim cut the distance quickly.

A looming darkness emerged behind him. Grinning Bear turned and yelled, "Stop swimming! Stop thrashing! He's right behind you!"

If he hoped to keep him calm, it had the opposite effect. He redoubled his efforts, churning the sea into a roiling boil.

Now they could clearly see the shark's dorsal fin cutting a thin line directly at Micah. He wasn't going to make the canoes.

Frank tore his eyes from the spectacle and pointed to Grinning Bear's waist. "Your pistol! Use your pistol, for chrissakes!"

Grinning Bear remembered. He clutched at the pistol, which had nearly become a part of his body. He had to crouch in order to get a clear shot. He aimed and his hand shook. Frank ducked, hoping he didn't accidentally put the round through his back or hit Micah instead of the shark.

The pistol made a pathetic click. Frank looked up and Grinning Bear cursed and worked the hammer back, hoping the next round wouldn't be a dud. Frank ducked again. Micah screamed, then the bang of the pistol. Grinning Bear fired two more times, the sound so close to Frank's head it made his ears ring painfully.

The water roiled and churned and Micah's screams suddenly sounded as though they came from underwater. The pistol roared again. Micah suddenly wasn't there. The water still bubbled and he could see the rings from the last bullet impact, but he didn't see any signs of Micah or the shark.

"Where—where is he? Where is he?"

Neil frantically moved over the pile of dried fish to the back. He still held his paddle, and he hefted it over his head, ready to bludgeon the shark if it reared its ugly snout. He stood there panting with the paddle, but there was nothing. No movement at all.

His voice came in panicked tones. "I saw it take him. I—I saw it bite him in half. Oh my God, no! Micah!" He screamed his name repeatedly, but Micah couldn't answer.

Grinning Bear still aimed the smoking pistol, but Frank could see in the light cast from the moon that the chambers were empty. "I think you're out, Larry."

Grinning Bear didn't look at him at first, just kept sweeping the muzzle over the water searching for a target. He lowered the muzzle and his wide eyes focused on Frank. He finally understood and opened the chamber. He pulled out the dud and chucked it into the ocean with a dull plop. He sat down heavily and dropped the pistol to the bottom of the canoe. He ran his hands through his greasy hair.

The canoes continued drifting south, but they spun lazily as the three men sat in stunned silence. Micah was gone. The wind stopped, and the sea returned to placid calm. It was as though he'd never existed.

Frank took up his paddle. "We need to paddle. Micah's gone. I hate to say it, but perhaps the sharks have had their fill for the time being."

Neil glared at him and looked ready to say something, but instead he simply sat where Micah had been and dipped his paddle.

Grinning Bear returned to his seat and they paddled in silence until the sun rose and brought a new day.

THE HORIZON SPREAD out before them like a massive green and blue canvas. Nothing but water and sky greeted them as they slowly paddled with the current. The sun grew hot and sweat poured off them. They drank sparingly, saving as much water as possible.

They hadn't seen any more sharks since daylight, but they didn't feel comfortable enough to venture into the water to cool themselves. Micah's screams as the shark took him still reverberated in Frank's mind. It didn't seem fair. He'd survived so much, only to be eaten by an alpha predator in the East China Sea. It sounded like something out of a dime store adventure novel.

By midday, their paddle strokes became desultory at best. They ate the dried fish and sipped the water. Frank held up one of the non-dried fish. It had shriveled and the large eyes had fallen out. "I wonder what the Shaman expects us to do with these?"

Grinning Bear looked over his shoulder. He stopped paddling and ran his hand through his hair. "Dammit," he muttered.

"What?"

"Remember when we asked him? How agitated he became? Remember?"

"Yeah, I guess so."

"Remember, he put his hand on his forehead like this?"

It hit Frank and Neil at the same moment. They said in perfect synchrony, "Sharks." Frank shook his head. "He was trying to tell us to use it to distract the sharks."

Neil gazed back the way they'd come. Somewhere back there, Micah would be making his way through the shark's intestinal tract. "Oh my God," he muttered. "All we had to do was throw in some chum. Micah'd be alive."

No one spoke as they realized their mistake. Frank rubbed his head and felt his body deflate. "I—I didn't know what he meant. I just nodded and pretended to understand."

"We all did," Grinning Bear added. "It's nobody's fault."

They took up their paddles and stroked silently for a few more hours. They switched positions to keep their arms fresh and sometimes took breaks, making sure the current continued taking them. They only had the sun overhead to guide them, but they thought their course stayed generally south.

As evening came, the sharks returned. In the broad daylight and clear water, they could see dozens of them gliding and darting beneath them. They kept a perfect cadence with them.

Grinning Bear reached for a fresh fish. He sliced its belly with the front sight of his pistol until it bled, then threw it overboard. The others joined in until there were dead fish sinking and floating all around them. The sharks didn't react right away. It started with one, slashing and grabbing a sinking fish, then quickly developed into a feeding frenzy. Shark bodies darted and sliced through the water as they tore into the fish.

"Time to paddle," Frank said.

They dug in with gusto for another hour. The sun set in an unforgettable shower of purples, oranges, and reds. The moon rose, and they stopped paddling to watch it rise majestically from the sea. Hours passed slowly. The sharks returned one more time, and they didn't hesitate to chum the water with bleeding fish and make their escape.

Frank paddled mechanically with his head down. His body on autopilot. Neil suddenly gasped, "What—what's that?"

Frank looked up, thinking he might've been asleep. His eyes took a long time to focus, but when they finally did, he rubbed them to make sure. A strip of blackness on the horizon held all their attention.

Grinning Bear finally said, "Land. It's land. We made it!"

Neil whooped and Frank nearly joined him before Grinning Bear shushed him.

"Knock it off. We don't know who's on it."

Frank's elation evaporated as he realized things had changed in an instant. They were moving toward the war. The war had seemed a zillion miles away after the Brain Ball competition, but now it flew straight into his face. The thought made his mouth go dry, and he reached for the waterskin and drank deeply.

"Grinning Bear's right. We have to be careful from here on out. Sharks are the least of our worries now."

They paddled toward the landmass. The moon dipped toward the horizon.

"We shouldn't get too close yet. The moon will be down soon. We'll go in after it sets," Grinning Bear stated.

They paralleled the shore for a few miles, searching for lights or signs of the enemy, but it seemed deserted. But they'd thought the last island had been deserted, too.

The moon finally succumbed to the warm ocean water and disappeared into it, plunging the world into darkness. The stars overhead seemed to pop with intensity. They paddled slowly toward the island, their senses on overdrive.

They paddled until they could see rocks and trees hanging over the water. They searched for a spot to land and finally decided on a rocky section. They maneuvered their way until they were close, then slowed and stopped. They listened for anything unusual, but heard only insects and skittering claws of crabs and the occasional night animal or bird. Nothing human. Nothing warlike.

Grinning Bear whispered, "I'll swim in from here. Stay put."

Frank didn't like it, but he said, "Okay. Be careful." Grinning Bear grunted and Frank realized how stupid it sounded. It went without saying.

He swam out of sight. Neil spoke in a whisper. "I don't think I can make myself swim. Not after what happened to Micah."

"Sharks wouldn't be in here—not this close to shore."

Neil didn't answer, and Frank didn't blame him. He didn't know the habits of sharks. For all he knew, there might be a pack of them waiting to eat them only yards away. He didn't think so, but he didn't really know. He kept his mouth shut and listened for Grinning Bear to return.

It seemed like a long time later when he finally did. He swam up silently to the side and launched himself into the canoe in one smooth motion, nearly causing Frank to yell.

"You scared the living hell outta me."

Grinning Bear rolled to his feet and crouched. “It’s clear. We can paddle through the rocks. There’s a little beach about a hundred yards straight in.”

“No sign of Japs?”

“No sign of anything. Pristine beach, but who knows? Let’s get in there and get these canoes hidden before the sun rises.”

Frank heard Neil’s relieved sigh. He reached across the canoes and patted him on the back. “We made it, Neil. Nothing to worry about now.”

Neil said, “I just wish Micah’d made it, too.”

“I know. Me too.”

They carefully paddled through the gaps until they beached with a soft hiss. Even though they hadn’t been at sea for more than a few days, the sand underfoot felt strange to him. He swayed slightly, as though still at sea. He breathed in deeply and wondered what dangers or wonders they’d face once the sun rose.

3

Camp Cable
Brisbane, Australia
February, 1944

Clyde Cooper sighted over the top of his M1 Garand at the distant target shaped like the top half of an enemy soldier. One of the range monkeys had painted a caricature of a Japanese soldier on the target . . . buck teeth, slanted eyes, and giant ears. He'd seen Japanese soldiers up close and knew better. Instead of making him laugh, it disgusted him.

A new batch of paratroopers fresh from the States had met them as they came off the ship, which had transported them back across the Coral Sea from Port Moresby, and deposited them back in Australia. They looked fresh, bright eyed, and green as spring grass.

He'd once looked the exact same way. Now he was a veteran and the new men looked at him and his fellow veterans as though they could walk on water. It bothered him at first, but he'd gotten used to it.

Now those same troopers crouched beside him, firing their rifles at the Japanese caricatures. The man next to him fired through his eight rounds and the clip pinged, signaling that the last round had been fired.

He looked sideways at Clyde and said, "Take that, Jap."

Clyde could see the tight pattern Private Hallon had scored. "Nice shooting, Hallon."

"Thanks, Corporal."

"You know they don't look anything like that, right?"

Hallon inserted another clip, careful not to pinch his thumb when the action sprang back. "Like what?" he asked.

"Buck teeth, big ears . . . they're not cartoons. They're skilled soldiers."

"I don't care what they look like. I just want to kill 'em all."

Clyde looked at his friend Gil Hicks standing nearby, clearing a jammed rifle. "Hey, Gil."

"What?" Gil said irritably.

"Private Hallon here thinks he's gonna win the war single-handedly."

Gil stopped what he was doing and looked their way. "Well, hell, looks like we can all go home now."

"That's not what I meant," Hallon protested.

"Maybe instead of the brass sending the entire regiment, we could just have 'em send you."

"A one-man wrecking crew," Gil added.

"Don't you wanna get back in the war, Corporal?" the young replacement asked.

Clyde thumped him in the back of the helmet and stood. "Shaddup, kid." Hallon glared at him, but soon turned away and went back to adjusting his sights.

Clyde walked the few yards to Gil's side and leaned on the table. "What d'you think of the new guys?"

"Liable to get themselves or us killed—but they *are* paratroopers. They'll do their bit. What d'you think?"

"I dunno. They're alright I guess. Were we this eager?"

"Yeah, I think we were. It's only natural—they're trained to fight. They wanna use their newfound skills, put them to the test. Hallon seems okay."

Clyde watched the new man line up the target and fire methodically through eight more rounds. "He can shoot. We'll see how he does when the targets fire back. He seems so damned young."

"He's only a few months younger than me. But you're the nonno paterno around here. Everyone except Huss is young compared to you."

Clyde marveled at how a few years of age made him one of the old men of Third Squad. He was second oldest only to Third Squad's squad leader, Sergeant Huss, who's twenty-five years made him ancient beyond measure. Clyde didn't picture his twenty-two years as being particularly old, but out here, he was older than dirt.

Clyde stretched his back. "I feel old. What's it gonna feel like when I hit thirty?"

Gil grinned and slapped his back. "That's the spirit."

"What do you mean?"

"You think you're gonna make it to thirty? You counting on getting out of here?"

Clyde clammed up. He didn't like this kind of talk. Superstition played a big role in combat and talking about it only tempted the fates to come down harshly.

He changed the subject. "How's Butler doing?"

Gil scanned the shooting range, searching for the newly arrived private. He'd been a pain in the ass since arriving at Third Squad. Sergeant Huss took a keen interest in him when he noticed his poor attitude and he'd been riding him hard for weeks.

Gil shrugged. "I don't see him. Probably getting his ass chewed out again. He better shape up or Huss'll blow out his eardrums."

"I've never seen such a bad attitude paratrooper. How'd he ever get through?"

Gil lowered his voice. "I hear his father has connections. Deep pockets, too."

"Coming from you, that's rich." Clyde often wondered how his friend would fit back into his mafioso lifestyle once the war ended . . . if the war ended.

"Not like my situation at all, Paisano. None of the brass knows my situation. Butler's father has *political* connections."

"Which makes it even more bizarre. Why isn't he back in the States at some cushy desk job?"

"Good question."

Clyde heard yelling coming from down the line. Even over the din from the smattering of rifle fire, he could pick out Sergeant Huss's harsh voice.

Since arriving back from New Guinea, he'd often heard Huss's voice railing against the new paratroopers and it was usually directed at Private Butler.

"Speak of the devil," Gil said.

Clyde tilted his head to the men still shooting. "Keep the men on task. I'll see what's up."

He walked behind the firing line, paying little attention to the rest of the squad's shooting. He kept his gaze on Private Butler's back as he stood at semirigid attention, facing Sergeant Huss's tirade. Huss gave him the business, using every dirty name in every conceivable combination he could think of. He must be running out of ways to demean the sorry son of a bitch, but he never seemed to find the bottom of his insults.

Clyde didn't want to get involved, but Butler was a new member of Third Squad, so he was his responsibility as much as Huss's. And besides, Huss had come to him a few days before, asking to help whip him into shape, something Huss had never asked before. Now might be an excellent opportunity to gang up on the surly private.

Clyde came up behind Butler. Close, but not close enough that he'd be noticed unless Butler turned. Huss ignored Clyde, continuing his ever increasingly sadistic insults. Spittle splashed Butler's face copiously, but he acted as though he didn't notice or didn't care. He stared straight ahead, looking far from cowed. He looked more bored than intimidated.

Huss finally ran out of insults and simply fumed. The veins on his forehead stood out like fat earthworms after a heavy rain and he breathed in and out like an idling freight train.

His eyes shifted slightly and locked onto Clyde's. "Take over, Corporal. I think the private's ready for a run up the hill."

Butler shifted, trying to see who was behind him. Clyde yelled in Butler's ear. "You ready to run, Private?"

Butler cringed both from the surprise of being snuck up on and from the piercing bellow. Clyde leaned in closer and yelled again. "I asked you a question, turd!"

Butler held his hand to his ear. "Yes, Corporal. I'm ready to run."

"Excellent," Clyde said. "Up Ullister Hill with you. Move out!"

Butler got his bearings, scowled, and trotted toward the looming hill. It wasn't much of a hill, but if you did it fast and often it took your wind and certainly built stamina and strength. Since arriving back in Australia, the company ran the three-mile circuit nearly every day, usually with full packs.

"Faster, Butler! Faster!"

Butler scowled at him but doubled his pace. Clyde kept up easily. As they started up the hill, Butler increased his speed. All the new men were in exceptional shape, having come straight from the rigors of Fort Benning's airborne school, but the veterans still had something on them—grit.

Clyde never wavered, keeping him within arm's reach, no matter how fast Butler pushed. Butler kept glancing back, seeing Clyde right on his tail, seemingly barely working at all.

With just a half mile to go, Butler asked, "Don't you wanna know why Huss is mad at me this time?"

"It's the same bullshit, Butler. Just a different day."

"Why does he got it in for me?"

"If you can talk, you're not working hard enough, Private." Clyde pushed him and Butler nearly face-planted, but caught himself at the last second.

If Butler had been armed, Clyde had no doubt he would've tried something, but instead he seethed and increased his pace, pumping his legs as fast as he could as they approached the peak.

Clyde doubled down and streaked past him easily. Butler flailed and strived to catch up, but when Clyde made the top and turned, Butler was still yards back. Clyde stood with his hands on his hips, breathing hard, but not nearly as hard as Butler.

Butler doubled over and nearly vomited. "If you're gonna lose your lunch, step away. You get my boots dirty—I'll skin you alive."

Butler looked up from his bent-over position. His good looks probably made the ladies back home swoon, but it didn't matter much out here at Camp Cable. So far, Butler hadn't procured a single pass out of the camp to try his hand with the beautiful ladies of Brisbane.

"Why—why you guys out to get me all the time?"

"Out to get you? Are you paranoid, Butler?"

"You don't bust any of the other guy's balls like you bust mine. What's Huss got against me?"

Clyde gave him his best glare, but Butler never looked away. "It's your shitty attitude. You're doing it right now for chrissakes. You've got a big mouth and you can't keep it shut. I don't know how you got through basic, let alone airborne school. They must be getting desperate. Guys like you normally get drummed out early."

"It doesn't make any sense. Lots of guys bitch."

"If you don't wanna run it again, you'll shut the hell up."

"Aw shit, Corporal. Come on."

Clyde shook his head as though dealing with a dense, highly disappointing three-year-old. He stepped right up to Butler's face and stared. Butler finally turned his eyes away and looked over Clyde's shoulder. It's what Clyde wanted, but he still had to teach him a lesson.

In a reasonable voice, Clyde said, "Run it again, Private." When he hesitated and his eyes burned with hatred, Clyde's rage spiked. There was something about the kid that just got under his skin. He yelled with renewed vigor, "Now!"

Sensing the danger, the young private turned and ran headlong back down the hill. Clyde watched him staggering and looking back furtively, as though fearing him. It was the same way his own men had looked at him after he'd killed the Japanese soldier in the foxhole back on New Guinea, but this spoiled little pissant hadn't been there. He had no right to look at him that way.

"I better not catch you, Private," he yelled after the streaking paratrooper. After giving him a decent lead, Clyde took off at a more reasonable clip. Butler saw him coming and sprinted down the hill. Clyde didn't increase his pace, but knew the stupid son of a bitch would run out of steam on the flats and he figured he'd catch up to him before he made it back to the camp entrance. He didn't know what he'd do then, but he was enjoying himself at the moment.

Back in the States, Butler would be one of the rich scumbags he'd met through Abby a few times. He loathed their imperious attitudes when they learned he hadn't grown up in the same social circles. It didn't take long, and invariably, they would treat him as though he'd crawled from beneath a shit-covered rock. Out here, the shoe was on the other foot. Yes, he enjoyed this duty immensely.

"Hurry up, Butler. You don't want me to catch you," he said the last bit in a sing-song voice. He felt like the bad guy in a scary novel chasing the good guy with a bloody axe. He nearly burst out laughing, but that would ruin the effect.

Sure enough, when they hit the flats, Butler slowed. He looked behind him more and more, and each time Clyde grinned evilly. He kept a steady pace, just enough to shorten the distance between them, but not enough to actually overtake him. He still didn't know what he'd do if he caught up with him.

He couldn't thrash him too much. That sort of thing was frowned upon once a paratrooper earned their jump wings. He still had to fight beside the bastard. Their lives would undoubtedly rely on each other someday and they had to have faith in one another or the whole thing would fall apart. They were supposed to drum these sad sacks out at Fort Benning.

Butler crossed through the archway signifying Camp Cable only yards in front of Clyde. He collapsed in the dirt and rolled onto his back, gasping for air. Clyde trotted until he stood beside him, looking down at him. Sweat dripped off his nose and plopped onto Butler's red face.

"You wanna open your mouth again, Private Butler?"

Butler's blue eyes stared back at Clyde in utter horror at the prospect. He looked terrified, but instead of speaking, he simply shook his head emphatically.

"That's the right answer, Private." He hardened his voice, drawing from the countless times he'd heard Sergeant Huss do the same thing. "Now get off the deck and clean yourself up."

Butler scrabbled like a crab on its back, then jumped up and trotted toward the barracks, looking back every so often as though Clyde might change his mind and simply gut him.

Gil sauntered up beside him. "Looks like you put the fear of God in him, Paisano."

"I hope so. He needs it."

"Hopefully, he won't put a bullet in your back."

Clyde watched Butler staggering away like a drunkard. Would the sorry son of a bitch be capable of such a thing? He doubted it. He had to know that no matter how connected his father might be, he'd be put up against a wall and shot if he even attempted such a thing out here.

~

CLYDE SAT OUTSIDE in the sun, reading the latest letter from Abby. It was a month old. She'd started flying for the WASPs and she sounded as excited and happy as he'd ever heard her sound. She said how worried about him she was, but he wondered if he should be more worried about her. Flying wasn't the safest thing in the world, but somehow he had no trouble picturing her doing the job. She must look cute in her flight suit, or whatever they had her wearing. He decided he'd ask her to send a picture.

Gil sat nearby, also reading a letter. Clyde asked. "I wonder what kind of suit they have the WASP girls wearing? I'm going to ask her if she can send a picture. Maybe I'll send her a picture of us. Know anyone with a camera and a way to develop it?" Gil didn't answer. He seemed completely engrossed in the letter he was reading.

Clyde threw his tin cup at him, and it bounced off his shoulder. Gil glared at him.

"Whoa, there." Clyde said, holding up his hands. "What're you reading?" He saw the hurt and anger for the first time. "What's happened?"

Gil held the flimsy piece of paper up. "It's from Melinda. She dumped me. Shacked up with some pilot officer in the RAF."

"She said that?"

"Not in so many words—no, but it's over."

"That's a raw deal, Gil. I'm sorry." He reached into his pack and pulled out a thin metal flask. "Here, this'll help ease the pain."

Gil caught it and looked around before opening the lid and tilting it back. He wiped his mouth with the back of his hand, then threw it back. "Thanks."

"That long-distance stuff doesn't always work out so well."

"Does for you and Abby."

"Yeah, but we're married. You weren't thinking like that, were you? Marriage, I mean?"

Gil considered for a moment, then shook his head while crumbling the letter in his fist. "Nah. I liked her, though. Gorgeous body and her hair . . . but you know all that."

Clyde blushed deeply. He'd slept with Melinda Hampstead before shipping out to New Guinea. A night he'd regretted ever since, but he couldn't deny her beauty or the desire she effortlessly sparked whenever he thought of her.

Gil said, "Sorry to bring it up again."

"Maybe if we'd landed in Cairns instead of Brisbane, things woulda been different for you."

"Yeah, who knows. Oh well, now I have a free hand here in Brisbane."

Clyde nodded his agreement, but didn't mention the fact that Gil hadn't let up on trying to hook up with other women since the day they landed. He wasn't a one-woman man.

"You have a pass this weekend, don't you?"

"Yeah. I plan on finding myself a Sheila, too. Are you coming to town?"

"Yeah, sure, but you know how it is. I'll need to spend most of the weekend getting ready for next week's jaunt into the countryside."

Gil shook his head. "I sure am glad they promoted you and not me. How long we going out this time?"

"We jump twenty miles from here and walk back. Since we're pretending we're behind Jap lines, we'll move slow, so at least three days, maybe four."

"Wonderful."

"Yeah, enjoy your weekend, 'cause next week won't be pleasant."

~

CLYDE WATCHED the ground coming up quickly beneath his jump boots. He'd jumped more times than he could count, but it still made him giddy. The feeling of floating through the air with just nylon and silk overhead never got old. Even the old-timers still seemed to enjoy it just as much as ever.

His landing zone looked clear of rocks, but he hoped the bush he descended toward wasn't one of the thorny ones. They cut like razors and could even puncture the sole of his jump boots if he hit just right—or wrong.

He slammed into the ground, his body twisting automatically, absorbing the blow across his legs, hips, and back. He grunted with the impact. As the dust settled, he evaluated his body. No large alarm bells blared in his head, although everything ached.

He carried almost as much weight as he would carry during an actual combat jump—sans ammunition. Despite the men grumbling about possibly needing ammunition if they faced wild animals or simply wanted to shoot a kangaroo to supplement their diets, the brass didn't want to take the risk that live ammunition added. So their weapons wouldn't be loaded, but to mimic the weight, they carried rocks. He doubted any of them would still be carrying the rocks by the end of the exercise.

He sprang up and unlatched his harness from the parachute that had hung up in the low scrub brush. As he rolled the chute into as tight a ball as possible, he watched the rest of the company floating through the sunny Australian skies like massive cherry blossoms. Different colored parachutes showed different platoons and squads.

Grunts and thumps filled the air as men landed all around him. Despite sounding like a torture chamber, no one yelled out in obvious sharp pain. He'd heard the loud pop of breaking legs more than once on these training jumps, and he hoped to never hear it again. It was normally followed by agonized screams that could rival those he'd heard from wounded men in combat.

He trotted to a growing pile of parachutes and deposited his own. Aussie truck drivers would pick them up after they left the area. The trucks and the few idling ambulances were the only things giving away that this wasn't the real thing. That and the absence of enemy soldiers and thick jungle.

Clyde heard Sergeant Huss before he saw him. He veered in that direction, unslinging his M1 carbine from his chest. He liked the new folding stock version much better than the old version. It felt light and small enough not to notice when he'd landed.

He trotted toward Sergeant Huss and the growing cadre of Third Squad. He noticed the men assembled were the veterans. The replacements must still be scattered. Perhaps Butler had broken his neck. That would solve one problem.

"Welcome, Corporal Cooper!" Huss bellowed. "Thought maybe you were catching a nap, or decided to take the truck home."

Clyde counted only four other paratroopers out of the twelve-man squad. He was early. "I wouldn't do that. I know how much you'd miss me, Sergeant Huss." He blew him a kiss.

Huss scowled, but Clyde knew he wasn't really mad. They understood one another, and it surprised both of them to find that they worked well together.

"Stay here and assemble the rest of the squad. I'm gonna find Lieutenant Milkins."

Clyde nodded his understanding and watched Huss trot off into the brush. "Anyone see any of the fresh meat?"

Janikowski and Gutiérrez both shook their heads. Private Wallace said, "I haven't heard any of 'em squealing for their mamas yet."

A panting soldier burst through the brush from the direction Sergeant Huss had gone. His face was red and sweat dripped off him as though he'd submerged himself in water.

"Jesus Christ, Hallon. What that hell's the matter with you?" Clyde asked.

"What—what d'you mean?" he panted.

"Looks like you ran four miles to get here."

Hallon looked confused. "I—I just saw Sergeant Huss and he pointed you guys out."

"Get some water and pull yourself together." He watched as Hallon worked to unscrew the lid of his canteen. His hands shook bad enough that he could barely hold it to his mouth.

Oliver and Gil pushed through the brush as though just finishing a Sunday stroll. They both kneeled and adjusted their packs, nodding and grunting to the others.

"Glad you could join us. You see Butler anywhere?" Clyde asked.

Oliver shook his head. Gil said, "He went out right before me, but I didn't see him after that."

"You and Guti go find him. He's probably trying to hitch a ride with one of those Aussie truck drivers."

"I wouldn't put it past him," Gutiérrez said.

They pushed through the low brush and spread out. Paratroopers still wandered, searching for their squads and platoons, but most had found their homes by now. Third Squad looked to be one of the last to fully assemble. That would turn Sergeant Huss into a bear.

"Oliver, head that way and see who you can find." Clyde pointed in the opposite direction the others had gone.

"On top of it," Oliver uttered as he trotted away.

Hallon finished drinking. His hands didn't shake as much and his red face had diminished to a pinkish tone.

"You okay?" Clyde asked.

"Yeah, I'm fine. Just excited I guess."

"It's a training exercise, for chrissakes. Calm down or you won't be able to shoot when the real thing comes."

Hallon licked his dry lips, and his eyes widened, undoubtedly thinking about adding combat to the drop. He took a deep breath and blew it out slowly. "I'm okay, Cooper."

Clyde flared at the familiarity. "*Corporal* Cooper," he corrected.

Hallon looked at the others. The veterans called one another by their names all the time, and he clearly thought he should be able to do so as well.

"You haven't earned that right yet, Private."

"Yes, Corporal."

"Now spread out and set security."

Moments later, more men streamed in, but still no Butler. The morning sun beat down on Clyde's neck. He fought the urge to pour cool water over his head. He'd need to conserve every drop for the twenty-mile hike back to Camp Cable. There would be water stations, but not many, and there was no guarantee they'd be able to find them out here in the vastness of Australia.

Huss came back and took in the assembled paratroopers. He noted Private Hallon with a slight nod.

Clyde said, "Including us, we have eleven men checked in. I sent Guti, Oliver, and Hicks to find Butler."

Huss's jaw rippled at Butler's name. A moment later, Oliver came trotting through the loose perimeter, panting slightly. "I went all the way to the edge of the tree line. He's not over that way."

"We don't have time to wait for that stupid son of a bitch. Guti and Hicks will just have to catch up. Milkins wants us out front right now."

It was normally the reconnaissance squad's duty to patrol out front, but Milkins liked using Third Squad sometimes.

"We're ready." Clyde eyed Hallon, who looked like a kid on Christmas morning. "Hallon, you stay close to me."

Hallon nodded, but Clyde could see the hurt in his eyes, as though he'd been reprimanded by his father.

They formed up in a loose formation and trotted north, weaving in and out of thorn bushes and scrub brush, some of which put off a sickly-sweet scent when touched.

They made it a few hundred yards when Gutiérrez and Hicks joined them, pushing Private Butler in front of them as though he were a prisoner of war. Butler protested each jab, half turning toward the veterans, who looked as though they might run him through with their knives.

"Where'd you find him?" Huss asked.

"Tucked in with some other new guys from First Squad."

"First Squad?" Huss sounded incredulous. "Don't you know your own damned squad-mates yet?"

Butler sidled in beside Clyde. He was about to respond and Clyde had no doubt it would be some snide remark that would send Huss into yet another tirade, so before he could respond, Clyde squeezed his arm and hissed into his ear. "Stow it, Butler."

Butler shook loose. "I thought . . ."

Clyde gripped his arm, pinching his tricep hard, making Butler wince and squirm, but it cut him short.

"No, sergeant—I mean yes, sergeant," Butler finally said, glaring at Clyde.

Clyde said, "That's more like it, Butler. See—you are trainable. Now fall in, keep your mouth shut, and do *exactly* as you're told."

4

Clyde let his mind wander as Third Squad swept the desolate swaths of Australian outback in front of Able Company. The sun's heat felt like a feverish hand pressing on his back. His uniform top had soaked through with sweat, changing the color from light green to dark green. His pack settled low on his back, chafing him in spots he didn't know could hurt, but he didn't complain or even slow down. In fact, the longer he marched, the less he felt the aches and pains. His mind felt foggy and the only thing that mattered was the next step.

He wondered what Abby was doing at that exact instant. He tried to remember what time of day—or even what day it was—back in the States, but his mind blurred and wouldn't focus. He lost the image of her and frustration overwhelmed him.

He shook his head and immediately regretted it as a headache he didn't know he had throbbed. He checked his watch, barely able to focus on the tiny face. They'd been marching for nearly three hours. He looked behind and saw Sergeant Huss plodding along with his head down. He looked as though he were on autopilot, just like he felt. Each soldier looked the same, one step in front of the other like robots from a sci-fi comic book.

Clyde slowed until Huss caught up. "The men need a break, Morgan."

He rarely used Sergeant Huss's first name, and it made the surly sergeant flare momentarily until he realized who it was.

Huss's eyes came into focus as though he'd been deep in thought, much the same way Clyde had been. He checked his own watch and stood up straight, coming to a stop. He looked as surprised as Clyde had been, like he'd just emerged from a fog and didn't know exactly how he'd gotten there.

"Criminy, it's past time," he mumbled. He raised his voice, and it cracked with dryness. "All right, you guys, take a break."

The squad came to a staggered halt, each man looking dazed. A few swayed uneasily, but they all eventually found shade and sat themselves down heavily. No one spoke a word. Their hands shook as they went for their nearly dry canteens.

Clyde unscrewed his canteen and took a long swig. He had to force himself not to down the entire contents. It was warm, and had a distinct tinny taste, but it was wet and felt wonderful as it coated his throat.

The men drank sparingly, and as the minutes passed, they slowly came back to life. Huss had his back against a scrubby tree. The thin branches provided some cover from the sun, but the heat still permeated the air and made it hard to breathe.

Clyde sat by his side. His headache subsided, and he thought he could feel the water bringing life back into his limbs and mind. "I feel like I slipped into some kind of dreamscape or a trance."

Huss said, "That's one of the dangers. I shoulda been more careful."

"What d'you mean?"

"These men have been through the toughest training the U.S. Army has to offer. They've pushed their bodies to their limits countless times. They'll keep going until they simply drop from exhaustion or heat stroke. I've seen it before. They're too well trained to quit. It can be a dangerous sometimes." As though remembering something important, he looked around at the men. "Get me a headcount."

Clyde didn't want to stand up, but he heaved himself upright anyway. He felt light-headed for a moment. He clutched the spiny tree trunk until the dizziness passed. His legs ached, but without the pack, he almost fell forward with each step.

He counted the men he could see, and when he came up short, he mustered the energy to yell. "Sound off, Third Squad."

He listened to their raspy replies but was still one man short. It took all his energy to figure out who was missing, and when he finally did, he wasn't surprised. "Anyone seen Butler?"

The men looked from one to another, then looked back at Clyde with blank stares and shaking heads.

He wetted his mouth with the little saliva he could muster and called out, "Butler! Butler!" No response. His throat felt dry as dust and yelling only made it worse.

Huss got to his feet, cursing under his breath. He stood beside Clyde. "I shoulda known that shithead wouldn't be able to keep up. We need to link up with the rest of the platoon. He could be anywhere out here." He dug into his pack and pulled the walkie-talkie out gingerly. "Hope the battery held up to the heat." He turned it on and the squelch answered that question. He called multiple times, but each time he heard only static in reply. "Shit, we must be out of range."

"Out of range? How long ago did you do a radio check?" Clyde saw anger in Huss's eyes, but only for a moment before it changed to something else.

Huss finally answered. "I've only done one." He gritted his teeth and seethed in self-loathing. "I lost my wits for a while, I guess."

The men were all coming back to their senses, although few attempted to stand just yet. They couldn't help overhearing the call on the radio that had no reply.

Huss fumbled for the map in his oversized paratrooper pants pocket. He glanced sheepishly at Clyde before studying the map. His grizzled, cracked hand shook slightly. He looked around the desolate country. No landmarks stood out, only flat scrubby brush and gnarled stunted trees as far as the eye could see.

Clyde's apprehension grew as Huss studied the map. He clearly didn't know where they were. Had they veered off course? After the first hour, he hadn't been checking either. It was the squad leader's responsibility, but the assistant squad leader was there to assist. Neither of them had done their jobs.

Clyde's stomach turned as he pulled out his compass and studied the face. "We were heading northeast when we stopped, not due north. I have no idea for how long."

"We need to backtrack. The rest of the company can't be too far off. Once we're in radio range, they can talk us back."

The thought of the trouble they'd be in, not to mention the razzing from the other squads that would inevitably follow, made his stomach turn even more. Would Captain Stallsworthy even want them in his company? Would they kick them out of the airborne? Was Butler dying in the baking heat somewhere back there? He didn't like the man, but he didn't deserve to die—not like that.

Huss gathered the men around. Everyone except Private Hallon sensed the urgency and danger. He looked at the veterans like a child watching the big kids play football from the sidelines—as though he wouldn't be the one getting hit by the defensive linemen.

Huss laid it out. "Okay, look. We're out of radio range from the company. Out here without mountains or jungle getting in the way, that means we're at least three miles away. We were moving northeast instead of north when we finally stopped." He pointed southwest. "We need to head that way. We'll follow our own tracks until we're close enough for radio contact. Butler's missing." He looked at each man and they stared back through bloodshot, tired eyes. "He's a pain in the ass, but he's one of us. He could be anywhere, so keep your eyes open for any tracks that veer off our own. Conserve water. I know we're down to our last few sips, but if we don't find the rest of the boys, we'll need every drop. We've got plenty of daylight, so let's move out."

Clyde searched the faces for any anger or blame, but found only stoic resolve. He felt awful and wanted to apologize, but knew it wouldn't be appropriate or appreciated. For the thousandth time, he wondered how he'd ever fallen into such a company of men. He and Huss had surely let them down. Would he react the same if he was still a private? He resolved never to let these men down again.

Clyde plodded along their dusty track, trying to keep his mind off his growing thirst. Their best man for tracking, Private Wallace, stayed out front. Clyde had confidence in Wallace, but he secretly wished Private Rogerson from the reconnaissance squad led them instead. He could track like no one else he'd ever met. He wondered if the entire situation would've been avoided if Rogerson had been with them. He gnashed his teeth, blaming and cursing himself. He shouldn't have let it happen, plain and simple.

They'd reversed their course for an hour and had yet to find when they'd veered off course. He wondered if he'd been the one to initiate the new direction or perhaps it just happened slowly over many hundreds of steps.

There was still no sign of Butler or a wayward track. If Butler had veered off, it would be difficult to find his single track among so many. Clyde hoped they'd simply come across him sitting under a shabby tree napping, but the longer they searched, the more hopeless he felt.

Huss tried the radio every ten minutes and still raised only static. It was as though they'd dropped off the face of the earth. He suspected an entire division or even an army could end up missing in this vastness. He gazed up at the sky and saw only empty blue. Even a distant sound of a distant aircraft would make him feel better, but he heard nothing but the breeze.

At the top of the hour, Huss called a halt. Everyone took a seat after taking off their packs. The purpose of the training had taken a backseat to the actual situation. They didn't set security or try to stay quiet. They wanted to be found even if it meant a harsh razzing and perhaps disciplinary measures.

Clyde carefully sipped his water, letting it coat his mouth before allowing it to gurgle down his throat. He only had a few mouthfuls left.

"We've got a few more hours until the sun sets," he said to no one in particular.

Huss pulled out the walkie-talkie and turned it on. Before keying the kidney bean–shaped button on the side, he said, "We'll find 'em before that."

Clyde nodded, hoping he was right. He didn't relish spending the night out here, even though it was in the original training plans. He wasn't nervous about the wildlife. They'd faced much worse in the New Guinea jungles, but without more water, it would be difficult to sleep. They were supposed to be linked up with the rest of the company by now and had their water resupplied.

"The others must be looking for us by now, too."

Huss transmitted on two different frequencies, but the set only squawked and squeaked as though being tortured. He tried one last time, and everyone sat forward when they heard a distant human voice. Huss transmitted again, but it was gone. He shut it down after five more minutes, but the brief contact buoyed them.

"We're getting closer. Let's keep moving. The signal will only get stronger."

"Maybe they've already picked up Butler," Clyde said.

"Wouldn't that be something? Cocky son of a bitch would probably tell a tale."

Their pace increased. Clyde studied the edges of their track, searching for any veering off the main group. In the dusty, dry conditions, it would be a miracle to find such a track, and it might not even be Butler's, but just someone taking a piss, or veering around a bush or tree. But he felt he owed it to him to keep looking. He'd want the men to search for him if the roles were reversed.

After ten more minutes, Huss didn't bother halting them before calling on the radio again. This time, he immediately heard a clear voice. Everyone stopped and turned back to listen.

Huss identified himself and his smile cracked his dry lips in several places when he heard the call-sign of the Second Platoon.

The paratroopers slapped one another on the backs and there wasn't a grim face among them.

Once he established who they were talking to, Huss asked, "Yankee One, have you come across Private Butler? Over."

The squad seemed to hold their breath, waiting for the response. None of them particularly liked him, but he was a part of their unit, so they all felt responsible for him.

"Negative Yankee Three. We've found no stragglers. Over."

Their smiles faded as Huss relayed what he knew about the missing man, then signed off. He stuffed the walkie-talkie back into his side pocket and addressed them. "We'll keep on this track. We should run right into Second Squad. They're out front of the platoon looking for us. But don't stop searching for Butler. He could be anywhere out here."

"Too bad we didn't bring any ammunition with us. Maybe he'd hear our shots. Sound travels out here," Gutiérrez said.

"Maybe a kangaroo took him out," Gil teased. A few men guffawed, but no one disliked Butler enough to write him off completely. They barely knew him.

Clyde suddenly felt a renewed determination to find him. He cupped his hands and yelled. "Butler!" His voice seemed to disappear in the vast arid countryside.

The men cringed. Their training didn't fully allow them to accept yelling during an operation that was supposed to rely on stealth, even though they were thousands of miles from the enemy lines. They looked at Huss, who shrugged, cupped his hands, and joined in the call. Soon, they were all calling for Butler as they plodded.

A half an hour later, they met Second Squad. Second Squad paratroopers leaped out as though ambushing them.

Sergeant Plumly, Second Platoon's platoon sergeant himself, stood there gawking at them, his fists firmly placed on his hips, rocking back and forth like an unhappy high school basketball coach after a lopsided loss. "What in the Sam's hell are y'all doing? What's all the yelling about? I could hear you a mile away, for crying out loud."

Despite the glare, Clyde couldn't help smiling. Even though they'd only been separated for a few hours, it felt much longer and seemed more substantial.

Huss didn't dare smile, though. He matched Plumly's angry growl. "We're searching for a lost man, Private Butler. I figured that was more important than pretending the Japs were around. We need to find our man. That's what's important."

Plumly ignored him mostly. He looked the squad over, then signaled his own men. "Give 'em your canteens. These men look thirsty." He handed his own off to Huss, who took it with a shaky hand.

Clyde finished the last few gulps in his own canteen, then drained the one offered. He felt the moisture coursing through his body, even down to his fingertips. He relished the coolness and the way his body seemed to absorb it, like a dry sponge. His vision sharpened, and the fogginess he didn't know had been there cleared. It was as though someone lifted a shroud off his head.

Plumly let them enjoy themselves for less than a minute, then barked, "Alright, let's get you worthless sons of bitches back. I'm sure lieutenants Milkins and Jameson are dying to hear how you fucked up so badly." He threw up his hands. "Not to mention Captain Stallsworthy. I'm not sure I've ever seen him so fired up. You've really stepped in it this time, Morgan."

PRIVATE BUTLER DIDN'T REMEMBER when he'd lost Third Squad. One moment they'd been there, and the next they were gone. He remembered trotting, then running to catch up, but it was like the dusty hot land had swallowed them. By the time he resorted to yelling for them, he'd drained the rest of his canteen and his dry throat made yelling difficult, if not impossible, so he simply kept treading along.

He lost all sense of time and direction. He wanted to sit down, but his body kept moving forward—seemingly forever and against his will. He stopped abruptly when his mind sharpened momentarily. He scanned the endless expanse of scrub brush and swirling dust devils. His mind screamed at him to find water—find the others, but the comforting fog slowly descended back over his mind and he forgot his purpose and continued his mindless wandering.

After a few endless hours, he stopped and sat down heavily. A tiredness overwhelmed him and he lay back, but something dug into his backside. He shed his pack, wondering where it had come from in the first place. He rifled through the contents. He found food, but no water. Every pore of his body craved water. He felt as though he'd blow away with the dust if he didn't find it soon.

Who had put him in this situation? His father? He tried to focus, but the world blurred then went to blackness. Footsteps approached. He wanted to sleep, but a sense of urgency made him pry himself back into a sitting position. He needed to see who was approaching. He felt it was someone important. Someone who'd help him. *Huss?*

A tall man dressed in an immaculate black suit took impossibly long steps toward him. The steps didn't bring him closer, but instead, brought him into clearer focus. *Father?* The sun blazed behind him so he couldn't see his face, but he recognized his voice. The heat and the dust didn't seem to affect him at all.

"Hello, boy."

"Father?" His throat hurt and he hacked a dry, violent cough. It felt as though his throat bled.

"You've always been worthless—a disappointment." The voice was hollow and devoid of emotion.

"Where? How did *you* get here?"

The dark outline seemed to shimmer, making the black suit somehow blacker than the deepest shadow. A coldness swept over him, but it didn't relieve the day's incessant heat.

"You'll die here, boy. Good riddance."

"Die? I—no, I can't die." The mere idea sounded ludicrous. He just wanted to sleep for a little while. "I'm so tired," he murmured. He looked down at his dusty boots. When he looked up, his father was gone. He looked around frantically. Where had he gone? He couldn't have gone far.

Hatred welled up in his guts. He'd show him. His mind cleared and he remembered what he'd seen in his pack. He laughed as he grasped what he'd been looking for. "I'll show him. I'll show him and make him pay for leaving me out here." The thought made him giggle as he staggered to his feet and started walking.

~

CLYDE STOOD at attention beside Sergeant Huss beneath a copse of shade trees. They faced Able Company's senior lieutenant, Lieutenant Jameson, and their platoon leader, Lieutenant Milkins, as they tore into them. Clyde stared straight ahead, planning on letting Huss answer questions they asked. But they didn't ask any that allowed him time to answer.

He took the absence of Captain Stallsworthy as a good sign that they wouldn't kick them out of the company, but it didn't make the dressing down much easier to sit through.

When both officers seemed to have spent all the insults they could stack upon them, Lieutenant Jameson turned to Lieutenant Milkins. "I want that man Butler found. Nothing happens until we find him. Understood?"

"Understood, sir," Milkins shouted back.

Jameson stalked off, beating his bush hat against his thigh with a puff of dust.

Milkins waited until he was out of earshot, then turned back to them. "You feel up to helping or you need time to recuperate?"

Huss barked, "We can help, sir. We're fine."

"Good. I've already sent the other squads out looking. We'll cover the final grid." He pulled out a corner of a map and pointed to a spot. "You think you can follow a map, sergeant?"

"Yes, sir!" Huss snapped. Clyde could hear the indignation in his voice. He hoped Huss didn't dig them into a deeper hole with an insubordinate slip of the tongue.

"Lead on, then."

Twenty minutes later, Third Squad walked through the bush again. They could hear distant voices calling Butler's name from the other squads. Clyde wondered if they'd ever find him. How would the army classify his loss—killed in action or missing in action, or something else? Training accident, he finally settled upon. How long would they wait before notifying his parents? If they didn't find his body, it would certainly complicate things.

He startled from his thoughts when a wraith of a soldier suddenly appeared from behind a gnarled, ancient tree. He leveled a carbine at his chest. The sallow cheeks and pale, pasty skin made him look otherworldly, but he recognized Butler instantly.

"Butler!" he gasped.

Butler's dilated eyes stared back at him dangerously. His cracked lips formed a sneering grin, and Clyde couldn't help thinking he'd seen a similar face in a horror comic book as a kid.

Clyde's relief at finding him quickly turned to fear as Butler's finger moved to the trigger.

"Butler, no!" he yelled, holding out his hand.

Lieutenant Milkins stepped out from behind Clyde and the barrel shifted off Clyde and onto Milkins.

"There you are," Butler rasped. "I've got something for you, daddy," he said mockingly.

Clyde yelled, "No!" He took one step toward him, hoping to bat the carbine from his hands, but too late. The crack of the carbine echoed in the vast Aussie outback. Clyde heard the bullet impact flesh and Lieutenant Milkins grunted just before he crumpled to the ground, clutching his stomach.

Clyde reached Butler just before he swung the smoking muzzle back at him. He gripped the barrel as he plowed into him, aiming it toward the sky. He landed hard on Butler's chest, pinning the weapon between them as they sprawled.

Butler fought like a crazed wild man, and Clyde thought he might escape his grasp. Only inches from his face, Butler lunged with his teeth, trying to bite Clyde's cheek. Clyde reared back and Butler's teeth clashed together with an audible snap. His bloodshot eyes darted side-to-side like a wild animal, and Clyde wondered if some wild dingo had bitten him.

A rifle butt smacked into Butler's face and his eyes lost focus, then finally shut. Clyde rolled off him, his breathing coming in quick gasps. He took Gil's offered hand and hoisted himself to his feet. Dirt and dust fell off him as he looked down on the man who had tried to gnaw his face off.

"Criminy sakes! He tried to bite me!"

"Milkins is hit! Medic!"

Clyde turned and saw Sergeant Huss stooped over the wounded lieutenant. A dark spot of blood spread out from Milkins's stomach. Milkins stared at the wound, his eyes wide, fearful, and unbelieving. Huss pulled his tunic apart, exposing the wound to the open air. Milkins's head fell back and he cursed, then screamed as Huss pressed his hand to the wound.

"Medic!" Huss screamed. "Medic!"

Butler moaned, and Clyde turned back toward him. Rage filled him. He dropped his knees onto Butler's chest and grasped his filthy uniform lapels, pulling his shoulders off the ground. He screamed in his face. "You filthy son of a bitch. I'll kill you!"

He slammed Butler's head into the dirt, hard. He reached for his knife, but Gil and Oliver each grasped a shoulder and pulled Clyde off the passed-out soldier. Clyde struggled momentarily, then regained control and shook them off. Gil and Oliver stood ready in case he tried again.

Clyde felt revulsion. He would've killed him if he'd pulled his knife. He had no doubt. A rage had come over him like a fast fever. It had passed just as quickly, but left him breathless.

His focus went back to his platoon leader. "We need a litter. We gotta get him outta here fast!" Private Wallace and Hallon took off back the way they'd come.

Huss was still applying pressure to the wound. His hands were red and sticky with blood. More men helped stem the flow, some wiping the excess blood and others dribbling water into Milkins's open mouth. All their faces were pale with worry. Milkins moaned and chewed his bottom lip as he stared up at the wide blue sky.

Gutiérrez pointed at the still passed-out Butler. "What about him?"

Clyde stooped and picked up Butler's carbine. He pulled the breech and peered inside. "Son of a bitch snuck in live ammo." A part of him still wanted to bury his knife in his chest, but his rage had passed. "He must be delusional. He called Milkins his daddy right before he shot him. See if you can get some water into him."

5

Nasira, India
February 1, 1944

Shawn Cooper swung lazily, tucked deeply into the hammock hanging between two stout posts on the deck overlooking the tennis courts in Nasira, India. Beside him, other members of Operational Group Bellevue sprawled similarly. Some snored contentedly, while others sipped gin and tonics.

Shawn adjusted his position so he could reach his drink. He drained the last vestiges and placed it back down on the little table. Instantly, an Indian man stepped forward and replaced it with a fresh one.

"Thank you, Salim."

Salim nodded and stepped away. He watched them like hawks, ready to help them in any way possible. It was discomfiting at first. Shawn wasn't used to being waited on hand and foot, but after two weeks at the OSS compound, he'd gotten used to it and learned to enjoy it.

His head swam a little from the alcohol. It was a pleasant buzz—one he'd also gotten used to having most of the time.

He addressed the others, swinging nearby. "I'm gonna miss this."

JoJo asked lazily, "Which part?"

"All of it, I guess." He swirled the sweating drink in his hand. "But mostly the bottomless gin and tonics."

"Leave it to the Brits to turn medicine into a drink, eh? We're getting a nice buzz and all the quinine our systems can handle."

O'Keefe chimed in, "I hear the alcohol kills the effects of the quinine."

JoJo threw his stir stick at him. "That's a nasty rumor. Don't let the officers hear you or they'll take the gin out of our gin and tonics."

Shawn pointed at the tennis courts where two men dressed all in white were in the middle of a robust rally. "They won't hear you unless they stop playing that silly game."

Veatch didn't open his eyes, but said, "I find the sound soothing. Puts me to sleep."

"Yeah, until Umberland puts one in the net and starts cussing and yelling again," Shawn stated. They all laughed at the memory.

JoJo said, "He's a stone-cold killer in combat, but an unforced error on the court is enough to send him into a rage. Too bad we can't harness all that rage and use it against the Nips."

"Japs don't play tennis," O'Keefe said flatly.

JoJo pulled the hammock edge down so he could see O'Keefe better. "How the hell d'you know, you stupid Mick? Of course they play. Why wouldn't they? It's a universal game."

"I can't picture it—you know? I mean, can you?"

"Japs playing tennis?" JoJo considered it a moment as he gazed at Lieutenant Umberland and Captain Burbank darting around the court, chasing a fuzzy green ball and smacking the hell out of it. "I'll bet they'd use a yellow ball. Or maybe bright red like their rising sun."

"Brilliant insight," O'Keefe murmured.

"I'll bet they're good, though. I mean, they're quick little bastards. Bet they have all sorts of underhanded strategies, too."

Shawn laughed despite himself. The alcohol felt good in his system. "How d'you cheat in tennis?"

JoJo sat up in his hammock and glared at Shawn. "I dunno. I've never even played, but I bet they cheat."

Umberland's voice rose from the courts. "Out!"

"What?" came the exasperated reply from Captain Burbank.

"It was out," Umberland insisted.

All eyes shifted to the court. Both men breathed hard, but Burbank leaned on his wooden racket, staring daggers across the net at his opponent. Umberland palmed a ball and stuffed it into his shorts pocket, then strode to the service line and prepared to serve. He noticed Burbank glaring and standing near the net, completely out of position to receive the serve.

"Are you ready?"

Burbank shook his head. "No, I'm not ready. How can you say that was out? It was in by mile. I could see it from way back here. It's my point."

The men who'd been snoring woke up feeling the mounting tension on the court. Like the others, Shawn watched in rapt fascination. Rank meant little in the OSS and certainly less on a tennis court, but he wondered how this would all play out. His slight buzz made it even more interesting and entertaining.

Umberland shook his head. "It's my call. It was out."

Burbank shook his head slowly, then looked around searching for anyone who might have seen the point and could corroborate. He glanced at the Indian staff member standing stoically courtside in the heat of the sun, but didn't ask him. The Indian would do anything to serve them, but he wouldn't take sides for fear of offending one or the other. Shawn had seen it before.

Burbank saw the men on the porch leaning out of their hammocks, watching their exchange. He lifted his chin and raised his voice. "Did any of you see that?"

Shawn knew better than to take the bait, but JoJo couldn't resist. He stood up with his hand raised high over his head, waving like a lunatic. "I saw it, sir."

Umberland turned around and glared acid at JoJo. "You couldn't of seen it from all the way up there. Stand down, Palance." He turned back to Burbank. "It's my call, Rex."

"In or out, JoJo?"

JoJo didn't hesitate. "In, sir."

Shawn and the others sniggered behind their hands. They knew JoJo hadn't seen a thing. He'd been wrapped up in his hammock, paying little attention to the game or the point.

"That's two of us that called it in, Danny. It's my point."

The look Umberland directed at JoJo made them all cringe. He looked ready to kill JoJo on the spot. His glare slowly turned to an insipid smile. He glanced back at Burbank. "Okay, it's your point." He turned back to the patio and raised his voice. "JoJo, since you're so interested in calling shots, why don't you come down here and shag balls for us."

JoJo's smile faded quickly and his eyes darted to his lounging comrades, then back to the courts. "Um, that's okay, sir. I'd rather just watch from here. You're both playing splendidly, by the way. Especially you, sir." He adopted a slight British accent somewhere, which made Shawn's smile spread wider.

"I insist," Umberland said with iron in his voice.

JoJo looked ready to bolt. "I'm afraid I don't know much about the game, sir. I'd most likely just get in the way."

Umberland pointed to the sideline. "You'll stand there and run after errant balls. You don't need to know the rules. Nothing could be simpler."

He gave one last desperate look at the others and cursed himself. "Shit, shit, shit."

"Have fun," Shawn said. "You might want to take your drink, though. It looks hot enough to fry eggs down there."

For the next hour, they watched JoJo work like a dog as they lounged and called out encouragement. JoJo kept plying himself with gin and tonics and after a bit, he played the part, darting, spinning, and jumping for the balls like a circus performer.

Burbank and Umberland soon took to hitting balls at him as he darted across the net to retrieve the game ball. He dove, somersaulted, and lunged to avoid being hit. They only hit him a few times, but when they did, the men hoisted their gin and tonics and drained them, no matter how full or empty. By the end of it, Shawn's guts hurt from laughing and JoJo's hurt from being beaned by tennis balls.

~

A WEEK LATER, Shawn and the rest of Operational Group Bellevue wrote their last letters home and prepared to return to the war in Burma. Shawn wrote his mother a long letter. He focused mainly on happy stories. He avoided any mention of combat or danger. His mother wasn't one to worry too much, but he didn't need to throw it in her face.

He also wrote to his aunt and uncle. He asked them for his cousin Clyde's address or at least his unit. He hoped he hadn't befallen some tragedy. His letter may take months to find its way back to the West Coast of the U.S. Even if nothing had happened to cousin Clyde yet, something could happen in the interim.

Rumor had it that airborne units in the European theater were heavily engaged, but he felt isolated from any news from back home and chanced upsetting his aunt and uncle, hoping to connect with someone outside his immediate sphere. It would be nice to correspond with his cousin, even if the time between letters might be long.

He thought about writing a letter to Ilsa, but he had no idea how it would ever get to her. Was she still alive? Every time he thought of their intense love affair, he yearned for her, but knew that even if the war ended tomorrow, he'd likely never see her again. Did she ever think of him? He hoped so.

He joined his team sitting beneath the shade trees of the Nasira tea garden. Despite the muggy heat, the tea garden grounds always seemed to be ten degrees cooler than everywhere else. Perhaps it was because there always seemed to be a pleasant breeze blowing through.

After a few minutes, Captain Rex Burbank waltzed out from an outbuilding. He took one last drag on his cigarette before stripping it down to grounds and spreading it around at his feet. A habit from being in enemy territory for long stints at a time.

Captain Burbank was the epitome of health. He had broad shoulders and stringy muscles with thick veins interlaced across his biceps. Shawn had seen him trot with a full pack all day without taking more than a five-minute break. Despite being older, he could out march every man, except perhaps Henry Calligan.

"Men, as you've heard, we'll be heading back into Burma tonight. Instead of dropping into Camp Knothead, we'll drop into the Hukwang Valley, near Zhang Htaw Naw's village, Taikri."

Shawn pictured Zhang Htaw Naw, the diminutive leader of the Kachins. When he'd first seen the man, he'd doubted someone so small and seemingly inconsequential could possibly be the leader of such a deadly force. The constant smile he wore made him hard to take seriously. But he'd seen the way the Kachin revered him and he'd seen the way they fought like tigers for him. They invoked his name in combat like he was a king of old.

Even the leader of the OSS, General Donovan, had met him and been awed. He'd been so impressed, in fact, that he recommended to General Stillwell, leading troops in China, that he could rely on him and his Kachin Rangers to lead the way in his push into Burma. That push had already started, but was gaining momentum. That was why they were heading back into the jungle, no doubt.

Captain Burbank continued. "You've had a nice little break, but it's time to get back to work. This time things will be different, however." He paced back and forth slowly now. "We'll still be working with the Kachin Rangers, but instead of training them, we'll be fighting alongside them." He let that hang there a moment.

Shawn thought of the raid on the ammo dump. It had nearly been a complete success. If they hadn't been caught on the road in daylight by the two Japanese fighters and strafed mercilessly, it would've been perfect. The Kachin had learned a valuable lesson, as they all had. *If only Umberland had listened.*

He liked and trusted his CO, but he'd messed up on that one. He should've gone with his instincts and forced the Kachin to leave the road before the sun rose. As it was, many brave men died. *Men? Some were only boys.* He couldn't shake the image of their young, torn bodies strewn like old spaghetti along the road. It made his stomach churn. But now Burbank was telling them they'd be taking a more active role? *What had they been doing?*

"General Stillwell and Chiang Kai Shek's Chinese are pushing strong into Burma. The southern portion of the Burma road's out of reach, so Stillwell's gonna build a new road behind his advancing Chinese, from Ledo, India, all the way to Myitkyina, then Lashio, where he'll link back into the original Burma road. That will reestablish the overland supply route from India to China. Flying over the gap is too damned costly in lives and equipment, and just isn't enough. The Chinese are hanging on by a thread up there. There's not enough aircraft or pilots and those numbers go down daily because of enemy activity and simple maintenance issues. They have to get that road built or the Chinese will wither on the vine and free up about a million Japs. So, they're taking the fight straight to them. The Chinese will do most of the heavy lifting, but the Kachin Rangers and ourselves will hit Jap supply lines and anything else that'll disrupt their response."

Murmurs went around the group. Shawn felt excitement but also a heaviness. He'd seen his share of death, even doled it out more than once, but it sounded as though he'd see a lot more in the coming months. The task seemed overwhelmingly daunting.

JoJo smacked his arm. "You hear that? We're gonna kill more Japs."

"Yeah, I heard him," he said, trying to sound excited but coming up short.

O'Keefe leaned in. "We're not all as bloodthirsty as you, JoJo."

JoJo looked ready to protest, but Captain Burbank cleared his throat to get their attention, then continued. "General Stillwell is also bringing in an American infantry unit to help with the attack." Eyebrows raised around the room. This was fresh news to them. "The 5307th led by Brigadier General Merrill will be attacking along the northern mountains and pushing on toward Myitkyina and Lashio." A murmur of discussion went through the group. So far, they'd been the only Americans in Burma. Stillwell had them in China, but none had ventured into their neck of the woods.

"That's tough terrain. Do they know what they're getting into up there?" Umberland asked.

"I doubt it. If they ask for help, we'll give it, but you know how those leg units are."

"Stubborn and stupid," JoJo slurred under his breath.

"These men are veterans and they've had extensive training for long overland marches and jungle fighting. But I don't think they fully appreciate that terrain up there. They're hoping to get behind the Japs while they're engaged with the Chinese, but they have to get there first."

Burbank wound up the briefing. "The Nips have increased their bombing raids into western Burma and even into parts of India. There's even been troop movements out of Myitkyina. Large troop movements. But the brass doesn't think it'll amount to much. They think their repositioning in order to better counter the Kachin raids and not to the impending push. By the way, General Stillwell wants to be in Myitkyina in just over a month."

Shawn's mind went to Henry Calligan. The veteran Task Force 101 man and the other two operatives watching the Myitkyina had undoubtedly been the ones who'd relayed the information about the enemy troop movements. Would they link up with Calligan during this operation? He hoped not. The man scared him sometimes. He was even more bloodthirsty than JoJo. Was Didi, the Kachin Ranger who'd adopted Calligan, out there, too? They made a deadly and fearsome pair. They hated the Japanese with equal hatred and were absolutely ruthless.

No one had any pressing questions for Captain Burbank, so they left the comfort of the shade trees and ambled back to their hammocks and cots. They'd be flying out at 2100 hours on a converted bomber and jumping into a spot they'd been to before, but never parachuted into. That prospect didn't make Shawn nervous. Jumping had become automatic and almost sedate. He'd certainly rather jump than walk.

He unpacked his parachute and repacked it, mostly for something to do. Something to keep his mind off the killing. He didn't want to see any more boys ripped to shreds by Japanese bombs and bullets.

JoJo sidled up beside him as Shawn put the final tucks into the parachute pack. "You okay?" Shawn startled, then looked at him with a question in his eyes. "It just seems like you're not too happy to be going back out there."

"You are?"

"Sure, why not? It's what we're trained to do. You nervous about the jump?" He pointed to the repacked parachute.

"Nah," Shawn almost laughed. Jumping into unknown swaths of land in the middle of Burma from a few hundred feet off the ground didn't faze him anymore. It had become almost routine. If something went wrong, they'd likely die, but that was a roll of the dice. "Are you?"

"Course not, but don't divert my question. What's the matter?"

Shawn turned to face him squarely. "You don't get sick of the killing?"

JoJo lowered his eyes and kicked the dirt before finally answering. "I know how it sounds, but no. Those slant-eyed little fuckers deserve everything they get."

"Is that how you do it?"

"What d'you mean?"

"I mean, it's easier to kill 'em if you don't think of them as humans."

"Yeah, I guess it helps. But you've seen the stuff they've done. They don't *act* like humans."

"But they can't all be like that. I mean the officers, sure, but not Private Dickhead from down the street. They're taking orders like everyone else."

JoJo thought about it for a while. "If Burbank or Umberland went into a village, even say a Jap village in Japan and ordered you to kill all the civilians, would you do it?"

Shawn chewed his lower lip. "Well no, I guess not."

"How 'bout a Jap prisoner all bound up and defenseless? Would you lop off his head if General Donovan ordered you to?"

"Jesus, JoJo."

"Well, would you?"

"I dunno . . ."

"What if they threatened to put you against a wall and shoot you for treason if you didn't?"

"That's a lot to think about."

"Well, the Jap privates already made that decision. They said, fuck yes! So did the Nazis, for that matter."

Shawn shifted on his feet. "I guess you're right, but it still feels wrong sometimes."

"Were you raised religious or something? I know that can be tough, but the holy rollers justify it by saying it's evil they're killing and it's true."

"I'm not anymore religious than anyone else. I mean, we went to church on Sundays and I know most of the songs."

"Well, tell yourself they're evil, which they are, or tell yourself they're subhuman, which is also true, and get on with it. It needs to be done and your head needs to be in it. We need to know we can trust you out there."

Shawn looked JoJo straight in the eye. "Have—have the others said something?"

JoJo's silence told him everything he needed to know. The thought of the others in Bellevue having concerns about him made his legs wobbly. He'd been through endless trials from training and even combat with those men. He thought of them as more than simply comrades in arms, but brothers—even that wasn't a strong enough description. Letting them down wasn't an option.

He stood more erect and put iron in his voice. "You can count on me one hundred percent. That's never been a question, JoJo. Let the others know, too. I'm in for the long haul."

JoJo slapped his back. "Good man. Now let's get some chow. It's not as good as Chef Watson's, but these Indians sure can cook."

~

SHAWN LEANED his head against the metal wall of the converted bomber. He'd jumped from this exact aircraft several times. The roar of the engines and loud whistling of air seeping through widows and rivets made him feel at home. He wondered how many flight hours this old bucket had on it and when it had been serviced last. Between flying the hump into China and these short hops into Burma, these birds got a lot of hard use, not to mention the pilots.

He leaned forward toward the cockpit. He could see the darkness beyond the cockpit glass. The pilot's hand rested on what he assumed to be the throttle. He wore a peaked, non–regulation style baseball hat with the emblem of some baseball team. He'd heard the pilot, Captain Clem, was quite a ballplayer. Even had a chance at the bigs, but the war put a crimp in those plans.

He stood and waddled forward past Lieutenant Umberland. Umberland glanced at him but otherwise ignored him and kept studying his maps using a red lensed flashlight. Shawn would never do something like stand up in the middle of a flight and approach the flight deck back in the 501st airborne, but this was the OSS.

He hunkered between Clem and Dave, the copilot. He looked out over the jungle only a few hundred feet below, which seemed to glow from the light of the half-moon. They flew low to avoid any patrolling Zeros.

"Hey, Clem," Shawn had to almost yell to be heard. Both pilots jolted, then looked at him.

Clem said, "Hey, Shawny. What can I do for you?"

"Rumor has it you're a decent third baseman. Who'd you play for?"

He took off his hat and shoved it closer. Shawn didn't recognize the emblem and shrugged. "I don't know that team."

"The Barons. It's a farm team for the Reds."

"The Reds, huh? You ever play in the bigs?"

"Nah, but the war started right after I got onto the team. Hell, the whole team quit and joined up when the Japs attacked Pearl. Even some guys who were in the bigs quit and are fighting these bastards."

"No kidding?"

"Sure they are. Lots of 'em, too." The copilot said something into his radio and Clem nodded. "Tell young Lieutenant Umberland that the drop zone's coming up in ten minutes."

Shawn nodded and turned, but Clem grasped his arm and said, "Good luck down there, Shawn. We'll see you back in Assam soon enough."

Shawn smiled at him and nodded emphatically. He passed the message onto Umberland and took his seat between JoJo and Sergeant Boyd.

Umberland yelled and held up ten fingers, "Ten minutes!"

JoJo yelled in his ear. "What was that all about?"

"You owe me five bucks."

"You asked him about playing ball?"

"He played for a Reds farm team called the Barons."

JoJo leaned forward and peered toward the cockpit, then back into his seat. "I'm supposed to believe a pilot? They're notorious liars."

Shawn laughed. "Well then, we'll have to wait'll we can corroborate his story somehow. Know anyone from Cinci?"

"Nah, they're all a bunch of squares over there."

A few minutes later, the crew chief barked orders, and they stood and readied themselves for the jump. This wasn't a static line jump, they had to manually pull their chutes. The plane bucked and swerved as it hit turbulence, but they'd all learned to stand with their feet spread wide for support and to hang onto something besides. Shawn glimpsed open fields just ahead, their landing site.

Without warning, an impossibly loud hammer sound banged on the outside of the plane. Shawn's blood turned cold. The bomber shuddered under the impact and slewed right, but soon corrected. He heard yelling from the flight deck. "Get out! Get out, now!"

None of them hesitated for even an instant. Umberland went out the door first and the others followed close behind, one after another. Shawn grasped his pull cord and went out the door. As he fell, he glimpsed a small bright flame coming from the left wing's engine cowling.

He pulled the cord and his neck tweaked with the harsh snap as his chute deployed and blossomed. He found the glowing flame again a moment later in the dark sky, but he had to look away as the ground approached quickly.

He landed painfully, but felt nothing snap or break. He sprang up and automatically unsnapped his harness and began hauling in his chute, but his eyes darted back to the sky. He couldn't see the bomber or the flame, but he could still hear the engines and a black streak left by the burning engine against the moon and clouds.

Men darted from the shadows and he recognized the diminutive Kachin Rangers, all dressed in uniforms provided by the U.S. Army. They always reminded him of children playing dress-up and playing army, but he never told them that. They spoke in excited whispers, but Shawn only caught snippets as he hadn't grasped their language just yet. They normally smiled, but not tonight.

They gestured wildly toward the sky. Shawn grasped the shoulder of the nearest ranger and when he had his attention, pointed to the sky. "Did you see what happened? What happened to the airplane?" He mimicked the plane and pointed and shrugged.

The ranger nodded emphatically and acted out two airplanes, one higher than the other, and then yammered, imitating a firing machine gun. Then he wobbled his hand back and forth and pointed south, then shrugged.

Shit, Shawn felt helpless. Had the plane gone down? Wouldn't they have seen an explosion if it had? Not if it didn't explode, he surmised. Perhaps they crash-landed and were okay. Perhaps they were injured and needed their help.

He trotted through the darkness, unslung, and loaded his M1 carbine with a fresh magazine, while searching for Lieutenant Umberland. He found Sergeant Boyd instead. "Boyd, have you heard anything? Did the plane go down? Are we going after them?"

Boyd's gruff voice had an edge of worry. "I dunno. It was on fire. I saw it make it over the ridge, but nothing after that."

"There's no friendlies over there. The Nips will be on them quick if they went down."

"We don't know what's happened yet. First things first. Assemble and assess."

Shawn didn't like it, but he understood. They couldn't just traipse off into enemy territory half-cocked. Assembling everyone seemed to take forever, even though it might've been a new record. No one had been injured, although Shawn's neck stiffened with each passing minute, but he wasn't going to mention that.

Umberland had gone to speak with someone while the rest of them gathered their gear. The flight crew had planned on dropping the men first, then make a second pass and drop more requested supplies, but the enemy Zero had negated the second part of that plan.

Umberland finally returned. He looked grim but determined in the light from the moon. "The village chief here got a radio report from the next village over. The plane went down just over that ridge another four miles or so. It didn't explode on impact, so there could be survivors. We're going after them."

Shawn wanted to run. The adrenaline from the attack, then the jump, still coursed through his veins. He took long, deep breaths until he found control. Instead of feeling nervous, he wanted to get the show on the road. He had friends on board that plane. The thought turned his mouth dry. He hoped they'd survived, but knew the odds weren't in the crew member's favor. It was a miracle it hadn't exploded on impact.

Finally, they were ready to move out. A squad of Kachin Rangers joined them, and they set a grueling pace through the moonlit countryside.

6

Shawn thought they should've brought more rangers when they set out for the bomber crash site, but he hadn't voiced his concern because he wanted to get a move on as quickly as possible. But now, as they hunkered on a low hill overlooking the scars from the crash, he wished they had an entire company of rangers.

From what he could infer with just the light from the moon and his slightly elevated vantage point, the bomber had skimmed the trees of the ridge they sat upon, then nosed forward and impacted into a long field full of kunai grass. The aircraft traveled a long way as evidenced by the deep trough full of bits and pieces of various sizes and description. It finally came to rest in the middle of the field. Most of the left wing had snapped off, but the engine still clung stubbornly to the stub of the wing, although it sagged nearly to the ground. Even in the moonlight, he could see smoke curling up lazily from one of the charred engines. It was a wonder it hadn't lit off the aviation fuel permeating the air, making his nostrils sting.

But the real concern wasn't the crash site itself, but the number of Japanese soldiers descending upon it from all sides. He stopped counting at fifty men. With the addition of the rangers, they nearly matched the Japanese force, but they'd only brought the ammunition they jumped with.

Enough for a few minutes, but nothing sustained. Besides, if they engaged, they'd undoubtedly risk killing the very men they came to save.

Besides the two pilots, Clem and Dave, there was also the navigator, Ben, the crew chief, Taylor, and his assistant, Bailey. He didn't know if anyone had survived, but they soon would as they watched the Japanese approach the stricken bird cautiously. Flashlights added to the moonlight, but it would've been better without them ruining their night sight.

"How the hell did they beat us here?" he asked no one in particular.

"Had to be bad luck. They must've been moving through the area. Maybe they're part of the Jap shuffle Burbank mentioned in the briefing," Sergeant Boyd whispered.

"Way up here? That was down in Myitkyina—days and days march from here."

"Maybe it's bigger than they thought."

O'Keefe laying on the other side of Boyd said, "What's the plan? We attacking or what?"

"Umberland wants to wait and see if they find any survivors."

"What if they just shoot 'em? We gonna sit back here and just watch?"

Boyd turned sharply and scowled at JoJo, then hissed, "We follow orders, Private."

Umberland crawled up to Boyd and whispered in his ear. Shawn strained, hoping to catch the conversation, but he only caught snippets, and none of it helped. It was probably too late to call for reinforcements, but they could ambush these bastards somewhere down the line if they correctly guessed where they'd go from here. But that's what it would be—a guess—and if they were wrong, they might lose the crew for good—assuming they'd survived.

Yelling wafted up from the crash site. Japanese voices called out sharply and the enemy soldiers aimed weapons and became agitated near the fuselage.

Umberland used his binoculars. "Someone survived. I see hands coming out from the cockpit section."

"Who is it? You see anyone else?" Shawn asked. The pilots weren't as closely knit as the men from the operational group, but they knew each other fairly well from all the times their paths had crossed. He considered them friends. Even though they were cocky pilot scum, they were good men.

"It looks like Clem. He's got that damned baseball hat on. I—I don't see anyone else yet. He looks shaken up."

More yelling and agitation from the Japanese troops near the main section drew their attention. Umberland shifted his view and adjusted the focus. "Okay, okay. I see more survivors. One guy's coming out with a hand up. Wait—he's pulling someone else along, so two. Three with Clem, so far."

JoJo hissed, "What are we gonna do about it, Danny?"

"At ease, JoJo," Boyd hissed back, but the question hung in the air.

Umberland dropped his eyes from the binoculars. He exchanged a glance with Boyd. "There's at least a platoon down there."

Shawn's gut wrenched, thinking he knew where this was going. He didn't know if he could just sit here and watch his friends be taken—or killed. But Umberland surprised him.

"We can take 'em—but not here."

Relief flooded through Shawn and he could feel the mood lighten in the others. Everyone felt the same way—they wanted to get their friends back.

Umberland growled low. "We can't set up an ambush until we know which way they'll take 'em. We don't know where they came from or where their base camp is. Hell, they might not even have one yet." He tucked the binoculars away, then added in a barely audible whisper, "Which makes it dangerous for our guys."

"What d'you mean?" Shawn asked.

Umberland ignored Shawn's question. "We might have to hit 'em sooner than later." He tapped Boyd's shoulder. "Take a squad down and to the right and I'll take the rest left. We'll try to get them in a crossfire and squeeze them."

"What about the flyboys? They'll be caught in it, too."

"It may not matter," he said with iron in his voice.

Shawn exchanged a worried glance with JoJo on his right. "What's he talking about?" he hissed.

"You know damn well what he's talking about. It's like we talked about before—they're not human."

"You mean they might just kill 'em? In cold blood? Just like that?"

Boyd slapped his shoulder. "Let's move out."

Shawn followed the others to the edge of the field. The kunai grass came to his waist and thankfully wasn't as thick as he'd seen in other spots. He could just make out the crash site in the hazy distance. Voices came in undulating clarity occasionally, but nothing sounded close.

Boyd waved them forward. Shawn hunched and stepped into the grass trying to keep his head just below the top. After only a few steps he felt his legs straining with the effort. Beads of sweat pinpricked his armpits, but he ignored the discomfort as they had trained him to do.

Boyd led them until the crash site loomed on their left, less than one hundred yards away. Boyd slowly rose until he could see clearly over the grass. He scanned while Shawn watched his eyes from his hunkered position.

Boyd slowly lowered himself, then signaled for them to spread out. Shawn moved carefully through the grass, assuring each step he took was soundless. The Japanese must have sentries out, but so far they had seen no signs of them. It worried and relieved him at the same time. It would be easier to get close enough for the engagement if they didn't have sentries, but the fact that they had seen no one could also mean there were skilled soldiers lying in wait somewhere.

At a passed hand signal, Shawn stopped and readied his mind for combat. He stayed down, but he could clearly hear talking and yelling now, although he couldn't understand the foreign language. He concentrated on keeping his heart rate and his breathing to a manageable level. Hearing the enemy so close had an immediate adrenaline response, which he needed to control.

He held his breath when he heard an American voice. He checked his carbine, making sure he'd released the safety and had a round chambered and ready to go. He did a quick readiness assessment. He had four magazines in his ammo pouch and two hand grenades dangling from his shoulder straps. It would have to be enough.

He raised himself inch by inch until he could see the wreckage. He saw shapes darting in the moonlight but also a large clump of soldiers standing in a semicircle with their rifles leveled. Just beyond, he saw two Americans with their hands up. Harsh, guttural yelling came from the Japanese. He heard another American voice, but he couldn't understand the words. It sounded scared and pleading.

What were they waiting for? The hastily put together plan called for Umberland's group to open fire first. Once that happened, they'd wait until the Japanese turned their backs toward the threat and away from Shawn's group. That's when they'd open fire.

They must be in position by now. He desperately wanted to start things off. The Japanese tirade had an edge of hysteria that made him nervous. The officer, or whoever the voice belonged to, sounded unhinged—as though trying to provoke some kind of response. He felt a foreboding in the pit of his stomach.

He risked raising his head a few inches more. Other Bellevue men did the same. He wondered if an enemy sentry had his sights squarely on his head at that moment. Even that thought couldn't keep him from watching.

A wave of dread swept through him as he saw an officer holding a pistol, assembling a staggered line of soldiers to face the only two flyboys he could see. They had to do something now, or it would be too late. He had no doubt the Japanese were about to kill their prisoners.

In some distant corner of his mind, it made perfect sense. The Japanese were exposed, moving to some unknown but undoubtedly new base of operations. They'd be slowed down and possibly compromised if they took prisoners along. But these were obviously American airmen. They'd be a bounty of information if they could get them to talk. Was that why Umberland chose this path? To keep them from falling into enemy hands one way or the other? Shawn's nerves felt electrified. They had to act now.

Over the yelling coming from the crash site, he heard Boyd's whispered iron voice. "Wait for the signal."

Shawn licked his lips. Everyone was on edge. He even saw a few carbines at shoulders, ready to fire. Boyd's hold command had come in the nick of time. Shawn's trigger finger had traveled from the trigger guard to the trigger without a conscious thought. He removed it now, but stayed in his mostly upright position. If there were sentries, they would've reacted by now.

Come on, Umberland! Come on! He silently pleaded.

The Japanese officer's voice rose an octave and Shawn saw his pistol go from aiming at the sky to aiming at the flyboys. Then he fired. It sounded like a toy gun, but the subsequent shots from the rest of the enemy soldiers filled the air with sharp cracks, which made his head throb.

He brought his carbine to his shoulder as he fought off a wave of nausea. He could only see gun smoke now. The prisoners were undoubtedly dead or dying, but still Umberland didn't open fire. *What's he waiting for?*

Boyd's voice again. "Hold. Hold. Wait for the signal."

It took every ounce of Shawn's control not to open fire. Only his extensive training, both in the airborne and in the OSS, kept him from disobeying a direct order. He suspected he wasn't alone in that. He expected someone to break—he hoped someone would, but nothing happened. He cursed their training. He couldn't make himself do it, somehow, although every fiber in his being wanted him to pull the trigger and avenge his friends, he simply couldn't disobey the order.

A full minute passed, and Shawn realized the signal would never come. Anger and confusion flooded his mind. Even this close to the bastards that had just murdered his friends, his anger shifted to Umberland. He was going to let these bastards get away with it?

Boyd moved among them. He tapped Shawn's leg. "Get down, you idiot. Fall back."

Fall back? He could hardly see straight. He wanted to strangle someone, and Danny Umberland was at the top of the list.

Boyd must've sensed his anger. He pulled him down to eye level. "Get a hold of yourself. Fall back, now. It's over."

Shawn glared back, but softened himself and gave a quick nod. Boyd moved off, relaying the message and making sure no one took matters into their own hands.

Before taking his first step back, he heard the Japanese talking and even a few chortles of laughter. He touched the grenade on his harness. It would be so simple to lob it into their midst. That would take care of their laughing. But he didn't act on the happy thought. He silently moved back through the kunai grass until he reached the relative safety of the jungle.

He turned back toward the crash site, but a thick band of clouds slid in front of the moon and he couldn't see much more than a dark outline. As his friends slid past him, he saw the same hurt and anger in their eyes that he felt. Even Boyd looked ready to tear someone's head off. Umberland had some explaining to do.

They met the rest of Bellevue back on the ridge where they'd first seen the crash site. Darkness hung on the land as though the foul deed they'd witnessed wouldn't allow the moon to ever illumine the area again. Permanent darkness would stain the crash site forever.

Umberland conferred with Boyd away from the men. Shawn watched them out of the corner of his eye, as did all the rest of them. He'd been through a lot of pain and hardship with Lieutenant Danny Umberland, but at that moment, he wouldn't have paid a penny for his life. He could feel the other men's hatred permeating off them like heat.

"What the fuck was that?" Shawn whispered to Ned Plano, who'd been in Umberland's group.

Ned looked ready to rip someone's head off, too. "I dunno, Coop. I really don't know. He just sat there watching it happen. When the Nips opened fire . . ." he paused and shook his head slowly. "It was like—it was like he was relieved."

"Relieved?" Shawn had to work to keep his voice under control.

Murmurs of conversation permeated the group despite their proximity to the enemy still loitering around the crash site.

Boyd stepped away from his private meeting with Umberland and seethed at them. "Knock it off. We're moving out. No more talking."

The order didn't sit well with any of them. They weren't used to being talked to as though they were just another line unit. The OSS didn't follow the same rules as a regular unit, but they complied and swallowed their pride and their anger until they were in a position where they could properly vent and not risk being ambushed.

The Kachin who'd guided them to the crash site veered from the main group and headed back toward the kunai grass field and the crash site.

Boyd addressed them again. "They're going to follow the Japs—see where they're going."

That at least helped a little. Shawn took one last look at the downed bomber. He couldn't see the Japanese any longer. They'd either moved off or hunkered nearby. He thought about Clem and his hat. He didn't want to leave the area. They deserved a proper burial.

He'd seen what the Japanese sometimes did to bodies—hacked them to pieces. Had they done that to Clem and the others? He steeled himself that they most likely had. They wouldn't miss an opportunity to mess with their heads. *They hate us as much as we hate them.* He felt his own hatred seal any remaining cracks of empathy he'd fought to maintain.

SHAWN INSISTED on joining the group tasked with recovering whatever was left of the airmen at the crash site. Only two days had passed and already the scene seemed old—even ancient—as though the crash had happened decades before in a long-forgotten war.

New sprigs of grass had already taken root in the deep gash left by the burrowing aircraft. They watched the area for over two hours before descending on the scene. No enemy presence remained.

He and nine other Bellevue men, along with two dozen Kachin Rangers, approached the site carefully. They would've seen the Japanese setting out booby traps on that fateful night, but they didn't know if they may have returned in the interim and left them lethal surprises, so they used caution.

Pockets of clouds kept the direct heat of the sun at bay, but it added to the stifling humidity. In broad daylight, the crash looked much worse. Large chunks of the aircraft dotted the area. The left wing had torn loose early on and it must have tumbled, shedding bits and pieces of the wheel and strut assembly. Large swaths of metal peeled back from the main cabin area where they'd sat and jumped from just a few nights before. It was a wonder anyone survived the crash, let alone the three they'd seen. Survived the crash but not the Japanese.

Shawn stepped around the massive rudder assembly. It was surprisingly intact. JoJo, Lawrence, and O'Keefe stood and stared at something he couldn't quite see, as though transfixed. Shawn stepped around debris and large clods of dirt to stand beside them. What he saw turned his stomach.

"Jesus, Joseph, and Mary," he muttered.

"I don't think they were involved," JoJo grunted.

Five bullet-riddled bodies were laid out as though for inspection. They had separated their heads from their bodies, as well as their hands, which held severed penises.

Shawn bent and heaved his breakfast into the dirt. The others didn't even glance his way, just kept staring at the aircrew.

Shawn recovered and wiped his mouth with the back of his hand. He stood and faced the carnage. "They—they must've hauled the other two out and shot them full of holes for the fun of it."

"Or maybe they weren't dead, just wounded. Doesn't really matter," JoJo said. "They're animals."

The lack of emotion in his voice struck Shawn. The rest of the men streamed in and had a long look. A few heaved their guts up, but most just looked on stoically.

JoJo said, "You ever get kindhearted toward 'em again. Think of this and you'll be cured."

Shawn swallowed the bile rising in his throat, not allowing himself to be sick again. He wouldn't give the Japanese the satisfaction again—ever.

He slid his pack off and pulled out his brand-new poncho. Before spreading it over their bodies, he searched for Clem's baseball hat, but it wasn't there. He went into the belly of the bomber. Wires and junk crisscrossed the floor and the ceiling. The seats they'd sat in remained mostly intact, although a few were completely missing. Congealed blood slicked the floor in spots and he stepped around it carefully.

He made his way to the cockpit, threading between gashes and unidentifiable piles of debris. The front windscreen had shattered and the cockpit controls were covered with blood—mostly on the copilot's side. What he figured must be Dave's still laced-up boot sat near the rudder pedals as though on display. He searched the cockpit, but he didn't find the hat. As he stepped out through the hole in the roof, he spotted something in the mud. He bent down and hefted Clem's hat. He smacked it on his pants and dirt and mud flew off in clods. He placed it on his head. It would remind him of every day of Clem and also the evil the enemy held in their hearts.

The Kachin had brought along stretchers and they were reverently placing the bodies onto them when he stepped from the wreckage, wearing the hat. Handling the severed heads and other bits proved difficult, but they managed without causing any undue disrespect. They did the job with stoic reserve. They'd seen this kind of handiwork before, after the Japanese ravaged their villages early in the war. They seemed used to it, somehow. The thought of getting used to such barbarity made Shawn's head spin.

A few of the others went through the wreckage while the Kachin walked the dead back toward their village, where they would be buried. Getting them out would be nearly impossible and not worth the risk involved. The air crew were past caring, but Shawn wondered about their families. *If I find a Jap with anything on him from the crash site, I'll kill them slow.* He jolted at the thought. It was as though it had come from someone else—someone he didn't know. *The new me,* he thought bitterly.

When the Bellevue men were done sifting through the wreckage, Boyd said, "Burn it. We're not leavin' nothin' for the Nips."

They'd brought white phosphorous grenades for the occasion. Soon the flames lapped at the sky and blackened the kunai grass as it swayed in the hot, artificial wind.

Shawn stepped back from the unbearable heat. He looked to where the Kachin marched with their grisly burdens. The heat and the flames felt like defeat.

He pondered the burning wreckage. The aircraft had started its life somewhere in a factory in the United States—each rivet attended to by some factory worker who went home each night to his wife. Perhaps one of their children fought for survival out here somewhere. Perhaps they'd already been killed or horribly maimed. All that work, all that effort, ended out here in a field of kunai grass in a country they most likely never heard of.

Each step back to the village felt like a death dirge.

7

Sweetwater, Texas

Sal Sarducci hated this small Texas town, but the thought of leaving never crossed his mind. Even if Beatrice Malinsky lived in the pit of an active volcano, he wouldn't have left her side. Particularly now that she had a beautiful baby girl to consider.

He'd dealt with stupid people plenty during his career, but he'd never seen such backward-thinking folks as lived in Sweetwater. Granted, they were old-fashioned about women having children while unwed and probably thought even less of a man living in the same house—living in sin—as his mother would've put it if she wasn't dust in a grave.

She would've sided with most folks in Sweetwater on that topic—but she'd never met Beatrice or Cora, the wonder baby. She might change her mind if she did. And perhaps one day, if she'd have him, he'd marry Beatrice and make it all better, but he almost didn't want to just to spite these small-minded people.

He accepted the scowls and outright hostility they faced when they took little Cora on walks in the park, which is what they were doing at the moment. Cora certainly didn't mind. Her bright blue eyes lit up with wonder, even if she felt a slight breeze on her face. Everything was brand new and intensely magical and infinitely interesting to her growing mind. Sal loved her dearly, and Beatrice even more, if that was possible.

"What are you thinking about, Sal?" Beatrice had her arm wrapped through Sal's beefy arm while he pushed the stroller along the pitted sidewalk. The bumps and jolts always made little Cora giggle and gurgle happily.

"Oh, nothing much," he lied.

"Oh, come on, Sal. Tell me."

He pointed at a cluster of women with young children playing at a playground. They were undoubtedly the parents. One or two men stood nearby, also chatting. "When they notice us, they'll do their normal nastiness—turn away, scowl, and talk behind our backs. The men are either too old for service or didn't pass the physical. The three there look disgruntled as all get out. They're itching for something to make them feel better, make them look good in front of the women who they think look down on them because they're not fighting the Japs or Krauts like their husbands are. They're not much of a threat, but they might try to cause trouble for us." Beatrice stared up at him. He looked down at her and shrugged. "You asked, sweetheart."

She shook her head. "You think you'll ever get over it? I mean, assessing threats all the time? It must be stressful going through life like that."

"I did it too long. It's just who I am now. Does it bother you?" He asked with an edge of worry.

"No. It makes me feel safe, but I wonder if it's healthy. You're liable to have a stress attack or something."

"It's only stressful if I don't think I'm up to the task." He shifted his chin toward the men. "And that bunch doesn't put undue stress on me."

"I received a letter from Abby," Beatrice said.

Sal broke his gaze away from the men, who were sizing him up. "You did? How is she?"

"I wasn't sure if I should tell you at first."

"What do you mean? Has something happened?" He felt a sudden pit in his stomach.

"She's fine, she's fine. She had a bit of a scare, though."

He wanted to ask her to spit it out, but he'd learned that she would eventually tell him what he wanted to know if he simply waited. Asking or pushing usually prolonged the pain, so he held his tongue. He'd learned a lot about Beatrice Malinsky in the past few months, and the more he learned, the deeper he fell in love with her. He just hoped she felt the same way. She was so much younger, after all, and young people tended to change their minds easily.

"She was towing targets for the navy gunners and one of them clipped her tail. She was able to land without trouble, but she said it scared her and made her think."

"I'll bet."

An image of a flaming wreckage falling from the sky over the waste-lands and trenches in France sprang to his mind, unbidden. It had been his first week in the trenches. He'd been young and dumb—he must've been to volunteer for such a thing—ages ago, now.

He remembered watching the planes dogfighting overhead. The others watched as though it was a free showing of a popular play. He remembered his pals gaping and slapping one another like they were watching a sporting event. The dogfight seemed sedate, even elegant for a while. But then one got the upper hand and laid a long burst of machine gun fire into the other. He realized he didn't remember who'd won the fight, but the inferno darting into the ground and the horrible screams as the pilot burned left an indelible mark. He shuddered to think of Abby in such a horrible situation.

Beatrice hugged his arm. "You look like you've seen a ghost. She's fine. Honestly, she flew again that same evening."

That didn't make him feel any better. "I just wish she'd chosen a safer profession."

She relaxed her grip. "It's what I'd be doing if—well, you know." She reached down and wiped a spot of drool from Cora's chin. "How would you feel if I got back into it? I think I could, you know. I mean, once Cora's ready for real food." She blushed slightly, and Sal marveled once again at her beauty.

"Um, well, I guess I hadn't really thought about it much. Who'd take care of Cora while you were flying?"

She looked at her feet, then back up at his dark eyes. "Well, we could hire a nanny, I suppose."

"We?" he asked carefully.

"Well, of course—we. Who else?"

They walked in silence for a few minutes. As he forecasted, the women turned away and gossiped, throwing them dark glances when they felt encouraged. The men puffed out their chests and said things just quiet enough not to be heard outright. The volume increased slightly as they passed and had their backs to them. Sal barely noticed. He beamed. *Perhaps she loves me the same way I love her.*

"I—well, I guess I could watch her. We wouldn't need a nanny. I could do it."

She stopped abruptly and turned to face him. Cora gurgled happily as he stopped the stroller.

"You'd do that? Are you sure? I mean, it's certainly not traditional. But it would save us oodles of money." They continued walking. He liked the way she said "us."

He had left Brooks Industries with plenty of money to last both of them a long time. He'd never told her exactly how much, just that he'd be able to pay for her rent and all her expenses until Cora reached an age that she felt comfortable going back to work.

Funds weren't bottomless, but being smart would allow them a comfortable, if not opulent, lifestyle. But he had broached nothing long term. He still didn't know exactly how she felt about him. She'd never mentioned the age difference but he wasn't a fool and they hadn't even made love yet. What if they weren't compatible?

The passion was certainly there, but between Cora's fitful sleeping and Beatrice's healing, it hadn't been a possibility yet. Soon, he hoped—very soon. But he didn't want to broach that subject either. It would have to happen organically.

He often found himself fantasizing about different sexual scenarios, and he scolded himself for being such a desperate romantic. He had to remind himself that he'd killed men with an entrenching tool for chrissakes.

He laughed. Beatrice gave him a curious look. "What's so funny?"

"I'm just trying to picture myself as a nanny."

Beatrice smiled broadly. "Well, you're more than a nanny."

"I am?"

She stopped him again. "Don't be a fool. Of course you are. You've been there every step of the way, Sal. I couldn't have done it without you. Honestly."

He loved how she slipped deeper into her Texas drawl the more passionate she felt about a topic. Her voice almost dripped with drawl.

"Well, not *all* of it," he ventured and immediately wished he hadn't.

But instead of brushing him off or calling him a male chauvinist pig with only one thing on his mind, she tilted her chin up at him and puckered her ruby-red lips.

He took her in his burly arms and kissed her passionately right there in the park for all to see. His world focused down on a single point encompassing Cora and Beatrice. Nothing else mattered at that moment. His troubles with Victor and Meredith vanished as he lost himself in her soft kiss. He floated in the clouds a million miles above the pull of Earth's gravity. They finally came up for air and stared into each other's eyes for a moment before continuing their stroll.

He didn't notice the men approaching from behind until the last possible half second and by then it was far too late. Something hard slammed into the back of his head and his world turned from light to darkness. Distantly, he heard screaming and little Cora crying, but everything was muted and far away. He felt himself falling, but there was nothing to hold on to. He glimpsed the gravel only inches from his face. How had he gotten there?

A harsh voice cut through the darkness. "Now you'll get what you deserve, whore."

~

Sal opened his eyes, but they didn't seem to work properly. He couldn't focus. He was in a bed covered in thin sheets. He shut his eyes, then opened them again. This time the room came into focus better, but it still had fuzzy edges, as though looking through water.

Someone touched his right arm, and he heard a cooing voice he thought he recognized but couldn't quite place. He looked that direction and saw a woman's fuzzy outline. It all came flooding back.

"B—Beatrice? Is that you?"

She leaned in closer, but something she held kept her from getting closer. "Oh, thank God. Yes, it me. Me and little Cora-belle."

He jolted upright, wanting to get a better look, but his head throbbed painfully and stars shot across his vision.

"Easy, Sal. You should rest. They hit you hard."

"Hit me? Who?"

Her voice became small, and he could hardly hear her over the rushing of blood in his ears.

"Those awful men at the park."

Sal laid back. The pillow cupped his head, but he felt deep pain near his spine. He adjusted and realized something kept his head from lying flat. He reached and felt a mass of bandages low on his skull.

"They'll have to change it soon. It's starting to bleed through."

He had a vague memory of men's voices. "They—they hit me?"

"With a billy club. I think that's what the police called it."

"Police?"

"Yes. After they hit you, I screamed for help and one of the women ran for the police. Bless her heart. She was the only one to help."

He remembered what they said to her before he must've passed out. His blood boiled, making his head throb even more. "Did they touch you?" he asked with molten iron in his voice. "Did they . . ."

"No." She blurted. "The cowards took off running when Gladys ran to get the police."

"Did—did they arrest them?"

Her voice took on its own iron. "No. They said there were no eyewit nesses, even though all those women must've seen it happen and this town's too small not to know who did it."

"You saw it. You can identify them."

"I told them that. I said I'd do whatever it took to bring them to justice."

His head swirled. "How—how long have I been here?"

"Two days. The doctor put fifty stitches in your scalp. He said you're lucky to be alive."

"Two days?" It sounded impossible. "Are you okay? You and Cora?"

She gripped his hand and although he couldn't focus well enough to see her eyes, he could tell she wept as she spoke. "Yes, Sal, we're fine. I'm just happy you finally woke up. I thought—well, I didn't know. The doctor didn't know." She choked back a sob. "He's worried about brain damage," she said carefully.

He assessed himself. Besides being a little fuzzy, he didn't feel brain damaged. *Would I know, though?* "Do—does it seem like I have that? Am I making sense?" For all he knew, he may gibber like an idiot.

She leaned forward and kissed his cheek. Cora gurgled and grunted as she pressed into him. "You're making sense. You're fine. I just knew you would be."

She pressed Cora against him and she snuggled into his chin, searching for food that she wouldn't find. He eased his arm and placed his hand against her warm, soft back. It nearly covered her entire body. Cora stopped nudging and calmed down with a little sigh.

"She loves her papa."

His vision blurred again, but this time from a tear of happiness. Beatrice leaned into him and he adjusted to put his hand on her head.

"I was so worried," she whispered.

"I'll have a headache, but I'm fine." Despite the pain, he could've stayed in that position forever. He had a family. A flash of anger ignited on the edges of his consciousness. Someone had assaulted his family and that couldn't stand, but he wasn't ready to deal with that just yet. He'd need to heal, and this was how he'd do it, with Beatrice and Cora at his side.

He felt Beatrice crying against his chest. He kept stroking her hair and calmed her. "It's okay, now. It's okay."

Hearing Beatrice refer to him as Cora's father melted his heart and made him love her even more. He could never be her actual father, but he'd do his best from here on out if she'd let him.

~

Sal didn't let the hospital staff keep him longer than one more day. The doctor lamented his condition, told him he needed more time to be evaluated, but Sal wouldn't have it. He felt he'd already been there too long. He felt coddled, and he hated it.

He sat on the old leather chair in the tiny house they rented, bouncing Cora on his lap while Beatrice cooked in the kitchen. There was a loud rap on the door.

Beatrice stuck her head out and looked at him questioningly. "Expecting someone?"

"No." He stood and shifted Cora into the crook of his arm. Her tiny body nearly disappeared into him. Four little Cora's could've fit in the space. She clutched at his arm hair and pulled with delight. He peered through the small window, looking out onto their tiny porch and the neglected dead grass. "It's the police," he grumbled.

Beatrice wiped her hands on her apron and said, "Be nice."

He'd already talked extensively with the police, yet they still claimed they didn't have a clue who assaulted him. It was almost a joke by now —almost.

He opened the door while unconsciously bouncing Cora. "Hello, Officer Blankenship. Here to tell me you arrested someone?"

"Hello, Mr. Sarducci. Uh, no. I'm here to ask you a few more questions, if you don't mind." He looked beyond Sal's shoulders, obviously expecting to be invited inside.

"I've already answered all your questions, officer. What else could there possibly be? You want me and Beatrice to come down to the station so she can point out the guy from a lineup?"

"We don't have any suspects yet."

"Sweetwater must be a lot bigger than I thought. Hell, if you brought in every male under fifty, it would barely fill this room. Just do that, Officer Blankenship." Sal glanced over his shoulder toward the kitchen, then lowered his voice. "Or would you rather I found the son of a bitch myself? Maybe I'll just start cruising around town and Beatrice can point him out to me. Since your department's obviously not interested, we'll do your job for you. How would that be?"

Officer Blankenship was one of the younger men on the force, which was undoubtedly why they kept sending him here—low man on the totem pole. He still had a few pimples on his chin between the sprigs of curly facial hair he'd somehow missed shaving. His scrawny arms and greasy hair must have made his high school days a living hell. Probably joined the force to earn some respect. Sal didn't ask why he wasn't serving overseas like most other young men his age.

Officer Blankenship had his pencil and paper out ready to take a statement, but he gawked at Sal. "You mean to take matters into your own hands? You know vigilantism is illegal, Mr. Sarducci."

"If I did, I'll bet you'd have plenty of witnesses then, wouldn't you? Lock me up and throw away the key."

Blankenship gritted his teeth, obviously trying not to become flustered like every other time they'd spoken. "You—you gonna cooperate or not?" he stammered.

"Not," Sal said simply. He went to close the door, but Officer Blankenship put his toe in the doorjamb. Sal stopped bouncing Cora, and she lunged forward and mouthed his arm with abandon.

He stared daggers at the officer, and Blankenship's Adam's apple traveled up and down his neck like a slow elevator. "Are—are you saying you're done cooperating? We can't continue the investigation unless you and Miss Malinsky—unless you cooperate."

"Doesn't seem like you're interested in getting justice for us. It's been a week and no suspects, even though everyone in the town knows who did it."

"I—we don't."

"Virgil Cummings, Gleason Baten, Hugh Clevenger, or Danny Cahill." He squared up to him and the officer's face turned even more pasty white. "You bring those men into a lineup and Beatrice'll identify which one tried to murder me."

"Murder? Now don't be so dramatic . . ."

"Hitting someone in the back of the head with a steel baton, nearly cracking my skull? What would you call it? Massage therapy?"

He slammed the door, and Officer Blankenship removed his foot in the nick of time. He heard the young police officer's squeaky voice from the other side of the thin door. "So you want us to close the case? Are you dropping the charges?"

Sal didn't respond. He resumed his spot on the chair. Cora gurgled and smiled at him, then gummed his hairy arm again.

Beatrice came in from the kitchen. "Well, that went well," she drawled.

"They're not interested in putting the son of a bitch behind bars. I'm sick of pandering to them."

She patted the back of Cora's little head. "I don't want you doing anything stupid, Sal."

He looked at her beautiful blue eyes. He could lose himself in those eyes.

She lowered her voice and said, "I don't want them to get away with it, either. When I think about what might've happened . . ."

"They won't get away with it," he said in a low dangerous tone. "But I'll do it carefully. Trust me. But we might have to leave here."

She sighed, then nodded. "I'm ready to leave. I enjoy all the airplanes flying overhead all the time, but it also makes me sad. Makes me wonder where I'd be . . ."

"Well, we can move someplace with airplanes. No problem there. Why not closer to Abby?"

"Virginia?"

"Sure, why not?"

"I've never imagined leaving Texas. But why not? Oh, Sal, what an adventure." Cora relaxed mid arm-maul and her head fell to the side. Her eyes closed and drool dribbled out the side of her mouth and down Sal's already drool-encrusted arm.

Beatrice clutched her chest. "She loves you so much, Sal. How adorable." She carefully reached for her. Sal held out his arm as though a bird of prey had landed there. Beatrice took the little bundle in her arms, gently rocking her. She didn't wake up. "I'll put her down for her nap." Sal nodded and reached for the paperback novel he'd been trying to read. She gave him a sultry look. "You think we'd both fit in that chair?"

His voice caught in his throat, and he had to clear it before he could speak. He finally said, "Um—I'd like to find out."

Her smile broadened, and she took Cora to the room with the crib they'd bought at a thrift store. She closed the door as she entered, but winked at him just before closing it.

His heart felt as though it would beat right out of his chest. Should he just sit there? Undress? Take off his shoes at least? He'd dreamt of this moment countless times.

A minute later, the door opened and she came out in just her underwear. She scolded him like a child. "Why are you still dressed?"

He gawked at her beautifully full body, then darted out of the chair, nearly tripping over his own feet.

"Close the curtains first," she said huskily.

He pulled the curtains, slipped off his shoes and started to unbutton his shirt, but his fingers suddenly felt like they were made from cast iron.

She moved to him like a cat, and her scent wafted over him. "Oh, let me do it," she admonished. "Honestly, you're all thumbs."

Her fingers worked deftly and soon she had his shirt unbuttoned and in a heap on the floor. Next came his undershirt. She paused and placed her palms against his broad chest. Her hands felt as hot as irons fresh off the fire. His skin prickled where she touched him.

"So strong," she cooed as she stroked his chest, shoulders, and arms.

Desire engulfed him, and he bent to kiss her. Her ruby lips tasted as though she'd eaten some kind of tropical fruit he'd never tasted before. Their tongues found each other and he couldn't get enough of her.

Before the passion consumed him completely, he broke away and asked through gasping breaths, "Are—are you sure you're up for this?"

She gave him a small smile and a tilt of her chin. "What are you saying, Sal? Are you . . ." she clutched his groin, feeling his hard manhood against his pants. "Gifted?"

He nearly crumpled at her aggressive touch, but he managed to say, "I mean from the baby. Are—are you healed?"

In answer, she pushed her tongue deep into his mouth. She smiled into his mouth. Her arms wrapped around his neck. She jumped and wrapped her long legs around his waist as they stood in front of the chair. He took her weight easily. It seemed the most natural thing in the world.

"Why don't you find out for yourself?" she murmured in a voice he'd never heard her utter before.

8

Two weeks passed since Sal's run-in with the steel baton. He still woke with a raging headache every morning. He worried perhaps he had permanent damage from the blow. But this morning he woke and felt different. Something had changed. He couldn't pinpoint it but it was a good change.

He rubbed the back of his neck. The doctor had shaved the back of his head to perform the minor suture surgery. The stubble had become more than just stubble, and he was thankful it didn't itch. Beatrice had removed most of the stitches already. He could still feel the puckered scar, though. It angered him that the perpetrators were still out there living their miserable lives as though they'd gotten away with something.

Beatrice stirred in bed beside him. She rolled into him and lay her warm arm across his chest. Her fingers played with his chest hair and he relished her touch. Through the curtains, he could see the dim light of early morning. The drone of an airplane barely registered in his subconscious. There always seemed to be an aircraft overhead. Even if he was outside, he barely looked up anymore, unless they were flying low.

"Your head still hurt?" she asked groggily.

That was when he realized what had changed. He clutched her hand. "No, it doesn't," he answered. "I couldn't figure it out at first. Something changed but I couldn't figure it out . . . the headache's gone."

Beatrice sat up and smiled up at him. "That's the best news I've heard all day."

"Did you feed Cora last night? I didn't hear you get up."

Beatrice took a moment to think. She sat up even more and said as though it might be the biggest revelation ever, "No. She never made a sound. I think she slept through the night." Her joy and wonder changed to fear. "I need to check on her."

She pushed the covers off and sprang out of bed, not bothering to cover herself. Sal watched the show in the dim light. Her butt jiggled seductively and her full breasts swayed. Despite himself, he became aroused.

"Hurry back," he said.

She glanced back at him and saw his growing manhood. "Hold that thought," she panted.

He listened as she moved to Cora's bedroom door. He heard the click of the door and the slight creak, which no amount of oil on the hinges seemed to fix. More than once that damned door squeak had woken Cora and started her fussing and crying. But he heard no squawking or crying this time.

He imagined Beatrice creeping in, not wanting to wake the sleeping baby. They'd both learned never to wake her if at all possible, or they paid for it with a solid hour of inconsolable crying. He loved Cora with all his heart, but he didn't relish her ear-splitting tantrums. They'd learned to simply leave her alone during these times. No amount of comfort or distraction cut the tantrum any shorter, so they stopped trying.

He decided he needed to know what was happening. He slid out of bed, slipped on some underwear, and avoided as many creaky floorboards as possible as he tiptoed his way across to Cora's room. The door was open and he heard Beatrice talking to her in low tones. He also heard little gurgles, grunts, and giggles.

He poked his head around the doorjamb, and his heart melted. Beatrice had her back to him and Cora's tiny face poked out above her shoulder. She'd learned how to hold her head up not too long before. Her eyes focused on him, and she gave him a toothless smile. Then she wiggled and dug her face into Beatrice's neck like a tiny vampire. She locked eyes with him again and gurgled in delight.

Beatrice turned slowly. When she saw him, she smiled too and the similarity was uncanny. "Is that your Dada? Is that Dada?"

He thought it couldn't get any better. His whole life had been building up to this one point, but none of the rest seemed to matter anymore. He didn't even resent his attackers at the moment. All that mattered stood six feet in front of him.

Cora reached her pudgy arms out for him and he was pulled in inexorably. He couldn't have stopped himself to save his life. He wrapped an arm around Beatrice's bare hip and the little family embraced. Cora lurched forward and her tiny hand found his nose and held fast.

"She's so strong," he marveled.

"She's growing fast. She'll be crawling before we know it."

"Then walking."

Beatrice broke away from him. Cora objected at first until Beatrice offered her breast. Cora abandoned all thoughts of Dada and dived into her breakfast with abandon. The little gulps and deep breaths of contentment filled his soul with wonder.

His mind suddenly wandered. He'd seen death and destruction on a massive scale in his life. He'd seen countless lives snuffed out in their prime in the trenches in France. He'd seen evil acts and performed his own share, too. He'd also seen heroism, bravery, and sacrifice. All those men had once been Cora's size. They'd once cooed and gurgled and ate from their mother's breasts. How could they turn into such violent abominations? The Kaiser, even that crazy son of a bitch Hitler, had once been just like Cora.

Beatrice asked, "Where are you?"

"What?" He shook his head. "Sorry. I'm getting soft in my old age."

She looked down at his crotch region, then back into his eyes. He'd come to recognize her different looks, particularly the lusty ones.

She teased, "I hope not."

He blushed. He'd never met a woman who could make him do that, but she did frequently. He felt like a schoolboy being teased by an older girl, even though the opposite was true.

"She'll need a nap in a few hours," she added.

"If we're not careful, we'll end up with another one of those," he pointed at Cora.

"Would that be so bad?" she said in a quieter voice.

He hadn't meant to say it, and he hadn't really even thought about it before. "I—no, it wouldn't be a bad thing at all."

His mother's nagging voice interrupted his train of thought. "It isn't right—you need to marry that girl, Salvatore Wayne Sarducci."

It came out of nowhere, and he fought the urge to look around the room. It sounded too real to just be inside his head, but he knew it couldn't be anything else.

Beatrice pouted her lower lip and her eyes flashed for a moment. "You don't seem too sure, Sal."

There was a rap on the front door that tore him away. They both looked. Morning light streamed through the windows, but it was early for a visitor. He gave her a questioning look, and she shrugged, obviously not expecting anyone.

He strode to the door. Beatrice said, "Put some clothes on first."

He put his bathrobe on, then opened the door just as another knock started. The neighbor stood there with his knuckles up in mid-knock. He and his small family of four lived next door in a similar-sized house. They'd exchanged pleasantries a few times, but he mostly minded his own business. Sal thought his name was Harold.

"Can I help you, Harold?" Sal asked.

"Sorry to visit so early, but . . ."

Sal saw him glance toward the small shed that faced the short driveway. Sal clenched his teeth and his jaw rippled. In big black letters, the word "whore" had been scrawled in large letters.

Harold looked apologetic and even a little scared. Sal outweighed him by at least sixty pounds of muscle. "I wanted to point it out before most folks were up. My kids, included." He gave an awkward grin, "I don't wanna hafta explain that over the breakfast table."

Sal broke his angry stare at the graffiti and leveled his gaze at Harold. "Did you happen to see who did it?" Harold gulped audibly and Sal added, "Or are you as blind as everyone else in this town?"

Harold's face turned white and he looked as though he might bolt. He stammered, "I—I uh . . ."

Sal closed his eyes and softened his tone. "I'm sorry. I shouldn't have said that. It wasn't fair." He placed a hand on Harold's shoulder. "Thanks for pointing it out. I appreciate it." He noticed a few early morning walkers and commuters staring at the graffiti. "I'll get it covered up right now."

He stepped past Harold and went to the shed, looking for any clues the artists may have left. Besides a few boot tracks in the dirt, there was nothing. It could've been kids for all he knew, but he suspected it was probably the same cowardly bunch who'd attacked him. Harold retreated to his own house and family.

Sal opened the double doors to the shed, splitting the offensive word into two. Inside, he found an old canvas tarp that looked to have been used for a painting project sometime in the last decade. He shook it out and hammered it up with a few well-placed nails.

When he turned around, he saw Beatrice standing there holding Cora. She'd put on a pretty blue dress and Cora had on a frilly pink dress and a little bow in her thin blond hair, which always reminded him of silk. Sal often marveled at how quickly Beatrice could change her and Cora's appearances.

Beatrice shook her head. Sal tilted his head at her. "Did you see it?"

She nodded, "Yep. At least they know how to spell."

He couldn't make himself laugh, but he was glad she could still joke. He looked at his handiwork. "It'll have to do for now. Looks like I'll be painting the shed today."

She gave him a thin smile. "I can help."

He nodded as though it's how he wanted to spend his day in the first place.

She sighed and said, "We're gonna have to do something about this, aren't we?"

He clapped the dust off his hands and said, "'fraid so."

FIRST SAL KISSED Beatrice on the forehead, then the back of Cora's head. Cora didn't wake from her slumber, propped against Beatrice's chest.

Beatrice said in a hushed voice, "Be careful, Sal. I need you whole."

"Don't worry, I'll be fine. You know the plan better than I do."

"I know, but it doesn't mean you can't get hurt."

"I can take care of myself."

"See that you do."

He closed the front door gently behind him and adjusted his coat. It wasn't cold, but it wasn't warm either. He glanced at the newly painted shed. They had had no repeat graffiti artists visit them since the first time over a week ago. He glanced at the neighbor's house. Behind the drawn curtains he could see shapes darting this way and that and assumed it was dinnertime.

He mounted the old bicycle and pushed it into the street. The bike didn't fit him well, and he always felt foolish riding it, but he didn't have a car and it was a short ride into downtown Sweetwater. He hoped he'd be riding back here a few short hours from right now, but it depended on a few factors out of his control.

He glanced back at the rental house. Beatrice had stepped to the window and had the curtain pulled back so she could watch him ride away. Cora was covered with a blanket, and he could see the outline of her tiny head. He smiled and waved. She waved back, but her smile didn't reach her eyes. She looked worried.

A tinge of worry turned his insides cold for a moment. What if the hooligans chose that night to play their dirty tricks on them? But he put it out of his mind. He'd done his research and knew his targets normally spent Friday nights in the bar playing pool and drinking until the wee hours. If they chose to graffiti or assault their house that night, it wouldn't be until they had enough liquid courage in their systems. If all went according to plan, he wouldn't let it get that far.

He teetered down the road, gaining speed steadily. The old bicycle needed the chain oiled, but he hadn't gotten around to it yet. The faster he went, the louder and quicker the cadence of the squeak became until he felt like some kind of circus clown, tooting a horn.

He pulled up outside the Flying Horse bar and leaned the bike against the side of the building in the alley's darkness. He checked his watch—right on time. Laughter came from inside. He suspected that wouldn't last much longer.

He stepped to the door, which had a well-seated sign that stated no minors allowed. Just below that, an army recruitment poster dangled precariously. He took a deep breath and let out it slowly, then pushed the door open and stepped inside. Even now, he still got the jitters before an operation.

A few folks turned to look at the newcomer, but his entrance went mostly unnoticed. He scanned the room out of long habit. The place wasn't packed, but it had a healthy crowd, as expected on a Friday night.

Everything seemed in place, but he didn't see his targets right away. Then he heard the meaty clack as one pool ball collided into another, followed immediately by voices he recognized. The one pool table sat in the far corner beneath a low-slung light with a beer logo emblazoned along the side. He saw the four men he'd come here to see. Two played while the other two watched. Each man held their own cue, using the chalk copiously on the pool cue tips.

He strolled to the bar and got the attention of the bartender. He remembered his name was Taft Bingham. It stuck with him because it didn't seem to fit the man at all. Far from aristocratic, the man had a massive belly that made him appear he'd swallowed a watermelon whole. Even in the dim lights, Sal could see the thin, dark red lines crisscrossing his oversized nose. His breathing came in heaving gasps, which made Sal think he might keel over and die at any moment.

Mr. Bingham noticed him, and a flare of recognition crossed his dull, bloodshot eyes. "What'll it be?" he said in his wet-laced voice.

Sal couldn't help clearing his throat, hoping it might remind Mr. Bingham to do the same and rid himself of the phlegm that must be lodged in his airway.

"A beer," he stated flatly. He didn't much like beer, and there was only one beer choice, but he needed to keep a clear head so he avoided hard alcohol.

Mr. Bingham pulled a mug and swiped his dirty rag through it before pouring from the tap. Sal took it and turned to watch the rest of the bar. He sipped the beer and pretended to enjoy the taste.

He took in the rest of the room. A few groups of friends huddled together, both men and women. The men outnumbered the women and were all older. The young men had joined the service long before. He didn't see any uniforms among the patrons, which was a good thing. He didn't need any young warriors with misguided loyalties around tonight—at least not that kind.

He set his focus on the pool players. He knew one or all of them were the men responsible for nearly cracking his skull. If they'd left it at that, he might have let them get away with it, but they kept pushing. He knew the type. They'd keep pushing until he put a stop to it once and for all.

These were weak men who preyed on weakness. That's why they attacked him by surprise and from behind. When Sal hadn't done anything about the attack, they took that as a sign of weakness to exploit—so the graffiti followed.

They were made even more dangerous by the fact that he'd run into a few of them when he'd first come to Sweetwater and beaten them to bloody pulps in the local eatery after they insulted Beatrice. He hadn't known her at the time, but she'd been very pregnant and very vulnerable and he'd done what any decent man would do in the same situation—defended her honor.

Now, they thought they'd gained the upper hand—as though he'd lost his nerve to fight. He imagined they'd become even more emboldened when the police did basically nothing. The police didn't seem to care and even seemed to secretly agree with the treatment. *That's the tricky part*, he thought. He had to teach them a lesson *and* stay out of prison while doing it. Teaching them a lesson would be the easy part—and the most enjoyable.

He gulped down most of the beer in one long gulp, then waltzed over to the pool table. A small group of women sat nearby, but they mostly ignored him. He stood a few yards back from the pool players, watching their game-play. None of them were all that good, even though they'd probably tallied up countless hours.

When they were between shots, he leaned forward and put a quarter on the corner of the table. "I'll play the winner," he said with a quick smile.

All four of them glared at him. The scrawniest one—named Virgil Cummings, the ringleader—sneered and said, "Well looky-looky, boys. The whore-lover himself is here."

Sal stepped away from the table and gave the small man his best smile. "It's ironic. I'd think about the only way a guy like you can get laid is by paying for it, *Virgil.* Do the actual whores in this town know how you feel about them? Excluding your sister, of course."

Virgil's eyes narrowed dangerously and they darted to his cohorts, then back to Sal. Sal didn't think he'd been the one to actually hit him, but he'd probably given the order.

Virgil said, "How's that little bastard baby girl doing? You think your little whore's ready for another one, 'cause I could do the honors. I'll show her how a real man feels."

Sal kept his emotions strongly in check. He knew he'd have to withstand some smack talk. Virgil was so predictable it nearly made him laugh out loud.

Sal shook his head as though perplexed. "Now, I'm just even more confused. Now you wanna screw her even though you think she's a whore?" Sal held up a finger as though he'd finally figured things out. "Or maybe you were *complimenting* me by calling me a whore-lover. Is that it? Are we friends now?"

He went to put his arm around his newfound friend, but Virgil quickly darted away. He held his pool cue like a baseball bat. "You stay away from me or I'll have to crack your skull again."

Sal lifted his chin. "So that was you? I thought you woulda gotten one of the bigger boys to do it. I didn't think you could reach that high."

Virgil glanced at his cohorts. All of them held their cues aggressively and stared daggers at Sal. They looked ready to jump him at any moment. Virgil had a bit more sense. He looked around the bar and noticed people watching.

"You really screwed up coming in here, old man. No matter what happens in here, no one's gonna turn us in. We could kill you and they'd swear up and down that you slipped and hit your head."

Sal turned and noticed the bartender staring at him with his dull, dead eyes. He'd added a toothpick to his meaty lips and his slow chewing reminded Sal of a cow chewing its cud.

"Is that true, Taft?"

The bartender's surprised look at hearing his first name almost made Sal burst out laughing again.

The bartender recovered and said in his wet, phlegmy-voice. “You slipped and fell, boy.”

Sal looked at the ground, then slowly nodded as though finally deciding on an unfortunate but necessary course of action. “Well okay. I guess I’ll just leave, then.”

He stepped toward the door, but Virgil made a motion and Hugh Clevenger, the biggest man in the group, stepped in front and barred his leaving. He smacked the pool cue into his hand with meaty thumps and said, “It’s too late for that. You ain’t leaving here in one piece, pops.”

Sal turned back toward Virgil and did his best to put a pleading fear into his voice. “Please, just let me leave.”

Virgil’s sneer could make a snake cringe. Hugh reared back with the pool cue and aimed to break it against the back of Sal’s head. Sal expected that. He ducked and sent his elbow back hard into the big man’s soft stomach.

The air went out of Hugh’s lungs and he dropped the pool cue with a loud clatter. Sal scooped it up with his foot and gripped the thin end. He swung the beefy end into the side of Hugh’s head in one flowing motion. The crack as the wood met skull sounded like a Babe Ruth home run. Hugh staggered, then dropped to his knees.

Sal didn’t stop. He pulled the pool cue in and extended it behind him. He felt the thin end drive into soft flesh and he heard Virgil blow out his air. Sal quickly pulled it back and spun back toward the Hugh, still the bigger threat. In a quick motion, he brought the cue down hard atop Hugh’s skull. The big man’s eyes crossed and he toppled over. A thin strand of blood seeped from his hairline and pooled in his eye.

Sal turned back toward Virgil, who was backing up, holding his stomach, still trying to find his breath. He had a hand up in a lame attempt to keep Sal away. Sal batted the hand away with the pool cue and he thought he heard bones break in his hand.

Virgil yowled like a feral cat and clutched his hand to his chest. When Sal lunged, he turned and lurched to get away. He tripped over his own feet and his chin bounced off the hardwood floorboards.

Sal was on him a moment later. His knees dug into his back as he gave him his full weight. He grasped his hair and pulled his head back hard.

Virgil struggled to breathe. Blood dripped off his chin and splattered as he tried to shake his head free, but Sal held on.

The other two men stepped forward to help their fallen leader, but Sal froze them with a look. "Don't make it any worse than it already is," he seethed dangerously.

They exchanged uncertain and fearful looks, then they both backed down. They placed their pool cues on the floor and backed away as though Sal aimed a loaded gun at them.

"Okay, okay. Take it easy there, fella," Danny Cahill said.

Sal focused his attention back onto Virgil. He put his mouth right next to his ear. "Leave. Us. Alone. If I even *suspect* you've insulted or threatened my family again . . . you won't be able to hide from me. They won't find your body. Understand?"

Virgil's eyes darted like a wild animal, but he nodded as best he could with his head pulled back. Sal loosened his grip and yelled, "You understand me, Virgil? I need to hear you say it."

"Y—yes, I got it. I understand."

"Good boy." He released Virgil's hair, and his bloody chin hit the floor again. Sal pushed himself upright and wiped the dust off his pants. Everyone in the bar stared at the spectacle. The only sound came from the buzz of the lights and Virgil's heavy breathing. Hugh moaned and his eyes fluttered open, but he stayed on his back as though trying to piece together how he'd ended up there.

The unmistakable pumping sound of a shotgun being fed a fresh shell shattered the moment. Sal raised his hands and faced the bartender.

"You're in a heap of trouble, you Yankee son of a bitch. Everyone saw what you did here. You started the whole thing—jumped these poor men while they were trying to enjoy their Friday night. Hope you like prison food, 'cause it's what you'll be eating for the next decade."

Sal looked from one patron's face to another. He saw their anger and their resolve to follow the bartender's lead.

A woman's strong voice from the table near the pool table filled the silence. "I beg to differ, Mr. Bingham."

All eyes turned to the unfamiliar voice. Four women stepped forward into the light from the pool table. They'd been wearing overcoats but they'd taken them off and their gleaming WASP uniforms adorned with officer's insignia were unmistakable.

The barkeep dropped the muzzle of the sawed-off shotgun. "Colonel Cochran? Colonel Love?" He stammered. His mouth hung open in stunned shock. "I—I didn't see you come in."

"We saw the whole thing, Mr. Bingham. We'll just wait here while you call the police so they can record our statements." She smoothed her uniform dress and looked at the fight scene with an air of disgust. When he didn't jump to do her bidding, she added with more heat this time. "Make it quick. I don't enjoy being around such awful men." She cut her eyes at Virgil and the others, and they hung their heads.

Mr. Bingham placed the shotgun on the bar and said, "I don't think we need to get the police involved, ma'am. I'm sure these fellas were just messing around and got a little out of hand."

Colonel Cochran stood nearly as tall as Sal. Her dark eyes and thick dark hair seemed out of place in the dingy bar. Indeed, all the women seemed to glow in the dim light. Confidence and grace exuded from their pores, making everyone else in the bar seem small and petty.

She raised an eyebrow at Sal. Sal smiled and extended his elbow to her. She pushed her arm through and led the other women out the front door of the Flying Horse bar. He walked them to the corner where his bike still leaned against the wall.

He held each woman's hand in both his and thanked them individually.

Colonel Nancy Cochran, who led the WASP program, gripped his hand back. "Tell Miss Malinsky that we miss her and if she needs any more favors, we'd be happy to help."

"I will. I promise. She wanted to be here, too, but . . ."

"Yes, how is the little one? Cora, right?"

"That's right." He beamed, thinking about her. "She's wonderful. Absolutely wonderful."

She leaned in close as though telling him a secret. "None of us wanted to see her leave, but she obviously couldn't keep flying in her condition. Does she ever plan on coming back? We'd love to have her."

"She'd be thrilled to hear that, ma'am. We've actually talked about it once or twice."

“Good.” She lifted her chin toward the front door of the bar. “You think you put your troubles behind you in there?”

“Thanks to you ladies, yes. Thanks again.”

“Our pleasure,” she spoke for all of them. “It was a pleasure watching you take care of them,” she said with an edge of something different in her voice.

Colonel Love stepped in. “Shouldn’t we be getting you back to the major . . . Colonel?”

They laughed and hustled to the army green car parked on the other side of the street. They waved as they sped off toward the airbase. He waved and mounted the rickety bicycle. He pedaled as fast as possible, eager to assuage Beatrice’s fear and burn some of his excess adrenaline.

9

Norfolk, Virginia
April 1944

Abby finished washing the dishes in the tiny house the government allowed her to live in rent free. She sighed and sat down heavily on the well-used sofa. She sank deeply into the cushion and wondered how many hundreds of others had sat in that exact spot over the years. The housing was new during the Great War, over twenty years before, but it seemed much older.

She had hoped to receive mail that day from Clyde, but had been disappointed. She loved her job, but she didn't like this part. She missed her husband and her WASP friends. She saw them at work, but their schedules differed and most of her evenings she spent alone. She'd gone out a few times, but instead of making her feel better, it made her miss Clyde even more. Occasionally men would make passes at her, which made her feel even worse—as though she were cheating somehow—so she stayed in most nights, unless she had a mission to fly.

She checked the wall clock. It was too early to get into bed. She'd finished a novel the night before and hadn't had time to find a new one. She wandered into the tiny bedroom and sat on the side of the bed. The bedsprings squeaked and complained and she wondered again how many other people had slept on the bed.

She opened the bureau drawer—perhaps she'd left a book there and forgotten. She saw a book, but not one she wanted to see. Miles Burr's journal poked out from beneath a flight handbook. She'd nearly forgotten all the drama she'd left behind in Seattle, but the journal brought it all flooding back.

She immediately thought of Sal. The journal documented his involvement in the arson at the Trask building. She hated to think about that—it still stung her to the core. When he'd showed up in Sweetwater just days after her graduation, it had incensed her. She wanted nothing to do with him or anyone from her family. But he'd taken such a liking to her best friend Beatrice that she could hardly stay mad at him for long. *I wonder if they're sleeping together?*

Even though a large age gap existed, she saw the way they both looked at one another. The sexual tension hung thick, even when Beatrice was as big as a bloated whale.

She held the journal and flipped through a few pages. Miles's handwriting was delicate and masculine at the same time. She loved reading his words, she just didn't like specific parts, but he wrote beautifully and eloquently about his feelings and outlooks on the world. Such a waste. She'd read it through once before, but hadn't done so again. She'd been so angry at her father and Sal that she nearly burned it.

That's what she'd told her friend Trish she'd done with it when she'd demanded the journal from her. What was happening in Trish's world at that moment? Would she hear if anything really bad happened to her? Not likely.

Perhaps she should send her a letter. Had enough time passed? They hadn't parted on friendly terms, but Abby didn't hold it against her. Trish had lost her lover Miles, and she clearly blamed Abby's father, Victor, for his untimely death.

That's why she wanted the journal so badly—so she could prove her father's guilt. But the journal wouldn't really do that. Other than the admission of committing arson at the direction of Victor, there was nothing in the journal that would indict him for Miles's accidental death. Her father's business tactics were brutal, but besides the arson, he hadn't broken any other laws that she could discern. *Perhaps I'll send her the journal. How would that impact Mother?*

The letters she'd received from her mother, Meredith, lamented that she and Victor continued to suffer through a loveless marriage. At first, Abby had been stunned and embarrassed that her mother would open up so much about something so intimate. It made her profoundly uncomfortable, and she didn't know how to respond. If she wrote back at all, she wrote bland letters—ignoring her mother's heartfelt admissions, but Meredith's letters kept coming, and she kept pouring out her soul.

Abby finally wrote a more intimate letter. While she wrote, she convinced herself that she wouldn't send it—she simply wanted to write it for her own edification—but she sent it. The letter that came back from her mother felt as though a long-lost friend had written it. Every letter since felt the same way. They opened up to one another and it even made Abby miss her, something she wouldn't have thought possible.

Sending the journal to Trish might hurt Meredith as much as Victor. She didn't want to hurt either of them. Even though she knew her father had done some bad things, she still loved him—and she didn't think he'd gone so far that he couldn't come back.

But perhaps the only way he'd ever come back to being a good person was by airing out his dirty laundry for the whole world to see. She'd gone back and forth on the issue. But now that she considered her mother a friend, she had more to think about. If Trish used the journal against him effectively, it would most likely lead to her father's business dying—which would affect her mother just as much as Victor. Would the journal be enough to indict her father? Probably enough for the police to at least do some investigating, but would they? His factory was helping the country win the war, after all.

She laid back on the lumpy mattress and stared at the cracks in the ceiling. Why did everything have to be so complicated? She hugged her pillow and imagined she held Clyde. She imagined his lips kissing her neck tenderly as they made love. *God, I miss him so much.*

Trish Watkins dropped the butt of her cigarette onto the wet street and ground the heel of her work boot into it, leaving a dirty smudge. She didn't know where or when she'd find another cigarette. She barely had enough money to buy food, let alone cigarettes.

She stared into the bustling street. Normally she saw opportunity—people to scam or simply rob, but not today. Today, she saw only her own desperation staring back at her.

No one gave her a second glance and that scared her the most. Perhaps she just hadn't noticed it before, but lately she felt invisible—like one of the street people. In a kind of bizarre switch, now she noticed the street people more than ever—as though the closer she came to becoming one of them, the more she noticed them. There weren't many of them, but she'd always ignored them for the most part, unless they could offer her something.

"I'm not one of them," she muttered to herself. An uppity businessman gave her a disgusted look as he passed, and she realized her muttering to herself only helped solidify people's perceptions. She cursed at him. "What're you staring at? Huh?" He hustled off, but he didn't look cowed, only more disgusted.

Maybe I should get another factory job. She'd had one for nearly six months, but she didn't consider it a real job since it was her cover while she tried to find dirt on Victor Brooks for the mob boss, Julius Trambolini. It was an important job that would've been the biggest payday of her life so far—but she'd failed, and it had ended in tragedy.

Instead of a payday, she'd only received threats. They'd paid her half in advance and she had spent most of that. She'd saved some from the factory job and she'd paid them out of that to keep them at bay, but they wanted the rest of their money and she had no idea how to give it to them.

The idea of clocking in and out of a factory job again made her angry. She hadn't minded the work, but she told herself that was only because of the Trambolini aspect. As long as she had a higher purpose, she felt she could stomach the monotony of the factory floor. She had to admit, though, that the money and stability had been nice.

"I'm not one of *those* types of people," she murmured to herself. She felt for another cigarette, but came up empty. A nagging voice in the back of her head said, *Maybe you should be.* It sounded like her alcoholic mother's voice, but she couldn't be sure, since that was an extremely distant memory. It didn't help that everywhere she looked in this thriving wartime economy, she saw prosperity.

She pushed off the wall, shoved her hands in her pockets, and slunk down the sidewalk. Maybe Vince had a job for her. He said he'd keep an eye out. She hadn't been into the little coffee shop on the corner in over a month. It was in her neighborhood, but she had spent little time there because more and more she saw the Trambolini boys waiting for her there. She'd been staying with a friend, sleeping on the lousy couch, but even that arrangement was fraying.

She walked the few blocks to Vince's coffee shop. She scanned the street, looking for trouble. She'd been doing that more and more often. Didn't they know she wanted to pay them off even more than they wanted to be paid off?

She saw nothing obvious, so she crossed the street and pushed on the heavy door. She heard a bell tinkle overhead. She glared up at it. Vince poked his head out from behind the kitchen area. He seemed flustered and instead of his normal glad-to-see-you smile, he glared at her. She glanced around the place and didn't see a single customer, though.

She pointed at the bell. "That new? I don't remember that."

Vince came from the kitchen glancing back the way he'd come, guiltily. Trish heard another voice, a female voice, call from the back. "I'll be right there."

Trish bristled and raised an eyebrow at Vince. "Who's that?"

Vince ignored her question and called back to the voice in the back. "Don't bother, Tina. It's not a customer."

Trish said, "You hire someone new? Sounds young."

"Yeah. What's it to you?"

"Last I heard, Morty could barely pay the rent, but now he's hiring people?"

A slim, handsome woman came from the back area. Her dark hair stacked on her head in tight swirls reminded Trish of Medusa. She smacked her lips as she chewed gum. Seeing Trish, she crossed her arms and leaned her hips against the counter, watching her the way a fox watches a rabbit.

"You must be Trish. Vince described you perfectly," she said flatly.

Trish did her best to ignore her. She focused on Vince. "Can I talk to you over here a minute?"

The woman answered before he could. "You can say whatever you're gonna say to him in front of me."

Trish raised an eyebrow at Vince. He shrugged his broad shoulders and glanced at the woman. He stood up straighter. "She's right. We don't keep secrets."

Trish checked to make sure there were no patrons she might've missed. The place was empty. "How's business?" she asked.

Vince answered. "Been steady in the mornings and at lunch, but it slows down about now. Isn't that right, Tina?'

"That's right, sugar." She pushed off the counter and draped herself over Vince's side. Vince dwarfed her, but Tina was taller than Trish by a few inches.

Trish crossed her arms. "You two an item?"

Tina put her lipstick-laden lips against Vince's cheek, leaving a messy, wet mark.

"Thought you told me you never got involved with the help."

"She's not the help. She's my business partner."

"Business partner? Jesus, what happened to Morty? You two got him stashed in the cold storage back there?"

Tina didn't look amused. She pulled away from Vince, pulled out a nail file, and started grooming.

Vince said, "You should come by more often. Morty sold his half to Tina. So, yeah, we're business partners now." They made goo-goo eyes at each other and Vince continued. "More than just business partners, though."

Tina smiled seductively and pressed herself into him again. She wrapped her arms around his neck and they kissed passionately. Trish stared—stunned. She'd never seen Vince act this way. He didn't even blush when they finally finished, and he saw her staring.

"You—you seen Johnnie recently?" Trish asked.

Vince gave her a sharp look. "Johnnie? Shit, Trish, you need to stay away from that guy."

"Why? Last time we talked, he had some kind of gig happening that kind of lined up with my own." She cut her eyes at Tina, who was doing her best to shoot daggers at her through her eyes. "You gotta problem, Tina?"

"Leave her alone, Trish," Vince growled dangerously.

"You seen him or not?" Trish pressed without taking her eyes off Tina. When Vince hesitated, she added, "Just tell me and I'll let you two get back to whatever business meeting you were doing back there."

"Yeah, I've seen him."

Tina cut her eyes to Vince. "You said you wouldn't tell her, you promised." She crossed her arms and puffed out her lower lip. Trish fought the urge to grab it and pull it off her face.

Vince gave her a pathetic puppy dog face. "She's one of my oldest friends, honey. She needs my help. It's the last time, though."

Trish narrowed her eyes. She hadn't been into the shop in a while, but somehow Vince knew she'd fallen on hard times.

"I don't need anyone's help . . ."

"Oh, knock it off. Those Trambolini thugs come in here once a week looking for you. I know you owe 'em money. I don't know how much, but it's enough to keep them interested. Johnnie came by looking for you, too. Not more'n a week ago. Said he might have a job for you. He wanted your help with something."

"And you weren't going to tell me that?" She shifted her eyes to Tina, who didn't break eye contact. Trish wanted to rip her pretty skin off her skull and shove it down her throat.

"I just did. But I don't wanna be involved anymore. The shop's finally working for me—us. No more harebrained schemes for me."

"The last one almost got him killed," Tina huffed.

Now Trish completely ignored Tina. She kept her gaze firmly on Vince. "He give you a way to contact him?"

He nodded and hustled back toward the kitchen. Tina continued her icy stare and continued to smack her gum annoyingly. Trish took a step toward her and they locked eyes.

Trish said, "Are you scamming him? If I find out that you are, I'll shove my hand up your pretty little ass and pull your heart out."

Tina pulled back and gulped noisily. Her rosy cheeks shone even brighter against her suddenly pale skin. She opened and closed her mouth several times, but no words came.

Vince returned and handed her a sealed envelope. She took it from him and gave Tina one last glance. Vince looked from Tina to Trish and back again. Before he could say anything, Trish held up the envelope and nodded her thanks. "See you around, Vince."

As she went out the door, the little bell rang again. She jumped up and ripped it off the doorjamb, then threw it onto the wet ground outside. She shook her head in disgust and didn't look back.

~

TRISH READ the note from Johnnie. He'd never been too good with reading, let alone writing, and a few words she couldn't decipher, but she got the gist. He wanted her to meet him at a local deli downtown. He left a phone number. That left her scratching her head. She didn't have a phone and—unless things had changed dramatically for Johnnie—she doubted he did either. Where would she find a phone?

She pocketed the note and strolled toward her apartment. She hadn't been to the apartment for almost two weeks. She hoped the locks hadn't been changed. She'd paid the rent last month, but she hadn't yet this month. Her landlord wouldn't put up with late rent. Maybe he'd already sold all her stuff.

She went through a mental checklist of everything she owned. She grew angry at the thought of her slob of a landlord, Joe, rifling through and selling it on the street. Perhaps she should do that. It wasn't enough to pay back the Trambolinis, but it might keep the sharks at bay for another week or so, just until she got her feet back beneath her.

She slowed as she approached her street. Her eyes darted to the alleyways and the shadows between streets, but she didn't see anyone who might be lying in wait for her. She saw some traffic cops on the corner discussing something while chomping on sandwiches. Each had a colorful thermos beside them. She imagined their wives packing their lunches in the morning for them. The peck on the cheek as they left for the day with a word to be careful. *Scumbags.* She hated cops, and they hated her—natural enemies.

She stopped at the top of the short, dark stairs leading down to her front door. The steps never seemed to dry out, even in midsummer. A tiny rivulet of water ran down them now and dripped into the steel grate at the bottom of the steps. She leaned on the railing and pretended to fish into her pocket for something. Beneath her wool sailor's cap, her eyes darted from side to side, but she saw nothing out of the ordinary. Perhaps the Trambolinis had given up on watching the apartment.

With one last glance around, she descended the stairs quickly. She dug deep into her pants pocket and pulled out a set of keys. With one more glance up the stairs, she slid the key into the lock, praying that Joe hadn't changed them. Relief flooded through her as the key entered easily and turned with a satisfying click. She undid the other locks and deadbolts and pushed into the small apartment.

She stopped at the entrance and used all her senses. The place smelled musty, but it always smelled musty. There was a hint of something else, though, something sweet. She couldn't place it. She couldn't see much in the gloom. Even at midday, the place felt like a dark cavern. The only light came from the window in the corner, but it was a basement window so allowed little light in.

She stepped in further, feeling blindly for the lamp she knew to be on the table to the right. She could see the outline of her one good chair, so Joe hadn't sold her stuff just yet. She imagined he must be going out of his head for the rent she owed. There weren't any threatening eviction notes on the door.

She found the light and flicked it on. The room lit up enough for her to know something was definitely wrong. She suddenly placed the sweet smell as a man's cologne. She didn't see anyone, but he had to be there. The skin on the back of her head crawled into her burned scalp. It made her itch, but she fought the urge to scratch. Instead, she lunged back for the front door, but too late. A beefy hand pushed it shut, and the deadbolts locked into place.

A large body blocked the door. The man slowly turned from the door and faced her. He smiled and showed off tar-stained teeth. The cleft in his chin deepened, and she had the urge to see how deep it went into his skull.

"Going somewhere, Miss Watkins?"

Trish didn't recognize him or the voice. He wasn't one of the Trambolinis she'd seen hanging around before.

"Who the hell are you?" she asked, trying to keep the hitch in her voice to a minimum. She'd dealt with thugs like this her whole life. The trick was not to let them see your fear. That's what they wanted—what they thrived upon. *I should write a damned book*, she thought.

The man's eyes never left her as he took a slow step toward her. "I've been waiting an awful long time for you. The others bet you wouldn't come back here, but I had a hunch you might."

"I'm not gonna ask you again," she pulled a snub-nosed .38 from her waistband and pointed it at his face. She aimed for the cleft in his chin. She only wished she had bullets for the thing, but he didn't know it wasn't loaded.

He stopped abruptly, the smile fading to more of a smirk. He held up his hands in surrender, but it didn't go to his eyes. "You don't want to do that, Trish. You really don't."

She pulled back the hammer. "I'm not going to ask again," she bluffed.

"Fine. My name's Howard Halcon. My friends call me Howie."

"Well, Howard. Step aside or I'll punch a few holes in your ugly face."

"Oh please, Trish. No need to be rude." He stepped aside as though he were an unskilled square dancer, unsure of his moves.

"Who do you work for? Trambolini?"

"Trambolini? The mob boss? Goodness no. I wouldn't work for such trash."

"Who then?" she pressed.

"Put the gun down and we'll talk. Please, it's the very least you can do, Miss Watkins. Or can I call you Trish?"

"What do you mean by that? The least I can do—I don't owe you anything. I've never seen you before."

"My employer paid your rent for the next six months."

That wasn't what Trish expected to hear. The muzzle wavered in her hand. "You did what? Who's your employer? Who do you work for?" When he didn't answer right away, she brought the muzzle up to aim at his left eyeball. "Talk."

"I work for a man who wants the same thing as you, my dear."

"That doesn't answer my question. You wanna die?" He shrugged, and she wasn't sure if it was in response to her first or second comment. "You don't think I'll do it? I've killed plenty of men before you."

He nodded and looked at the floor as though he knew her past. "Yes, I know you have, but that was far different than this, wasn't it?"

His eyes lifted to hers, and she saw empathy and understanding there. *Who the hell is this guy? He couldn't know about that—could he?*

"I'm done playing games Howie."

Her finger tightened on the trigger. He lifted his chin and said, "I know about your mother's boyfriend, and like I said, you had no choice. You acted to preserve the life of yourself and your mother. Surely you did the right thing back then and you'll do it now. You've killed, certainly, but you're not a killer. Not like they are."

Trish felt like her head might explode. This stranger seemed to know things he couldn't know about. No one knew those things . . . but that wasn't entirely true. Johnnie knew. The realization struck her like a two-by-four across the face. This son of a bitch knew Johnnie.

Ice filled her veins as she understood what it meant. Johnnie wouldn't simply tell this guy about that incident. They'd taken a blood oath to never tell a soul. As far as the cops knew, Dougie, her mother's abusive boyfriend, had shot himself in the mouth with his old service revolver from the Great War.

"What have you done with Johnnie?"

"I can assure you I . . ."

He struck much faster than she thought possible. Before she knew what was happening, he slapped her hand, took the .38, and reversed the muzzle to aim into her face. She knew it wasn't loaded and needed to use that against him. But she hesitated.

His eyes blazed with fury, but only for a moment, then they softened. He opened the cylinder and dumped it into his palm. He snorted a quick laugh.

"You're a cheeky gal, you know that? It's not loaded. You had me convinced, and I'm not easily fooled. You should be proud of yourself."

"Fuck off," she said as she rubbed her stinging hand. "What have you done with Johnnie?"

"Still with the questions? You are a brave one."

She deepened her scowl as she pictured her fist smashing his nose flat.

"Johnnie's fine. He works for the same man I do."

Trish wracked her brain. Johnnie had told her months ago about a job. It paralleled her job with the Trambolinis, but she couldn't quite remember the name. Then it popped into her mind.

"Trask," she stated flatly. "He wants to put Victor Brooks out of business. Correct? That's who Johnnie works for—or did."

"He still does. No need to be so paranoid. Johnnie's fine."

She didn't believe him. Johnnie would never tell anyone about Dougie's demise. They'd both been involved, which made it easier to keep a secret. If it ever got out, they'd both spend the rest of their lives in prison.

"Can I see him? Take me to him. Can you?"

"Why the sudden interest? He told me you hadn't parted on the best terms last time."

She thought about the last time she'd seen the big gangly son of a bitch. He'd picked her up from the country club after she confronted Abby's mother, Meredith, about Victor's wrongdoing. That had been months ago. She remembered Johnnie had been upset about something and it was true. They hadn't parted on the best of terms. She was convinced this bastard standing here with her gun had killed him.

"Let's just say I don't trust you."

"That'll come in time. Johnnie's on an errand for Mr. Trask. He's out of the state at the moment, but he'll be back soon. You can see him then."

She felt it was all bullshit, but she nodded her head in understanding.

"Now what?"

"Mr. Trask would like to meet you. He has some questions for you."

The way he said it made her skin crawl, but it couldn't be worse than being picked up by the Trambolinis—could it? She fought the fear growing in the pit of her stomach. Suddenly she wished the mobsters had picked her up. At least they were a known entity. *What have you gotten me into, Johnnie?*

10

Northern Philippines
April 1944

Frank Cooper watched the darkness for anything human. Nearby, Larry Grinning Bear and Neil Winstad slept soundly. He couldn't see them, but he could hear their steady breathing and the occasional grunt or moan.

They'd landed on the island nearly a week before. Their stores of fish and water had run out, but they'd found fresh water in a good-sized stream and even speared fresh fish from the shallow shoals. It was enough to keep them alive, but they needed more food.

They'd only explored a small portion of the island. So far, they hadn't seen any humans, but they'd seen a few sets of large footprints, so they kept watch at night and moved cautiously during the day.

Frank's eyelids drooped and he fought to keep them open. He clutched the sharpened stick he'd carved from the bone knife one of the women from the previous island had given him. He realized how pathetically inadequate it would be against a Japanese soldier with a modern rifle, but it made him feel better to have something resembling a weapon.

He squeezed the spear until his hands hurt. The grogginess subsided. They'd managed to carve out a little piece of the thick jungle and set up shelters made from massive leaves and weaved grasses—skills they'd learned from the Shaman and his people. It had rained hard three times and only a few drips came through. The bigger problem was keeping the snakes, centipedes, and other nasty creatures out, but they were used to such things by now. They'd heard larger creatures yowling at night, which sent shivers down their spines, but they hadn't found whatever caused the racket.

The first hint of dawn tinged the eastern skyline. He wondered what the day would bring. They planned on climbing to the top of the highest peak to get a better feel for the rest of the island. They hoped to see villages or towns from the higher vantage point. If they saw Japanese, they didn't really know what they would do. Perhaps get back in the outriggers and seek another island further south. *We need to make a plan.*

Grinning Bear jolted awake. Frank still couldn't see him, but he knew it was him after countless hours spent together. He knew every sound and grunt. He whispered to him. "How'd you sleep?"

He didn't answer in words, just grunted.

"It'll be light soon."

"I thought I was back with Bree," Grinning Bear murmured.

It wasn't her real name, but it was what Grinning Bear called his woman from the other island.

"Do you miss her?"

Grinning Bear guffawed, like it was a ridiculous question. "Course I miss her. You don't enjoy getting laid?"

"That all she was to you?"

Frank heard Grinning Bear pushing himself to his feet. He shuffled in the confined space until he stood next to him. He could barely see his outline in the dim light.

"Are you judging me?"

"No, course not. Just wondering what she meant to you. I mean, you could still be back there with her."

Grinning Bear's deep chortle started low and slowly grew in volume. If he didn't know him, he wouldn't know he was laughing, but might think he'd gone insane.

"What's so damned funny?"

Grinning Bear finally controlled his laughter. He said, "I'm not sure what my mama would say if I brought her home with me. My father would raise an eyebrow and maybe grunt, but I think my mother might have some words for me."

"She wouldn't approve? Hell, she's probably more Indian than you are."

"Maybe not quite as bad as bringing home your sister, but she's not from our tribe."

"I don't have a sister, you know that. Besides, Bree's as tribal as they come."

"If you had a sister, I wouldn't date her."

"Why the hell not?"

"You'd want me to?"

"Well, no—but why wouldn't you? She'd be cute."

Grinning Bear just grunted, his way of saying he didn't agree.

"You don't think she'd be cute? Oh—she'd be cute. Cuter 'n Bree by a mile."

"You don't even have a sister, but I don't like the way you're talking about her. You sound like a perverted uncle."

Neil stood and stretched. "This is the stupidest conversation I've heard in my entire life. How the hell did I end up marooned with you two maroons?"

"You just come up with that, or have you been waiting for the right moment?" Frank asked.

"You like it?"

"Not too bad."

Neil slapped Frank's shoulder. "If it's any consolation, I'd screw the living daylights out of your sister—if you had one."

"Ah, now you're just trying to make me feel good."

They hunched near the edge of their shelter and watched the sun rise seemingly straight out of the ocean as they munched on dried fish.

"What d'you think we'll find on that mountain?" Frank asked.

"Probably more mountains," Grinning Bear answered.

The jungle around them changed from darkness to light in seemingly an instant. The sounds changed as nocturnal animals found shelter and day animals came to life. The buzzing from the incessant insects never changed.

"Let's get this done," Frank hissed.

Grinning Bear pointed at Frank's whittled spear. "You planning on cooking some weenies with that?"

"Better'n nothing."

Grinning Bear patted the pistol tucked into his tattered pants. "I'm outta bullets, but they won't know that."

Neil said, "Hope we don't find anyone."

"Someone made those prints," Frank said.

They moved from their shelter and found the game trail leading west. They'd explored it in both directions for a few hundred yards and found nothing except the prints. They'd been old and nondescript, but definitely human.

They crept. Frank led the way. He held his spear but wished he held his old Springfield—or even better—a Thompson submachine gun. *Nothing better for close jungle work.* But he may as well wish to sprout wings.

The trail angled upward for a hundred feet, then dropped back toward the water. They'd explored up to this point. From here on out, they'd be in unknown territory.

Frank hunkered and waited for the others to catch up. When they did, he pointed up. "Ready?" Both men nodded. He stepped off the game trail and wound his way carefully through the jungle. With each yard, the jungle thinned. He couldn't decide if it had been cultivated in the distant past, or thinned naturally.

He made sure of each step. It wasn't steep, but if he fell, he'd likely roll and he didn't relish the thought of having to climb what he'd already climbed, not to mention the razzing he'd get from Neil and Grinning Bear.

Sweat stung his eyes. The effort of climbing made his breathing more labored. It annoyed him. He'd once prided himself on his physical fitness, but the long incarceration and dismal diet had combined to make this kind of effort brutal. The time on the other island had helped, but he still felt weakened. Would he ever get back to normal?

He climbed slowly but steadily. He couldn't see the top, but figured they'd made it at least halfway. He glanced back at the others. They kept good spacing like the professionals they were. They didn't simply follow, but watched their surroundings as closely as Frank. They made very little noise. If the Japanese lingered nearby, they'd be hard-pressed to notice their passing . . . at least he hoped so.

A few uneventful minutes passed. The terrain thinned even more, exposing large swaths of lush ferns. Sunlight streamed through the thin overhead canopy and lit the ground in fluorescent green. It would be a wonderful place for a picnic with one of the native girls.

He came to a much larger swath of ferns. He crouched and waited for the others. They soon arrived and watched the open space for nearly a full two minutes.

Satisfied that no one waited to ambush them on the other side, he wound his way through the ferns. Pearl-sized drops of water rubbed off on his bare legs as he passed. They dripped down his leg like blood, but cooled him. He automatically checked himself for leeches every few seconds. The act had become as natural as breathing. *How long will that habit linger?*

Successfully across, he crouched and watched the open space he'd just passed through. The others came across stealthily and soon joined him. They watched in all directions in silence, focusing their senses on anything out of the ordinary.

"I think we're alone," Frank finally whispered.

He turned away from the ferns, ready to keep moving up the slope, but Grinning Bear reached out and stopped him with a firm grasp on his shoulder.

Frank looked back, annoyed, but the look in his friend's eyes made him freeze. He slowly turned back toward the ferns. A light breeze swayed them slightly and thousands of water droplets sparkled in the sun. The beauty nearly took his breath away, but that wasn't what had seized Grinning Bear's attention.

From the far side, two small brown figures emerged. They appeared like apparitions and their wide eyes stared as though surprised or deathly frightened.

"What the hell?" Frank hissed. "Where'd they come from?"

Even though the three stowaways had blended in with their surroundings without even thinking about it, the two men seemed to stare directly at them—as though the stowaways wore flamboyant colors and danced around waving their arms.

"They see us," Neil said. "And they have rifles."

"Don't move a muscle," Grinning Bear said through gritted teeth.

Frank sensed something else besides the men coming across the field. He turned slowly back toward the jungle and let out an involuntary yelp. Two more men crouched only feet away. Each aimed an ancient rifle at them, and both grinned like crazy people.

"Shit," Frank said. He stood, dropped his spear, and raised his hands to show he wasn't armed. Grinning Bear and Neil saw them too and both slowly stood.

The two others bounded across the field with exuberant smiles on their faces. In seconds, the four native men had them surrounded.

Although they aimed old weapons at them, they weren't Japanese soldiers. They reminded him of Filipinos he'd worked with in the Philippines, but less refined. They wore no shirts but had on shorts, which reminded Frank of British or Australian troopers he'd seen. Their skin was the color of rich coffee and their hair was short, straight, and dark as night.

Frank smiled broadly, hoping to ease any thoughts they had of shooting them. Hopefully, they didn't work for the Japanese.

He pointed at himself and said, "American, American."

The word didn't seem to register. Frank uttered the word for a friend he'd learned from the other natives on the other island, but their faces didn't change. Grinning Bear tried a few words he'd learned along the way with the same result.

One native finally spoke. He had a high, thin voice. Frank didn't recognize the words, but recognized they spoke pidgin. He'd become familiar with the language, but couldn't speak it or understand its many vagrancies. The pointing and gesturing made their intent clear, however. They wanted them to move up the hill—the same direction they'd already been heading. They aimed their rifles at their backsides, but their smiles never left their dark faces.

The three Americans exchanged glances. Despite the rifles, their captors didn't seem threatening. They kept gesturing up the hill and the one who seemed in charge kept talking in his high, reedy voice. It almost sounded like he was singing.

"Guess we'll see what happens," Frank said with an edge to his voice.

Grinning Bear nodded. "They don't seem dangerous. I think they're Filipinos."

"That would make sense," Frank added.

"They might work for the Nips," Neil suggested.

A long silence ensued as they slowly climbed up the hillside. Frank went through different scenarios in his head. He finally said quietly, "If I see Japs, I'm going for a rifle. I'd rather die than be a POW again."

Neil nodded gravely and Grinning Bear added, "I'm with you on that."

THE HILL PROVED to be much taller than the Americans imagined. The natives kept urging them along like dogs working cattle. Their rifle muzzles never wavered from their backsides, but neither did their smiles.

Finally, the supposed leader trotted into the lead and held up his hand for them to stop. The other three natives kept their places, but they spread out and adjusted their aim. Frank wondered why they'd march them all the way up here just to shoot them.

The lead man spoke quickly, then ran up the hill as though gravity had no effect on him. He didn't sprint, but moved quickly. Frank marveled, and the word "grace" popped into his head. Frank wondered if his feet left a mark in the soft ground or if he simply used the spines of the ferns for leverage. The natives soon disappeared into the jungle, leaving the Americans breathless.

Frank muttered under his breath, "If he comes back with Japs, I'm taking the guy on the left."

"Middle," Grinning Bear said.

"Right," Neil added.

Frank figured if he could get close enough, quick enough, he'd have a chance, but he didn't like his odds. If they were as deadly as they were graceful, they'd have zero chance of success. Were these his last moments on Earth? He took in the lush jungle. The various shades of greens, reds, yellows, and everything in between dazzled his senses. It wouldn't be a terrible place to die. He idly wondered how long it would take for the jungle to consume his body.

Noise from up the hill made him turn away from the rifle muzzles. His heart rate increased noticeably. His ears burned hot. Whoever came was quiet, but not nearly as graceful as the natives. If he saw a soldier of Imperial Japan, he'd make his move.

His mind and body buzzed with anticipation. He pictured disarming the native quickly and turning the ancient rifle on the enemy soldier. He'd kill the natives second. Even in his mind's eye, it seemed outrageously impossible. He wasn't a trained assassin with the skills of a Ninja—he was a common infantryman. Sure, he could hold his own in a fight, but he wasn't magic, and he felt far from deadly at the moment.

The pounding in his ears eased when he saw a tall Caucasian man step from the jungle. Compared to the native leading him, he seemed like a giant. He towered over the Americans, too. He wore shorts and a shirt tucked neatly into his waistband. He wore a holster, and his hand rested lightly on a pistol grip. He smiled at them and swept his jauntily askew Aussie-style hat off with a flourish.

With a heavy German accent, he said, "Güten täg. I'm Valentine Gustav. It is good to finally meet you face-to-face."

Frank's jaw dropped. Questions abounded, but he couldn't form words. Valentine Gustav looked as though he'd stepped straight out of a fantastical fairytale book. His hair, although on the longish side, was combed perfectly. He almost shone with cleanliness. Frank nearly laughed out loud when he had the bizarre thought that perhaps Gustav was some kind of living doll. A walking, breathing, brand spanking new doll.

Neil was the first one of them to come to his senses and speak. "Uh, hi. I'm—I'm Neil Winstad and this here's Larry Grinning Bear, and this is Frank Cooper. Uh, nice to meet you, too."

Gustav stepped past the lead native. He raised his chin and spoke to the natives in their same pidgin language. The natives immediately slung their rifles over their shoulders. Their smiles broadened.

Gustav said, "Ach, sorry about that, but I had to be sure you were not the enemy."

Frank finally found his voice. "Are—are you German?"

Gustav nodded and smoothed his perfect mustache. "Ja, but do not worry, I am not a Nazi. I am on your side, I suppose."

"You suppose?"

"From your accents, I assume you are American?"

The three of them nodded, still stunned to meet this giant of a man.

"Güt. I mean, good. Sorry, sometimes I slip back into my native tongue, especially when I have not spoken English in a while."

Frank said, "You speak their language, too." He stated it as a fact more than a question.

"And many others. But that is beside the point. You must be hungry."

At the mention of food, any remaining doubt or fear dropped away. All three of them stared hungrily, and Frank heard Neil's stomach growl at the mere mention of food.

"Come. There is food at the outpost." He turned and waved them to follow. The natives stepped past them too, as though they'd known the Americans their whole lives and didn't mind turning their backs to them.

Frank exchanged looks with the other two and shrugged. They shrugged back, then hustled to keep up as the natives and the German strode up the hill quickly.

The small entourage crested the hill, but they didn't stop there. Tall trees hid the view mostly, but Frank could see flashes of the sparkling sea in the distance. He wanted to find a better view, but Gustav waved to them to keep moving.

They followed him to a spit of land leading south from the top of the hill. They moved along it for a couple hundred yards before they stopped.

"Here we are," Gustav stated.

Frank looked around, bewildered. He saw nothing but more jungle, although he could see a larger portion of the island. It wasn't as big as he'd suspected. Green trees spread out all the way to a relatively narrow channel of sea. Across the channel, another much larger island loomed.

Gustav pulled aside a green wall of vegetation and stepped into darkness. When they didn't follow, he stuck his head back out and gestured. "Well, come on then."

Frank stepped through the vines. A lit oil lamp flickered in the corner, throwing weak yellow light onto a cramped room. A large glassless window looked out over the channel and the island chain beyond. Thick trees overhead kept the room shaded and relatively cool.

Gustav pulled a canvas tarp off a large square lump sitting on a makeshift but sturdy table. It was bigger than any radio he'd ever seen. It looked powerful.

Frank's eyes bugged out. "A radio," he said in awe. "An honest-to-goodness radio." He beamed back at Grinning Bear and Neil, then turned back to Gustav. "Does it work?" he asked hopefully.

Gustav looked offended. "Of course it works. It is the whole reason I am here."

"How'd you get it up here?" Grinning Bear asked.

"With a lot of help from these men," he pointed his thumb toward the natives who still stood outside, as though on guard duty. "There is a lot more than just those four," he added. "It nearly took the whole town."

"They live on this island?" Frank asked.

Gustav pointed to the large island across the strait. "No, on that one. We had to move the radio here, though. The Japs were getting too close."

"What do you mean? The Japs are after you?"

Gustav scowled and gave him a cutting glance. "Well, of course they are. Been looking for us since the beginning of this cursed war. How do you Americans say it? 'We're a cut in their side.'"

"Thorn. You're a *thorn* in their side."

"Thorn," he said with some obvious difficulty. "Yes. They would love to get their hands on us. We have been reporting their every move for years now."

"So, you're in contact with command? With the allies?"

"That is correct."

"So, you could tell them about us?"

Gustav raised one eyebrow. "Yes, of course. But that is not a priority. I only contact them once a week—sooner if I see something urgent."

"We're not urgent?"

Gustav looked from one to another in obvious confusion. "Urgent? Why would you be urgent? Have you seen something to help the war effort?"

"We were on Corregidor when it fell. We escaped from a Jap POW camp."

Gustav looked at them with more understanding. "I assumed you were from a sunken naval vessel—or perhaps a long-range bomber crew." He rubbed his chin in thought. "I called in this morning with my regular report. I vary the times and days to keep the Nips guessing. I can report again tomorrow. They may be interested in hearing your circumstances."

Frank felt a welling of emotion in his chest. "Could, could they get word to our parents? To our families?"

The German smiled. "Yes—and perhaps they will send a submarine for you."

The American's mouths dropped open. Neil said, "Really? They'd do that?"

Gustav shrugged, as though it was a common occurrence. "Since the fall of the Philippines, they have brought in spare radios and supplies occasionally. It is dangerous for them, obviously, but sometimes necessary. We can make do with very little, but some radio parts are impossible to reproduce out here."

The thought of rescue had never really occurred to Frank. He only hoped to be free and able to fight the Japanese until the end. He never imagined he'd be whisked off the island and returned home to his family. The thought made his knees weak.

Grinning Bear stepped forward and placed a hand on Frank's shoulder. "Don't get your hopes up. I can't imagine them sending a submarine just for the three of us." He focused on Gustav. "You act as though you've seen us before, but we've never met."

The big German smiled and nodded. "Yes—we knew about you the moment your canoes landed on the beach." He indicated the men outside with a lift of his chin. "They reported your arrival to me and they took me to you a few days ago."

"Why the hell didn't you say something, then?"

"Sometimes it is better to observe than to act."

"We coulda starved out there, or been eaten by a tiger or some jungle cat."

"No tigers here. We would not have let such a thing happen."

The mention of starvation brought food back to the forefront. Frank's stomach growled and Neil's and Grinning Bear's answered as though their stomachs spoke a secret language only they knew.

Gustav smiled. "You are hungry."

He walked to a corner and opened a small stove Frank hadn't noticed. The smell of cooked meat wafted over them and nearly sent the men diving toward it, but they maintained their manners and only drooled and rubbed their hands together in anticipation. First, the possibility of going home and now meat? The day couldn't get any better.

~

AFTER THE AMERICANS gorged themselves on roasted pig meat and some kind of cooked tubers, they sat back, completely satisfied. They'd eaten outside the stuffy little shed, in the broad daylight of midday. Frank took in the magnificent view.

A buzzing caught their attention. Valentine burst out of the shack and gazed up at the cloud-dotted sky. The Filipinos faded into the surrounding jungle and were out of sight.

Valentine took off his hat and pulled a pair of large binoculars from a case nearby. He carefully put the strap over his head. He scanned with his naked eye first, then he pointed and raised the binoculars.

"There it is."

He swept the binoculars slowly until he found what he was looking for, then he adjusted the focus wheel. He mumbled to himself in German as he watched.

A few seconds later, he let the binoculars swing around his neck. He pulled a pad of paper from his pocket, licked the tip of a pencil, and jotted something down. "Right on schedule," he said.

Frank saw the notepad was filled with line upon line of tiny script in a neat hand, but in German.

"Bomber?" Frank asked.

"Transport."

"For the past two weeks, it flies over at the exact same time on that exact heading."

"You think it's important?"

"Maybe. I don't know. I have told my controllers. It is up to them to act on it or not."

Neil's eyes drooped and he struggled to stay awake after eating the heavy meal. He asked, "You ever see American planes up there?"

"Seldom," he said. "Sometimes they fly so high that I cannot see them at all."

Grinning Bear asked, "So this is what you do all day? Report on air traffic?"

"It is one job, yes. But I mainly report on enemy ship movements." He pointed across the strait at the larger island. "The enemy has five thousand men garrisoned there. Sometimes ships come and go. I report the name, what they offload, load, and their direction of departure."

The Americans looked more closely at him. Frank said, "You'd have to get pretty damned close to see all that." Valentine simply nodded. Frank added, "You don't really fit in. How do you manage it?"

"My network knows what to look for. They bring me the information and I relay it to control."

Grinning Bear looked at him out of the corner of his eye. "How'd you get this job? Are you military?"

"They call us coast watchers. I am but one of hundreds of coast watchers scattered throughout the South Pacific and beyond. We report on enemy movements, but I have never served as a soldier."

"They drop you in from one of those submarines you were talking about?"

"No. I was a missionary before the war. These people are my flock."

Frank scowled. The thought of a religious cult made him uneasy. "They don't seem too Christian," he stated.

"I was not the best missionary." Valentine's grin turned into a laugh. "I fell in love with the culture . . . and a woman." his laughter stopped as quickly as it had started. "But she died." His eyes had grown dark and foreboding beneath his large forehead and bushy eyebrows.

Frank could hear the bitterness in his voice. "I'm sorry to hear that. She must have been a special woman."

"Every time I report a Japanese ship or aircraft, I pray it ends in their deaths." He cleared his throat and looked at his feet. "Not very Christian, I know. God and I are no longer on the best terms. He allowed those monsters to kill my wife—now I kill them back."

The three Americans stared at Valentine. They'd all seen Japanese brutality up close and personal. They understood his anguish.

Grinning Bear spit onto the ground and said, "Amen."

11

Colonel Glen Borill hadn't received good news for ages, but the bombshell report he held made him smile.

He looked up at Captain Nols, who'd handed him the report. "Is this accurate?"

"Yes, sir. It's from Mr. Gustav."

Borill nodded. If Gustav reported it, it was gospel. "This could be a boon for the folks back home. This kind of story is just what they need to hear—boys risen from the dead. Do we know anything about these men?"

Nols shrugged. "All the records from Corregidor and the Philippines, in general, are a jumbled mess. The Japs barely allowed the Red Cross access, so the records of who survived and who didn't aren't reliable. But the names check out—they were certainly there."

"And now they're with Gustav. Unbelievable. I'd love to hear that story."

Nols asked, "So, what's the plan? Are we getting them out of there?"

Colonel Borill sat in the high-backed leather chair and cleaned his glasses while he considered. The only successful method to get men out that deep behind the enemy lines was by submarine. They'd successfully delivered radios and other essential items to various far-reaching islands—they'd even delivered men—and even taken a few men off, but it was dangerous work.

"Where's the *Nautilus*?" Borill asked. The USS *Nautilus* was a Narwhal Class submarine specifically designed for such delicate missions. It had already performed many. Borill knew the captain personally. Commander Baskin would relish this kind of mission.

"She's on a mission up north."

The door opened abruptly and a major stepped in and barked, "Attention!"

Both Borill and Nols snapped to attention. Borill raised his eyebrows as General Pericles entered the room. "At ease," the general grumbled.

Borill exchanged a glance with Nols. It was unusual to have General Pericles, the CO, come out to the intelligence shack. He'd made it clear that he considered it to be a backwater. He didn't trust their intelligence and as long as they stayed out of his way, he'd stay out of their way—but here he was.

He cut straight to the point. "I heard about the report from Gustav concerning the escaped POWs. Where do we stand?"

Someone had only decoded the report an hour before. How had the general gotten word so quickly? He held up the paper. "Yes, sir. We were just discussing what to do about it. The *Nautilus* would be our best option. We . . ."

"Scratch that," the general said flatly.

"Sir?"

General Pericles lifted his jiggly chin and his ice-blue eyes leveled at Borill. "We're leaving them there."

The colonel and the captain exchanged confused glances. Borill said, "But sir, we were thinking it would be good for morale to . . ."

"Morale? No. We're leaving them there."

"May I ask why, sir? They've been through hell and back. Surely, they deserve to come home—and they'd have information about other POWs—camp locations, Jap numbers, all sorts of . . ."

"Not happening, Colonel. This Gustav fellow is invaluable. He's built his own little army right in the enemies' backyard." He glanced at a file he held. "This Corporal Cooper, PFC Nols, and the marine, PFC Larry Grinning Bear, have excellent records. They're just what this Gustav fellow needs to shape his army of informants into something more lethal."

Borill understood now. The higher brass had been pestering them to step up not only Gustav's reconnaissance but also to take more direct action against the Japanese occupiers in the Philippines. Borill thought it would be suicidal and might bring an invaluable source of information to a complete stop. He'd told them so in no uncertain terms. Without support, they would squash Gustav and his men like bugs.

"But sir, we've talked about this before. What's changed?"

"We've never had this kind of opportunity before. Those men are skilled soldiers. They'll be a tremendous asset in their training."

"One's a marine, sir—and unless I'm mistaken, none of them have been trained to train indigenous people to fight a guerrilla war. Private Winstad's a clerk, sir."

General Pericles's face reddened. "This is not a discussion, *Colonel*. I have already decided. Now give the order, or do I need to find someone who will?"

Borill thought about stomping out in protest, but it would mean the end of his career, and that was the last thing he wanted to happen. "No, sir. I mean, I'll do it, sir."

"Good."

He turned to leave, but before he made the door, Colonel Borill asked, "What about the parents, sir? What'll we tell them?"

The general stopped and clenched and unclenched his fists as his assistant held the door for him. Long seconds passed before he finally said, "We won't tell them anything. Nothing at all."

Borill couldn't believe his ears. "We're not going to tell their families that their sons are alive?"

The general turned and looked both officers up and down. "That's correct. I don't want a word of this getting out. If it does," he held up a finger. "I'll know where it came from."

Borill wanted to throttle the general, but he knew when to shut his mouth. He bit back his anger, lifted his chin, and snapped to attention. "Yes, sir. I understand, sir."

The general slapped his hat into his other hand and left the room. The major gave them one last scowl before closing the door.

Nols waited until he heard their footsteps receding. "*Do* you understand? 'Cause I sure don't."

"Deniability. The son of a bitch wants deniability." Nols lifted a questioning eyebrow, so Borill explained. "If it ever gets out that he left parents and relatives in the dark about their sons being alive, it wouldn't go over too well. The fewer people that know about it, the better. He feels he can control the two of us, apparently."

Nols shook his head. "Can he?"

"His word against ours. Besides, if we go over his head, he'll just have us canned—he'll put someone in place that'll do all his bidding like a lapdog."

Nols stared at the door. "I feel real bad about this. Can you imagine your own parents in a similar situation?"

"I know. It stinks."

"What'll we tell Gustav? I mean, what if he asks about their families?"

"Leave it to me," Borill said stoically. If it came to that, he wouldn't make Nols tell the lie.

~

FRANK LISTENED as Gustav talked on the radio. He felt almost giddy to hear another American voice on the other end of the radio. He hadn't heard a new American voice in ages, and even though it was tinny and distant, it sounded good. He wasn't alone out here. He and the rest of them hadn't been forgotten, and now the rest of the world would know they were still alive. The three of them all sat there listening and none of them could wipe the goofy grins off their faces.

Gustav went through a litany of code words, most of which sounded like nonsense, especially with his German accent. Gustav removed the headset and tapped the Filipino, cranking the generator handle to stop. The loud grinding stopped, and the jungle noises outside the little shack continued as though nothing had happened. When Frank first heard how much noise the generator crank produced, he'd cringed, but Gustav assured him that the jungle ate the sound quickly. He'd tested it himself. Unless the enemy was within ten yards, the sound wouldn't be noticed over the cacophony of insects and screeching jungle birds.

The young Filipino fellow left the shack and joined his friends outside. Gustav clapped Frank on the shoulder. "I told them all about you."

Frank raised his eyebrows, wanting more. When it didn't come right away, he asked, "And? What did they say?"

Gustav pressed his lips together and shook his head. "It doesn't work that way. They will decode my message, then respond with their own coded message. We should know by tomorrow morning."

"That long?" Neil asked.

"Sometimes longer, although I have never reported this kind of news before. Perhaps they will respond earlier than normal."

"How will you know? Do we stay here and wait?"

"No. I do not wait. There are response times." He checked his wristwatch. It looked old, the watch face scratched enough to make it nearly impossible to read. "I will check back in two hours. That is the earliest."

Frank looked at the hard-dirt floor. He wanted to know right now. Would they be getting onto a submarine and sailing home? It sounded fantastically impossible.

"When was the last time they sent a submarine out here?"

"Many months ago. I needed a radio part. It was essential to my mission."

"Do you think they'll send a sub for us?" Neil asked.

Frank gave him an annoyed look. "We'll just have to wait and see."

Gustav added, "It is very dangerous for the submarine."

Grinning Bear hefted his large frame from the makeshift stool he sat upon. "Well, there's no use stewing about it. Can you show us around your island?"

Gustav smiled. "A wonderful idea."

Frank followed them out into the bright sunlight. The day had turned hot, but a slight breeze coming off the straits kept it tolerable. He gazed at the view. The large island across the strait didn't look real. It sparkled greens, yellows, and reds, and from a distance looked like a knobby mat of carpet. It reminded him of the carpet his mother insisted they never eat meals over back home.

He realized he hadn't thought of home for a long time. Would he be home soon? The thought made him dizzy, but it also sounded slightly ridiculous. He'd learned through harsh reality not to get his hopes up for anything. He'd seen the carpet swept from beneath his feet too many damned times. *More like thatch instead of carpet.*

Would his parents even recognize him? He hadn't seen himself in a mirror in ages, but he must look different. He'd certainly lost weight, but had his face changed? What about his brother, Clyde? He must be in the war effort by now. Was he still alive? Was he fighting, or did he land a cushy desk job working for his father-in-law? He didn't know a damned thing. It hadn't bothered him before, but now, being on the cusp of so much potential, he burned to know more.

Gustav hunkered beside one of his Filipino friends and they talked in that odd pidgin spinoff.

Frank asked, "You get any news out here? I mean, are we winning or losing this war?"

Grinning Bear's and Neil's eyes sharpened. They wanted to hear the answer as much as anyone.

Gustav said, "Yes. The allies are making it tough on them, but they have a long way to go. Your marines kicked them off Guadalcanal and moved onto Bougainville Island and beyond. I have heard your marines have attacked as far north as the Marshall Islands. I do not hear everything, but occasionally we pick up distant radio reports on our set, and my network hears conversations from Japanese soldiers sometimes." He grinned, "They do not know some Filipinos understand their language and often talk freely. I have even heard Guam and Saipan may be next."

Frank tried to remember his geography, but it wasn't his best subject. He asked, "Are they close to here?"

"They have not crossed into the Philippines. They are still thousands of miles from here."

That sobered Frank. Thousands of miles. "But they must be getting closer if they're using your reports."

"I have no idea what happens to my reports. I hope it is useful and leads to Japanese deaths, but I do not know for certain. They do not tell me such things."

"You're a grunt, just like the rest of us," Frank said.

"Grunt?"

"Yeah, you know . . . a cog in the wheel. You're a foot soldier like the rest of us. You only know what's in front of you."

Gustav nodded slowly, as though trying to understand what Frank meant. "Yes, I suppose, but I am not a soldier."

"You said that before, but you're in a dangerous situation. Have you killed the enemy?" Frank asked carefully. "I mean personally, not through a report."

Gustav's large forehead furrowed and his bushy eyebrows condensed, sending long strands of hair in every direction. "I have had to kill, yes."

A silence lingered. Frank knew killing, even killing the enemy, was a deeply personal experience. He'd dreamed of killing his guards so often that he'd almost forgotten what it was like to end another human being's life—almost.

"I'm sorry. I didn't mean to pry."

Gustav lifted his chin and stared at Frank. "It is okay. I killed the man who killed my wife. I strangled him with these hands." He lifted his hands and turned them back and forth as though they didn't belong to him. "These two hands. I gripped his neck and squeezed. He was not a large man. I could feel his spine in my palms. It did not take long. I remember his eyes."

Grinning Bear said, "You did the right thing."

Gustav looked at him with surprise in his eyes. "Yes, of course I did. He was evil. He needed to die. But it did not bring my wife back."

"No, I don't suppose it would," Grinning Bear said softly. "But you avenged her death."

"No. Not until all these vermin are dead will I have avenged her," Gustav said with venom in his voice.

Frank said, "Then why haven't you attacked them more? I mean directly."

"I take orders the same way you do. I am not in the military, but I help them. The best way to do so is to follow orders," he stated in his clipped German accent.

Frank could imagine this giant of a man strangling a Japanese soldier, but despite his anger at losing his wife, he didn't seem the type to go on a murderous rampage. Despite his size, he seemed more like a teddy bear than a bloodthirsty grizzly, but just like Grinning Bear's stoic quietness hid a violent streak, he supposed the same was true for Gustav's size. He wouldn't want to get on the wrong side of him.

FRANK STOOD inside the radio shack as Gustav stood by, awaiting word from what he called control. He'd asked him where exactly control was, but Gustav only shrugged and said the less he knew, the less he could tell the Japanese if they ever captured him. Frank doubted they'd capture him alive.

After fifteen minutes passed, Gustav clutched the earphones tightly and listened intently. He grasped a pencil and wrote what looked like gibberish onto a sheet of paper already full of such gibberish. If a stranger came across the paper, they'd think it was doodling or the rants of a crazy man, or both.

After nearly five minutes of frantic yet precise writing, Gustav removed the headset and stood. He clutched the paper as though it might hold the secrets of eternal life.

"They have responded early. They rarely are so fast."

"What do you suppose it means?" Neil asked. He'd been picking at a scab on his elbow and it bled onto the dirt floor. Ants swarmed the bloody spot.

Gustav said, "I do not know. I need time to decode the message."

Frank could hardly contain his excitement. He wanted to know what it said right now, or at least ask him what he thought it might say, but he didn't open his mouth. Anything he did would only delay the message.

"Come on, fellas. Let's give Gustav space so he can get to work."

The three of them left the shack and found seats in the little clearing. The day had passed into evening, but the air remained hot and humid. The breeze had stopped and massive cumulous clouds built on the far horizon.

They tried to make small talk while the minutes ticked by agonizingly slowly. They quickly slipped into silence—the only sound the high-pitched buzzing of insects in their ears.

Frank reluctantly ate the offered meat from the Filipinos. He felt the way he did right before combat, or right before the guards chose who to beat the crap out of that day—slightly nauseous. But he ate it anyway. He'd experienced too much starvation in his life to ever refuse food again, no matter how he felt. If he ever made it home, he supposed he'd become very fat very quickly.

Thinking of home made him remember all those who'd never get home. So many had died. Nearly everyone on Corregidor. Those that had survived and been sent to the same prison camp had either perished from malnutrition, beatings, or simply lost their will to live, or they'd gone down with that damned ship. The irony of his own countrymen killing so many of them in the end nearly made him laugh. It sounded comical. *A tragic comedy, like some kind of deranged Shakespeare play*, he supposed.

Finally, Gustav pushed his way through the flap and stood holding the piece of paper. His dark eyes went from the paper to the men. Frank didn't know him, but he could read that something wasn't right.

"What does it say?" he asked.

"I deciphered it twice. It is accurate, but . . ."

"But what?" Neil asked irritably.

"They are not sending a submarine. They want you to stay here with me . . .with us."

Frank looked at his friends, who looked equally confused. "Did—did they say why?"

"They want you to train these men to fight."

Frank felt gut punched. "Train them? Train them? What the hell? We're escaped POWs. Did you tell them that?"

"Yes, of course. I gave them your names and ranks. They know who you are."

Neil said, "There must be some mistake. We don't know how to train your men. We don't even speak the language, for Pete's sake. I'm a clerk!"

Grinning Bear spoke in his laconic slow way. Frank recognized it as his 'it doesn't have to make sense' voice. "They want us to train them to fight in their own jungle? I think they could teach us a thing or two, not the other way around."

Frank added, "We don't have weapons or ammunition. What do they expect us to train them with? Bows and arrows? I'm with Grinning Bear. This is ridiculous."

Gustav lifted a thick finger. "That is not true. We have weapons and ammunition."

All three Americans stared at him as though he'd grown wings out of his backside.

"It is true. But we have not used them. Headquarters told us just observe and report. No attacks."

Frank couldn't believe his ears. He felt conflicted. On the one hand, he yearned for vengeance, but on the other hand, he wanted to go home and end this nightmare once and for all. Despite trying to keep a level head, he'd let himself dream of home. He kicked himself for the slip. *I'm not meant to make it home.* He reminded himself.

He hardened his heart to the tiny seedling of softness that had planted itself in the coarse ground of reality.

"You better show us these weapons, Gustav."

12

Oro Bay, New Guinea
April 1944

Clyde lit a cigarette and let the smoke sift out the side of his mouth. He'd been smoking more and more often. The long boat ride from Australia back to New Guinea had started on April 5 and ended on April 14. In that time, they'd traveled two thousand water miles. Besides training and gambling, the only other thing to do was to smoke cigarettes. He felt it cut his wind on marches, but it calmed his nerves. *Besides, I'm not gonna live forever.*

Gil Hicks sat beside him, listening to nearby officers go back and forth about officer stuff. "You think they'll ever let us get back in the war, or just bicker until it ends?"

"They didn't send us all the way back out here just to twiddle our thumbs."

Gil looked sideways at him. "We've been here in Dobodura for a month now. I haven't seen any sign of Japs—just the constant drone of our flyboys in and out and in and out. It's enough to drive me crazy."

"There's a reason they have us near an airfield, I suppose."

"Well, then why the hell aren't we training? We trained for a full month for the jump onto Cape Glouster."

"Yeah, and we didn't even go. Maybe they think that's enough, like it'll carry over. You don't feel ready?"

"I'm ready for anything, you know that. We all are." He shook his head. "Damned marines. They really screwed us over."

The paratroopers still bristled at missing out on the jump onto Cape Glouster. They'd trained hard right up to the day of the jump when the whole thing had been called off because the marines overran their jump zones. The chafing wasn't caused as much from missing out on another combat jump as it was that the marines were the ones that messed it up for them.

"I don't think we'll have that same problem out here."

"Why's that?"

"'Cause MacArthur isn't using the marines over here on New Guinea. It'll be an army show, through and through. When the regular leg guys get in trouble, they'll send us in to bail 'em out."

"We don't need the damned marines, that's for sure."

Clyde stubbed out his cigarette. "They're good for absorbing Jap bullets for us. But yeah, we don't need 'em."

Gil gave him a cutting look. "Damn, Coop. That really the way you feel?"

Clyde shook his head. "Nah, but I'm sick of them always talking about being the only ones fighting the Nips. If you read the papers, you'd think the army was back in the States cooling our heels."

"Yeah, you got that right. But I think it gives us more credibility."

"How do you mean?"

"I have an uncle, Uncle Ignacio. He's the best chef you'll ever meet. I mean, he can do things in the kitchen you just have to see to believe. His knife skills are beyond anything you can imagine. Quick hands—just incredible."

"Yeah? So what?"

"You'd never know it unless you saw it. I mean, he doesn't say a word about it to anyone. He just does it, and since it's mostly behind closed doors, no one really sees it. He could call himself a master chef, but he doesn't. In fact, he rarely speaks about it." He pushed his index finger into his knee for emphasis. "And that makes it even more impressive."

"So, you're saying he's modest."

"Exactly! He's modest, and it makes his skills that much more impressive. That's what we are—modest."

"The marines are showboaters and we're modest professionals. I like that."

Gil spit into the jungle dirt. "Only problem is, if no one knows how good you are, you don't get the ladies."

"Not all women like showoffs, Gil."

"Well, we're not all as lucky as you. You heard from Abby lately? How's her flying going?"

Clyde's eyes lit up at the mention of his wife. Gil barely knew her, but he asked about her a lot. It made Clyde happy to take about her, but it also made him worry. "Yeah, the letters finally caught up to me here. She's finished flying targets. She applied for a transfer to an airplane delivery service, or something like that, and they scooped her up. She hadn't started yet, but that letter was about three weeks old, so I assume she has by now."

Gil gave a low whistle. "You mean a ferry pilot?"

Clyde gave him a surprised look. Few people knew that term. In fact, he hadn't known until Abby explained it. "That's right—a WASP ferry pilot." He glanced up at the clear blue sky. He guessed today would be a good day to fly, but he didn't see any flights overhead. "How d'you know about ferry pilots?"

"Time magazine had a story about them before the war really heated up. Men used to do it, but I suppose it's mostly women now, since the men are overseas."

An engine roared to life from the airfield. Both men looked in that direction. It was a dull-green P-38 Lightning. Since they'd been stationed there for quite some time, they'd become familiar with the aircraft flying out of there. The P-38 looked lethal, but in a sexy way. Clyde wondered how it would feel to fly one of them.

"Maybe your Abby flew that very plane. Wouldn't that be something?"

Clyde hadn't thought about that. "They don't deliver them overseas.

That'd be too dangerous. They ship 'em here on ship transports. She doesn't leave the States."

"Sure, but maybe she delivered it to the ship. Will she fly all over the country?"

"Yeah, I think so." Clyde looked at his feet. He didn't like thinking about her out there all alone in an aircraft, crossing the country from one end to the next. He didn't know a lot about aircraft, but he *did* know that more casualties happened from malfunctions than actual combat with the enemy. "That scares me. She's all alone out there."

"Really? They don't fly in groups?"

"Nope. She's all alone and sometimes she's gone for weeks at a time."

"Well, they must know where she is. They know her route."

"Sure, but what good does that do? If she goes down, they might find her body, I guess."

"Jesus, Clyde. You can't think like that."

"I can't help it. I love her, but I—I hate worrying all the time."

Gil lit another cigarette. He offered one to Clyde, but he refused. The thought of smoking right then almost made him sick.

"Tell her to quit, then."

Clyde cut a glance at his longtime friend. He'd thought about doing just that many times. She would listen and she would understand, too—but something kept him from doing it.

"She's worked so hard for it. I just can't stand the thought of her disappointment."

Gil shrugged it off as though his comment meant less than nothing. "It's your right as a husband. You can't have babies if she's dead."

"Jesus, Gil. Quit that crap. I worry enough as it is without you adding to it."

"It's true and you know it. I'm just saying what you already know."

"It's more than just that. She really loves it and she's glad to be helping the war effort in such a unique way."

"Unique and dangerous."

The P-38's dual engines roared as it taxied from parking and moved to the line for takeoff. They could see the pilot sitting in the bulbous canopy. The twin propellers spun only feet from his head. The powerful struts on the landing gear moved smoothly up and down as it taxied across uneven ground.

"I wonder if she's flown one of those? Does it matter if there are two engines?"

"I think it does. Abby talked about it, but I can't remember if she has that rating or not."

"I know I couldn't do it."

"Do what—fly?"

"No. I mean, I wouldn't allow my wife to be a pilot. No way."

"You gotta get married first," Clyde said, trying to divert the conversation to something more comfortable.

But Gil would have none of it. "When I do, she'll stay home and cook, clean, and raise the ten kids we'll have." He winked at Clyde, who blushed.

"Yeah, we'll see about that. If you meet the right woman, you might find yourself compromising on occasion."

"Ha, no way, Paisano. With the right woman, it won't even be an issue."

"Maybe you're right, but I wouldn't trade Abby for anyone else. She's amazing and this whole flying thing only makes her more amazing."

"Well, I suppose she's probably good at it. And it'll keep her out of trouble, hopefully."

Clyde hoped that was true. Abby's letters didn't talk too much about her skills. In fact, despite it being her job, her letters weren't full of flying stories, but mostly how much she missed him and the plans she had for after the war with him. Even those didn't necessarily involve flying.

"When I get home, things will go back to normal."

Gil grunted his agreement, then asked, "I saw Butler the other day."

Clyde snapped his head toward him. "Butler? You mean the guy that shot Lieutenant Milkins?"

Gil nodded. "Yep. Saw him waltzing around like a damned peacock."

"You sure? I thought he'd be rotting in Leavenworth by now."

"I'm sure. I even asked Perkins from First Platoon about it—it's him."

"I guess it pays to have a daddy in high places."

"You can say that again. If that had been you or I, they woulda put us against a wall."

"Does Huss know?" Sergeant Huss would blow a gasket when he found out.

"Huss knows everything about this company. I'll bet he does."

Clyde nodded his agreement. "I can't believe they allowed him to keep his jump wings, let alone kept him in the same company."

"You hear anything about Milkins?"

"He's back in Australia, I guess. He didn't make the trip out here."

"You think he'll ever rejoin us?"

"I sure hope so. He was a good leader."

Gil looked around and lowered his voice. "Damn sight better than Palinsky."

Clyde winced, thinking about Milkins's replacement. He wanted to jump in and talk about all the new officer's many shortcomings, but he bit his lower lip and ignored Gil's comment. It wasn't proper for an NCO to talk negatively about an officer to an enlisted man.

When he didn't get a response, Gil clammed up about it. "Well, when do you think we'll get a mission?"

"There's something brewing up north. I'm hoping it leads to something for us, but I haven't heard anything." He slapped his old friend on the shoulder. "But rest assured, I'll be sure to tell you last."

~

WITH THE CHANGING of April into May, there was definitely something brewing on the horizon. Flights out of Dobodura increased by a factor of ten. Not only-bomb laden P-38s taking to the skies but also A-20 bombers. Most came back unscathed, but many had holes from shrapnel and small arms fire, and one even came in with an engine out.

Clyde made a point of getting to know a few pilots stationed at the airbase. They were good guys and loved to talk, as long as the conversation remained firmly on flying or women. Besides basic conversation, they also gave him insight into what might wait for them over the horizon.

He saw one of his friends emerge from the debriefing shack. He flew a P-38 Lightning and had just returned from an early morning mission, or sortie, as they called them.

He waved, then saluted, "Hey there, Lieutenant. How'd the sortie pan out for you?"

Lieutenant Bowers gave him a quick salute back. "How ya doing, Corporal?"

"Fine, fine. Just enjoying this wonderful tropical weather." It was an old joke, but they both laughed. "You fly up north again?"

"Yep, up near some islands off the northern coast. Dropped some eggs on an airfield on a tiny little island."

"Noemfoor?" Clyde asked. He'd been studying maps of the area, and even though he didn't know the tactical situation as well as he would've liked, he'd gotten enough reports from other pilots to put two and two together.

"Yeah, that's the one."

"Much resistance?"

Paul Bowers took long strides toward his tent. Clyde had to nearly trot to keep up.

"Some. Mostly ack-ack and small arms. Didn't see any Zeros this time around. I think they've mostly left or been shot down."

"You think they're softening it up for a landing?"

Bowers stopped in his tracks and looked him up and down. "You working for the Nips, Corporal?"

The comment almost made Clyde sick. He stammered for something to say. The accusation was almost as outlandish as asking him if he was the man in the moon.

Bowers's face turned from serious to laughter in an instant. He slapped his knee and pointed. "You shoulda seen your face, Cooper. Ah, that's rich."

Clyde burst out laughing, too. The thought of conspiring with the hated Japanese was a complete fantasy—hysterically funny—in fact.

"You had me going there for a second, Lieutenant. I thought maybe you'd flipped your lid."

Bowers slapped Clyde's back and kept walking. "To answer your question, I don't rightly know. I mean, there's a few islands up there. We already took Biak, but Noemfoor isn't too far away and it's still full of Japs. I doubt old Mac wants to leave 'em there, hoss."

"Thanks, sir. I don't mean to pester you, just pulling our hair out here waiting for a damned mission. Maybe that'll be the one."

"Yeah, I get it." He pointed a bony finger at him. "Just be careful what you wish for, Corporal."

Clyde nodded and watched the tall aviator duck into his tent. It wasn't definitive information, but it added to the scuttlebutt that a mission might be in the works.

He sauntered back to camp and found Sergeant Huss whittling a figurine out of a bamboo stalk. "Just had a word with Bowers."

Without looking up, Huss asked, "That the P-38 pilot?"

"Yeah. They hit Noemfoor again by the sounds of it." Huss nodded, but went on whittling. "Think we'll get sent there?"

Huss finally looked at him. "I may as well tell you. There's a plan to take Noemfoor. Operation Cyclone. The 158th is landing there sometime in early July."

"The 158th? Not us?"

"Nope. There're troops on Biak that are much closer than us, but Captain Stallsworthy seems to think we'll be held in reserve for the operation."

"Well, at least that's something. The men are going stir crazy."

"I know it. That's why they're gonna increase our training—well, that and the possibility of a jump."

"I never thought I'd hope for a mission, but I feel like we've been out of the war so long, it might just pass us by."

"There's little chance of that. Keep the men sharp and ready to go."

"Are you gonna tell 'em about Noemfoor?"

"Lieutenant Jameson wants to address the platoons one at a time tomorrow. Word is, he'll be giving us a combat readiness order."

"Well, hot damn," Clyde slapped his hands together.

"Don't get your hopes up, though. From what I hear, Noemfoor's a tiny island with only a small enemy presence—the 158th should be able to handle it on their own. But just in case, they're sending us further north to Hollandia."

"Another boat ride?"

"'Fraid so."

"We've got more nautical miles under our belts than some navy guys."

"Make sure the men are ready. That's our focus right now."

"You hear about Butler?" he asked carefully.

Huss stopped whittling. "Yeah, I heard he's back. First Platoon, right?"

"Yeah. Hicks saw him the other day."

"Shitbird shouldn't be allowed to keep his jump-wings."

"I agree. I can't believe he's not cooling his heels behind bars."

"I guess it pays to have a bigwig father. I don't wanna hear any more about him, though. He's not our problem anymore."

"Understood. We'll be ready to move when the time comes."

~

THE MOVE north to Hollandia took the 503rd a few days. The five hundred nautical miles took them past battlefields they'd fought on only months before. Clyde watched Finschhafen pass by in the early morning. It brought back memories of brutal fighting, but from the safety of the troopship, you wouldn't know anything extraordinary had ever taken place there. He thought about the enemy soldier he'd killed in the foxhole. He'd tried to put that out of his mind, but it returned to him almost nightly as a nightmare.

They settled into their new, although temporary, home in Hollandia. They set up near another airfield, this one called Cyclops, for reasons he couldn't begin to explain. They passed the time training. The month of May passed into June and the fervor around the Hollandia aerodrome reached a crescendo.

News of the invasion of France came to them, but it barely made a ripple for the men of the 503rd, beyond hearing about their airborne brethren having a hard time of it. Clyde wondered how it must've been for those men jumping into the French countryside, but beyond that, his mind was firmly planted on his own theater of operations.

Then, on June 30, the news went out that Operation Cyclone: the amphibious assault on Noemfoor Island would proceed on July 1. The 158th would embark from Biak Island aboard eight LSTs—nearly seven thousand men—and land on Noemfoor on either the first or second of July.

The Able Company CO, Captain Stallsworthy, told them about the operation kicking off himself. But instead of being excited, Clyde felt let down. Certainly seven thousand men would have no trouble defeating the estimated two thousand enemy soldiers on Noemfoor. What would they need paratroopers for? There were other closer army elements who could bring heavy weapons to the game in a matter of days.

Clyde and the rest of Third Squad lounged under the shade of the trees around Cyclops Airfield. They'd just completed a four-mile run around the compound in their boots and packs. The men were dusty, sweaty, and ornery.

Despite Clyde's doubt about being activated into the assault on Noemfoor, he didn't show it outwardly. He did his best, but doubted he fooled anyone, since he heard the same grumbles from the enlisted men he heard from the NCOs.

The droning of aircraft in and out of Cyclops Airfield remained nearly constant all day long. Parked in well-constructed hangars sat several C-47 transport planes. But the air traffic consisted mostly of fighters and bombers. The few transports they'd be using, if called upon, sat collecting dust.

Lieutenant Palinsky burst from an old building they'd turned into an HQ. The door slammed against the siding, making them all turn to look.

"What's got him in such a fuss?" Sergeant Huss asked bemusedly.

"I didn't know he could move that fast," Clyde whispered to Huss so no one else could hear.

"Me neither. Something must be up." He pushed himself to his feet and Clyde followed suit. The rest of the men only watched the show.

Palinsky raised a piece of flimsy paper in his hand and yelled as he ran past, doing a pretty good impression of Paul Revere, just without the horse. "We're going in! Saddle up! We're going in!"

Sergeant Huss couldn't contain his derision for the young officer. He kept his voice low, "Oh, for crying out loud. Is that any way to act? He's the most unprofessional prick I've ever come across."

Palinsky kept running and kept yelling. Sergeant Plumly, the platoon sergeant, stepped in front of Palinsky and forced him to stop in his tracks.

Palinsky tried to push past him as though Plumly wasn't there. It wasn't a good decision.

Plumly put his hand against Palinsky's chest and barked into his face. "You have orders, sir? You have something you want me to pass along to the men?"

Palinsky sputtered and his face turned red, but he finally nodded and remembered how to be an officer. "Yes, Sergeant Plumly. Gather the men quickly for a briefing."

"Right away, sir," Plumly said with a quick salute.

Huss shook his head at the spectacle. "How'd we get stuck with this asshole?"

"It's like an officer version of Butler," Clyde answered. Huss scowled at him for bringing Butler up again.

Since most of the company had seen Palinsky's spectacle, it didn't take long before they were formed up. Clyde heard the men snickering and talking about Palinsky. It made him angry. They were laughing at Lieutenant Palinsky, but it felt like they laughed at Second Platoon. Clyde missed Lieutenant Milkins more than ever.

Soon, Lieutenant Jameson and Captain Stallsworthy stood before the assembled company. Stallsworthy said, "Men, I know we've been sitting on our hands for months now, but we finally have a mission. Operation Cyclone has kicked off. The 158th boys are kicking Jap butt. They've already overtaken Kamiri Airfield, one of three airfields on the island, but they've received intel that a large enemy force landed on the other side of the island and is advancing to retake the airfield and push them back into the sea. They've asked for our support." A murmur of approval and surprise went through the assembled paratroopers.

"Elements of the 503rd will jump tomorrow morning onto Kamiri Airfield to bolster the 158th defenses. As you probably noticed, there are only a few transports available to us, so we'll do this jump by battalion and broken up by days. First Battalion will jump tomorrow, Third Battalion the next day, and Second Battalion the day after that." Another murmur of approval from the men.

Clyde leaned forward to talk into Huss's ear. "I don't care how they do it, so long as we get it done." Huss grunted and nodded his agreement.

Stallsworthy went on for a few more minutes before wrapping up. "I know you men will do the 503rd proud. Tomorrow we make history. Geronimo!"

They met the last word with three loud Geronimo cheers from Able Company. Clyde felt a surge of pride and adrenaline course through his veins again. It felt good. Tomorrow, he and the rest of First Battalion, Able and Charlie Company, would jump back into the war.

13

Over Noemfoor Island, New Guinea
July 3, 1944

It felt good to be inside a C-47 high over the jungles of New Guinea again. Clyde had done countless practice jumps over the years and months, but nothing compared to the real thing. No amount of training could mimic the combination of heart-stopping thrills and crippling fear. His emotions undulated like the C-47 as thermals buffeted it up and down violently.

Clyde could see the obvious fear in Lieutenant Palinsky's face. He tried to hide it, but every bump made his eyes nearly bug out of his head. Huss, sitting beside Palinsky, must've noticed too. He elbowed the young officer in the ribs and shouted over the din of the engines. "Don't worry, Lieutenant. This'll be easy."

"How do you know?" Palinsky yelled back with genuine fear in his voice.

"'Cause we usually drop *behind* enemy lines—but this time we're dropping onto friendlies. You don't have to worry about getting shot—just landing. Piece of cake."

Palinsky nodded his understanding, but his face didn't look any less pale. The aircraft bucked like a bucking bronco in the turbulent air. Clyde's stomach was full of pancakes and eggs. Normally he had little appetite before a combat jump, but this morning had been different. Perhaps it was what Huss spoke about that kept his nerves at bay. But he wished he hadn't eaten so much.

He had to swallow his rising gorge when another less fortunate paratrooper lost his breakfast on the floor. The vile stuff sloshed up and down, causing more men to lose their meals. Soon even the roaring wind couldn't wash the stench away, and Clyde struggled even more to keep his breakfast down.

Near the back of the plane, the jump master listened to his headphones, nodded, and held up a hand—five more minutes. Through the small windows across from him, Clyde could see another C-47 edging up beside them. Normally they lined up in single file, but for efficiency and speed, the brass wanted a side-by-side drop. They'd practiced it a few times in Australia and it went okay, but if the winds were swirling over the airfield, it could toss men into each other on the descent and tangle their lines. They had reported the winds as light over the drop zone. Clyde hoped to hell they knew what they were talking about.

He felt the transport slow and descend. The turbulence eased until they flew along in smooth air. He breathed a sigh of relief. It would make it much easier to exit the aircraft quickly.

The jump master yelled, "Stand up!" The paratroopers went through the sequence automatically. They'd done it countless times. Even to the new guys, it was second nature now. Clyde noticed Palinsky no longer looked as though he'd die of fear. Sometimes a guy just needed to keep busy. They went through the pre-jump checks, hooked themselves to the static line running the length of the aircraft, and sounded off that they were ready.

Thirty seconds later, the light near the door turned from red to green. "Go! Go! Go!" the jumpmaster shouted, slapping men on their backs as they catapulted themselves into space.

Clyde shuffled his way to the door, flung himself out, and started counting. His chute snapped open. He checked his canopy, then looked at the ground and knew immediately that something was wrong. The ground came up far too fast and the airfield was strewn with destroyed aircraft and deep holes from naval artillery and bombing runs. The flyboys had dropped them too low, and it looked like he'd be landing in a junkyard.

He swung beneath his chute only once before he slammed into the ground, hard. His legs buckled and his lungs felt as though they'd been deflated like a balloon. He rolled into a bomb crater. At the bottom, he gasped for air and thrashed side-to-side. Besides the wind being knocked from his lungs, he felt something strangling him.

He gripped the risers that had twisted around his neck as he'd rolled into the crater. He finally pulled enough slack so he could breathe. Awful sounds greeted him as men hit the ground or worse—metal hunks of aircraft. Screams of agony told him he wasn't the only one who'd landed hard.

He scrambled to release his harness, but that didn't free him from the risers. The roll into the pit had twisted him up like a mummy. He finally resorted to his bayonet. He slashed and cut until he freed himself.

He panted at the bottom of the crater. The sky directly overhead was empty, but he still heard screams and the dull droning of aircraft approaching. He'd been in the first stick of paratroopers. More paratroopers would follow until all seven hundred and thirty-nine men were down.

He assessed his body for any major breaks. He couldn't believe he'd come out unscathed. Perhaps landing on the edge and rolling down the crater had helped cushion his fall. Besides nearly being strangled to death, he'd avoided a broken leg.

He scrambled up the side and crested the lip. He spun in a circle, taking it all in. Paratroopers dotted the airfield. Most were still down. Some screamed in agony and some were immobile.

He went to the nearest screaming soldier. He writhed back and forth on his back. When he was still ten yards away, he could see the unnatural bend to his leg. It was Private First Class Geyer. He'd been one of the first wounded men from the Markham Valley drop. He'd rejoined the unit just in time to move to Hollandia. He'd been ecstatic to be back in the fight after so many months spent in hospitals, and now this.

Clyde slid in beside him. Geyer's pain-filled eyes locked onto his. His face was bloody from biting through his lower lip. Blood covered his chin and bled onto his uniform and harness. His eyes reminded Clyde of a wild animal caught in a trap.

"You're okay! You're gonna be okay," he said, but he couldn't keep the horror off his face when he saw off-white bone sticking through Geyer's paratrooper pants. "Medic!" He yelled. "Medic!"

Geyer clutched his shoulder hard. "Fucking hurts! Oh God, it hurts!"

Clyde dug into his combat harness for his med-pack. His hands shook, but he found what he was looking for. He held up the syrette of morphine so Geyer could see it. "You're gonna be okay," he said as he pressed it into Geyer's uninjured leg.

Geyer's eyes immediately turned glassy, but he still took shallow breaths and remained in obvious discomfort. His eyes continued to dart wildly.

"Medic!" Clyde yelled again. He heard others yelling for medics from other parts of the airfield. *How many more were injured?* He stood and waved at a group of paratroopers. "Over here! I need help over here."

Soon a group surrounded Geyer. A medic he didn't recognize finally arrived. He wasn't a paratrooper, but an infantryman from the 158th. He took one look at the break, mumbled, "Oh geez," and went to work. He felt around the upper leg above the break. His hand came away bloody, but Clyde had seen worse. The medic applied a tourniquet and Geyer grimaced as he tightened it.

"I gave him a shot of morphine. One shot," Clyde said.

"Okay, good. We need to get him to a med station. I can't do much more out here." He marked Geyer's forehead with a marker, so the medical corps would know he'd already received one dose of morphine.

A stretcher arrived with two bearers from the 158th. In no time, they hefted Geyer onto it and carried him away. The medic lingered, repacking his supplies. From the sounds of agony all around him, he'd be busy for the next few hours.

"Is he gonna be alright, doc?"

The medic didn't look up from his packing. "There wasn't a lot of blood. I don't think he punctured any major vessels or he'd already be dead. I put a tourniquet on him just in case. The surgeon will know more." The medic stood and asked him, "What the hell happened?"

Clyde shook his head. "The flyboys dropped us too low." He spread his hands at all the detritus dotting the airfield. "And they told us the landing site was clear of debris." He felt his anger mounting. "Does this look clear to you?" More agonized screams tore through the air and the medic ran off to help.

Despite the carnage, Clyde still had a job to do. He moved to the rally point at the leading edge of the airfield. He saw horror after horror, but each man had medics attending to their wounds. He stopped counting broken legs at ten.

More lines of transports came in side by side and disgorged paratroopers over the airfield. At least these aircraft had corrected the altitude problem. But the obstacles on the ground would still create hazards.

He weaved his way through, picking up men from the platoon and even a few squad members. Two men needed help from buddies. Even though they wore their jump boots, Clyde could see swelling—they'd either broken or badly sprained their ankles.

"Cooper—is that you?"

Clyde saw Huss waving at him. "Yeah, it's me," he hollered back.

"How many you got with you?"

"Five from Third Squad and two from First and Second."

Huss pointed, "First and Second are forming up over yonder."

The paratroopers peeled off and joined their respective squads.

Huss looked him up and down. "You doing okay? No dings?"

"I got lucky—fell into a bomb crater. But there's a lot of casualties. Geyer broke his leg badly. He didn't look good."

"Poor devil just got out of the damned hospital," Huss said. "Where's your weapon?"

Clyde hadn't even thought about his weapon until that moment. Even though they weren't behind enemy lines, they were in enemy territory. He pulled it from his backside and loosened the sling. He unfolded the metal stock and loaded a magazine, but didn't pull the charging handle.

"With all the injuries, I forgot all about it."

More parachutes billowed over the field. Most landed well, but a few swung into and onto burned-out enemy aircraft. The sounds of clanging metal as bodies slammed into them made him cringe.

"There's gonna be more casualties before this jump is in the books," Huss said bitterly.

"At least the pilots fixed their altitudes. I barely had time to take a breath before I hit."

"No shit, same here."

More paratroopers filtered into the rally point. Clyde counted the men and checked their status. He reported to Huss. "All troopers accounted for, but Geyer and Mosby won't be joining us."

"What happened to Mosby?"

"Blake told me he shattered his ankle. He's in bad shape," Clyde answered.

"All right. Let's move out and find the rest of Second Platoon."

"You seen Palinsky?" Clyde asked.

"Yeah, he doesn't have a scratch on him. Beginner's luck, I guess."

The roar of low-flying C-47s drowned out any more talk. They moved off the airfield and followed a road into the jungle.

Gil came up beside Clyde and said, "Good thing we didn't land in a bunch of Nips. They woulda chewed us up."

"I think we have more casualties from this botched jump than we lost so far fighting them."

He pointed his carbine muzzle at the highest peak they could see in the distance. "They're probably up there laughing their asses off at us."

THEY DUG in on the outskirts of the airfield that night in foxholes that the 158th had dug and abandoned once they'd moved forward. The paratroopers scraped them deeper and wider and settled in for the night. It had been a long time since they spent the night facing the enemy.

The distant sounds of gunfire and the low rumble of mortars and artillery almost made Clyde feel at home. The thought spooked him, but there was no denying that he felt like he'd entered his element. He suspected that would change once they met the Japanese.

Most of the 158th was positioned in front of them, so no one expected much to happen that night. Once the rest of the regiment joined them, they'd push to contact and things would get more interesting.

They'd chosen a relatively open area, so the half-moon overhead gave them plenty of light to see far in front of them. If an enemy soldier sneaked past the 158th, even in the darkness, they would have a hell of a time sneaking across the grassy plain without being seen. But the paratroopers took nothing for granted, so they'd posted outposts and had a three-hour guard rotation in place.

Sergeant Huss called out to Clyde from the right. "I'm coming to you, Cooper."

It was never a good idea to move around at night, too many itchy trigger fingers, but in the half-light conditions, it felt safe.

"Okay, come on then."

Huss loped his way across to him and sat on the edge of the foxhole. Clyde scooted to the other side to give him room. "What's the scoop?"

"Got the numbers from the jump."

Clyde could tell by the long pause that it wasn't good news.

Huss continued. "We had seventy-nine casualties."

Clyde couldn't believe his ears. He knew it was bad, but he didn't know it was that bad. "Holy Shit. I didn't think it would be so high."

"A lot of broken legs and ankles. Tucker in Fourth Squad hit his head hard on the side of a Jap Zero. He's unconscious but alive. Doc thinks it's a brain bleed."

Clyde pointed back toward the airfield. Even from here, they could hear tractors working. "Well, at least they're clearing the airfield for tomorrow's jump. Third Battalion should have a better time."

"I sure the hell hope so. I heard some more news."

Clyde listened, knowing Huss enjoyed some buildup when he had information to pass along.

Huss finally said, "You remember those intel guys got the word about a large Jap force being landed a few days ago?"

"Yeah, it's why they sent us in. What about it?"

"Well, and this isn't confirmed, but the scuttlebutt says it was all bullshit."

"So, this was all for nothing?" Clyde guffawed.

"I don't know about that, but there wasn't a need to hurry things the way they did. They don't think there's an attack coming."

"What about the rest of the regiment?"

"They're still jumping in as scheduled. Nothing's changed for us. Besides, it might be true. You know how they are. Sneaky sons of bitches."

The night passed without incident. Clyde even managed to get some sleep. He couldn't explain it, but sometimes he slept better out here in the jungle, facing an unknown future. Not as deeply, but he didn't normally suffer the same nightmares he experienced in safer areas. *What will it be like once they send us home?*

As the sun rose and brought a yellow glow to the world, the senior NCOs were called to HQ. Clyde and the rest of the squad found a hot meal nearby and ate with abandon—not knowing when they'd get another.

Sergeant Huss found them back at their holes, shooting the shit. "Stop playing grab-ass and listen up." The men quieted and listened. "Command doesn't want us to wait for the rest of the regiment to arrive. We're moving forward to that big hill you probably noticed yesterday. The 158th has run into stiffening Jap resistance around it and they want us ready to support their push."

The day had taken on a decidedly serious tone. To stress it, a flight of A-20 bombers suddenly streaked overhead at two thousand feet, heading straight for the three-hundred-meter-high hill. They unleashed machine guns then dropped bombs that shook the ground, even from this distance.

Clyde felt relief. After hearing about the easily avoidable casualties and the possibility that they didn't even really need to be there, he had felt let down. He was glad to have a new mission. He couldn't believe it, but wanted to fight.

"What're you grinning about?" Gutiérrez asked.

"Nothing. Just thought of a joke. Mind your own business."

Gutiérrez held up his hands as though offended. "Okay, okay, Corporal."

Second Platoon marched along the road, winding its way through the jungle toward the hill. The 158th had brought lots of trucks and even a company of Sherman tanks, and their heavy frames and treads had left deep muddy ruts. Soon the paratrooper's pants were muddy up past their knees. The mud dried on their rifles and carbines, making them look as though they'd been painted dull white.

After an hour, the sounds and atmosphere changed. Soldiers darted between cover and didn't stand out in the open any longer. A few idling tanks faced the hill and occasionally fired off a 75mm round, making them all cringe. Clyde saw the distant impact on the hill the 158th soldiers had been tasked with taking. The heavy smell of gasoline and gunpowder replaced the loamy jungle smells.

Clyde could see why they wanted the hill. It was easily the highest peak around and would be an excellent observation post for directing artillery and even airstrikes. He suspected the Japanese wouldn't be easily dislodged, especially if they'd dug in.

Officers barked and soon the paratroopers moved into fighting positions. Despite the occasional roar of a 75mm tank round, there was no return fire. In fact, Clyde heard no small arms fire at all.

The hill smoked in spots where small fires had started. Sections of jungle had been denuded by bombing raids, and the top was dotted with dark craters from naval shelling.

"All right, don't get too comfortable," Sergeant Plumly barked while standing beside Lieutenant Palinsky. The word passed down the line and soon all of Able Company sat watching the smoking hill.

The droning of more aircraft made Clyde think another bombing run might be inbound, but when he looked up, he saw the familiar outline of C-47 transports making climbing turns after disgorging their sticks of paratroopers. "Third Battalion must be jumping," he stated to no one in particular.

"They'll be sorry," Gil chimed in his best singsong voice.

"They can't have it as bad as we did," Private Hallon said.

The droning of aircraft became a constant roar as more and more transports dropped their loads onto Kamiri Airfield. They couldn't see the airfield or the drop, just the empty transports turning back for Cyclops where they'd originated.

Noise and commotion up ahead of their position drew their attention. Soldiers from the 158th were up and advancing toward the hill. The tanks fired volleys over their heads and unseen mortar teams arced rounds skyward. Puffs of explosions dotted the hillside. Mounds of dark dirt, interspersed with flashes of fire, erupted high up the hill.

Clyde watched countless soldiers moving carefully through the jungle. A machine gun on the far-left flank opened fire. He flinched until he recognized the staccato of a Browning .30-caliber machine gun. He still hadn't heard any return fire.

"Maybe they up and left," someone called out hopefully.

"They saw us and skedaddled," Private Wallace, the self-described cowboy from Montana, called back.

"Shaddup," barked Sergeant Huss.

"Aw, you're no fun," Wallace yelled back.

Huss let it go. The men were keyed up and if they wanted to burn some energy in friendly banter—why not?

Clyde felt his own heart racing wildly, making him want to run up the hill and conquer it all by himself. *Where's my fear gone?* The last time he'd faced the enemy, he'd been scared to death. What had changed? He hated being scared, but he didn't like this antsy feeling any better. *Don't get reckless. Do your job,* he reminded himself.

The last of the 158th soldiers he could see faded into the jungle. The tanks continued hammering the hillside, but still no return fire. A few tank commanders fired their mounted .50-caliber machine guns. Another .30-caliber machine gun joined the first. He couldn't see if they had targets or were simply laying down suppressing fire. He guessed the latter.

Finally, the crack of enemy rifle fire seared the air. He ducked despite being well out of range. Answering rifle fire from the 158th rose to a crescendo of sound. More machine guns opened up, and the tanks elevated their muzzles and slammed rounds into the upper areas. Clyde wondered if the commanders sitting in their top cupolas staring through binoculars could see the enemy positions now that they'd opened fire or were still guessing.

Listening to other men fight was almost worse than doing it himself. He heard yelling and firing, but he did not know how things were going.

An enemy Nambu machine gun opened fire. The distinctive woodpecker sound couldn't be mistaken for anything else. He hated that sound.

It grated on his nerves. He strained to see where the dreaded sound came from, but it was too far away.

Over the din of fire, he heard the whine and grate of the nearest Sherman's turret turning. He watched the tank commander pointing and barking into his crew radio. The turret stopped and the muzzle adjusted slightly. The boom from the 75mm added to the already incredible noise of battle. A distant blossoming explosion on the right side of the hill pulled Clyde's attention. He listened for the Nambu. For a moment, he didn't hear it and thought the tanker had taken it out, but then he heard the damned thing, and more Nambus added their weight to the battle.

"Those boys are really getting it," Gil yelled from his crouched position nearby.

"I hate just sitting here listening," Clyde said. "Driving me crazy!"

Gil looked at him with raised eyebrows. "You wanna go up there?" he asked incredulously.

"I'd rather be up there than down here sitting on my hands. Yes, dammit. Don't you?" Gil just shrugged and turned back to the show.

What the hell's the matter with me? He really wanted to join the fight.

An insufferable hour passed. The fighting continued, but the intensity of fire diminished as both sides seemed to lick their wounds and reset. Yelled orders came down the line, and Clyde waited anxiously. He either wanted to head back to the airfield or attack, but sitting here in between was for the birds.

Huss waved him over. Clyde was happy to finally be able to do something besides watch. "What's the scoop?"

"We're moving to the right flank. They found a weakness in their lines and they want us to exploit it."

"Hot damn!" Clyde couldn't keep from blurting out.

Huss looked hard at him. "Keep your shit together, Corporal."

Clyde swallowed his smile. "I'm ready, sergeant. Glad to finally do something."

IT DIDN'T TAKE LONG to settle into their new position on the right flank of the 158th. Able Company had spread out in a deep line facing the hill. Tank fire and the occasional burst from a machine gun continued hitting the enemy. The soft thump of mortar rounds exploding gave Clyde a surge of confidence. The mortars would keep the Japanese heads down while they advanced.

The front line of paratroopers rose from cover and crept forward. Clyde waited until it was Second Platoon's turn. First Platoon led the way, Second would follow, and Third would stay in reserve and fill any holes that needed filling.

Sergeant Huss hissed at Third Squad. "Okay, let's go."

Clyde licked his dry lips and rose from his crouch. Now that they moved toward the enemy, he felt the familiar fear, but it had changed slightly. Instead of straight fear, he felt more anxious than anything else, eager to get it started.

He gripped his carbine and watched the men advance steadily. This side of the hill hadn't seen as much artillery or tank fire and the jungle was still relatively intact. They slipped through the jungle easily. The ground cover wasn't as thick due to the high layer of trees blocking the life-giving sun's rays. It provided easier movement and had decent cover, but that worked both ways. The enemy could see them easier.

The island felt different from New Guinea. He couldn't place his finger on the difference, but it felt less alive and less dangerous, somehow.

They'd moved one hundred yards when the line stopped. He crouched and focused all his attention forward. He could hear the thrumming of his heartbeat in his ears. Besides the occasional burst of machine gun fire, there was no sign of the enemy. A few tense minutes passed before the line moved again. He wondered who was on point.

They moved another fifty yards and the hill steepened. He figured they might be close to halfway up already and still no contact.

Huss spoke in a whispered hiss, "First Platoon sees the enemy positions. We're waiting here so the 158th can push. We'll attack soon after, so be ready."

The men nodded their understanding. Clyde noticed Lieutenant Palinsky crouched nearby. The back of his uniform was soaked in sweat, making his uniform look black instead of green. He wished it were their old platoon leader, Lieutenant Milkins. He trusted Milkins. He'd proved himself in combat multiple times. Palinsky had done little to impress him so far. He wondered how he'd hold up once the bullets flew in their direction. Some men crumbled and some men shined—Palinsky was still an unknown.

The Sherman tanks opened fire almost in unison. The roar of machine guns followed soon after. Clyde watched Palinsky's back, waiting for him to wave them forward into combat. The wait seemed to last forever. He could hear the distinct rifle shots of M-1 Garands and even the distinctive pings as the clips emptied.

The Japanese didn't wait long to counter. Multiple Nambu machine guns opened fire all at once, and this time, Clyde thought he could see muzzle flashes to his left and high up the hill.

He pointed. "Looks like a trench line up there." He hadn't directed the statement at anyone, just thinking out loud.

Finally, Palinsky looked back at them and waved his hand forward. It was a weak and timid gesture, but it reminded him of some medieval attack with swords and spears. How often had that gesture sent men into battle? *Since the dawn of humanity.* The thought made him feel connected, but also insignificant. Would any of this matter in one hundred years?

He shook the thought from his head and focused straight ahead. Any moment now, the Japanese would notice the first line of paratroopers moving up on their flank. He expected to hear the battle join with each step, but the only sound still came from the main battle. Perhaps the enemy soldiers wouldn't see them until they made the top of the hill.

That fantasy shattered a moment later when he heard yelling followed immediately by enemy rifle fire. A bullet smacked a nearby tree and he flinched and ducked lower. With paratroopers to his front, he couldn't do much but wait. He aimed his carbine up the hill, but couldn't see anything but jungle and the backs of his own men.

The front line of paratroopers responded to the incoming fire quickly. Carbines, Garands, and submachine guns opened fire, drowning out the enemy's paltry rifle shots. A moment later, he heard shouted orders from

First Platoon. He stayed hunkered, knowing they'd be ordered forward as First faded right.

Palinsky yelled orders, "Okay, Second Platoon, move up!" To his credit, his voice sounded commanding, despite the slight quavering. He just might rise to the occasion after all.

Huss yelled, "You heard him. Let's get in the war!"

Clyde wanted to charge, but he controlled the urge and he strode along with measured steps, keeping pace with Huss. The paratroopers automatically spread out, making it difficult for the enemy shooters.

Second Platoon pushed forward. First Platoon had pivoted right, and the small force of Japanese turned to meet the threat. Clyde glimpsed a Japanese soldier about fifty yards from him. He faced First Platoon, had his long bolt-action Arisaka rifle to his shoulder, and fired over and over.

None of the Second Platoon had opened fire yet. He wanted to fire, but didn't. Finally, Second Platoon stopped and hunkered. Clyde aimed at the enemy rifleman, still oblivious to the danger. He saw other enemy soldiers moving into position next to the rifleman—some pointed out targets and others brought rifles to their shoulders.

Finally, Lieutenant Palinsky yelled, "Open fire!"

Before Clyde could pull the trigger, the rifleman had already been mortally wounded and dropped out of sight as bullets riddled the position. He found a new target, the top of a soldier's pith helmet. He fired four rounds. The impacts spread dark soil and debris and momentarily obscured his target. When it cleared, the helmet was gone.

"Move up!" Palinsky yelled.

Clyde saw Palinsky stand and fire his Thompson submachine gun on full automatic from the hip. He doubted he'd hit much more than dirt and thankfully he burned through the magazine in seconds, or he might've hit his own men. It reminded him of a comic book hero, but it seemed to energize the men. Those near the front gave war whoops as they ran forward.

Clyde couldn't help himself. He heard his own war whoop erupt as he leaped over deadfall and ran headlong toward the enemy position. Paratroopers in front fired into the enemy foxholes and terrified screams filled the air, then abruptly cut off.

Clyde ran past the first foxhole and glanced inside. A dead soldier stared back at him. Blood seeped from a bullet hole in the side of his head. The bottom of the hole glimmered with fresh blood.

Clyde stepped over the hole and ran uphill, searching for targets. Paratroopers ran up the hill, firing intermittently, but not finding much resistance. Orders and frantic yells stopped the mad dash up the hill.

He wanted to keep going, but he heard Huss yelling at Third Squad to slow down and reform. Clyde understood they'd overextended their line and if they didn't do something about it, the Japanese could cut the platoon in half.

He joined Huss's yells. "Third Squad, hold up! Hold up!"

Most of the men stopped, but some of the new guys continued their wild foray up the hill, firing their carbines from their hips as they went. The veterans finally got control of them and they soon stopped and found cover.

"We're waiting for First Platoon to form up on our right flank," Huss called out. "Fire at will, but only if you've got a target."

"Aw, hell. We've got the rabbit on the run, sergeant."

"Shut up, Wallace, and do as you're told."

Wallace shut his mouth, but he'd voiced what a lot of the others felt.

Gil kept his carbine at his shoulder and said to Clyde, "He's right, you know. We could roll 'em up right now."

Clyde wanted to agree, but he had to follow orders and keep the men in line. "We're just waiting for First Platoon. Shouldn't be long now."

The firing from the 158th remained steady from their left. The tank shots could be felt in the soles of their boots now and geysers of dirt erupted along the trench line, which had become much more obvious as more and more jungle had been blown to oblivion.

Just as First Platoon formed up on their right flank, a great roar of yelling enemy soldiers erupted from up the hill. It sent a shiver through Clyde's spine. He'd heard and seen this insanity before.

He checked his carbine and yelled, "Here they come!"

Every man found cover and leveled their weapons at the growing crescendo of sound from the attacking Japanese soldiers. The jungle seemed to come alive as soldiers covered in jungle flora and fauna raced straight at them. Their rifles had bayonets attached and Clyde wondered if he should do the same, but there wasn't time.

Huss called to them, "Kill the back row first."

Clyde aimed his muzzle at the furthest back line of attackers. He steadied himself and fired into a soldier's chest. The man kept coming and Clyde kept firing until he dropped out of sight. He found the next man back and pulled the trigger methodically until that man dropped. Fewer soldiers came from the jungle or were slow to do so after seeing their comrades cut down.

The leading soldiers didn't get far. The paratroopers cut them down before they got within thirty yards. Clyde could see outlines of soldiers in the distant line of jungle. He fired at them, but doubted his shots did much more than keep their heads down and make them reconsider their life choices.

They'd stopped the attack, and bodies littered the ground. A few writhed in agony, but most remained deathly still. Multiple Japanese officers screamed and yelled commands, and Clyde wondered what they were saying. Were they screaming for the attack to continue? If so, they must be insane. He couldn't fathom seeing his own men slaughtered so wantonly. *Are they even human?*

They stayed hunkered in cover for a few more minutes. The volume of fire from the main attack dropped off considerably and mortar rounds thumped the top of the hill and the other side.

Palinsky put the radio headset down and the smile on his face said it all. "The Japs are retreating. They're bugging out."

Clyde relished the news, but his blood was up. "We could push 'em off this island today if we attack now," he said excitedly to Huss.

Huss gave him his best glare, but it quickly softened. "I know that as well as you, but they're sending the 158th boys after 'em. We'll hold the hill in the meantime." Those that heard the exchange moaned and griped. Huss held up his grimy hands for calm. "I know, I know, but command thought they earned the right since they got chewed up worse'n us."

The men settled down and moved up the hill. They carefully made sure the Japanese soldiers were actually dead before leaving the area.

Clyde and Huss watched the men sifting through the bodies. "Pretty slick idea you had shooting the ones in the back row first."

Huss smiled as though he'd received kudos from an elementary teacher he had a crush on. “Me and Plumly talked about doing that. I’d say it worked pretty damned well.”

“Guess the Nips didn’t much wanna charge over their dead comrades as much. Took some of the fight out of ’em,” Clyde said.

“Yeah, I guess it proves they *are* human, after all.” He shrugged and amended, “Well, at least a little.”

14

Hukwang Valley, Burma
March 1944

Shawn Cooper and the rest of Operational Group Bellevue watched the Kachin Rangers stream past them. They'd just returned from a four-day patrol. They wore green U.S. Army–issued uniforms. Despite the mud and sweat stains, the unit looked sharp and deadly. Most beamed broad smiles at them, but a few had stoic faces, as though they'd seen and done grisly acts.

JoJo leaned toward Shawn and said, "I heard they had another successful ambush. Claim they killed twenty, but it's probably more."

Shawn raised an eyebrow. "More?" he asked.

"Yeah, they'll give you an accurate number of kills from the initial contact, but they don't tell you about the ones that died soon after."

Shawn nodded his understanding. "Yeah, those punji stakes are nasty."

"I came across a Jap body who hadn't been dead more 'n a couple of hours. The only wound I could find was a punctured foot. Figured it was one of them poisoned punjis. His leg had ballooned to at least triple the normal size. Looked ready to burst if I'd just touched it. The infection probably killed him."

Shawn gulped. The thought sent shivers up his spine. Stepping on one of the sharpened stakes that the Kachin placed all around their ambush sites in shallow hidden pits would be awful. They used a deadly poison extracted from a plant, or if that option wasn't available, they simply dipped the punji tips in their own excrement to assure infection. Like much of the Kachin fighting methods, it was brutal, but highly effective.

"I sure wouldn't wanna step on one of those things. They give me the willies."

JoJo agreed. "Yeah, I'd rather get blown to smithereens or shot in the head. That Jap I found—his face was frozen in sheer agony. Terrible way to go." He shrugged it off. "But they sure earned it."

The image of the bomber crew's dismembered and bullet-riddled bodies flashed into his mind. He felt the old anger rising in his belly and he touched the tip of Clem's baseball hat that he'd found at the crash site.

"I can't wait to get back out there. We still haven't gotten payback for what they did to Clem and the rest."

JoJo's mouth turned down. "By the sounds of it, Merrill's boys are in the thick of it at Walawbum."

Shawn had heard the same scuttlebutt. He wasn't surprised. Since Bellevue had arrived back in the area, they'd seen sizeable forces of Japanese moving from Myitkyina, directly into the path of the two Chinese Divisions. The Chinese 22nd and 33rd Divisions had hit a wall that included thick jungle and veteran Japanese forces.

"Well, we're doing our jobs—at least the Kachin are. Look at 'em," he indicated the men still streaming past. "They're happy as clams."

JoJo said, "Yeah, they're having a field day out there. Hitting supply lines and rear echelon troops is easy pickings for them. I suspect the Nips'll start beefing up their supply convoys, though. They've been hitting them hard for almost a month now. The Nips'll catch on soon enough."

"Yeah, but I don't think it'll make much difference. You've seen these guys at work as much as I have."

"You're probably right. More Japs just means more dead Japs."

The final Kachin Ranger waltzed past and gave them a happy wave. The M1 Garand rifle he had slung over his shoulder nearly touched the ground.

He looked like a child. He probably wasn't even fourteen, but was already a seasoned warrior.

"They don't get much of a childhood, do they?"

"Hell, I played army all the time with my kid brother and the neighbor kids. We'd have huge battles that lasted days. I imagine he's having the time of his life."

Shawn gave his longtime friend a sideways look. "You're a real piece of work, JoJo. Did any of your friends die while you were playing?"

Before JoJo could respond, a whistle came from up the hill near the village. They both turned and saw Veatch waving for them to come up the hill.

JoJo thumped him on the back. "Maybe this'll be a new mission for us. Maybe we'll finally get some payback."

An hour later, the entire Bellevue group huddled inside the long community hut where they sometimes took their meals with the Kachin elders. But today, only OSS men occupied the area. Captain Burbank stood in front, looking grim, as he discussed something with the other OSS officers.

He finally turned to the seated men and raised his voice over the din of murmured conversation. "Alright men, listen up." A map of northern Burma and eastern India adorned the wall.

Shawn exchanged furtive glances with several men seated nearby. Normally Burbank had a happy-go-lucky air, usually starting a briefing off with friendly banter or even a joke. But when he addressed them seriously, it was never good news. The room went silent.

"The Chinese are having a tough time breaking through the Maingkwan area to Walawbum. They've taken heavy casualties and are backing off until they can figure out a way to punch through. General Merrill and his marauders are hitting Walawbum effectively and, from early reports, they've got the Japs thoroughly flustered. To their credit, they made it to the rear without being noticed and are taking advantage of the surprise. They've cut off the road the Japs rely on to keep the front line supplied. But command is worried that the Chinese might not get there in time to relieve them."

The OSS men listened intently. The fresh, in-depth information would not have been given to common infantry soldiers. The grand overall plan didn't matter to most infantrymen. Following orders and survival mattered —but the OSS men weren't simple infantrymen. The officers trusted the strategy and the planning to all of them. It was privileged information that each man knew they'd take to the grave with them. Capture was out of the question.

"The marauders have been through hell just getting there, but their training is obviously paying off. Despite their unfortunate choice to travel overland, they are doing their job effectively."

Shawn and JoJo shook their heads in disgust. Scuttlebutt had it that against advice from OSS officers familiar with the area the American unit's leadership opted to march overland from Ledo, India, through to Shingbwiyang via the Naga Hills, a one-hundred-and-twenty-five-mile march through the most inhospitable terrain known to man, carrying all their own supplies on horseback, donkeys, and mules, instead of using vehicles or even aircraft. The commanders considered it a shakedown march to test the men. Weeks later, they emerged from the jungle with few horses, hundreds of sick and injured soldiers, and little will left to fight the Japanese.

The OSS men had been hearing about the unit, filled with veteran combat soldiers, who'd been branded 'Merrill's Marauders' by the press for weeks now. The horror stories from their march reached almost unbelievable levels, but Shawn had seen that terrain and didn't doubt the stories at all.

Burbank continued, "The weeks in the mountains has whittled them down considerably. They are fighting rear echelon troops at Walawbum, but once the Nips figure out that they're causing a big resupply problem, they'll pivot and attack with their veterans. Possibly even bring in fresh troops." He pointed to the map hanging behind him. "The Chinese are close, and they should be able to link up now that some pressure has been taken off, but there are no guarantees. So far, the marauders' first encounter has been a success, but command thinks they could use some help."

"More like Merrill's morons," O'Keefe crooned from the back. The snickering laughter quickly faded with Burbank's withering scowl. "Sorry, sir," O'Keefe murmured and lowered his gaze.

"As I was saying, they are doing well at Walawbum, but Stillwell doesn't want them to suffer the same fate as our Chinese compatriots, and he can actually do something about it this time. So, Bellevue and some Kachin Rangers will head down there to Merrill's position to assist them."

Shawn's jaw dropped. He didn't relish being a part of a line unit, but he relished passing along everything he knew about jungle fighting to the men who just might listen.

Umberland asked, "What's the command structure, sir?"

"Bellevue is still under the purview of the OSS. You are there to assist, but you are not under Merrill's command."

"What if they don't wanna listen?" Umberland persisted.

"You can only try. They are trained jungle fighters, but I'm sure they can use some refinement. They are veterans, so act accordingly." He leveled his gaze at O'Keefe. "I don't want this to turn into a dick-measuring contest."

O'Keefe stood up and said, "Aw, come on, sir! I'd win that hands down."

The men burst out laughing. O'Keefe took multiple punches from the men surrounding him, and he finally sat down, rubbing his shoulder.

"I'm sure you'd give them a run for their money, son."

More snickers, but the men quieted quickly when Burbank turned serious again. "Those men down there have been through the wringer. From all reports, they're at the end of their rope. They need a win, and so far Walawbum is just that, but it could change quickly into a rout. We need to help them hold on until the Chinese arrive."

~

SHAWN HUNKERED in the scrub overlooking a wide area of sparse jungle. He and the rest of Operational Group Bellevue, as well as half a platoon of Kachin Rangers, had been traveling south a day. The 5037th had set up to the northeast of the village of Walawbum, where they continued to harass the Japanese garrison there.

As they'd moved north, they'd come across a few Japanese outposts and even dodged a roving patrol of some twenty enemy soldiers. The Kachin wanted to ambush the patrol, but Captain Burbank wouldn't allow it.

He wanted to link up with the 5037th without enemy detection, but he marked the enemy positions and promised the Kachin they'd have plenty of opportunities to hunt and kill Japanese soldiers *after* the linkup.

Sergeant Boyd, who hunkered nearby, spoke with Burbank. "They're down there somewhere."

"Yep." He had his binoculars up and he scanned slowly. "The town's still out of sight. I don't see any Japs or marauders. I guess that's a good thing. At least they know how to keep a low profile."

"I was thinking the same thing."

Burbank pointed to the right. "We'll split up. You take a team right and I'll take a team left." He checked his watch. "We'll check in by walkie-talkie in an hour unless one of us finds them before that."

Boyd sent Shawn forward as the point man. He, and a Kachin everyone called Wayne because his actual name sounded somewhat similar, moved silently through the low scrub. If the Japanese were down there and looking for them, they'd likely see them, but the Kachin, who had an innate feel for such things, didn't think there were any Japanese nearby.

They moved into a grove of tall trees. The wind shifted the top branches and made unseen birds squawk loudly. Wayne suddenly stopped and froze in place. Shawn smelled woodsmoke. He crouched and held his carbine loosely. It could be another Japanese outpost, a village, or the American unit. He suspected the latter.

He signaled the men behind to hold and he and Wayne pushed forward slowly. Shawn smelled cigarette smoke a moment before he spotted the sentry. Wayne had also noticed and had his eyes on him. He held his rifle ready.

Shawn knew right away that it was a U.S. Army soldier. His uniform hung on him loosely and had ragged edges, but there was no mistaking the way the man stood and smoked. The soldier's face had an unnatural hollow gauntness, which made Shawn wonder if he was sick.

The sentry hadn't noticed them and Shawn figured it would be child's play to get close enough to slit the man's throat without being seen. He seemed as clueless as some Japanese soldiers he'd seen. Many had paid for their inattentiveness with their, and sometimes their comrades', lives.

Shawn wondered what the best course of action would be. He held up his hand until Wayne noticed, then signaled that he should stay put. It might be better if a white man approached the sentry, after all, the Americans had been sparring with the Japanese for days now.

Wayne nodded, and Shawn stood and took a few careful steps toward the American. When he got within twenty yards, he stood to his full height and looked around the area for any surprises. Satisfied, he cupped his hand near his mouth and hissed, "Hey, fella. Hey, you."

The sentry immediately clutched his Thompson submachine gun and crouched. The cigarette still hung from his lower lip as he frantically scanned. Even from here, Shawn could see the alarm in his eyes.

"Don't shoot. I'm an American," he said a bit louder. He waved his hands and the sentry finally zeroed in on his position. He had the Thompson tucked tightly into his shoulder and the muzzle aimed squarely at Shawn's chest. "Don't shoot, I'm an American!" He forced himself not to duck even though he thought he might mow him down at any moment. The gaping maw at the end of the Thompson's muzzle looked like the entrance to a volcano.

"Come on out where I can see you," the soldier said with a quavering voice. "Or I'll kill you."

"Don't shoot," Shawn repeated. He held his carbine in one hand and held it up and away as he took a few more steps. He smiled when he saw the tautness in the soldier's frame disappear.

"Who the hell are you?"

"PFC Shawn Cooper, formerly of the 501st airborne, now with Operational Group Bellevue."

The soldier moved the muzzle off his chest, but only a fraction. His face showed no recognition, only more confusion. So Shawn added, "General Stillwell sent us."

It wasn't completely true, but he doubted the man would know anything about the OSS and he didn't know if he was allowed to mention it in the first place. They'd drilled operational secrecy into their skulls back at the OSS training camp in Maryland.

"Are you with General Merrill's group?"

The sentry's eyes widened. "How the hell d 'you know that?"

"We're here to help you fight these Nip bastards. Didn't anyone tell you?"

The Thompson's muzzle aimed straight for the sky and he reinserted the cigarette back into place. "No one told us a thing about any force from Vinegar Joe."

The rest of the squad, including a few Kachin, stepped forward and revealed themselves. The cigarette finally fell from his mouth as his jaw dropped open again in astonishment.

"Well, I'll be damned," he finally said. "How'd you get so close?"

Shawn stepped forward and extended his hand. "I'm Shawn Cooper. Nice ta-meetcha."

The stunned soldier took his hand and shook. "PFC Stan Ludwig, 5037th."

Shawn smiled. "Merrill's Marauders."

The soldier's face hardened. "What?"

"That's what they're calling you. You didn't know?"

"Yeah, I knew, but I've never heard it outside my own unit."

"Well, like I said, we're here to help."

"We didn't ask for any help," he said with iron in his voice. PFC Ludwig looked the ragtag group over carefully. He still didn't seem too sure about their intentions.

Sergeant Boyd stepped forward and waved. "I see you already met Cooper. I'm Sergeant Boyd."

Ludwig stiffened at the rank, but his eyes shifted back and forth, searching for some proof of his rank. "Why don't you fellers have any rank insignia?"

Boyd ignored the question and said, "Why don't you take us to your HQ. I'll call in Captain Burbank and he'll fill in General Merrill."

Ludwig looked beyond the Kachin and the other OSS men. "You mean there's more of you?"

"Course there's more of us. You think they'd just send you a squad?" he said gruffly.

Ludwig's attitude changed when he heard Boyd's bark. With or without rank insignia—no one else sounded like an NCO except an NCO, and Ludwig immediately recognized his authority.

"Uh—I'm not supposed to leave my post."

"I think they'll make an exception. Besides, we didn't see any Japs and we'd know if they were any nearby." He thumbed toward the Kachin. "At least, they would. They can smell 'em a mile off."

"They look like children dressed up to play army," he said out of the corner of his mouth.

Shawn snickered, and Boyd leaned close to Ludwig's ear. "I don't know you, soldier, but I'd wager any amount that any of those children, as you call them, can run circles around you. I've never met finer soldiers."

"Yeah? Well, we've had a few of 'em with us, too, but they weren't wearing uniforms. They know their way around this place, but I don't know that I completely trust 'em."

Boyd exchanged a sour look with Shawn, and they both followed Ludwig deeper into the jungle.

The closer they got to the bulk of the American unit, the more obvious their presence became. They passed a few fighting positions, strategically placed to cover trails and even a road leading into the town. The marauders stared at them as they passed. Their eyes looked sunken and dark circles ringed them, making them look as though they'd all fought and lost the same monster.

Boyd leaned closer to Shawn. "They look like beaten dogs and they only just got here."

"Why the hell didn't Merrill have 'em drive in? Why'd he walk? I mean, it's hard enough when you've got Kachin helping and you only have to worry about carrying enough for yourself—but an entire regiment's worth of equipment on horses and mules? My God . . ."

Boyd lowered his voice as they wound their way through the haggard line of soldiers. "I guess Merrill thought they needed a warm-up."

"Look what it got him. These men look ready to fall over."

"Well, that's why we're here. To make sure they don't."

~

SHAWN MARVELED at how quickly they sprang into action. They'd only arrived a few hours before and already they were set up in ambush.

From the moment they stumbled onto the marauders, they'd been met with apprehension and even outright anger. He understood their anger. No one wanted to be told how to do things. Umberland and Burbank understood the situation immediately, as did the rest of the OSS men. They kept a low profile and only offered suggestions when asked.

Now, he lay on top of a small rise behind a wall of bushes, watching over a trail that the Kachin had chosen as their ambush spot. To either side of his overlook position, men of the 5037th Combined Unit hunkered and watched.

When he'd first seen their haggard condition and sensed their low morale, he'd doubted they'd ever amount to much of a fighting force, but he respected them. Most had come from other units, thus the combined unit. Many came from the 164th Regiment—a unit that had seen heavy fighting on Guadalcanal. Listening to their encounters with the Japanese reminded him of conditions out here, with one large exception. The U.S. Navy wasn't parked nearby, assuring plenty of resupply and even fire and air support. Out here, you had to be much more self-sufficient.

Shawn pointed at the portion of the trail they could see. He whispered to Corporal Higgs, the closest American from the 5037th, lying beside him, watching intently. "We won't see much from here, but we'll hear it and see the aftermath. Pay close attention to edges."

"I can't see the Kachin at all."

"Course not. If you could, so could the Nips. Trust me, they're there and ready."

Two hours passed. The heat of midday tempered a few degrees and made their perch almost pleasant. Shawn noticed Higgs had to catch himself a few times as his head bobbed. He didn't blame him; they didn't have enough to eat, and it affected their sharpness.

"Won't be long now," he hissed.

Higgs's head snapped up. "How'd you know?"

Shawn slowly pointed across the field to the far hill. The dim shape of the trail snaking down from it was just visible.

Higgs focused his attention and must've seen movement. His body tensed and his breaths shortened. "I think I see them." He moved his rifle up closer to his body.

Shawn touched his shoulder. "You won't be needing that. Just watch." He handed him a set of binoculars.

Higgs made himself comfortable on his elbows and held the binoculars to his eyes. Shawn made sure no direct sunlight touched the glass lens. A hush fell across them as they waited for the ambush to finally be sprung.

Shawn counted fifteen Japanese soldiers in the patrol. Perhaps two squads. They didn't move fast. By now, they'd learned nowhere was truly safe in the Burmese jungle, and these men would be especially careful since the arrival of the marauders.

He lost sight of them once they came off the hillside and entered the high-treed jungle where the ambushers waited. As long as they continued following the trail, they couldn't help falling into the Kachin trap. Any moment now.

Higgs hissed, "I lost 'em."

He offered the binoculars back to Shawn, but he shook his head. "Keep 'em for now."

The only sound came from the squawking birds and chirping insects. Long minutes passed, and it appeared the jungle had simply consumed the enemy patrol. The thought wasn't as far-fetched as it sounded. Shawn had seen and felt many disconcerting and even inexplicable things in these unforgiving jungles. Life seemed to balance on a knife's edge here.

Almost at the same instant, a raucous chorus of gunshots erupted from the calmness below. Muzzle flashes sparkled here and there, and gun smoke wafted through the tops of the trees or leaked from the bushes. The shooting lasted less than a minute, followed by a crushing silence that was finally filled with terrified screams. A few shots rang out and Shawn guessed the surviving enemy soldiers were probing for the Kachin positions. No return fire from the Kachin gave anything away.

A full minute passed. Higgs had the binoculars pinned to his face and he swept them side to side. He finally said, "Where are they? I can't see anything. Is it over?"

"Keep watching—watch the edges."

Even without the binoculars, Shawn saw movement—just flashes of tan and green uniforms as the surviving Japanese tried to move out of the killing zone, attempting to flank the ambushers. Shawn could imagine the carnage. Bodies strewn where they'd been shot—some men wounded and calling for help—survivors wondering what to do next—nearing panic.

Even the most experienced soldiers could break when facing a Kachin ambush.

A loud boom cracked the air, and fire and smoke pinpointed the spot. "Booby-trapped grenade. They string line across and when someone walks across it, it pulls the pin and rolls it from cover," Shawn said. He put his hand to his ear. "Listen."

More shots rang out, but not the recognizable crack of M1s but Japanese Arisaka rifles. Men yelled to one another—a few still screamed in agony. More frightened and even panicked voices joined in.

Shawn said, "Now they're getting in close and killing them with their knives. This is their favorite part."

Higgs dropped the binoculars from his eyes and looked at him as though he were kidding. "What? Really?"

Shawn simply nodded, his face grim. "Keep listening."

Soon, the screams became hysterical. He saw more flashes as Japanese soldiers fired their rifles, then cut and run. They didn't get far before the panicked screams changed to agonized screams.

"They're running into the punji stakes now."

"Jesus, they sound like they're being butchered," Higgs observed.

Shawn pointed to the right. "Over there. See 'em?"

Higgs shifted his gaze. He finally nodded. "Yeah, I see 'em. Are they done? Why don't they finish them off?"

"The only survivors are most likely wounded. They likely never even saw their attackers." Shawn couldn't keep from grinning. Higgs looked at him as though he'd lost his mind. He wondered if he'd looked at the veteran 101 Detachment man, Calligan, in much the same way when he'd first arrived in Burma.

"They'll report back to their HQ, and the fear will increase by a notch or two. Unless they're treated quickly, the Nips who stepped on the punji stakes will die from infection in a few days—maybe a week. Regardless, they'll spend precious resources trying to keep them alive, and the longer they do, the more the story and fear will spread."

Higgs gulped loudly. He looked pale against the black soil. "Brutal," was his only response.

Shawn gave him a sideways grin. "Now you're getting the idea. You can't play fair. There's not some bullshit code of honor out here. Kill and maim quickly and efficiently." Shawn pushed himself into a crouch. "Come on. Let's get down there and I'll show you how they did it."

"Aren't you worried about a follow-on force?"

"Nah, if there was one, the network of Kachin villages would've told us."

"There's a network?"

"Of course. How do you think we found you guys out here in the middle of nowhere?"

Higgs looked embarrassed. "I fought the Nips on the Canal—saw a lot of combat—some of it face-to-face, but out here I feel like I'm fresh out of basic. Fresh meat for the meat-grinder."

"You guys'll do fine once you've learned a few things. That's why we're here." Shawn bounded down the hill. Higgs and the rest of them tried to keep up, but mostly ended up making excessive amounts of noise.

15

Early Spring 1944
Sixty miles east of Sweetwater, Texas
Fifteen thousand feet AGL

Abby sat in the cockpit of the brand-new P-39 Airacobra flying at fifteen thousand feet on a westerly heading. She'd flown other P-39s but only locally to get acquainted with the handling, but now she'd fly it across the country.

After her stint pulling targets for the navy, she'd put her chit in for a slot with the WASP ferry program. She hadn't expected such a quick response. She still hadn't unpacked all her things before they wanted her to familiarize herself with different aircraft. She'd flown four times a day for seven straight days.

Flying the P-39 to Seattle would be her first real ferry pilot mission. She thought they might break her in slowly, but no. She'd been sure to map her route through Texas.

She loved her time pulling targets, but this was something she loved even more. This is what she'd been trained for, and she immediately knew she'd made the right decision. Not only did she enjoy the work more, but she also found that old spark with the other women in the group. They came in and flew out almost like a revolving door, but their excitement and love for flying was contagious and reminded her why she'd fallen in love with flying in the first place.

Despite a few fresh faces she didn't know, she knew most everyone, making each meet feel like a reunion with a long-lost friend. She'd only been at the airbase a few weeks and already she'd seen three dear friends from Bay 7, Margie Wills, Alice Cathart, and Eberdeen Huss.

But the only person on her mind at the moment was her dearest friend, Beatrice Malinsky. She hadn't seen her since she'd given birth to little Cora. She'd only been able to stay a day or two after the birth before she had to board a train for the long haul back to the east coast. *Now I'm flying there.* She felt like a queen or a superhero.

She'd written a few letters to her friend about her plan to move to the ferry pilot program, but she doubted the letters had even arrived yet. She might land at Sweetwater and completely surprise her. Her mood darkened slightly when she thought about seeing Sal, too.

Despite the age gap, they seemed like a happy couple. In her letters, Beatrice talked about him almost as much as baby Cora. It galled and delighted her at the same time.

She checked her gauges, then the map strapped to her thigh. The summer sky was clear, and she matched obvious features like lakes and towns to her small map. Right on course. She didn't need to land in Sweetwater. It wasn't her destination, but she would not miss such a golden opportunity to see her best friend. Perhaps she'd meet up with some of her instructors, too. She didn't know if they still worked there or not, but she couldn't wait to get on the ground.

She felt her pulse quicken as she recognized features from her training flights. She'd flown countless hours over most of Texas, and the closer she flew to Sweetwater, the less and less she needed to check the map.

She dropped her altitude and finally saw the tower sticking up from the flatness of Sweetwater. It always reminded her of a white pin stuck into an ultra-realistic contour map. She wracked her brain, trying to remember the air traffic controllers in the tower. Most of the trainers she'd flown in didn't have radios. They'd communicated through slow flybys and light signals, but she still knew them well from tours and even a few lectures. The P-39 had a radio, and she felt a wave of nerves pass as she pressed the talk button. *It's like I'm back in training,* she thought.

"Sweetwater Tower, this is Airacobra three six four at four miles and three thousand feet to your north, requesting landing clearance. Over."

There was a pause, but finally a voice she recognized came back. "Flight Airacobra three six four, this is Sweetwater Tower. You're cleared to land on three two. Wind calm. Over."

"Sweetwater Tower, Airacobra three six four. Is that you, Larry?"

"That's affirmative, three six four. Whom do I have the pleasure of speaking with?"

The excitement of seeing old friends made Abby laugh out loud. She keyed the mic. "It's me, Abby. Abby Cooper . . . over," she added as an afterthought.

She could hear the joy and laughter in his voice. "Abby Cooper? Well, I'll be damned. Come to bust our chops again?"

She couldn't keep from laughing. She remembered one of the last times she'd seen him. She'd reproached him for referring to them as airmen instead of airwomen. It had been a joke, but she'd delivered it seriously and Larry had apologized effusively before he realized she'd been joking.

"As long as you can tell the difference between a man and a woman, we'll be just fine, Larry."

"I've learned my lesson, believe me," he laughed back.

She approached the tower from forty-five degrees and leveled off at pattern altitude. As she entered the pattern, she could see movement in the tower. Despite the heavy glare on the glass, she saw workers waving at her as she passed. She waved and blew them all a kiss as she floated by.

She slowed and entered final. Even from here, she could see folks streaming from the tower and other buildings as word spread that one of their own was coming for a visit. She lowered the gear, which came down in a three-point configuration rather than a fixed tailwheel.

It always felt odd to land with such a flat attitude, but she had to admit it seemed easier, especially if there happened to be a quartering crosswind. If you ground looped with the tricycle gear, you might damage the wheel struts, but the entire empennage wouldn't bend in half like it would with a tailwheel setup.

She touched down with barely a squeak. She taxied along the old strip and noticed fresh paint and even a few more hangars. The place felt the same even though it had obviously grown as the WASP program grew. The air smelled the same: dust mixed with fuel, oil, and a hint of manure. It made her smile—some things never changed.

She parked and waved at the growing crowd of faces. She hurriedly unbuckled, then sprang from her seat and stepped onto the wing just as a crew chief lunged up to help. She recognized her crew chief from training and a tear blurred her vision.

"Holy cow! It is you!" Henrietta Kincaid burst out while she opened her bulky arms and lifted Abby in a bear hug. Abby opened her mouth to speak, but the hug took her breath momentarily.

When Henrietta finally put her back on the wing, Abby said, "I can't believe you're on duty, Hennie. It's so good to see you."

"Ha, they can't do anything without my help around here. You know that better than anyone." She leaned past Abby and admired the cockpit. She gave a low whistle. "Wow, just get a look at this sweet girl." She rubbed her oil-greased hands together as though getting ready for a meal. "Can't wait to get a look inside her guts."

"Well, we've got a long trip ahead of us. I have to leave in the morning."

"Any problems?"

"Nah, she purred like a kitten all the way." She leaned into Henrietta and elbowed her in the ribs, "But I don't mind if you give her a once-over. You're the best there is at this stuff."

Henrietta helped her off the wing, even though she didn't need it. She put her hand over her mouth as she saw more old friends approaching with wide-open arms. More tears clouded her vision as she embraced one after another. She felt as though she'd come home.

~

ABBY STOOD in front of Beatrice's rental house and took it all in. She didn't see anyone through the open curtains, but she could tell the place was lived in. The front grass had been cut and the edge of the little concrete pathway had been edged. A small shed at the edge of the property looked to have been freshly painted. She wondered if Sal had done the work. She had trouble picturing him doing such menial tasks, but perhaps the prospect of fatherhood had changed him.

She placed the straps of her small backpack over her shoulders and walked to the front door. She heard a squawk from inside. A flush of joy swept through her. It had to be little Cora. How old would she be now? She did the quick math, four months old. How was that possible?

She knocked tentatively at first, then louder when there wasn't a response. She heard footsteps approaching, but they didn't sound light like a woman's but heavy like a man's. Her smile faded as she wondered what it would be like to see Sal again. Had he changed? Could she forget about his role in the arson attack back in Seattle?

From the window over the top of the door, Sal peered out. His face changed from scowling to smiling in an instant. He called to someone behind him, then flung the door open. There he stood, just the way she remembered him—but no—that wasn't true. He beamed at her with a broad smile. She'd never seen him smile that way. He'd never been a brooding or angry man, but he didn't wear his emotions on his sleeve like she saw now. His smile made him seem ten years younger.

"Abigail! Holy cow, what a surprise."

From behind him, Beatrice came skidding around the corner. She held a bundle of blankets and, tucked inside, Abby saw Cora's wide, bright blue eyes taking it all in. Beatrice wore socks, and she skidded into the wall, jostling Cora, who giggled.

Sal stepped aside and Beatrice ran the last few yards. "Abby! Is it really you?"

Abby took her best friend into her arms and kissed her gently on the cheek. "Yes, it's me. I'm in the middle of a ferry flight and I thought I'd drop in for a visit."

She took a step back, and Cora stared at her. Abby's heart melted. She looked nothing like she remembered. She'd grown a lot and her face almost looked angelic, despite the bit of drool and possibly dried breast milk on her chin.

Abby's mouth hung open, and she tore her eyes from the child and focused squarely back onto Beatrice. "She's gorgeous. Absolutely gorgeous." She opened her arms tentatively. "May I?"

Beatrice immediately unwound her from the blankets and handed her over. "Of course. She's been quite the little hellion today. Maybe Aunt Abby will have the answer."

Abby took her into her arms and Cora continued to gawk at her as though Abby were the most interesting thing in the world. Her head bobbed and her pudgy little hands gripped Abby's hair.

"She's so heavy," Abby exclaimed. "How'd you get so heavy?" she cooed at Cora, who gurgled in answer.

Sal reached across and smoothed Cora's thin blonde hair. Cora locked onto him and lurched for him, nearly making Abby lose her grip, but she quickly recovered. "Not yet, little one. Not yet."

Sal stepped behind Beatrice, trying to hide from Cora. "Sorry 'bout that," he said.

Cora swiveled, trying to keep her eyes on Sal. She fussed, but Abby bounced her and kissed her forehead and Cora forgot about Sal for the moment.

Beatrice leaned into Sal's chest and said, "She loves her daddy. I've got what she needs, but she's a daddy's girl all the way. If Sal had breasts, I'd be out of a job," she teased.

Abby blushed deeply, but she kept bouncing Cora.

Beatrice smiled at her reaction. "Sorry. I can be so crass—even more with her around. I swear sometimes I forget how to act in public. I guess it just doesn't matter what other people think."

"It's okay. No need to apologize. I'm all grown up."

Sal stroked Beatrice's messy hair. Streaks of food and milk told her she hadn't showered in a while. Beatrice had never been a girl to be over the top about her appearance, but Abby didn't think she'd ever seen her more messy—or as deliriously happy.

"You look amazing," she said.

Beatrice gave her a wry smile. "You're a good liar, Abby."

"You do," she insisted. She cut a glance at Sal. "You, too, Sal."

Sal said, "You seem surprised."

"I—I guess I am. I don't mean anything by it, but you've never seemed the fatherly type. You never even married."

She saw hurt in his eyes for just a flash before he recovered and said, "I guess I just never met the right woman." He squeezed Beatrice's shoulder and she turned and they kissed as though Abby wasn't standing right in front of them.

Abby pushed her nose into Cora's and talked nonsensical baby talk to her. Cora gurgled, but soon lunged for her mother, or possibly, Sal.

Beatrice unlatched her lips from Sal's and turned back to Cora. But Cora rejected her and reached her small arms out for Sal.

Beatrice stepped aside and Sal took Cora into his muscular arms. Cora seemed to disappear into him. Sal's eyes took on a fresh glow. He was obviously head over heels in love with both the girls in his life.

Beatrice crossed her arms across her ample breasts and huffed, "I swear she hates seeing us hug or kiss. She breaks it up every time. If she wasn't a baby, I'd take her in the back and have a few harsh words for her."

Abby laughed, along with Sal and Beatrice. The laughter intrigued Cora. She stared at Abby, the person with the new-sounding laugh, and soon she joined in, too. It made them all laugh even harder and soon tears streaked down Abby's face.

~

Abby sat back on the couch and rubbed her belly. Sal had served a wonderful pasta dinner. He'd even found real butter for the thick slices of bread.

Cora had sat in her highchair and mostly thrown whatever Beatrice offered her onto the floor. She stuffed a few bits of pasta into her mouth, but for the most part, she wasn't having anything to do with the meal.

Now Beatrice was in the other room trying to nurse Cora into a food coma. The house had quieted. The smells of garlic and spicy red sauce hung in the air. Sal sat in his big leather chair. He tapped out a pipe, then stuffed it with fresh tobacco.

"Since when do you smoke a pipe? And where'd you learn to cook like that?" Abby asked.

"I always had a pipe in my house, but I didn't smoke it while I worked, so I guess you never saw it. I find I enjoy it more now, though." He struck a match, lit the pipe, and puffed until it smoked readily. "As far as the cooking bit goes, well, I always enjoyed helping in the kitchen." He pointed the end of the pipe at her. "And I still remember my mama's cooking. It's all about the sauce, she used to tell me."

"It's unusual to see a man cook."

Sal said, "It didn't make sense to have Beatrice cook for me since she's busy with the baby."

Abby stared at him as though he'd just arrived from outer space. She finally managed to say, "Well, I guess that makes sense."

"You don't think Clyde will cook for you if—well, if you have a child?"

Abby felt as though a dagger had been thrust into her belly. His hesitation made her wonder herself if this damned war would even give them the chance to find out. Would Clyde survive the war, or would it rob them of ever having a family together? She couldn't imagine starting over with someone else—it seemed impossible.

Sal placed the pipe on the ashtray and leaned forward. "I didn't mean to bring up a sore point, Abby. How is he? Have you heard from him?"

Abby swiped the tear that threatened to drop from the corner of her eye. She hadn't cried over Clyde in public in ages and it angered her for some reason. "Yes, of course. He writes all the time. He seems fine, but . . ."

"But you don't think he's telling you everything," Sal stated as though he could read her mind.

"Yes. Yes, that's right. He makes it sound like a lark. Well, that's not entirely true. There was one letter that really shook me up. I—I got the feeling that he thought he was going to die. But since then, it's all just anecdotes and funny things that happen with his buddies. I don't know what to think."

"He's a soldier. It's tough." He sucked on the pipe until it smoked heartily again. "I remember writing to my parents from the trenches in France." He paused and stared out the window for a moment. "I couldn't tell them the truth. Even if I was smart enough to write the words to describe it, no one would believe me."

Abby watched Sal drift off. He crossed spans of time and space and she knew he was back in those filthy trenches fighting a filthy war. Why did her husband have to do the exact same thing all this time later? Hadn't they learned their lesson the first time? What made men go to war? Glory? That sounded ridiculous. What had Sal seen and done that could make this stalwart brick wall of a man look this way from just a distant memory? Would Clyde come back and look the same?

"It's bad, isn't it?" she asked. "I mean the fighting."

Sal looked momentarily embarrassed by his foray into the past. "I can't imagine it being much worse than nineteen eighteen—but yeah—it's bad. They've had twenty years to make their killing machines more efficient."

"Cora is such a miracle," she said, softly changing the subject.

Sal's smile returned. "She is. She makes it all worthwhile."

"You won't hurt her, will you? Either of them?"

The look Sal shot at her nearly made her run out of the room. His face reddened and his scar seemed to pulse and shine. "Hurt them! Of course not—how dare you even . . ."

She cut him off. "I read the journal, Sal. I read Miles's journal. I know what you did. I know what you're capable of doing."

Instead of anger or confusion, she saw what she could only describe as relief. His eyes softened, and the scar stopped pulsating. He sank further into the chair and he suddenly looked every bit of his fifty-five years.

"You don't look surprised," she said.

Beatrice sang softly from the next room. The sweet sound almost made Abby tear up again. She wanted to join her friend, help her put Cora to bed, but she wanted to know how Sal would respond even more. So far, it wasn't the way she'd pictured. She hadn't meant to bring it up at all, but here they were.

He finally answered, "I saw the journal on your nightstand when you still lived here. Before Cora was born. I didn't know what it was at first, but I knew I'd seen it before. I'm sorry, but I snooped. I'd heard there might be a journal somewhere, but it never came up, so I forgot all about it, until that day." He stared straight into Abby's eyes. "I finally understood why you suddenly seemed to hate me."

Abby stared at her hands as she wrung them mercilessly. "I do—I did. Oh, I don't know anymore. It's all true then?"

"I didn't read it, but yes—I assume it's all true."

She flung open the top of the backpack and yanked out the journal. She held it up and shook it as though it held the secret sins of millions.

Sal reared back as though she'd slapped him. "Why do you have it here? What's going on?"

She drew it to her chest reflexively. "Don't try to take it."

"No, of course not. My God, Abby. You think I'm some kind of monster? But why do you have it here?" He seemed to realize something, and his curiosity melted away. "Is that why you're here—to put me in my place by waving that thing around?"

"No. I didn't even know if you'd still be here. I'm flying the Airacobra all the way to the West Coast. I'm going to hand it over to Trish Watkins. You remember her?"

Sal's face changed to a mask of confusion, then understanding. "You must really hate your father."

The words hurt badly. Did she hate her father? Did she really? She didn't know for sure. She hadn't decided yet. "I want justice."

Sal leaned back and puffed on the pipe. "Justice? For who?"

"For Trish." Anger welled in her belly and she fought to keep her voice down. "I'm sick of my father always getting away with everything. I've read the journal. He's not a good man. He needs to pay for his crimes."

"What does Trish have to do with anything? How does this give her justice?"

"Miles Burr. She loved him and he died trying to keep up daddy's quotas."

Sal leaned forward and tapped out the remaining tobacco ash into the ashtray. He sighed and said, "Your father is unscrupulous, but he's not responsible for Miles Burr's death. That was an accident."

Abby felt the heat rising again. How dare this arsonist sit and lecture her on scruples. "He'd be alive today if father hadn't pushed the numbers to impossible standards."

"No judge in the world is going to indict your father for trying to increase production during a national war crisis. Hell, they wouldn't do it if there *wasn't* a war on. It's a dead end."

"They can put him away for ordering the arson. That's still a crime the last I checked."

Sal nodded in grim agreement. She knew what he must be thinking. He'd go down too. In fact, her father might even put the whole thing in his lap. He could probably manufacture witnesses without too much trouble. Enough money could buy anything—and anyone. The fact that Sal left the company soon after made it look as though he'd fled. The jury would eat it up and her father might get a slap on the wrist for hiring such an unscrupulous man.

She expected him to plead, but instead he simply said, "Well, you should do whatever you think's right."

The door to Cora's bedroom creaked open and they both turned toward it. Beatrice's hair shot in all directions, but her smile went from ear to ear. She listened at the door, making sure the squeak hadn't woken Cora. When she heard nothing, she did a silent dance of joy. She danced all the way to the living room, then sat heavily onto Sal's lap.

"I need a drink."

Sal nuzzled her neck and asked quietly, "Is she down?"

"Yes, finally. I think she was excited to see Aunt Abby. She was all wound up."

"I wanted to come in to help, but it sounds like it's better that I didn't."

Beatrice nodded emphatically and blew a strand of hair out of her face. "I love you, but if you'd come in and got her all excited again—I woulda killed y'all."

She said it in such a deadpan, matter-of-fact way that Abby couldn't help laughing. But it was short-lived as she glanced at Sal, who stared at the floorboards in deep thought.

Beatrice looked from Sal, then back to Abby. "Okay, what the hell happened out here?"

Abby tried to smile, but she wasn't feeling it and she knew it was obvious. Sal pushed Beatrice's hair from her face.

He finally said, "Abby was just telling me she's flying her bird all the way to the West Coast. We were talking about her family."

Beatrice seemed to understand, but she obviously couldn't know the whole thing. "Aha," she said, raising a finger. "That explains why things are so glum all of a sudden. Still not getting along?"

"I haven't seen them in over a year. I thought since I'm going to be nearby, I may as well drop in. It's the right thing to do."

"Of course," Beatrice said. She leaned forward and rubbed her hands together. "Now, tell me your flight plan. That's a long trip over some wide open, desolate country. You want me to check your work? Did you bring your maps?"

Abby couldn't help laughing again. Beatrice clearly missed flying. "As a matter of fact, I did bring them along." She stuffed the journal back inside the pack and pulled out carefully folded maps.

Beatrice looked like a kid in a candy store. She scooted off Sal's lap and cleared the low coffee table. "Spread 'em out here," she said with mounting excitement. "How many miles is it?"

Abby fielded her questions as best she could. Beatrice dove into the maps with abandon. Abby noticed Sal watching Beatrice and she saw the bottomless love in his gaze. He seemed like a completely different person from the man she'd known back in Seattle, but had he really changed?

He stood and stretched his back. "I'll clean up the dishes," he said.

Abby watched him walk to the small kitchen. He didn't look at her, didn't plead for forgiveness with a harried glance. He seemed to take it all in stride. He must be thinking the same dire thoughts, though. He knew what her father was capable of, even more than she did.

He could snatch the journal from her in an instant. It would be child's play, but she knew he wouldn't. He'd simply let it happen. He'd let her ruin his new, idyllic life. Can I do that to him? Can I do it to Beatrice? Surely it would all come out and Beatrice would hate her more than she could even imagine. And what about Cora? She'd grow up without a father figure. Why did everything have to be so damned complicated?

16

Sal listened to Abby and Beatrice going over the flight plan in the small living room. Wisps of tobacco smoke still clung to the air. Beatrice knew little about his past. He'd told her the basics, that he'd work for Abby's father. She already knew as much. She remembered him from her childhood. But he hadn't told her anything about the shadier side of things.

He doubted she'd care to know, but perhaps he should tell her. Perhaps it might ease the pain if it came out later. He couldn't quite understand why Abby wanted to give the journal to Trish. He remembered her, of course. She'd grown up on the wrong side of the tracks, but his intuition told him that despite her hard outward appearance, she had a kind heart. She was a crook with a slightly bent moral compass, but she was basically harmless. At least, she had been.

What would she do with the journal? Hand it over to the police? Hand it over to the press? The press would be far worse. He knew for a fact that at least one judge, and possibly even a police chief, owed Victor Brooks favors, but he didn't think he owned any news editors in the same way. But there was a war on—would they run with a story of corruption during such a trying time? The war news had gotten better, but who could say if that would continue?

He rubbed at a stubborn piece of dried-on pasta sauce. He didn't know what would happen if the papers or the police took the journal seriously and ran with it. Would they seek him out? Judging by Abby's reaction to reading it, he had been named as a person who'd helped set up the arson. He wondered if those other two young men had been dealt with yet.

He wracked his brain for their names and finally came up with them: Bart Hanready and Mathew Clevenger. When he'd last spoken to Victor, he'd told him he would set the two men up for a fall. They'd find themselves in hot water and they'd stand trial in front of the honorable Franklin Hornsby, who happened to owe Victor Brooks a few favors. He'd give them a choice, jail or military service. They'd be sent to the front lines and that would be the end of that. They'd either survive or they wouldn't, but for the time being, they'd be out of Victor's hair.

Sal didn't know if that little incident had occurred or not, but he supposed he could call in a favor and find out easily enough. If Abby went through with delivering the journal and Trish knew what to do with it, Hanready and Clevenger might become important pieces. They'd name Sal, but they'd also name Victor. Without their testimony, Victor could easily pin the entire thing on him. Would he do that to his oldest friend? He nearly laughed out loud while he scrubbed the dishes. To save his own ass? Of course he would.

Abby must know how this might affect him and her best friend, Beatrice. He loved Beatrice and Cora with all his heart. He stopped scrubbing the dishes as the weight of losing them hit him hard. He felt faint for a moment and he gripped the side of the sink.

He glanced behind to where the girls were completely consumed by the maps. They hadn't noticed him nearly dropping a plate. Abby's eyes flashed away for a moment and he felt her sharp-as-a-razor-blade glance. This was the reaction he felt she'd been hoping for.

He straightened himself and resumed his job as though nothing had happened. Had she noticed? Would it be better if he showed some emotion? Perhaps she'd show him mercy, but that wasn't like her and it certainly wasn't like him.

He didn't know how to react. He could easily take the journal from her —he could probably do it without her even knowing until it was too late, but he didn't want to do that either. It might help cement her hatred for him. He still felt her hatred, but it had dissipated somewhat. Perhaps she still had hope for him and he felt she really *wanted* to forgive him—but she was too damned stubborn.

He knew her seeing him acting as a father to Cora and, even though they weren't married, a husband to Beatrice had an effect on her, but he wasn't playacting and he refused to do so just to make her change her mind. He'd meant it when he told her to do whatever she thought was right, but he didn't know what that was either.

Certainly, Victor was unrepentant and deserved whatever he got, but did he himself deserve the same treatment? Before the arson incident, he had done nothing outwardly illegal—not really. And hadn't he made sure Miles and his blundering idiot friends hadn't gotten themselves or anyone else hurt in the process?

Anger flooded him. He dried the last dish and smacked it into place too hard, causing a loud clatter. He didn't bother looking back at Abby. He didn't want her to see his anger. *I'm trying to justify my own bad behavior. Why do I deserve any less than Victor?*

He felt arms wrap around him and the subtle smell of flowers and clean baby filled his senses. He clutched Beatrice's hands and he felt her press into his back. She felt so good. He loved when she hugged him this way.

"Thanks for cooking *and* doing the dishes, Sal. I'm sorry I didn't help."

He turned and she loosened her grip to allow it. He looked down at her beautiful face. He pushed a strand of hair from across her eye and kissed her on the forehead. He took all of Beatrice in. He'd never felt this way about anyone in his entire life. Even his misdirected love of Meredith didn't hold a candle to the way he felt about this woman in his arms. Her big brown eyes stared up at him and her pouty lips glistened and begged to be kissed.

He leaned down and kissed her lips, which always seemed to taste of honey. He didn't know how she did that, and he always forgot to ask, because he forgot everything and everyone else when he kissed her or even held her close. She consumed his entire being, and he gave it willingly.

Abby cleared her throat loudly. Beatrice broke away from him. He felt the separation and immediately wanted it back.

She gave him one last fiery look and turned back to Abby. "Sorry 'bout that," she gasped. "You must think we're quite the pair."

"Whatever do you mean?" Abby asked.

"Well, we're always making goo-goo eyes at each other and sneaking kisses and hugs like we're high school lovers."

Abby shook her head, then tilted it. "You remind me of how Clyde and I are together. The world seems to melt away—it's the same with you two."

Sal couldn't have said it better himself, but he didn't say a word, just kept his eyes on Beatrice and yearned to kiss her again.

Beatrice flashed her sultry eyes at him, then turned back to Abby. "You've known him your whole life. It must be kinda—well, kinda awkward for you, I suppose."

Sal watched for Abby's reaction. He'd never really thought about how his relationship might make her feel uncomfortable. To him, it was as natural as the rain, but Beatrice was absolutely correct. It would be incredibly awkward. After all, he'd been there when she took her first steps and her first drink of alcohol and now here he was sleeping with her best friend. He could recall sleepovers, for crying out loud.

Did this add to her dislike? He cared a great deal for Abby. Did she know that? Could she possibly know just how much he cared? Should he tell her? Would that change her mind about the journal?

No, he couldn't tell her. It wouldn't be fair, and she might not even believe him. In fact, she may think he was trying to influence her, and besides, he wasn't one hundred percent sure himself, but how could she not see the resemblance?

He shot a glance at Beatrice. Did she see the resemblance? She'd never once brought it up, but Cora took most of their time and any free time they had they spent either making love or catching up on much-needed sleep. But now that he and Abby were in the same room, would she notice such a thing? Would it change the way she felt about him? He doubted it, but it might be awkward for her.

Abby woke, swung her legs off the couch, and sat on the edge staring into the early morning darkness. The only light came from a distant streetlight. The diffuse yellow light came through the window and made the windowsill glow slightly. She let her eyes adjust and guessed at the time: 0400 hours.

She flicked the light on and squinted. She rubbed her eyes and checked her wristwatch: 0355 hours. She smiled. Ever since WASP training, she'd been able to set an internal alarm clock, and it hadn't failed her yet. She simply concentrated on when she wanted to wake up the next morning and it just worked. She kept a backup alarm clock in her bag just in case, but she rarely heard its annoying chime. She hadn't set it the night before because of Cora. Beatrice had enough trouble with Cora's sleep patterns without her throwing a wrench in the works with a blaring alarm bell.

She glanced at the closed door to Cora's room and beside that, the room Beatrice and Sal shared. After lying on the couch for a few minutes the night before, she'd heard Sal and Beatrice talking and giggling. They sounded happy. She couldn't shake the wave of loneliness that swept over her. She'd fallen asleep yearning for Clyde's strong embrace.

She stretched and sighed, still not knowing what she should do with the damned journal. Before coming here, she'd been sure. The trip to Seattle was almost a sign from God. She'd give it to Trish and let things play out—good or bad—she'd be done with the whole thing once and for all. But after seeing the happy family, her doubts resurfaced.

She hoped a good night's sleep might help, but she hadn't slept all that well and she was no closer to deciding than she'd been before. Perhaps it would be best to simply drop the journal over the side of the P-39 as she barreled over the wastelands of west Texas . . . or perhaps Utah. Let God do with it what he would.

She shook the thoughts from her head. It would be light in another hour, and she needed to get to the airfield and prep her aircraft for the long flight ahead. Beatrice had insisted that she should wake her up so she could cook her breakfast. She'd agreed, but now she felt like a heel. Beatrice needed her precious sleep even more than she did.

She decided not to wake her. She'd simply sneak out the front door, but she realized her plan had a serious hole. She'd taken a cab here, but she'd need Beatrice or Sal to drive her back to Avenger Airfield since no cabs would run this early in little old Sweetwater, Texas.

The bedroom door clicked open softly and Abby stood abruptly. In the semidarkness, she saw Sal's broad outline. He stepped carefully and it reminded her of the term a bull in a china shop, but he didn't make a sound.

He crept around the corner on his bare feet. He had on a bathrobe and he smiled when he saw her and put his finger to his lips for quiet. The scene brought a flood of memories back. He'd done the same thing when she'd been up before everyone else during her middle-grade school years. He somehow always seemed to know when she was up, even if only lying in bed staring at the ceiling. Of course, back then, he'd already been fully dressed since he'd come from his house.

She loved their early morning talks back then. She'd forgotten all about them until that moment. How had that happened? Had she suppressed them or had time simply stretched her memories until they were paper thin and faded?

"Hi," she whispered. "I didn't want to wake anyone, but I need a ride to the airfield."

"Yes. But first I'll make you breakfast."

She wanted to protest. It seemed so out of character for him, and she still wasn't entirely comfortable.

"You've become quite the homemaker," she said and immediately regretted her huffy tone. She quickly added, "I only heard Cora once. Was that a good night for her?"

"Yes, exceedingly good, but mostly for Beatrice. She puts on a brave face, but she's exhausted."

"I don't know how she'd do it without you, Sal." She hadn't meant to say it, but she realized she meant it. How could she ruin all that? In the early morning darkness, reality seemed to come in stark clarity.

He plopped a spoonful of lard into a warm pan and it sizzled. "It's the best job I've ever had. But of course, it's not a job—but a joy. Too bad you won't see Cora when she wakes up. All smiles and gurgles, I can assure you. She's fussy in the evenings but mornings . . . she's a completely different person. Reminds me of you in that way. A real morning person."

She wrapped her bathrobe around her pajamas and sat in one of the wooden chairs surrounding the little dining table. Sal cracked two eggs into the pan and even laid two strips of bacon. She felt transported.

"I remember our mornings together," she said quietly. "I'd forgotten until just this morning. Isn't that strange?"

"We had some good talks. I remember, too."

"Why'd you do it, Sal?"

He stopped smiling and stared into the crackling pan of meat and eggs. He flipped the eggs and they sizzled in the bacon grease and lard. "It was the job. I know that's not an excuse. Men have committed some of the most heinous crimes, saying they're just following orders."

He pulled a plate down from a cupboard and expertly scooped the eggs onto it. "Over easy, just the way you like them, if my memory serves." He turned the strips of bacon and added, "They'll be done momentarily."

He wiped his hands on a hand towel hanging from the oven handle, then set the plate of perfectly cooked eggs in front of her. She never took her eyes off him.

"So you don't really have an answer," she stated flatly.

"No, not really."

"Is that why you left? Guilty conscience or something?" She didn't mean for it to sound so harsh, but he didn't seem to notice.

"I left when he wanted me to take care of the only two witnesses left. I told him I was done doing his dirty work. He could clean up his own mess."

Abby reared back as though he'd spit in her face. "What do you mean by 'take care of,'" she demanded.

"He wanted me to set them up. Wanted me to get them into hot water somehow, then be given a choice between being sent to the front lines or face jail time." He stood, shut off the stovetop, and held the two dripping strips of bacon over the pan to let them drip.

"I read about them in the journal. Bart and . . ."

"Bart and Mathew," he finished for her. He placed the bacon on the plate beside the eggs. "I don't know if he ever went through with it, though."

She stared at breakfast, and her stomach growled. She felt his gaze. She didn't feel uncomfortable around him anymore. He'd been completely honest with her and he had done nothing to dissuade her from giving the journal to Trish.

"That's awful," she managed to say. "I'm glad you refused him. It must've been difficult."

His eyes softened. "Best decision I ever made." He held up his hands as though they sat in a palace instead of a rundown two-bedroom postage stamp. "It brought me here. It brought me to Beatrice and Cora. And I've even managed to see more of you."

"You've changed, Sal. I've never heard you talk this way. What happened to the hardened trench warfare soldier I used to know?"

His smile faded. "Eat your breakfast before it gets cold."

She cut into the eggs and let the yolks mix with the bacon, then she cut the bacon into bite-sized portions and scooped the slurry into her mouth. She closed her eyes and relished the taste. She hadn't had fresh eggs and bacon in eons.

"Well, at least you haven't changed the way you eat bacon and eggs," he said, his smile returning. But it faded again when he asked, "What do you think Trish will do with the journal?"

She gulped down the bite with some difficulty. She wished he'd waited until she mopped up her breakfast before asking about it again.

"I'm not even sure I'm going to give it to her anymore."

Instead of relief, he looked truly surprised and even a little disappointed. How could that be?

"You should give it to the police, but not the Seattle police. Maybe Tacoma's far enough away."

"You want me to give it to the police? But you'd be implicated, Sal. You might go to prison."

"I'm prepared to pay for what I've done. It might be worth it to see the look on Victor's face."

She lowered her voice and peered back toward the closed doors. "But what about them? You might lose them forever."

He sighed. "Only for a little while."

Abby suddenly felt like throwing her eggs and bacon back up, but she gulped against the rising nausea. She finally said, "Beatrice would kill me."

Sal's head thrust backward and he had to put his hand over his mouth to stifle his laughter. When he got control, he looked her straight in the eye and said, "You're right, she may. I hadn't thought about that."

"You think it's funny?"

He shook his head, but he still had a goofy grin. "I think she'll be madder than a hornet, but she'll get over it." He stroked his chin as though thinking hard about something. "I should probably tell her myself. It might blunt her reaction toward you."

She'd wanted to know if he'd told Beatrice any of this, but realized that, of course, he wouldn't have. With the new baby and them getting to know one another better, they probably hadn't had much time to talk about their pasts. They were too busy falling in love.

"Are you worried she might . . ."

"Hate me?" he finished for her.

Abby nodded.

"I don't think she's committed any felonies, but I don't think she's as pure as the driven snow, either. She's got a rough edge to her. It's one reason I've fallen in love with her."

"You really have, haven't you?"

He shut down as though a light switch had turned off. He scowled and his scar protruded more than normal, and his lips thinned into a tight line.

"What did I say?" she asked.

"I've changed alright, but I'm not going to get more gooey-gooey than I already have. I still have some pride, for chrissakes."

"Aha, there's the old Sal I know." She scooped up the rest of her eggs and bacon and pushed the plate away. "Well, for a hard ass, you sure know how to cook," she giggled.

She suddenly knew exactly what she needed to do with the journal. It all made sense. She pushed her chair back and went to her backpack, still leaning against the couch. She rifled through it until she found the journal. She stared at the ornate leather-bound cover for a few seconds, then handed it to him. "Here, take it."

He didn't move, but the corners of his mouth turned down. He crossed his arms and shook his head. "I don't want it."

"Take it. It's perfect."

"What are you talking about? You won't get the justice you're after."

"I guess that depends on what you do with it."

"What if I throw it away or burn it?"

She looked around the room. It was a small place, but she could feel the love they'd put into it. She could see the life they were building together.

"I think it's your choice." She stood close to him. She pulled his arm to her, then placed the journal in his hand. "I think you'll do the right thing."

"Destroying it might be the right thing."

"It's not fair for me to decide. It's your decision."

SAL DROPPED Abby off at Avenger Airfield. Since handing him the journal, they hadn't spoken any more about it. Instead, she'd asked him about the incident with the local tough guys. Apparently, Beatrice had told her about it the day before. He mostly just answered her questions. He wasn't one to brag, but he felt proud of the way things turned out. But he also felt like he'd tangled with men who had no real idea about his background, which made it seem almost unfair. Abby relished the story and while she listened, seemed to forget that she was supposed to be upset with him.

They said their goodbyes, and he watched her saunter past the gate guard after flashing her identification card. She wore a one-piece flight suit with a leather coat and he had to admit she looked stunningly beautiful. Pride swelled in his chest and he wished Meredith could see her. She'd be proud, too.

He thought of Victor, and his mood soured. Would he allow himself to be proud of her, or would he stick to his belief that women shouldn't aspire to such nonsense? Sal knew the likely answer. Victor never saw the good side of things unless they directly benefited himself and Abby flying for the WASPs definitely didn't fit into his grand plan for her.

He remembered how angry he was when Abby announced she planned to marry Clyde—virtually a nobody. He'd nearly blown a gasket. Sal had never seen him turn such a vibrant color of red. He grinned at the memory.

Abby had always known exactly how to needle her father. At first Sal thought the marriage announcement was all an elaborate ruse, but then he saw Clyde and Abby together and realized it was the real thing. It may have started out that way, but people couldn't choose who they fell in love with.

Thinking of Clyde reminded him of Victor's failed plan to have Clyde fail out of Army Airborne training. Victor had asked Sal to reach out to an old military friend.

Sal had served with a little rat of a man named Nigel Manchester in the Great War. Now a general, he had assured Sal that he'd put a word in and something would be done. But despite all that, Clyde had prevailed. It was tough training, made even tougher by Victor's manipulation. But by making it through anyway, Clyde had earned Sal's respect.

He wondered how much Manny could have interfered. The airborne was a frontline unit and his old friend wasn't a frontline type of general. In fact, he doubted he'd even left the States yet. Even in the trenches, Manny hadn't been too keen on getting his hands dirty. He'd been a private, just like him back then, but he had a knack for positioning himself where he could do the officer's bidding—not assaulting positions and other combat-related tasks, but more like darning their socks and making their coffee. He soon found himself elevated to the rank of corporal. Soon he got himself assigned as a sort of assistant to a captain and he'd risen through the ranks, making himself too valuable to be wasted as cannon fodder when the others went over the top.

Despite his loose morals, Sal didn't hold it against him like most everyone else in the company had. He figured they all had to find some way to survive and Manny had found his by sticking his nose up officer's well-coiffed asses. Manny was the only one that had to live by his choices.

Just before the war ended, he'd received a battlefield commission to second lieutenant. He remained in the army and made it his career. Sal supposed he'd brown-nosed his way to the rank of general and now probably enjoyed his own ass being nuzzled by lower ranks with similar ambition.

Sal's mood soured as he thought about what Abby would think if she found out about his role meddling in Clyde's life. Surely, Miles wouldn't have known about setting up Clyde, so it wouldn't be in his journal, but that knowledge would surely put the nail in the coffin of his relationship with Abby. She'd never trust him again. He looked at the journal sitting on the seat beside him. He could easily toss it in the trash bin and never worry about it again.

As he waited for Abby to fly off, he read a few pages of the journal. Miles could write and he found himself drawn into the words. A full hour passed. Countless aircraft took off and landed, but they were obviously students with instructors flying in the back of bulky two-seater aircraft.

Finally, he heard a different sounding engine that tore him from Miles Burr's words. A sleek, deadly looking aircraft came roaring down the runway. He stepped from the old truck and shielded the sun with his hand over his brow. He watched the P-39 Airacobra dart down the runway, then lift into the sky. The tricycle-configured landing gear snugged up into the nose and wings. He could see the outline of the pilot's helmeted head and he knew it had to be Abby.

He felt a thrill of pride all over again. He vowed to himself right then and there that he'd never let her down again, and he'd do whatever it took to protect her. He also realized that Abby had given him the journal as a test. If he dumped it, he may never get her fully back.

As she climbed away into the clear blue sky, he wondered what Victor would do if he knew he had the journal. Sal still felt a loyalty to the man. After all, they'd been friends for most of their lives. Victor had changed for the worse, but Sal didn't think it was forever. Remnants of his friend still lingered. But was it too late?

He watched the aircraft turn gracefully back toward him. The P-39 leveled off and roared toward him at only a thousand feet. When it was abreast of him, Abby waggled the wings in greeting, or rather, farewell. She beamed a smile down at him and he couldn't help waving back. He felt like a spectator at a carnival and he quickly pulled his hand down.

He knew exactly what he'd do with the journal.

17

Seattle, Washington
May 1944

Abby stroked the side of the P-39 Airacobra and whispered to it as though it wasn't an inanimate object. "I'm gonna miss you, girl. You took good care of me." As if in answer, the cooling engine clicked steadily. Her first cross-country ferry flight had gone off without a hitch, thanks to good weather and excellent maps.

She didn't know what would become of the aircraft, but she supposed it would be partially dismantled and sent across the sea. She fantasized that it would fight the Japanese and perhaps save Clyde from some horrendous banzai attack. She'd read about banzai attacks in *Life* magazine and the thought of crazed soldiers carrying long rifles with bayonets attached terrified her.

After signing the aircraft off to the airbase, she checked with operations. She'd be flying another aircraft back to the East Coast, but not for two days. Two days in her hometown.

The thought of spending time with her mother and father gave her an upset stomach. She'd rather fly through a horrendous thunderhead, but she knew she had to see them. It simply wouldn't be right not to. She also planned on seeing Clyde's parents. She actually looked forward to that prospect.

Trish was another thorn in her side. She wanted to see her, but they hadn't parted on the best of terms all those long months ago. She wasn't even sure if she'd be able to find her. If she'd moved, she'd have no idea how to proceed. First things first: parents.

She stripped off her flight suit and donned her civilian clothes. It always felt odd doing so now. Would she ever feel comfortable in regular clothes again?

Outside the base, a green sedan with a bright white star on the door idled. She didn't give it a second glance, but the young soldier inside leaned his head out and asked, "You Mrs. Cooper?"

"Yes."

"Well, I'm assigned to drive you wherever you need to go." He hopped out and took her small bag and backpack.

"Really? I wasn't expecting this. How nice."

"Oh sure, you WASPs get anything you want."

She hopped in the passenger side and smiled as the soldier hopped behind the wheel. He gave her an awkward look and she supposed he probably expected her to sit in the back.

"I'm Private Lou Connor and you've got me for the duration, ma'am. Where to?"

She gave him the address of her parents, and he gave a low whistle.

"Do you know it?" she asked.

"I know the area. I grew up in Tacoma. That's where the rich folks live." His face reddened, making him look like a child. "I—I didn't mean nothin' by it, ma'am."

"I'm not offended. You know your geography."

"Yes, ma'am."

"Please stop calling me that. You can call me Abby, if you like."

He talked her ear off as they drove through the outskirts of Seattle. She mostly nodded and gave short answers when he asked questions, but mostly she gawked at her hometown. It hadn't changed much, but she sensed a change in the people walking along the streets. She saw more smiles and friendly waves than she remembered. It felt almost prewar, yet even more so.

During one of his lulls to catch his breath, she said, "People sure seem happy today."

He shrugged as though he didn't really know what she meant. "Sure, I guess so."

"When I was here last, everyone seemed glum."

"Well, the war news is better. I guess folks can see the light at the end of the tunnel. A year ago we didn't know what was gonna happen, but now the papers are full of one victory after another. Those Nazi bastards are taking a beating from the Russians and we're socking it to 'em in Africa and Italy. We have them in a real pinch. And the Japs aren't doing any better. They're on their heels, too."

"Yes, maybe that's the difference. It's refreshing to see so many smiles."

"I hope to get sent over soon, too." He said it without much conviction and she wondered if he meant it or said it to seem more manly and accepted.

"You don't like your job here?"

"Yes, I like it okay, but the action's overseas."

"It doesn't matter where you serve, as long as you serve. Everyone has a role to play."

"Yes, ma'am, I suppose so."

She didn't correct him calling her ma'am. "The turn's coming up." The vehicle slowed and turned onto the long driveway leading to the Brooks estate.

Private Connor gave a low whistle and gawked at the long row of thick trees along the sides. The lawn and bushes had all been manicured. Even when the business had been struggling, her father insisted on constant upkeep, but it seemed even more manicured than normal.

"What's it like to grow up in a place like this?" he asked unashamedly.

She gave him a wan smile. "It has its ups and downs, just like anywhere else, I suppose." To complain about such opulence would be blasphemous, but she would've given it all up to have a normal loving family.

The sedan came to a halt at the steps leading to the double front doors.

Lou hopped out and retrieved her bags. She asked, "I may be a while. Can I call you when I need you again?"

"You're my assignment until you fly out again. I'll just wait in the car, if that's alright."

"You're welcome to walk the grounds if you like. I'm not even sure if my parents are here. It might be a quick in and out. I haven't seen the house staff in ages though, so I'll visit with them if my parents aren't around."

He nodded his thanks and she went to the front door. Should she knock? It was home, but it didn't really feel that way—not for a long time. She used the large knocker. The door opened and there stood Mr. Hanniger in all his grace.

His face changed from chiseled stone to a bright smile in an instant. "Abigail, you're home."

Abby thrust herself into his arms and he draped her with his long arms. "It's so good to see you, Mr. Hanniger."

His deep rumble of a laugh rolled over her. "And you, too. You come unannounced—nothing's prepared."

"It's only for a short while. I didn't even know if I'd have time to come here, so I didn't ring." She broke from his embrace and indicated the sedan with the star on the side. "They gave me a driver, so it made things possible."

"The army?"

"Yes. Apparently, they have a high regard for us WASP flyers."

"As well, they should. We've heard so little about you, but it thrilled us to learn you'd passed all your flight qualifications." It wasn't meant as an admonishment, but she immediately felt bad.

"I know I've been awful about that sort of thing." She shrugged and looked at her feet. "But it's been hard. Mother and I have been corresponding, though."

"Yes, she's kept us informed."

"Is she here?"

"Why yes, she is for a change. She's normally out and about, but today she stayed in. Perhaps she had a premonition of your arrival."

"Abigail? Abigail, is that you?"

Abby looked to the sweeping stairs and saw her mother standing at the top, gawking. She looked beautiful as usual, wearing a dress that would be fancy enough for most gala parties.

"Hello, Mother." She touched Mr. Hanniger's hand, went to the base of the stairs, and made her way up.

Meredith hurried down, one hand on the railing, the other clutching her necklace. They met in the middle, hesitated for only a moment, then hugged. Most hugs from Meredith were austere and light occasions, but this one was deep and meaningful.

They had continued their letter correspondence and now they seemed more like sisters than mother and daughter. They'd shared experiences and bounced ideas off one another in those letters, and it had transformed their relationship.

They finally parted and Abby saw tears in the corners of Meredith's eyes. "Stop it, Mother. You'll make me cry, too."

"I can't help it. They're tears of joy. I'm so happy to see you."

"I'm only here for two days, then I fly back to the East Coast."

"Listen to you, you sound like Amelia Earhart, or a female Lindberg. It's all so exciting. I want to hear every detail."

Meredith led Abby down the stairs and into the sitting room. Staff came in and out with teas, coffees, and treats. Abby greeted and hugged each person. They were like old friends. She'd forgotten how much she loved them.

She remembered Private Connor waiting outside. After greeting Melody, a young, unattached woman on the kitchen staff, she pulled her close and said, "There's a handsome young soldier outside waiting for me. Would you be so kind to take him some of this lovely fare?" Melody blushed, but promised to do so.

After the flurry of joyful reunions and a bit of food and drink, they were finally alone.

Abby asked, "So has it gotten any better with Father?" Meredith had gone into gritty detail in her letters, but face-to-face was different.

"No, not really. I tried, Abby—I really tried. Occasionally, I'll see the man I fell in love with. Sometimes I'll see him smiling as he reads something that tickles his fancy. He never laughs anymore, but that impish smile still appears from time to time. It gives me hope that he's still in there somewhere beneath his brash exterior."

"Cripes, Mother, it sounds hopeless. Why do you stay with him?" She wanted to ask if it was about the money, but she didn't want to insult her and she didn't think it was true.

"I don't know, really. I—I guess I'm worried about him."

"Worried? Worried how?"

"I'm worried about his well-being."

"Is he sick? What do you mean?"

"No, no, nothing like that." She checked to make sure they were truly alone. "I never told you this 'cause I didn't want to upset you, but your friend Miss Watkins paid me a visit."

"Trish?"

"Yes, Trish Watkins. She told me awful things about your father. She holds him personally responsible for Miles Burr's death. She tried to blackmail me to give her information."

A coldness settled into the pit of Abby's stomach. The sweets she'd eaten suddenly felt heavy in her gut and the coffee stung like acid. She finally managed to say, "Blackmail?"

"Yes. You remember Calvin, I suppose."

Abby cringed even more as the image of her mother bent over the stacks at the country club library filled her mind.

Abby only managed to nod, and Meredith continued. "She threatened to expose the affair if I didn't cooperate. But it was a ridiculous and desperate attempt. I certainly didn't care, and it would've been her word against mine if it had escalated. Of course, nothing ever came from it. I haven't seen her since. But she also implied that Victor's life might be in danger from whoever she worked for."

Abby didn't know what to say. Her mother obviously didn't know how much Abby already knew and she wasn't sure she wanted her to.

With her mind reeling, Abby finally said, "And that's why you're staying to protect him?"

"I know, it's silly. I mean, what can I do? Besides, he hired a man to replace Sal."

Abby lifted an eyebrow. She hadn't even thought about that eventuality, but of course it made sense.

"He's a wisp of a man named Guy Hastings. Compared to Sal—well, there is no comparison. He seems too full of himself for his own good. He's awful, always slinking around, but Victor says he comes highly recommended."

"Hmm, can't wait to meet him. Did—did Trish say anything else?" Meredith stiffened, and Abby locked eyes with her mother for long seconds.

Finally, Meredith nodded while wringing her hands. Her eyes changed as though she'd decided something momentous. "She mentioned a journal you destroyed. She said it implicated your father in a crime."

"Arson," Abby stated flatly. "He ordered Miles to burn down the Trask factory. He did it with two friends of his."

"Yes, that's what she said," Meredith said in a quiet voice.

Abby felt a strange relief wash over her. It felt good to share the burden of this knowledge with her mother. "So you know, too," she reached across the short distance separating them and their hands intertwined. "So do—do you know about . . ."

"Sal?" Her lips pursed and she nodded. Abby saw deep sadness in her mother's eyes and it brought out her own feelings. She couldn't keep the tears away. They leaned into one another and hugged and cried for long minutes.

When they finally parted, Abby wiped her tears away. Meredith's eyes were puffy and red and Abby knew she must look the same. Abby dabbed her eyes with a cloth and swiped at her runny nose.

She said, "I didn't destroy the journal. I lied to Trish to stop her from doing what she wanted to do."

"What? Oh my. That changes things. What do you plan on doing with it?"

"I gave it to Sal back in Sweetwater." She'd detailed Sal's arrival in Sweetwater and his newfound life with Cora and Beatrice in a letter to Meredith a few months earlier. It had been a therapeutic letter to write. It helped lessen some of her negative feelings toward him. Meredith had written how happy she was for him and wished him the best. Had she known about the arson when she wrote that? She supposed it didn't matter.

"Oh," Meredith said. She stared at her hands and concentrated on the new information.

Abby could see her mind working. Her mother would understand her decision better than anyone.

She finally looked up at Abby and smiled. "He's a good man, Abby. He'll do the right thing."

"I agonized over it. It could ruin so many lives, yours included."

She swished her hand. "Pshaw. Nonsense, I'll be fine."

"But what if they take away the business? What if they shut it down and put Father in jail? You'll be left with nothing."

"You underestimate me. Don't forget, your father married me out of love, but also because he saw an opportunity in my parent's wealth. It's how he started his business in the first place. Your grandparents, God rest their souls, didn't leave me with nothing—far from it."

Abby sighed in relief, both from knowing her mother would be alright no matter what happened and that she wasn't staying with Victor just for the lifestyle.

"I—I'd forgotten that. I had no idea they left you with such means."

"It's not something I've ever spoken about."

"Does Father know?"

"Not as far as I know. He thought it all went to your Uncle Garret. I saw no need to correct him. You know how men are. They have to be the bread-winners and all that tripe. He mentions sometimes how he could throw me out and I'd have to live on the street like an urchin. It confounds him when I don't react."

"I don't know how I'm going to face Father tonight," Abby said absently.

"You won't have to. He's on a business trip. He's thinking of opening up another factory on the east side of the state. He won't be back for a few days. You'll be gone by then."

Abby felt relief and guilt all at the same time. "How do you do it every day? Doesn't it tear you up knowing he's a criminal?"

"Honestly, I've come to terms with it. I'm just thankful no one got hurt."

"I don't know if I could be in the same room with him without telling him how I feel."

Meredith pondered that for a moment. "It might be good for him to know that you know. Maybe it would be better for him if he had to face it. His daughter's wrath might knock some sense into him." Meredith checked the wall clock. "You'll stay for dinner."

It was still morning. "I will, but first I'd like to go downtown. Care to join me?"

"I'd love to, but I have an appointment. I'm sorry, but I've already committed and they're expecting me."

"I understand. I'll be back for dinner."

"I'll have Mr. Hanniger drive you."

"No need. They assigned Private Connor to me as long as I'm here."

They said their goodbyes and left the room. Neither of them saw the lithe figure of Guy Hastings standing in the dark corner as they passed.

ABBY SLID into the front seat of the army green sedan. Lou Connor had crumbs on the side of his mouth and a broad smile. "Where to, ma'am?"

"Take me to Third Street. I want to see my old apartment and maybe an old friend."

"Third Street? That's a rough area."

"It was all my husband and I could afford when we first married." He gave her a quizzical look but she didn't want to explain it to him. She already had too much bouncing around in her head. He drove without the constant talking this time, as though he understood intuitively that she had too much to think about—or perhaps he was too busy thinking about Melody.

Twenty minutes later, they neared her old apartment. "Slow down." She pointed, "It's right there." It looked the same, but it still felt like a lifetime had passed since she and Clyde had lived and loved there.

He glanced at it but didn't make a comment. He obviously wasn't impressed.

She sat back and gazed at the people on the sidewalk, hoping to glimpse Trish, but it would be a miracle to spot her. She could be anywhere. They drove a few more blocks until they came to Trish's block.

"Pull over here a minute. My friend lives down there," she pointed at a set of dingy stairs leading into darkness.

He braked and the sedan lurched to a stop. He eyeballed the area skeptically. "You want me to escort you? I've got a sidearm." He touched the butt of the holstered service pistol strapped to his waist. She hadn't noticed it before.

"Goodness, no. I'll be fine. She might not even live here anymore."

"I hope you're right," he muttered under his breath.

She left the sedan and Private Connor at the edge of the sidewalk. She pulled her light coat tighter around her collar. She wasn't used to Seattle's wet climate anymore. It wasn't raining, and it was rather springlike, but still chilly.

She hesitated at the stairs. She glanced to either side then descended them, being careful not to slip on the heavy moss. She looked for some nameplate that might tell her if Trish still lived here, but there was nothing but a blank door in need of new paint.

She knocked and listened for any response. She stared at the tiny peephole, but condensation had settled inside, making it next to useless.

She heard a voice. "Who's there?"

She smiled despite not knowing how she'd be received, but she recognized that voice.

"It—It's me, Abby. Is that you, Trish?"

The door suddenly flung open and Abby stared down the barrel of a pistol. She threw her hands up as though being mugged.

"Bullshit!" Trish blurted. "Abby's off winning the war."

Abby kept one hand up but pulled the coat lapels away from her face with the other. "Trish, it's me!"

The barrel never wavered, but Trish peered around her, as though looking for anyone hiding behind her. "You alone?"

"Of course I'm alone. Who else would I have with me?"

"Whaddya want?"

"Could you put the gun down, please? I can't talk with a gun pointed at my face."

Trish reluctantly lowered the pistol, but she didn't put it away. The light she'd been blocking with her gun hand lit up Trish's face. Abby took in a sharp breath when she saw the two ugly black eyes.

"Oh my God, Trish. What happened?"

Trish waved it off as though it didn't mean a thing. "It looks worse than it is. Happened weeks ago. It's just not healed yet."

"Is that why you answer your door holding a gun?"

Trish didn't answer, but motioned. "Have a seat. I don't know why you're here, but I've got a feeling you're gonna tell me, so lay it on me."

Abby didn't expect a welcoming party, but she at least expected some kind of warmth. After all, they were friends. "You look good, Trish. I mean, besides the black eyes."

"Blah, blah, blah. Why are you here? I know you like to sit and chat, but I ain't got time for it, so spill it."

"I just flew in. I'm—I'm a pilot now. A WASP."

"And I'm a bumblebee, so what?"

This wasn't the way she'd hoped this would go. She didn't know how it would go, but she didn't expect this kind of treatment. "Aren't you even a little interested in . . ."

"No, I'm not. I've got a lot going on at the moment, so for the last time, what are you doing here?"

"I didn't burn Miles's journal," she said it softly, but it stopped Trish's coming tirade before it ever started. "I still have it, or at least I did."

Trish sat down heavily on the nearest chair. It creaked and Abby thought it might collapse. Trish just stared at her in disbelief.

She raised the .38 and aimed it at Abby's face, her own face losing any semblance of goodwill. "Give it to me, now."

Abby reared back, but the seat back kept her in place. "I—I don't have it with me. I gave it to someone."

"Who?"

She wanted to protest the gun in her face, but she blurted, "Sal."

"Sarducci?" She tightened her grip on the pistol and Abby could see her finger touch the trigger. "He'll just give it to his boss, your father. Why didn't you give it to me?"

She shook her head emphatically. "No, no. Sal left the business. He doesn't work for my father anymore. He's in Texas, with Beatrice and Cora," she blurted.

"Who the hell's Beatrice and Cora, and what's he doing in Texas?"

"It's a long story. She's my friend and Cora's their—or I mean *her* daughter. She's just a baby and she's the most adorable . . ."

"Stop!"

Abby bit back her words and nearly choked on her own spit.

"Why are you telling me this? The journal's probably already in the incinerator." She lowered the pistol and threw it on the table with a loud bang. Abby cringed, glad the pistol hadn't accidentally fired. "Relax, it's not loaded. Ammo's scarce these days."

"It's not in the incinerator . . . or at least, I don't think it is."

"You shoulda brought it to me. All my troubles would be over." She indicated her two black eyes.

"Who did that to you?"

"Trambolini's boys."

The name brought nightmare scenes of men with Tommy submachine guns, blasting shotgun blasts, and blood and gore. She hadn't thought about the incident at the poker club in months. Learning to fly had taken every ounce of her concentration. She wished it had stayed that way.

"What? Why?"

"'Cause that's who I was working for. That's why I had the factory job, to get close enough to get dirt on your daddy. I already told you all this at the funeral."

Abby remembered, but she was still confused. "They beat you up because you didn't produce the journal? That was almost a year ago. Why are they still beating you up?"

"Because I owe them money. They gave me half my fee upfront and since I didn't produce the journal, they want the money back, but I already spent most of it. They keep reminding me," she indicated her face.

"How much?"

"Three grand," she said in a low voice. She felt her front shirt pocket, then the next one. "You got any cigarettes?"

"No. I don't smoke anymore."

"Lucky you."

"You want me to ask my father? He'd do it if he thought the money was for me." She kept her mother out of it.

Trish looked as though she might be sick. "God, no! Are you crazy? I'd rather die than be grateful to that asshole. Sorry, I know he's your father and all, but he's still an asshole."

The comment sounded like the old Trish she knew, and it made her feel a little better. "Well, if you don't do something, you may end up dead."

"Nah, I have a new employer now. They'll take care of me."

"Doesn't look like they are. Who is it?" She wasn't sure she wanted to know any more about Trish's life, but she couldn't take the question back.

"I can't tell you, but you know 'em. They're after the same thing the Trambolinis are, but just want different outcomes."

Abby's head spun. She'd only been back in Seattle a matter of hours and already she was being mired in filth and she hadn't even seen her father yet.

"I don't wanna know." But she couldn't help asking, "Trask?"

Trish pointed her finger shaped like a gun and lowered the hammer of her thumb. "Give the woman a prize."

She changed the subject back to the journal. "He'd be mighty grateful to get his hands on the journal. It woulda been so easy if you'd just brought it with ya. Like I said, all my troubles would melt away, just like that," she snapped her fingers.

"You got yourself in this pickle. Don't blame me."

Trish sneered at her and said, "Where'd you say Sal is in Texas?"

"I didn't. What, are you gonna send someone to get it?"

"It's just a train ride away." She placed her hand on the gun and spun it.

"Are you threatening me with an empty pistol?"

"Works well as a bludgeon, too," she said with a wink, but her eyes had gone cold—almost unrecognizable.

Abby struggled to keep the fear from overtaking her. She'd met danger head-on in the skies, but this was different. This was out of her control. Would her old friend really torture her for Sal's address? A cold spike grew in her belly as she thought about Beatrice holding little Cora. The anger grew in her belly. Trish had always intimidated her, but that was before. She thought she'd risen above this kind of fear.

"I was wrong. You *have* changed and not for the better."

Trish leaned forward, leaving the pistol spinning on the table. "Tell you what, why don't you get back in your little aeroplane and bring me back the journal? Then we can part ways and never see each other again."

"I think you said the same thing the last time I saw you."

"It's still good advice."

Abby stood abruptly. She'd been through too much to be bullied by Trish Watkins. "I came here to tell you that Sal will do the right thing with the journal. I think my father will pay for his crimes and you'll get some justice for Miles's death, but you don't really care about any of that. You only care about getting paid. Do you even care about Miles?"

Trish leaped to her feet and held her arms straight down her sides with her fists clenched. Her hat fell off and Abby saw the ugly scarring from the same fiery explosion that had taken Miles's life.

"How dare you preach to me. You have no idea what it's like for me! No idea! If I want to survive—if I don't want to become some floozy for the Trambolinis, I have to worry about being paid. I don't have a choice! You're on some high-horse bullshit. Did you read the fucking journal? Sal would go down, too. You really think he'll 'do the right thing?' Jesus, Joseph, and Mary, when are you going to grow up?"

"It was a mistake coming here." She stood abruptly, not liking where this conversation was headed.

She turned to leave, but Trish launched into her back and slammed her into the door with a loud bang. They both crumpled to the floor, grappling. Trish was smaller than Abby, but she'd been around the block more than once and knew how to fight. But Abby had gained weight in WASP training, mostly muscle from the daily physical fitness regimen, and the male instructors—mostly army sergeants—taught them how to defend themselves as part of their daily routine.

Abby broke free, spun, and before she knew what she was doing, she dropped her elbow into Trish's back. Trish cried out, but Abby didn't stop. She stepped behind her prone body, straddled her, and punched her in the back of the head with a quick jab from her right fist. Trish's head smacked the floor and all the fight went out of her.

Abby stood over her, breathing hard but ready to punch her again. She felt as though someone else had taken over her body. Reality came rushing back and she nearly vomited when she didn't see Trish moving. Had she hit her too hard? Had she killed her?

She stepped to one side and kneeled. She shook her. "Trish, Trish! Oh my God, Trish are you alright?"

Trish suddenly came back to life in a torrent of flying fists, kicks, and curses. Abby shot backward and tripped over the ottoman. She fell hard and the low coffee table went flying into the wall with another loud crash. Trish came at her. In the low light, her eyes seemed to be tiny flames, as though a devil possessed her. She had her fists clenched and blood dripped from a cut on her forehead. Combined with the raccoon eyes, she looked like a crazed death clown.

The door suddenly burst open behind her, letting a beam of daylight through. The silhouette of a man holding a pistol with two hands filled the door space. "Freeze!" Private Lou Connor yelled.

Trish stopped and faced the gunman. She couldn't see any better than Abby and must've assumed the Trambolinis had finally come to take her life, because after a moment's hesitation, she went for the gun illuminated by the beam of sunlight still resting on the dining table.

Private Connor tracked her. "I said freeze!" but she kept right on going. She clutched the .38 and brought it around. The roar in the confines of the small apartment took Abby's hearing and she only heard ringing and Private Connor's distant anguished yells.

Trish fell headlong onto the table. The empty .38 flew out of her hand and into the air, then thumped into Private Connor's chest. But he kept his weapon squarely trained on the heap lying on the floor.

Abby saw Trish's motionless body, and she screamed, "Trish! No!"

18

Northern Philippines
March 1944

Frank Cooper felt ridiculous. He led a mixed group of Filipinos along a trail near where they'd first landed on the little island the month before. The Filipinos ranged in age anywhere from nine years old to one hundred and nine years old—he couldn't really tell. The older ones looked much older than they probably were and the young ones were just kids. He concentrated on the ones in their twenties and thirties. They'd be the ones doing the fighting when it finally happened—if it happened.

The young men held rifles, a mix of Lee Enfields and Springfields, which looked like they'd seen service in World War I. They were loaded, but only with one round in the chamber. The Japanese were on the bigger island across the strait, not here, so they didn't expect real trouble. The others carried spears and a few of the children had bows and arrows, but they looked like toys rather than real weapons.

The evening light shone through the leaves and turned the landscape a warm, greenish hue. He came to a bend in the trail. He held up his hand for the formation to stop. They did, but not all at once, and a few men bumped into each other. The children grinned and a few couldn't keep from laughing. This was all fun and games for them.

Valentine Gustav kneeled beside Frank and Frank whispered, "Tell them I think the ambushers are straight ahead. See how the trail straightens out after the bend and there's good cover on either side? Perfect ambush setup. The enemy would have clear fields of fire and an easy escape route."

Gustav nodded his understanding and raised his voice a little so the knot of young men could hear. Despite the grinning children and the bored-looking elders, the young men took it seriously. They listened intently and noted the area of interest.

The most intense warrior of the group, the designated squad leader named Antonio, spoke, and Gustav passed it along.

"He says he will sneak around them and attack from behind."

Frank shook his head. "You don't want to commit your whole squad yet. Send one man to check it out."

Antonio listened to Gustav and spoke. Gustav translated. "He understands and he will check it out."

Frank shook his head. "He's the squad leader. Send someone else, so they still have a leader if he gets himself killed."

Antonio looked crestfallen as he listened to Gustav's translation, but he pointed at the nearest man and spoke curtly. The Filipino nodded and slowly moved along the trail's edge.

"Tell them to spread out and be ready to fight. Keep close enough to see one another. But remind them it's not the real thing. No firing."

Gustav passed the information along, and the group spread out into the jungle. The children never stopped smiling and the old men simply stood by and leaned on their spears, watching the charade with mild interest. Frank decided he wouldn't bring such a large group next time—just the fighting-age men. The others were too much of a distraction.

Frank watched the young man slowly working his way along the trail. He held his rifle at port arms, but they had strict instructions to keep their fingers on the trigger guard and not on the trigger. The last thing they needed was a friendly fire incident.

The limited ammunition didn't allow for much target practice. Each fighting-age man had practiced firing through one clip of ammunition, so they could practice not only shooting, but reloading. When one weapon jammed, everyone gathered around so they could demonstrate how to clear the jam. Frank felt like it was a shoestring operation at best.

When the scout made it halfway down the trail, he suddenly stopped and aimed his rifle. Frank nearly shouted, wanting to remind him that this wasn't the real thing, but before he could, six men yelled and jumped out from the cover with their rifles aimed at the scout's back.

Grinning Bear burst from cover and Frank had never seen him so mad. He fumed, spouting curses and waving his arms. The Filipinos cowered at his antics as he continued to color the air blue with combinations of curses that Frank would never have thought of in a million years. He pointed up the trail toward Frank's position.

Frank stood and waved. The rest of his squad rose, too, and waved their rifles in the air. The message was obvious. We could've killed you if it was the real thing.

Antonio glanced at Frank as if asking permission to rub it in a little. Frank nodded and Antonio and the others descended the path waving their rifles haphazardly and taunting their would-be ambushers. The children ran in circles, war whooping and having the time of their lives. The elders shook their heads and murmured among themselves.

Grinning Bear finally ran out of taunts and joined Gustav and Frank. "Christ almighty, how the hell are we gonna fight the Nips with this bunch?"

Frank added, "I don't know if they'll ever be ready."

Gustav rubbed his chin. "I think they need a real mission. This is play. They need real."

"But look at 'em. It's all a big joke to them," Frank said.

"No, our island is far north in the chain, but we are still part of the Philippines. They know what happened on Luzon. They know how to fight. Training is like a game to them. It is difficult to explain, but they will take a real fight seriously."

Grinning Bear said, "Well, I guess there's only one way to find out."

"A mission?" Gustav asked.

"I think it's time to have your network of informers on the main island give us a target. The first one should be relatively easy."

"Easy?"

"Well, yeah. Like cutting a communication line, or cutting fuel lines on trucks, that sort of thing."

"Sabotage," Gustav said.

"Yeah, we'll start with that and go from there."

Gustav left to tell the others. Frank asked, "You think they're ready? You think they'll rise to the occasion?"

"This whole thing's crazy. Right now, they're in a perfect position to gather intelligence and send it along to whoever's listening on the other side. The Nips are oblivious. As soon as we start killing troops, that'll change everything."

"I agree. But that's what HQ wants. They must be getting closer."

Grinning Bear shook his head. "I don't know. Gustav knows the situation and he says they're still thousands of miles away. Why're they having us expose ourselves? The Nips'll sweep the island and make it rough on the locals. If it gets bad enough, they'll sweep our little island, too."

Frank didn't like it either. He wished they'd just send a submarine and get them off this hunk of rock—but he also felt excited to finally hit back. They'd been taking abuse for ages, and it would be nice to dole out some payback. But he understood what that meant for the locals. As soon as the Japanese suspected a resistance movement, they'd crack down in their customarily brutal way, and they wouldn't limit their punishment to the actual resistance fighters. Every civilian would be affected.

"We could just ignore the orders," Frank said. Grinning Bear gave him a sideways glance and Frank quickly added, "They don't know the situation out here. Hell, we barely do ourselves. This could unleash a bloodbath for the locals."

Ignoring orders wasn't something he'd ever considered before, but it felt different out there. They weren't a part of a normal unit. They were now —effectively—a guerrilla unit, operating far behind enemy lines. Taking orders from regular army chumps stationed back at some cushy base with air-conditioning and mosquito nets over their racks didn't sit well. Who were they to dictate how they operated?

To Frank's surprise, instead of giving him a lecture about the chain of command and where they sat in it, Grinning Bear said, "Let's do the sabotage and see how it goes. No killing—not yet."

"Okay, agreed. That way at least we can tell command we're doing something and it might not lead to civilian deaths."

"Exactly."

A WEEK LATER, Frank huddled in the darkness near the edge of the strait on the main island, trying to catch his breath. It was his first time across the strait, and he found the experience harrowing.

A significant current whipped through the strait. It was only a half mile across, but they had to paddle hard and keep an angle into the current to keep from being pushed out into open sea. If that happened, they'd have to deal with breakers crashing into cliff faces to land on the main island. He had no doubt the small outrigger canoes would be smashed to pieces along with their bodies.

Five other outriggers beached nearby. They carefully pulled them into the jungle and did their best to hide them. They erased their tracks in the sand, but the wind that sliced through the straits would do most of that work for them.

Frank clutched his Springfield rifle. It was a reliable weapon that he was intimately familiar with. He would've liked to have fired a few more rounds through it, but he'd zeroed it as best he could with the limited ammo and he felt confident he could drop any target within range in good conditions. But that wasn't the mission.

He spotted Grinning Bear trotting up the edge of the beach toward him. He was a dark silhouette, but Frank would recognize his lope anywhere. He and Grinning Bear would lead their two half squads of men, a total of twelve men, to the target: a cluster of parked trucks on the outskirts of a small town with enemy troops garrisoned inside.

Neil stayed back with the radio. He'd had some radio training before the war broke out and he served their needs much better doing that job.

He'd been forced into combat on Corregidor, but he was a clerk. He didn't protest the decision.

Gustav insisted on coming along, even though Frank and Grinning Bear didn't think it was a good idea. The Japanese would invent a national holiday of celebration at the intelligence boon they'd receive if they captured him, but he wouldn't be dissuaded. He promised he'd stay out of the way and would die before being taken captive.

They moved into the jungle. The stars had provided some light as they crossed the strait, but now the darkness enveloped them like a wet blanket. It took a moment for Frank's eyes to adjust. The world appeared as dark blobs interspersed with brief bits of clarity.

He was pleased that they made almost no sound as they passed through the jungle, and there were no smiles or banter—just serious game faces. The bit of charcoal he'd streaked on his face itched, but he resisted the urge to scratch.

He felt a thrill as he realized he was finally on the offensive. He hadn't patrolled like this in years, but it came back to him as though he'd been born to it. Years of captivity and deprivation hadn't blunted his edge too much. He still wasn't back to his normal fighting weight—he doubted he ever would—but he felt good.

They came to a road and the group stopped and hunkered. Somewhere out there, their contact waited to guide them into the truck park. This was the most dangerous part of the operation. If their Filipino contact was working with the Japanese, they'd all be captured and most likely tortured or simply shot. Gustav assured them that the contact was trustworthy, but you never really knew.

He strained to see anything in the gloom. The edge of the jungle pushed right up against the road. The Japanese had obviously improved the road, but it still had large potholes and puddles from the occasional rain showers. There was no traffic at this hour.

A warbling whistle came from down the line. It mimicked a common night bird and was a decent rendition, but he doubted it would fool an alert enemy soldier. An answering warble came from across the road, almost directly in front of Frank's position.

He leveled his muzzle at the sound and placed his finger beside the trigger. This particular Springfield had a relatively heavy trigger pull, but he didn't want to take any chances with an accidental discharge. He hoped the Filipinos did likewise.

A shape emerged from cover. To Frank, it appeared as though the jungle came alive. One moment nothing, the next a smiling Filipino appeared and waved. He doubted he could see them any better than they could see him. Frank rose slowly, Gustav right beside him.

Gustav whispered something and the contact hustled across the road and stood in front of them. He was significantly shorter than Frank and Gustav. He shook Gustav's hand as though old friends.

They exchanged words, and Gustav relayed. "This is Mandio. He says we should follow him. There are no enemies between here and the trucks."

"Okay," Frank whispered back. "Move out." He waved his hand and the rest of the squad broke from cover and crossed the road quickly. Frank was happy to see a few hold back and cover their advance. Grinning Bear would be with them, he supposed.

The jungle opened up the closer they got to the town. More and more pathways crisscrossed the area and there were signs of habitation all around, including a few dilapidated houses and sheds, but no light emanated from the bare windows. They looked abandoned.

They moved steadily and didn't see any signs of the enemy. They finally came to another road. This one was in much better shape. The squad hunkered and spread out. Frank felt pride seeing them taking defensive positions. They hadn't had a lot of training time, but they seemed to have absorbed the lessons. So far, Gustav had been correct about them: they were taking the real thing seriously.

Mandio whispered to Gustav and pointed. Gustav leaned close to Frank's ear. "The truck park is just ahead. It is unguarded."

Frank felt a pit in his stomach. This was it. He pointed at Antonio, the ranking Filipino. He'd earned the rank because he seemed the most serious and the others respected him.

Antonio hustled over and hunkered beside him. "Send two men to search the area for any guards."

Before translating for him, Gustav said, "Mandio says there are no guards."

Frank wanted to throttle him, but he gulped back his anger. "Just tell him. We do this my way." Gustav relayed the message, and Antonio sent two men forward.

As they disappeared into the gloom, Frank wracked his brain for anything he might've missed. He was a corporal, so used to leading a team of a squad, but it had been a long time and he didn't have a squad leader sergeant to rely on.

The minutes ticked by slowly. He didn't like how long it was taking. He signaled for Gustav and the others to stay put, then he moved along the edge of the road until he found Grinning Bear. He had planted himself directly in front of his section of Filipinos. Judging by their faces, they'd grown to respect the surly marine.

"I sent two men forward. They haven't come back yet."

"Trouble?"

"Mandio says there aren't any guards, but I think you and I should check it out."

Grinning Bear nodded. "Good idea."

Frank relayed his plan to Antonio via Gustav. He could see the agitation in Antonio's eyes, but he nodded and relayed the information to the others.

The pair crossed the road and followed it until they saw a turnout. A rickety gate stretched across the driveway and lines of silent trucks sat there like black blobs.

They hunkered near the gate and searched for the wayward scouts. They couldn't see to the far side. They were about to move forward when Frank sensed movement to their right. They both froze and waited.

Frank saw two figures emerge from around the corner. He guessed it was the scouts, but he couldn't be sure, so he watched them come closer. He shifted the muzzle of his rifle slightly.

The pair veered away from the truck park and headed straight toward the other Filipinos. It had to be the scouts.

Frank hissed, "Hey, over here."

Both men turned their way, leading with their rifles. Frank stood, showing himself fully. Their smiles shone through the darkness as they hustled to them and crouched. They spoke quickly, pointing and gesturing toward the trucks the whole time. When they saw the incomprehension, they tried to act it out. One of them finally said, "Jap," and he held up two fingers and pointed.

"Shit," Frank said.

"What're your orders, Corporal?" Grinning Bear asked.

He wanted to abort the whole thing, but he didn't feel it would go over too well with the Filipinos. They'd come all this way and they wanted something to show for their efforts. What would Mandio think? He'd spread the word that the resistance was a paper tiger. Would that be such a bad thing?

Frank touched the other Filipino's shoulder and pointed back to the main group. "Go," he said. To the other, he pointed to the truck park and pointed to his own eyes, conveying that he wanted to see the guards. The Filipino nodded emphatically that he understood.

The first scout left them, and the second waved for them to follow. He led them around the edge of the truck park. It felt odd being so close to the enemy's equipment. He saw the red sun symbol clearly marked on the doors and hoods of the trucks. It sent a shiver of excitement up his spine, as well as a foreboding dread. These belonged to the enemy.

The Filipino slowed when they came near the end of the line of trucks. He pointed, then leaned into the side of the truck, allowing them to peer past him. Frank crept to the edge, then leaned out. He nearly choked. The sight seemed far too familiar and brought back horrid memories of guards and beatings. But no, this wasn't the POW camp. Here, he had the advantage.

The two guards sat on overturned fuel barrels. Between them, they'd tipped an old wooden spool carrier sideways to fashion a table. The low light of a lamp glowed and they seemed to be playing some sort of game. Their rifles leaned against a stack of fuel barrels some ten feet away. They clearly didn't expect any trouble.

They watched them for a few minutes. It wasn't clear if they were actually guarding the trucks or simply found a quiet place to play a game together. They barely looked up from their game. The lantern light would keep them blind.

Frank pulled back and so did Grinning Bear. Frank signaled for them to follow. He wound his way back through the trucks, his mind sifting through the different scenarios. He could easily kill the soldiers, but that might elicit a brutal response from the Japanese. If he was going to kill enemy soldiers, he wanted to do it in a more spectacular and impactful manner than two hapless guards, who might not be guards at all. But he couldn't scrap the mission, either.

By the time they returned to the main group, he had a plan. He gathered the men around. He could sense the tension seeping from each one of them.

Mandio had his head down, obviously ashamed about his misinformation. The Japanese had obviously shown up after he last checked, but that didn't seem to ease his shame.

He whispered to Gustav. "One team will watch the Japs while the rest work on the trucks furthest away from them. Keep noise to a minimum. Cut lines, slash tires, but be quiet. We'll kill the guards if we have to, but that's a worst-case scenario."

Gustav relayed the information, and Frank noticed the tension evaporate. Broad smiles replaced worried looks, and he knew he'd made the right decision. These men wanted to fight back as much as he did.

~

THEY TOOK their time getting into position. Frank kept his sights on the two guards. They continued to play their game. They occasionally talked and laughed and remained completely oblivious to anything outside their little sphere of light.

He strained to hear any noises from the others, but there was nothing. Grinning Bear led the team of saboteurs. They had knives and a few wire cutters. It would be too loud to open hoods, so they went from beneath, cutting and slashing anything that looked important.

An hour passed and he supposed the saboteurs must be nearing the end of the truck line. They'd have to leave the final two trucks intact for fear of the noise carrying to the enemy soldiers.

Frank cringed when the distinct smell of spilled gasoline wafted over him. The intensity increased and he hoped the Japanese wouldn't notice, but he thought they must.

Watching them had almost become boring, but now he worried. It was time to leave. This fleet of trucks would need serious work before they'd be operational again. They'd done enough for one night.

He signaled the nearby men to move back. They slunk away silently. Frank took a few steps and stepped into a puddle of gasoline. It was flowing like a small stream directly toward the guards. It shimmered and reflected the vibrant stars overhead. The smell burned his nose as he moved back. They'd notice the smell at any moment. They had to get out of there now.

He angled toward the trucks, where he still saw men working. He went to the front of the nearest one and saw Grinning Bear standing there with his rifle at the ready. He waved to get his attention.

Grinning Bear approached quietly and said, "We're almost done."

Frank shook his head and hissed, "We have to go now. The gasoline is flowing straight toward them. They can't help but notice. We've got minutes to get outta here."

"Shit," Grinning Bear hissed back. "Hadn't thought of that."

"Get 'em outta here."

"I'm on it."

He lunged away and soon men joined Frank in the retreat. He'd made it to the gate when he heard what he'd been dreading—yelling Japanese soldiers. At first, they sounded alarmed, then enraged. Had they seen them?

He turned and kept waving at men to keep moving. Perhaps they could still get out of there without being seen. But that fantasy ended with the crack of a rifle. The bullet whizzed past the gate and smacked into the road. A second shot, and he saw the muzzle flash at the end of the truck park. They must've seen someone. Another flash, much closer, drew his attention, but it wasn't the crack of a rifle.

In the flare from a lighter, he saw Grinning Bear's face. Grinning Bear yelled, "Fire in the hole," and chucked the burning lighter onto the river of gas.

"Oh shit," Frank yelled. "Run! Go! Go! Go!" He high-stepped his way across the road and kept right on going. The Filipinos darted all around him as they sprinted toward the safety of the beach and the outriggers. They hadn't planned on leaving the area so quickly, perhaps hanging around and scouting out more targets of opportunity, but that notion had come and gone.

He heard screaming from the truck park. He hoped it wasn't one of his men. He stopped and turned back. Against the black sky, he saw a growing glow. Tops of trees swayed side to side as they lit up with fire. A muted whump sound followed immediately by three more added to the conflagration.

He saw Grinning Bear come out of the darkness. He earned his name in that moment. He looked pleased as punch. Frank stood and Grinning Bear veered his direction.

"Christ almighty, Larry," Frank complained.

"Figured we needed a distraction," he said as he stopped to watch his handiwork.

"Well, so much for keeping a low profile. Let's get the hell outta here."

19

Frank's body ached and he needed sleep, but he knew he wouldn't be able to yet. Even though they'd been back for hours, he couldn't stop thinking about the botched raid. Looking around at the other raiders, he wasn't alone. Men paced back and forth around the crest of the hill beside the radio shack. The only man he didn't see was Grinning Bear. He could sleep no matter what. He rarely passed on an opportunity to do so. Frank couldn't take his eyes off the island across the straits.

They'd watched the glow from the fire die down as the sun rose, but even now they could see plumes of smoke rising in the distance. Frank finally sat down and tried to eat the offered food. His gut still felt like someone had tied knots, but he did his best to eat. More and more raiders slunk away to find their beds, but Frank lingered.

Neil sat down beside him. He looked at the smoke and gave a low whistle. "Well, so much for not making a big scene."

Neil had been helping the Filipinos with a spare radio on the other side of the island and hadn't seen the results of the raid yet.

Frank couldn't help chuckling. "Yeah, it didn't go quite as planned."

"They never do. Grinning Bear said no one was hurt, though, so that's good."

"I'm pretty sure the Japanese got hurt. I heard them screaming."

"Well, nobody important, I mean."

"Yeah, I guess so. Bad way to go, though."

"They woke me up when they saw the glow. I knew something wasn't quite right. Must've been an inferno if we could see it from here.

"It was. Looks like it might still be burning."

"You might be right. What do ya think they'll do about it? I mean, they're gonna be madder 'n hornets."

"I guess we'll find out soon enough, but I'm guessing they'll start working on the locals. That's worrisome. They might just round 'em up and start shooting until someone talks. I don't know how I'd ever live with myself."

Neil gave him a long look, then said, "It wouldn't be your fault. The Nips are the ones at fault."

"Yeah, but still."

"I don't know if you noticed, but these people are ready to fight back. The ones that woke me up were jumping around as though you'd single-handedly won the war. I can't understand a word, but they were downright giddy. They're not afraid. And another thing: they know better'n anyone that they're gonna have to fight like tigers to kick the Japs outta here, and people are gonna die." He let that sink in before he added, "Besides, Grinning Bear said they might not even know it was sabotage. The trucks probably burned to cinders. All that cutting and slashing you did won't be visible. All the evidence burned up."

Frank hadn't thought of that. He might be right. "But someone started the fire. And the guards fired off a few shots."

"I'm just spitballing, but Nip soldiers smoke almost as much as we do. One spark from a cigarette coulda set it off. They've got no reason to suspect sabotage. As far as the shots, Grinning Bear said it was only one or two. It coulda been missed that late at night."

Frank felt better, like a weight had been lifted. Maybe they'd get away with it scot-free. His eyes suddenly felt heavy. The worry had been keeping him from sleeping, but now he felt like he might fall asleep right there. His head fell onto his crossed arms and he closed his eyes.

Neil nudged him. "Come on. You'll be stiff as a board if you sleep like that."

Frank stumbled along, letting Neil lead him. He didn't remember lying down, and he slipped into a dreamless sleep.

It felt like only minutes had passed before he startled awake. He lay there for a moment, disoriented. Something had startled him into wakefulness, but he didn't know what. He heard voices nearby, excited or perhaps fearful voices.

He didn't remember how he'd gotten to his little thatch bed. The day had passed into evening, so he must've slept for at least a few hours. He desperately wanted more, but no, something was happening. Perhaps the Japanese were on the way.

He pawed for his rifle and found it lying nearby. He checked the breach and stumbled his way toward the racket. Bits of thatch dropped off the side of his face and he supposed he must look quite the mess.

He saw Valentine Gustav tromping from the radio shack. Unlike himself, Gustav looked as though he'd just stepped from a tailor shop with a freshly made suit—creases and all. He had no idea how he kept himself so clean.

"What's going on?"

Gustav turned to him and gave him a quick up and down. He always gave him the same—almost, but not quite disapproving—look. Frank supposed he should work on his appearance more.

"We have a visitor."

Frank's gut clenched, and he gripped his rifle tighter. "Japs?"

"Goodness, no. Constance, a woman from the town where the truck park used to be."

Frank let out a long breath and lowered his rifle. "Oh, thank God. I thought we were under attack."

"You must have faith in the network. We would have ample warning."

"I'm just a little on edge since the raid."

"Yes, well, Constance will have information for us, I'm sure."

Frank slung his rifle over his shoulder and followed Gustav down the hill a little way. Filipinos darted this way and that. Those that saw him smiled and a few even saluted as though he were an officer. He'd have to nip that in the bud quick.

A group had formed and he saw Grinning Bear and Neil sitting on stumps, facing a young woman. A strikingly beautiful Filipino woman that made him stare.

Gustav noticed his abrupt stop and his gawking stare. "That's Constance. She's quite the fraulein."

Frank shook his head as though clearing cobwebs. He ran his fingers through his greasy hair and tried to keep from staring. He strode into the group and stood next to Grinning Bear. Constance smiled at him and he suddenly didn't know where he should put his hands. He grinned back and she covered her mouth and snickered.

Frank blushed deeply. She was laughing at him. A few of the others were also snickering, and he felt he was the brunt of some unknown but cruel joke.

Grinning Bear stood and put a hand on his shoulder, sensing his growing unease and embarrassment. "Easy does it, pal. It's your face."

"What about my face?" He touched his cheeks as though he might have a leech attached.

"You've got thatch-face. Your cheek looks like a checkers board."

He rubbed his cheek, trying to make his skin forget the thatch weave pattern he'd fallen asleep upon.

He smiled at her and said, "Sorry 'bout that, I just woke up."

Gustav translated for her, and her grin widened. Frank realized she must think him the laziest man in the world, just waking up in the late afternoon, but he didn't try to explain himself.

Gustav spoke to her in quiet conversation for a few minutes. The other Filipinos listened in, too. Frank couldn't understand a word, so he waited and took her in. He thought she might be the most beautiful woman he'd ever seen.

His mind flashed to Bernice, the nurse from the POW camp. He hadn't thought of her in a while, and her image was hazy at best. Sometimes he thought he might have dreamed her in his state of malnourishment, but Constance wasn't a mirage. She was real.

"Easy, big fella," Grinning Bear said.

He was staring and he couldn't have been more obvious if he had his tongue hanging out. He pulled himself together and did his best not to gawk.

Gustav finally finished his conversation. It was difficult to judge what she'd said based on the other Filipinos, but it obviously wasn't horrible news or there would be more reaction.

Gustav waved the Americans over. Frank forced himself to let Grinning Bear and Neil go first.

Gustav introduced them and she smiled at each of them and shook their hands. Her hand felt warm in his hand, but she had hard callouses. She obviously worked with her hands.

In stilted English she said, "It nice to meet you."

"It's nice to meet you, too," Frank said too quickly.

Gustav said, "She has come from Tavista, the town next to the truck park. She says the whole town came out to watch the trucks burn. They are destroyed."

"Well, I guess that's something," Grinning Bear said.

"The Japanese came soon after the fire started. They forced them back into their homes. They tried to put the fire out, but they could not. She says parts still burn. The soldiers stayed nearby, making sure the fire didn't spread to the town. When they finally left, she came here."

Frank held his breath, waiting for the other shoe to drop. Surely there must've been some sort of reprisal, but Gustav stopped talking.

"That's it? That's all? Did they ask any questions? Interrogate anyone?"

Gustav relayed the question. She shrugged and spoke. "She says they met with the mayor and spoke for an hour. Then they gathered the remains of their soldiers and went back to their camp. She said they left a small group of men to watch the fire."

Frank cringed at the mention of the charred soldiers. They'd been guards, maybe just like the sadistic bastards that made their lives miserable back at Bilibib, but it was still a horrible way to die. He'd seen too many men burned alive on Bataan and later on Corregidor. Those that survived wanted to die.

"Holy shit, we got away with it," Frank marveled. He slapped Grinning Bear's back, but instead of looking relieved, he looked worried. Frank knew his looks and when he was worried, everyone should be worried. "What's wrong?" he asked with an edge of dread.

Grinning Bear stroked his chin. "Well, she says it's still burning, so they probably haven't gone in there and done a thorough check on things."

Frank thought he knew where he was going. "All the cut wiring, tubes, and slashed tires will be burned. Neil was right. They won't find anything incriminating." Grinning Bear squinted at him and it suddenly hit him. "Your lighter."

"A Zippo. I've seen those things survive worse fires than that—says U.S.M.C. right on it."

"Semper Fi," Neil added.

"Yep."

The joy and relief evaporated. The Filipinos didn't know what had been said, but they knew something was wrong. Constance's eyes darted from one to the other in confusion and growing concern.

Frank said, "We need to go back there tonight. They'll go to work in the morning." He turned on Constance and her eyes widened. "Ask her about the men they left. Are they guarding the sight? We need to know everything she can remember."

FRANK AND GRINNING BEAR sat near the beach with six other Filipinos, including Antonio and Constance, waiting for the sun to set so they could paddle across the straits. They had two boats this time, not including the small boat Constance had paddled across earlier. She'd travel across with them and come back for her boat later. She'd been sent by Mandio, her uncle. She wanted to get back to town before the next day, so she'd cross with them.

Frank couldn't help whispering, even though the enemy was far away and the Filipinos couldn't understand them. "We gotta be smart. Constance says the Nips are in town, but if they moved and there's even a chance of them seeing us, we gotta abort. They might not find the lighter, but if they see us, it's a guaranteed shit sandwich."

"I agree. We'll be careful."

The colors in the west turned a fiery red as the sun dipped lower toward the horizon. The wind always seemed to blow near the straits and this evening was no exception. Despite the warm air temperature, the wind made Frank shiver. He couldn't keep his eyes off Constance.

"You better stow that shit," Grinning Bear grumbled.

"Stow what shit?"

"You keep making eyes at Constance. Don't get attached."

"You're one to talk. You and that native gal back on the island . . ." he raised an eyebrow at him.

"I left her there, didn't I? And that was different. She wasn't living beside a Jap garrison." Frank rolled his eyes, but Grinning Bear added, "Sooner or later the Japs are gonna know about us, and when they do, they're gonna take it out on the locals. It's best not to get attached. You've gotta stay impartial."

"It's too late for that." He spread his hands to all the Filipinos lazing around watching the sunset. "I'm already partial to all of them. Constance is just one more civilian."

Grinning Bear raised a skeptical eyebrow. "Bullshit. Don't sleep with her."

Frank blushed. Here he was about to cross a dangerous strait to an occupied enemy island to extract a piece of damning evidence from beneath the enemy's noses and he was blushing like a freshman at the high-school dance.

His eyes glazed over as he glanced at her once again. The breeze blew her thick brown hair and she flicked it to keep it off her face. She plucked a strand from her mouth and caught him staring. She smiled and he nearly fell off the log.

Grinning Bear rolled his eyes. "Criminy sakes, get your head out of the clouds. Your life might depend on it." Frank hardly heard him—he was lost in that smile. Grinning Bear reached across, grabbed his shirt, and pulled him until their noses nearly touched. "My life depends on it, too," he hissed. Finally getting through, he released him and added, "Not to mention hers."

Frank gulped and shook his head as though he'd just woken from a dream. His eyes hardened. "I hear you, brother. I hear you."

He looked around at the darkening sky. The final tip of the sun sank into the sea and twilight shifted to darkness. "It's time to go."

"I don't like leaving this early in the evening."

"You heard Gustav and the others. They don't wander down to the straits, the current's no good for swimming."

"Yeah, I know, but I still don't like it."

"We need time to search. The lighter could be right where you tossed it or it coulda been blown anywhere."

The Filipinos watched the exchange, waiting for them to send them into motion. Gustav wasn't with them this time. He'd sent along Antonio's younger brother, Elarno. He spoke passable English and could translate if needed.

Grinning Bear said, "Okay, let's go."

Frank touched Elarno's shoulder, signaling to him it was time. Elarno raised his voice and gave the order. Antonio glared at his younger brother, and Frank wondered if it was a good idea to have brothers on the same force.

Elarno was two years younger than his much bigger brother, but he seemed to have a chip on his shoulder. His words had an immediate effect, though. They dragged the outrigger canoes from cover and hauled them to the shore, cutting deep creases into the beach sand. The remaining Filipinos would cover their tracks.

Frank shimmied into the nearest canoe and took up a paddle. He remembered how hard they had to paddle to make it across without losing too much ground the night before. He couldn't help notice Constance slipping in right behind him. She clutched a paddle, too, and held it like she knew how to use it.

Frank tried to ignore her, but he could smell her sweat and sensed her breath on the back of his neck. He fought the urge to turn and smile. Grinning Bear sat on the other boat, and Frank hoped he didn't notice.

The Filipinos on the beach angled the boats upstream and pushed them off. Without a word, they paddled, and Frank thrilled at the power as the canoe surged into the strait.

He was aware of Constance's steady breathing. He reminded himself to stay focused, but she made that difficult. The crossing seemed to take less time than before. The beach came up quickly and the two men in front hopped out just before to keep the canoe from completely beaching.

Frank replaced the paddle with his rifle and scanned. He saw nothing out of the ordinary, but it was dark enough that an entire regiment might wait for them and he wouldn't notice. He hopped out and felt the coolness of the water up to his shins. His sandals sank into the sand and he trudged onto the beach. Filipinos followed him and soon they made it to the edge of the jungle. They barely made a sound. The wind whipped the dry sand into his wet legs and it stuck there. He'd have to scrub it off once he was back at the other island. Something to look forward to. *But Constance won't be there.*

They approached the truck park along a slightly different path than before. It took longer, but even if the Japanese didn't suspect foul play and weren't waiting for them, it didn't sit right to retrace their exact steps. It was another good lesson for the Filipinos to learn. Never use the same path twice.

They stopped when they butted up to the edge of the road. Constance spoke to Antonio in a light whisper. Frank hadn't meant to, but he'd subconsciously kept her in sight. His ears perked up, trying to hear her, even though he wouldn't be able to understand her words.

Antonio gave her a brief hug, then called Elarno to his side with a wave. Frank felt an irrational jealousy sweep over him. Antonio spoke into Elarno's ear.

The younger brother scurried to Frank's side and said, "Constance, back home. Home," he repeated.

Frank understood. They'd talked about it before they'd left Gustav's camp. She wasn't a part of the resistance, at least not in the way Antonio and the others were. She needed to be back home before anyone noticed her absence. If this operation went south and she wasn't where she was supposed to be, the Japanese couldn't help but suspect her. There were also a few townsfolk who'd thrown their hats into the ring with the Japanese, and they were likely more dangerous than the Japanese themselves. They called them Makapili. She had to be careful.

Constance stalked her way to his side. She touched his arm and he felt as though he'd been electrocuted, but in a good way. "Goodbye," she said carefully.

"Goodbye," he said back. He patted her shoulder as though he were a teacher giving kudos to a student who'd recited the alphabet correctly. He felt himself flush with embarrassment and he was glad for the darkness. She flashed a smile, then moved into the darkness.

Frank watched her shadowy shape until it became one with the darkness. He looked toward Grinning Bear, who watched him with dark eyes.

Frank flushed with anger, remembering the marine's words about pulling his head out of his own ass. *Pull it together, Cooper.* "Alright, let's go," he whispered.

Their smaller size allowed them to move more easily than the night before. They followed the edge of the road toward the truck park. The fires must've gone out because the sky didn't have a glow. As they got closer, the smell of charred metal and wood filled the air.

The sound of an engine made them stop and crouch. It was still early evening, so it wasn't unusual for there to be traffic. Headlights lit up the road and jungle shadows danced, grew, and shrank as the light swept over and through.

Frank hugged the ground, even though he knew they'd be invisible to anyone in the car. He shut his eyes to preserve his vision as the beams sliced through the night. Whoever it was, they weren't worried about being bombed or strafed.

He raised his head as the vehicle passed and he saw it was small, like a jeep. He glimpsed three Japanese. He only got a brief look, but he thought the man in back must be an officer. His blood rushed to his ears and he had the absurd impression that perhaps they steamed.

He glanced at the others nearby. Even in the darkness, he saw their smiles. Being so close to the enemy and remaining undetected made for a thrilling night. Worry accosted him as he thought about Constance. Surely, she found cover in time.

He signaled for them to continue forward. He could feel their excitement. Every second out here, they gained more confidence. He hoped it wouldn't go to their heads. If they didn't find the Zippo and the Japanese did, they'd need to keep their discipline. He respected their skills and discipline so far, but they hadn't been tested yet. Once the bullets flew and lead met meat, all that confidence might vanish in an instant. They were civilians, after all.

They finally made it to the truck park. It felt eerie seeing the destruction they'd wrought. The trucks still sat there in the darkness, but they'd been transformed. The dim light from the stars showed a scene of desolation. Some trucks still smoked. The tires had burned, so they sat on their scorched rims. Every shred of fabric had burned to cinders, making them look skeletal. The ground they stood on just outside where the gate used to be was scorched and puffs of ash floated up with every step. Frank had to stifle a cough.

Frank signaled for them to stay put. He found Grinning Bear and pulled him away from the others. "It's no good. The ash has covered everything. We'll never find the lighter."

Grinning Bear scowled and kicked at the ground as though to prove or disprove his theory. Great puffs of ash rose and covered his feet. "Worse, they'll see our tracks in the morning. Even if we tried to cover them up . . . I don't think it'd work. It's like walking in snow."

"Well, the good news is, they won't likely find the lighter. It's buried in six inches of ash."

"Unless they step on it," Grinning Bear said.

"It's a chance we'll have to take."

Grinning Bear clutched his shoulder. "I'll go in. One set of sandal prints won't cause a fuss and the wind might cover them up by morning. I know right where I threw that thing."

Frank chewed his lower lip. He was the ranking man. They'd both agreed on that, but it was still Grinning Bear. They'd been through too much to simply discount one another's suggestions.

"It was my mistake. I'll fix it."

"You know I don't blame you for anything. No one does." Grinning Bear continued to stare at him, waiting for his decision. "Let's make sure there aren't any Japs nearby. If not, you've got ten minutes, but I'm going with you. Two sets of prints won't make a difference." Grinning Bear gave him one of his rare smiles.

Frank passed along the plan to the others. He sent them out in two groups to search for any enemy soldiers. Antonio returned after ten minutes. He had his brother in tow.

Elarno said, "Antonio says, no Nips" He shook his head emphatically to help get his point across.

"Good man," Frank said. "Keep watch," he mimicked, watching by placing his hand over his brow and looking side to side. "Watch for Nips."

Elarno's relayed it to his brother. Antonio smacked the back of Elarno's head. He'd obviously understood what Frank meant and didn't need the translation. Elarno glared and rubbed the back of his head.

Frank and Grinning Bear watched them move off into the darkness alongside the road. Grinning Bear said, "That's brothers for ya."

"Let's get this over with."

The gate that had marked the front of the truck park the day before had burned. The only evidence it had ever been there was a bit of twisted wire. Frank carefully stepped around it. Ash puffed with every step. He stopped at the front of the first truck. He crouched and held his rifle at the ready. He didn't see any sign of life, only burnt ground and smoldering trucks. The burnt smell was overwhelming and heat still radiated from the metal.

Grinning Bear kept moving deeper into the carnage. He stopped several times, obviously trying to get his bearings. Nothing looked the same. He'd been at the second truck when he threw the lighter.

Frank watched him crouch and sift through the ash. The darkness combined with the deep ash made the chore seem impossible. He doubted ten men could find it in the light of day with rakes. This was a waste of time and an unwarranted risk. If the Japanese jeep came back and pulled into the park, they'd be spotted immediately. He bit his tongue, though. He told him he'd give him ten minutes and he would.

When he figured ten minutes had passed, he waved, trying to get Grinning Bear's attention, but he kept right on sifting through the ash. Frank took a few steps. His legs must be covered in a layer of sand and ash, which would be difficult to remove. He looked forward to a swim once they were safely across the strait.

He froze when a shot rang out from the direction of town. The night birds and insects stopped for an instant, then resumed. Grinning Bear's eyes were wide as he looked at Frank.

Another shot came from the same vicinity. It was too far away to be Antonio and the others—at least, he hoped so. Perhaps a civilian was chasing off some apex predator. He suddenly worried about Constance.

"Forget the lighter. We gotta move."

He hustled back the way they'd come, not worrying about footprints. He heard Grinning Bear right behind him. They ran past the burnt gate and searched for the others, but they weren't in sight. He supposed that was a good thing.

A sudden flurry of shots rang out and he heard yelling. He didn't know if it was Filipino or Japanese, but it was harried. He sprinted toward town, hoping he'd stumble upon his men.

When he didn't find them where he expected to, his worry and anger vied for supremacy. Had they gone into town? Why would they do such a thing?

More shots rang out and muzzle flashes sparked in the night.

"The stupid sons of bitches are shooting it out with the Japs," he hissed to Grinning Bear.

"Seems that way," he answered in his laconic way.

Frank checked his breech. He'd loaded the Springfield before they'd left the small island, but he checked out of habit. He exchanged a nod with Grinning Bear. They spread out and hustled along toward the firefight. As they approached, dark figures lined either side of the road. Occasionally, one would stand and fire a shot. It was met with instant return fire from town.

They veered toward the Filipinos on the right side. A stray bullet whizzed down the road. Frank hadn't felt the sensation since Corregidor and he didn't relish the memory. He ran faster.

He slid in behind a shadowy figure. He smacked him in the back and barked, "What the hell's going on here?"

The Filipino jumped. Relief replaced fear when the Filipino recognized him. He jabbered words Frank couldn't understand. Frank shook his head and said, "Stop! Cease fire. Move back, now." But the Filipino didn't understand him. "Elarno! Where's Elarno?" he asked in desperation.

"Elarno?" He pointed forward.

He pushed through the underbrush, trying to get to his interpreter.

More gunfire crashed as the Filipinos took potshots. Bullets whined and whizzed back at them. He wanted to scream at them to stop, but it might just egg them on to keep shooting. He hoped the townspeople weren't being peppered with stray bullets.

"Elarno!" he yelled.

Elarno stepped out from the brush. His eyes were wide and he looked ready to bolt.

"Where's Antonio? Antonio!"

Elarno pointed toward town. "Antonio. He go."

Grinning Bear growled his frustration. He yanked men out of the brush and pulled them back, forming a growing cadre of scared Filipinos. He made them stay put with his burning eyes and hand signals.

"I've got five men here. Antonio must have the other five with him."

Muzzle flashes further up the road, pinpointed their location. "That's gotta be him," Frank said, and took a step in that direction.

Grinning Bear stopped him. "I'll go."

Frank wanted to argue, but it was the right call. "Okay. I'll take these guys back to the truck park. We'll wait for you there."

"Roger that."

Frank pushed and shoved the five Filipinos until they understood what he wanted them to do, then he ran ahead, waving for them to follow. They did so willingly, almost sprinting to get away from the firefight.

He stopped at the burned gate. He hunched and thought about his options. They were too exposed, so he crossed the street and sank into the thick jungle across from the truck park. The others gathered around him like scared children after hearing a ghost story.

He pushed and shoved them. "Spread out, dammit!" They finally complied, but their eyes darted side to side as though expecting to die at any moment.

The firing subsided and finally stopped. Grinning Bear had obviously gotten some control of the situation. He expected to see him trotting down the road at any moment. He strained to see them coming. Shapes finally emerged through the gloom. Grinning Bear had them running straight down the middle of the street, taking the fastest route out of there.

In the gloom, he did a count and thought he counted everyone. No one appeared to limp or carry anyone along. Perhaps they'd get out of this with nothing hurt but their pride.

His hopes were dashed when he heard the unmistakable sound of a whining engine. He turned and only had a moment before the jeep careened around the corner. The headlights flooded the road and Grinning Bear and his Filipinos ground to a halt like the proverbial deer in the headlights.

The jeep skidded to a stop only yards from Frank and his band. The passenger side door and the driver's door opened and the two soldiers stepped out. The passenger had a submachine gun. He quickly propped it on top of the door and took aim.

Frank stood, his rifle at his shoulder. He aimed over the top of the jeep and found the soldier's head. He couldn't miss at this range. He pulled the trigger and the soldier's head snapped to the side and he dropped out of sight. The driver's eyes grew to plate size as he saw Frank work the bolt action. The Filipinos fired and the driver crumpled from multiple impacts. He heard screams from the officer in the back, but they silenced him with a shot to the head.

Frank kept his rifle at his shoulder and marched out of the jungle. He walked through the headlights over to the man he'd killed. The soldier lay in a pool of expanding blood.

Through his ringing ears, he heard shouting and more shots from town. Grinning Bear pushed his men and they sprinted to the jeep, which had stalled. It hissed and pinged as it cooled.

"We gotta get outta here, now!" Grinning Bear panted.

"No shit. Come on. We'll lead them down the road. We can't go straight to the boats or they'll know."

The Filipinos faded toward the beach, but Antonio cursed them and pushed them to follow Frank and Grinning Bear.

"We'll lead them on a wild goose chase," Frank said. Elarno made a face of incomprehension, and Frank amended. "Away from home. No home."

Elarno spoke with Antonio, who seemed to understand. He relayed it to the others and they nodded stoically.

Frank desperately wanted to know what the hell had happened, but it would have to wait until Gustav could translate. He tried to read Antonio, but the stoic warrior only stared back at him with cold eyes. He wasn't gonna get anything from him out here.

"Well, I guess they know about us now," he said to Grinning Bear.

"Yep. I hope these assholes are ready."

"Me too."

20

Noemfoor Island
July 1944

Corporal Clyde Cooper sipped coffee and watched the sunset from the top of the highest hill on Noemfoor Island. Despite the charnel house of destruction all around his position, the view took his breath away.

The 158th had chased the Japanese from the hill with a little help from the paratroopers a few days before. From the hill, he could almost see the entire island. Smoke wafted up from various spots and he could still hear the occasional bout of machine gun and rifle fire, but the Japanese seemed to have lost some of their vigor after losing the vital hill. No one expected the operation to last much longer.

Members of Third Squad sat nearby, making busy work for themselves or simply lounging. Gil scooted close and sat beside Clyde. “Coffee? Where’d you get coffee?”

Clyde held up the tin cup. “Perks of being a corporal, I guess.”

“That’s hardly worth it,” he teased. “Now, if it was whisky, that’d be different.”

“I’ll take what I can get.” He sipped as the edge of the sun seemed to touch the flat surface of the sea. He'd watched countless tropical sunsets by now, but they never ceased to amaze him. "Beautiful, isn't it?"

"Yeah. Sure is, but I prefer the sunrise."

"Yeah? Why's that?"

"Less likelihood of a Jap attack."

"Ah, I see. What about back home?"

"Sunset. I'm not awake at sunrise back home."

"The Japs have had it here. I don't think you need to worry about an attack. Besides, they'd have to get through the 158th to get to us."

"I'm not as optimistic as you, I guess."

Clyde did a double take when a paratrooper approached. He nearly spilled his coffee. "What the hell's he doing here?"

Gil turned and cursed. "Butler? He's got a lot of nerve coming up here." He got to his feet and balled his fists. Other men from Third Squad saw him and reacted similarly.

Clyde put a hand on Gil's arm. "Easy does it. Let's see what he wants before we beat the shit out of him."

Butler waved at the men facing him as though he were greeting old friends. "Hiya, fellas."

No one returned the greeting, but they moved a few steps closer and a few men unslung their rifles.

"You lost, soldier?" Clyde asked.

"Not if this is Second Platoon, and I'm pretty sure it is," he smiled at his own joke, but no one smiled back.

Clyde felt the hatred dripping off the men. They wanted to put this son of a bitch on his backside, and he couldn't blame them. He seriously considered turning away and leaving Butler on his own. Third Squad would make quick work of him.

"What're you doing here, Butler?" he asked, not hiding the edge in his voice. He'd lost all interest in the precious coffee.

Butler finally noticed the hostility. He raised his hands. "Hey, take it easy, fellas. What's the matter with you guys?"

Clyde wanted to throttle him. "Answer my question, now."

Butler focused on Clyde, but he looked spooked. "I'm—I'm a runner. I had a message for Captain Stallsworthy."

Clyde hoped Sergeant Huss didn't see him. He might do something he'd regret later and this shitbird had already destroyed one man's life.

"He's at HQ. You went right past it on the way up here."

"Yeah, I know. I already gave him the message. I thought I'd come up and visit my old unit."

"Jesus, Butler. You really think you're welcome here after what you did to Lieutenant Milkins? I'm shocked you're not in prison, or worse."

Butler looked from one man to the next. Fear grew in his eyes and Clyde found satisfaction there. The circle tightened around him as the light faded to dusk. It would be so satisfying to let the men take their aggressions out on this bastard.

Butler stammered, "That—that was an accident. I was out of my head with heat stroke and dehydration. I don't even remember doing it."

"Milkins is still in the hospital. He should be here with us right now, but here you are instead."

Butler shook his head. "But it wasn't my fault."

Gil stepped right up to his face. "Who's fault was it then? You pulled the trigger."

Clyde added, "You snuck in the ammunition, or was that someone else's fault, too?"

The light faded, and only a quarter moon shed light on them. Butler didn't answer right away, but his Adam's apple bobbed slowly as he swallowed nervously.

"I—I shouldn't have done that. I . . ."

Gutiérrez stepped in front of him and punched him hard in the stomach. The air went out of him and he doubled over, hacking. Clyde had a moment to put a stop to it, but he turned away. Suddenly, the prospect of his coffee sounded good again. He sipped and listened to the men landing punches again and again. The darkness hid anyone else from seeing the action.

It ended quicker than he would've thought. He turned and saw Butler curled in a ball, clutching his stomach with one hand and his face with the other. He softly moaned and rocked side to side.

Clyde crouched beside him. "Looks like Private Butler fell down. Shame, but you need to be more careful out here, Private."

Butler kept rocking and moaning. Clyde said, "I don't think you're fit to travel back tonight. You'll stay with us till morning. That okay with you, Butler?" He nodded. "Good, good. I'm sure Sergeant Huss would love to have a talk with you, too."

Butler uncurled himself and sat up shakily. Even in the low light, Clyde could see his face swelled. "I don't wanna see, Huss."

"He doesn't wanna see you either. He's afraid he'll kill ya."

"Jesus, I—I didn't know you guys were so mad. I—I feel awful about the shooting."

"I'm sure Milkins feels worse," Gil grumbled.

"*If* he ever recovers and returns to us, you better crawl under a rock," Clyde said.

Butler pleaded, "You gotta believe me. I feel awful. I don't remember doing it, but I know it happened and you're right about the ammo. I've learned my lesson." He spit when his mouth filled with blood.

"You gonna tell anyone about this?" Gutiérrez asked.

He shied away from him and shook his head. "Uh uh. Like the corporal said, I fell." He touched his face and winced.

"I'll radio HQ and tell 'em you won't be coming back tonight. You may as well make yourself comfortable, but I'd keep out of sight. Huss is bound to come by at some point," Clyde said.

"I'll just leave then."

"Nope, you're staying here. These foxholes need some work."

Gil chucked his entrenching tool at him, and it clattered at his feet. "Here you go, you can start on mine."

~

THE HOURS PASSED. The moon darted in and out of high clouds, alternating between bathing the island in a gentle glow and darkness. Clyde stared at the sky. He'd relieved Butler of digging foxholes an hour before. He'd been in obvious pain, but he'd struggled through.

He reflected on the way he'd treated him. Before the war, he never would have dreamed himself capable of such mistreatment. It felt too much like bullying. He hated bullies, but if anyone deserved it, it was

Butler. He should never have come looking for them. He wondered if he was stupid, but decided that rich people didn't think of themselves like everybody else. He probably still couldn't imagine why everyone was so upset. He wouldn't cause any more trouble for them. He hoped he'd learned his lesson.

He closed his eyes, hoping for sleep. He wasn't particularly tired, but he'd give it a try. The sounds of the island surrounded him. The insects and night animals weren't as loud here. He wondered if it was because they had blown much of their habitat to kingdom come by relentless shelling.

The sporadic and inevitable sounds of gunfire still pierced the night occasionally. He suspected the 158th was shooting at ghosts again. He heard a series of low thumps. *Grenades?* He remembered sitting in his room with his brother Frank guessing at car types from the sound of their engines as they drove by. Frank would sit at the window and tell him if he was right or wrong. This was kind of like that, but instead of cars, he identified weapons.

He opened his eyes and stared at the moon, wondering if his brother, Frank, was looking at the same moon. The last he'd heard, his older brother was in some hellhole POW camp far away. He yearned to talk with him one more time. They talked about everything. It was an advantage to have a few years between them. Frank knew more stuff—especially about girls. He missed him terribly. *I don't even know if he's alive.*

The crump of more grenades in quick succession and much closer brought him to a sitting position. He instinctively clutched his carbine and peered down the hill. That didn't sound quite right. It wasn't far off, but near the base of the hill. The moon was behind a cloud at the moment and he couldn't see much. He hoped the outpost was on their toes. Would it be prudent to call for flares from the mortar team? That wasn't his call to make.

He noticed other troopers sticking their heads up from foxholes and slit trenches. Something didn't feel right and the veterans reacted. He peered into the gloom, then up at the moon. The cloud currently blocking it would pass any moment now. He heard the radio squelch and Sergeant Huss's voice. He must be talking with the outpost.

"What's going on?" he heard Gil's groggy voice from the foxhole beside him.

"I don't know yet, but get your ass up. That didn't sound right."

"Yeah, no shit."

The clouds slipped past the moon and bathed the chewed-up field below them in grayish light. Artillery had chewed the grasses and trees up, but there was still ample cover to hide behind. But he saw nothing dangerous.

Butler was suddenly beside his hole on his belly. "What's going on? Japs?"

Clyde instantly regretted keeping him here. If there was a firefight, he was the last person he wanted to rely upon. "Get back in your hole and stay there," he hissed with as much venom as he could muster.

Butler slithered off without another word. Maybe he *had* learned his lesson. The old Butler would've had a snide remark for him.

Soon after Butler left, he heard movement nearby. He was about to curse Butler out when he saw Huss. Clyde asked, "What's going on down there, Sergeant?"

"The outpost says they're hearing all sorts of sounds they don't like. Palinsky wants them pulled in. Pass the word so they don't get their asses shot off."

Two grenade explosions blasted the lower slope. Clyde saw the flashes. Two men emerged from the ground halfway down the hill and hustled up the hill. "I see the outpost. They threw grenades and they're hightailing it!"

Huss yelled at Third Squad, "Hold your fire. The outpost is coming in."

"Oh shit," Clyde said. He saw shapes further down the hill rise into crouching positions. He heard the thump as they launched grenades from knee mortar tubes. He rose and yelled, "Get down! Grenades!"

The two scrambling soldiers either didn't hear him or chose not to respond. They kept churning up the hill, but the chewed-up soil and downed trees hindered their progress.

"Who's down there?"

"It's Spaulding and Hammerson."

He couldn't see the arcing grenades but he saw the explosions bracket the two men. They both dropped, and he had a sinking feeling deep in his guts. He put his carbine to his shoulder and fired down at the distant enemy. They dropped out of sight, but he doubted he hit anyone. More paratroopers joined in. They'd seen the same thing. For a few seconds, lethal fire raked the lower slope.

Clyde finished off his fifteen-round magazine and reloaded. Huss said, "You see 'em? You see Spaulding and Hammerson?"

"The grenades hit all around them, but I don't know if they're hit. It was damned accurate, though."

Huss said, "Take your team down there and get 'em out of there."

It was the order Clyde wanted to hear. "Leave it to us."

From behind Huss, Butler said, "I wanna come with you."

Huss spun as though someone had stabbed him in the back and wanted to face his attacker. He could hardly speak. "What—what the fuck're you doing here?"

Clyde thought Huss might tear Butler's head from his shoulders. He didn't want Butler with him, but he also didn't want to have to explain himself just yet. "Come on then," he said.

Huss was left gawking and speechless as Clyde hauled Butler along by his shirt. "Stay out of the damned way. You get any of my men killed. I'll kill you myself." He raised his voice. "Come on, Team Two, we're gonna pull Hammerson and Spaulding out of there."

They spilled from their foxholes and formed on him. A few leveled simmering looks at Butler, but said nothing. They wound their way through the barbed wire, keeping low and staying quiet. The firing from the other paratroopers ceased instantly at a barked order from an exasperated Sergeant Huss.

"Spread out and keep your eyes peeled. I saw where they went down," Clyde ordered.

Clyde slid around mounds of dirt and slithered in and out of the bomb craters. He kept his eyes on the base of the hill where he'd seen the grenadiers, but he saw nothing. The smell of sulfur and burnt gunpowder intensified the lower he went. The moon tucked in behind a cloud again and the night darkened considerably. That was both good and bad.

When he neared where he thought the troopers should be, he stopped and leaned against a dirt berm and a shredded palm tree. His senses were on high alert. He glanced back up the hill. It looked dark and ominous and he couldn't see any of the paratroopers he knew to be there. The rest of

Team Two filtered in around him. Butler stayed in the back, keeping his distance.

Clyde called out in a hoarse whisper, "Spaulding, Hammerson. Hey, where are you?"

He heard a mumbled something coming from the left and down the hill a few yards. The others heard it, too, and shifted their weapons.

Clyde got to his knees and strained to see. "Where are you?" he repeated.

"Over here." He saw a hand waving from the blackness. Clyde pointed. "There they are. With me, Guti and Ollie." He rose and slid down the other side of the berm. He waited for any response from down the hill, but there was still nothing. Gutiérrez and Oliver rolled down the berm and joined him.

Clyde saw one of the outposts waving at him only a few yards away. Hammerson said, "Spaulding's hit bad. I need help getting him outta here."

Clyde lunged the last few yards and slid in beside them. Gutiérrez and Oliver were close behind. Clyde checked Spaulding. He was unconscious. Even in the darkness, he could see blood glistening from multiple wounds.

"He doesn't look good."

"We need to get him outta here. He'll be alright, he's okay," Hammerson said with an edge of hysteria in his voice.

Gutiérrez handed his carbine to Hammerson. "I'll take him." He maneuvered himself closer and they helped flop Spaulding's dead weight onto his back. He grunted with the weight, but he stood. "I can hack it."

"We'll swap if you get tired," Clyde said. "How 'bout you? You hit?"

Hammerson shook his head. He didn't take his eyes off Spaulding. "I'm fine—I got a scratch. He took the brunt of the blast. Saved my life."

"You can thank him once the doc patches him up. Come on. Let's get outta here."

They helped Gutiérrez maneuver through the destruction, pushing him up the hill when he staggered. They made it to the rest of the team only a few short yards away. Everyone wanted to help, but Gutiérrez insisted he could handle it even though he was already breathing like a winded racehorse.

Gil whispered, "I saw movement down there, Coop."

Clyde spun and checked while the others helped Gutiérrez maneuver the steep slope. Gil pointed. "Right about there. I saw something."

Butler was suddenly beside them, leaning on the same berm. "I saw it, too. They're down there."

Clyde glared at him, but he didn't have time for him. Butler propped his carbine on the berm, aiming at the spot. Clyde put his hand on the barrel. "Don't you dare fire. You'll give away our position."

"I wasn't. Just getting ready."

The moon popped out from the thick clouds, and the darkness retreated. The others made headway, but it was slow going and Gutiérrez's breathing sounded like a wheezing freight train. He peered back down the hill. The moon lit the area with surreal light.

Clyde couldn't discern what he was seeing at first. His mind processed the image, but it took a moment for it to register. It appeared that the entire hillside was moving slowly up the hill. He could hardly breathe as he recognized Japanese soldiers strewn with vines and brambles for cover, crawling slowly up the hill only forty yards away.

He snatched a grenade from his harness, but didn't throw it yet. Gil did the same, and they exchanged worried glances. Butler's eyes shone wide in the moonlight. He didn't have any grenades, but he clutched his carbine tightly and looked ready to bolt or charge.

Clyde looked up the hill at the rest of the team. They hadn't noticed the mass of enemy soldiers yet, and the enemy soldiers hadn't noticed them yet.

Clyde hissed, "Wait. We gotta give our boys time to get up the hill." Both Butler and Gil nodded their understanding. "The first sign they've seen 'em, throw all your grenades and get up the hill."

Clyde peaked over the berm, not daring to expose his head more than a few inches. He wished he had a radio to warn Huss and the others, but he supposed they'd know soon enough. How had they gotten past the 158th? This was supposed to be a safe zone. There was no such place in this war.

He watched the Japanese continue their slow slog up the slope. When would they be too close? Another five yards—ten? If they got any closer, he'd be able to stab them. The thought nauseated him.

The rest of Team Two and Spaulding and Hammerson were halfway home. He could see them clearly, but somehow the Japanese hadn't noticed them yet. Should he try to break away unseen? Perhaps they were so intent on the sneak that they weren't even looking up the hill. Once he threw the grenade, all hell would break loose. He needed to decide now.

He whispered into Gil's ear, "Let's get outta here. Save our grenades." He stuffed the one he held into his oversized paratrooper pants pocket.

Gil nodded and looked relieved.

Butler shook his head, though. "I'll stay here."

"Bullshit," Clyde hissed. He had an urge to push his fist straight through his skull. Why did Butler have such an effect on him? "You're coming with us."

When he didn't come right away, Gil grabbed him by the hair and pulled him away from the berm. Butler struggled, but he didn't call out. He broke loose and followed their lead up the hill, his eyes shooting daggers at Gil.

Clyde hated turning his back to the enemy. He stepped up the hill and felt sure he'd be shot in the spine at any moment. He could feel the fear and panic rising. He forced himself to stay calm and take one step at a time. Now would not be a good time to trip.

He fought the urge to look back at the enemy. He felt like he walked a tightrope. He prayed the clouds would obscure the moon once again, but a glance skyward dashed that hope, at least for the next few minutes.

He glanced back to make sure Butler kept pace with them. He couldn't help looking beyond him. He shuddered seeing so many enemy soldiers so close. How had they not seen them yet? Perhaps they had, but didn't want to break cover. Perhaps they were letting them climb away so they could attack them in force and from much closer.

The thought made him freeze for a moment. Was he being a coward? Were his actions endangering the rest of the company? If he opened fire on them now, Able Company would be alerted and have plenty of time to react. If he waited until they made the top of the hill and safety, they'd have far less time to react. Perhaps they'd be overrun. His urge to survive was putting the others at risk.

Gil and Butler caught up to him, and Gil gave him a harried look. Clyde couldn't ask him to sacrifice himself. He said, "Keep going. Don't stop, no matter what."

"What the fuck're you planning?"

"Nothing. Just get up the hill."

"Yep, but you're coming, too."

"I'm right behind you."

"Don't bullshit a bullshitter. I know that look."

"No time. Just go."

Despite the danger, Gil grabbed him by the lapel and pulled him close. Clyde could smell stale cigarette smoke and the spaghetti he'd had for dinner. "I won't allow it. Abby'd never forgive me. Think of her."

Clyde flushed. He didn't want to think about Abby. She was the last thing he wanted to think about at that moment. She'd be heartbroken. "If I don't do something, they'll get too close and overrun our position."

Gil turned and faced back down the hill. "Then we'll do it together."

Butler elbowed his way in. "I'm with you." Clyde had never heard such steel in the young socialite's voice. He sounded like a paratrooper. But he didn't have time for more discussion. The enemy closed.

He could see the rest of the team getting closer to the top. He guessed they'd be there in ten more minutes. By then, the Japs would be at least halfway up.

He yanked the grenade out of his pants pocket and handed it to Butler. "How's your arm?"

"I pitched for my prep school baseball team," he grinned.

Clyde unlatched the last grenade from his harness and felt the weight. "Okay, on three, we throw and run our asses up this hill without waiting for the fireworks."

They separated, giving themselves room to throw. Clyde licked his dry lips, and the pit in his stomach seemed to grow heavier. "One, two, three . . ."

He pulled the pin and threw the grenade as far as possible. It disappeared into the gloom, and he didn't wait to see where it landed. He took off up the hill as fast as his legs would carry him.

Gil and Butler followed close behind. He leaped past downed trees and waited to hear the grenades. What seemed like an eternity later, the grenades went off in quick succession. Screams of alarm and pain rose from the Japanese. He fought the urge to fling himself into cover. He needed to make it as far up the hill as possible before they forced him to cover.

He made it a few more yards before the crack of rifles and the buzzing of bullets passing close forced him to dive into a hole he guessed had been formed by a mortar shell.

He rolled into the deepest portion and stayed down. Bullets smacked the dirt and debris all around him and he wriggled, trying to get lower. He pulled his carbine out of the dirt and held it to his chest as he faced the skittering clouds.

"Stay down!" he yelled.

Gil yelled back from somewhere close, "No shit!"

The distinct pop of a carbine nearby told him Butler was nearby, too. The crazy son of a bitch fired continuously. Bullets smacked around the lip of his hole, and the carbine shots stopped and he heard Butler cursing, "Shit, shit, shit!"

Clyde rolled onto his stomach and scooted his way to the lip. He didn't aim, but fired through half his magazine, spreading bullets downhill haphazardly. The muzzle flashes seemed far too close, and he wished he had more grenades. He ducked back just as more Japanese bullets turned the air into hot, buzzing hell.

Gil opened fire, but he only fired a few rounds before he was forced back into cover. He yelled, "They're firing knee mortars! Stay down!"

Clyde cringed, waiting for the grenade to land in his hole and blow him to hell and gone. Over the din of incoming fire, he heard the thumps from multiple knee mortars. He'd seen these deadly weapons in action multiple times and hated them with a passion. He wished someone had a rifle grenade to answer them.

He curled into the fetal position and waited. He felt the soft impacts of the first grenade through the soil, followed immediately by the crashing explosion. Dirt and debris cascaded over him like a great blanket. He choked and gagged and spit dirt from his mouth. That was too damned close. Anger swept through him. He didn't want to die in the bottom of a hole. He rolled to his knees. He barely registered the smoking hole only a few feet in front of his position. He focused instead on the enemy soldiers covered in flora and fauna rushing up the hill.

He pulled his carbine tight to his shoulder and found the nearest man. He pulled the trigger over and over. The bullets sank into the soldier's torso and disappeared, seemingly with no effect. The enemy soldier finally stumbled and fell, his rifle flew forward and stuck into the dirt.

Clyde shifted slightly and found the next target. In the soft light from the moon, he saw the soldier's gritted teeth and his churning legs. He leaped over a downed palm tree like an Olympian. Clyde pulled the trigger steadily, and his bullets found their mark. Even with a massive dose of adrenaline coursing through his veins, he couldn't miss from this range. His target fell out of sight. The ground seemed to swallow him. He pulled the trigger again and nothing happened.

"Reloading!" he yelled. He dropped into the hole and struggled to pull another magazine from the pouch attached to his belt. He didn't know how many more he had, if any, but he didn't have time to check.

He lay on his back, working to shove the magazine in, when a looming form appeared next to his hole. He thought it might be Butler since he was on that side, but the scream and the gleaming bayonet on the end of an Arisaka rifle dispelled him from that illusion.

He had the drop on him. Clyde dropped his carbine and tried to deflect the blade thrusting toward his guts. Fear gripped him as he waited for the cold steel to enter his intestines. But it never came. A shape slammed into the enemy soldier and tackled him off the lip of the hole. He heard grunting and cursing behind the hole.

He found his carbine and his feet. He aimed, but he couldn't tell one soldier from the next. Bullets singed past his ears. He turned away from the wrestling match and fired indiscriminately into the nearest soldiers running up the hill. From the corner of his eye, he saw Gil firing into bodies only yards away. They wouldn't last long.

He spun back to the struggling men behind him. One man got the advantage, but he couldn't tell who. He straddled the other and raised a gleaming knife. Clyde nearly fired, before the moon lit up Private Butler's crazed face and he eased off the trigger. Butler slammed the knife into the enemy soldier's chest over and over like a jackhammer. The doomed soldier convulsed and gasped with each new thrust, and blood and gore followed the knife each time he drew it out.

A flare popped overhead. The shock of it made Clyde freeze. For a moment, he couldn't understand what had just happened. The entire scene took on a surreal feeling. His senses returned, and he dropped onto his belly and unloaded the rest of his magazine into sprinting enemy soldiers. He felt into his belt for another magazine and came up empty.

"I'm out!" he yelled. He flipped the carbine and gripped the muzzle, preparing to swing it like a baseball bat, but he quickly dropped it when his hands burned.

He pawed for where he'd seen the Japanese drop his rifle. He found it and tucked it into his shoulder. He pulled the trigger, but nothing happened. He worked the bolt, happy the airborne trainers thought to familiarize them with enemy weapons. He jacked a round in and fired. His target spun as the bullet slammed into his shoulder, changing his war scream into a pain-filled grunt. But he kept on coming. Clyde worked the bolt, but when he thrust it forward, he felt the round twist and jam in the breech.

Bodies lay strewn all around. Gil continued firing his carbine and Butler joined him, pouring lead into the nearest enemy soldiers, but there were too many of them. When they ran out of ammunition, it would be over.

The soldier he'd wounded came rushing on with murder in his eyes. Clyde hefted the rifle, leveled the bayonet, and charged. He could see the surprise in the soldier's eyes. But neither of them hesitated. Clyde remembered training for close-in bayonet fighting, but he never dreamed he might actually have to draw on the skill for real. But here he was, charging a Japanese soldier. Unfortunately, this enemy didn't stand still like the dummies they'd practiced on at Fort Benning.

He closed the distance quickly. He had the advantage of the downhill and he wasn't wounded. He saw a flash of fear in the enemy soldier's eyes. He thrived on it. He thrust the bayonet toward his injured side. The Japanese planted his feet and parried the thrust. Clyde flew past, expecting to feel the butt of the rifle slam into the back of his head. It would be lights out, then the feel of steel in his back. But it didn't happen. Clyde stopped and turned, slashing with the blade as though he wielded a sword.

The Japanese soldier had tried to smack him in the back of the head, but his injured shoulder made his effort weak. Clyde's blade slashed into the soldier's side. He felt it cut into him and it exited his body with a great gush of blood and a ripping sound. All fight went out of the Japanese. He dropped his rifle and toppled to the side, gasping and gripping his torn-open side.

He suddenly heard Gil yelling, "Get down! Get down!" Clyde lost his wind as Gil slammed into him, wrapping his arms around his waist and taking him down in a classic open field tackle. They both slammed hard and Clyde lay beneath him, gasping for breath.

A moment later, the air overhead sizzled with tracer fire from the top of the hill. The heavy weapons team opened fire with their .30-caliber machine guns. The storm of tracers just feet over his head looked as though he could walk across it. Heavy impacts made sickening sounds as bullets met bone and meat mercilessly.

The onslaught continued for a full minute. It finally slowed down as crews reloaded, but rifle fire filled the void. More flares overhead mixed with high explosives as the mortar crews added their deadly ordnance.

Clyde heard yelling from up the hill. "Get your ass out of there!"

He fought his way from beneath Gil and they both looked up the hill. Clyde saw Sergeant Huss waving for them to retreat up the hill.

"Time to go," he barked. "Where's Butler? Butler!" he called.

"I'm here. Get me outta here!"

Gil and Clyde crab-crawled up the hill a few yards. Butler had somehow ended up underneath an enemy soldier. "I'm stuck!"

Clyde grabbed his hand, and Gil shoved the dead body off him. Blood covered the front of Butler's shirt. "You hit?" Gil asked.

"No, it's not my blood."

"Get up the hill," he barked at them. "Go!"

"My weapon," Butler said.

"Leave it!"

Gil was the only one who'd hung onto his carbine. "I've only got a few rounds left."

Bullets smacked into the dirt as they climbed, but the intensity of the American machine guns kept their heads down and made their fire inaccurate.

They finally made it to Huss and the rest of the Third Squad. They were out of breath and dripped sweat.

Gutiérrez looked ready to burst. "I thought you guys were with us. I'm so sorry we left you."

"Not your fault. Now get us the hell outta here. I've had enough of this damned hillside."

Clyde saw Huss glare at Butler. He corrected him. "Butler saved my ass back there. He fought like a tiger. Leave him alone, Morgan."

Huss's expression changed from anger to surprise to business as usual. "Well, I guess even the worst airborne soldier's better'n anything else."

They made it back to the relative safety of their lines. Harassing small arms from the Japanese continued, but now mortars began raining down on them. They found cover and Clyde felt he could finally breathe easy. But it was short-lived.

Lieutenant Palinsky looked pale and dirty, but his eyes had hardened since the last time Clyde had seen him. "You men okay?" he asked with genuine concern.

Clyde answered for all of them. "Yes, sir. It was a close, but we're fine."

"Well, don't get too comfortable. The Japs aren't finished with us yet, and all our artillery is positioned to support the 158th. We're on our own tonight."

"Yes, sir. We just need a minute for water."

Palinsky nodded and left to attend to more pressing matters. Huss lifted his chin at his departing backside. "He's the one that sent us down there to get you."

"No shit?"

"No shit. Tonight's full of surprises," he said, smiling sideways at Butler. "Get yourself cleaned up, Butler. You look like something from a horror comic."

"Yes, sergeant."

Huss turned away, muttering to himself, "Wonders never cease."

21

Clyde's hands shook as he gripped his carbine. Now that he found himself back in the relative safety at the top of the hill, surrounded by Able Company, he had time to reflect on his harrowing encounter, and it terrified him. How many times had he cheated death down there? How many bullets had missed him by mere inches? What would have happened if Butler, the most unlikely of heroes, hadn't been there to take out that enemy soldier? He'd be lying in a pool of his own blood either long dead, or dying a slow, painful death—but instead he sat here without so much as a scratch.

A fresh flare burst to life overhead and bathed the night in stark white light. He peered below. He thought he might see better without the flare—it created too many deep shadows. The moonlight alone seemed to bathe the landscape more evenly, but with the clouds, it wasn't reliable. He didn't see any movement, but he saw bodies.

Lieutenant Palinsky hustled along the line of fighting holes and trenches, checking on the men. Clyde still didn't trust him completely, but he was doing his job at the moment. He lingered near Huss, and he nodded and pointed as they talked.

He came to Clyde's hole next. "How you doing, Corporal? Holding up okay?"

"Yes, sir. So far, so good. Any word on Spaulding?" He'd heard he was still unconscious when they first returned, but that had been a few hours ago.

Palinsky shook his head sadly. "He didn't make it. He lost too much blood. He died on the way to the infirmary."

Clyde felt gut punched. He wasn't a close friend but he was an Able Company man and that meant he was a brother. "Damn."

"He was a good man." The silence lingered between them. Finally Palinsky said, "I wanna speak to you about that Butler fellow." Clyde stiffened and Palinsky continued. "I understand he used to be in this unit, but I don't understand why he's still here."

"He was, sir. He's a runner for the regiment now. He just came by to say hello and got caught up in the attack."

Palinsky's eyes narrowed. "Is that so? He's pretty bruised up. He looks like he went a few rounds with Joe Louis."

"He fought a Jap down there hand to hand—must've taken a few shots to the face," Clyde lied.

"He's the guy that shot my predecessor, right?"

"Uh, yes, sir. Lieutenant Milkins. But I guess they acquitted him—heat stroke and dehydration caused him to go bonkers." He felt odd defending him. Only hours before, he'd turned a blind eye while the squad beat the shit out of him.

"I want him out of here in the morning."

"Yes, sir—I'll see to it personally."

"See that you do. We might need his rifle tonight, though."

"Any movement?"

"Yeah, plenty. They probed Third Platoon's position. We think they're gonna make another push. Captain Stallsworthy wants us to hold here and be ready to support anyone that needs it. He also heard what happened down there and wanted me to tell you and Huss personally that he's proud of Third Squad's actions tonight."

Clyde swelled his chest. "Thank you, sir. It was touch and go there for a while. Thanks for sending the rest of the squad down to get us out."

Palinsky seemed to shrink from the praise. If he wasn't mistaken, he thought he saw him blush.

"Be ready to move and stay vigilant, Corporal."

"Geronimo, sir."

"Geronimo," he answered automatically.

Palinsky shuffled out of sight. Beside him, Gil, Gutiérrez, and Oliver watched him go.

"He might just work out after all," Gutiérrez said.

Oliver said, "We'll see. We still haven't seen him under real pressure."

"He made the right call sending you guys back for us," Clyde said.

"I think he knew we woulda gone no matter what and he just wanted it to look like his idea," Oliver said.

"Always seeing the worst in people, Ollie."

Oliver scowled, "I've come by it honestly, Guti. Besides, you gotta agree —Huss was going down there with or without orders."

"Yeah, I know. But I'll give the lieutenant the benefit of the doubt."

"Wait'll he calls in artillery on the wrong grid, or gets us lost on patrol. You might change your tune."

Gutiérrez punched Oliver's shoulder. "I'm an optimist, you're an asshole."

Oliver smacked him back. Clyde had seen this play out countless times. It was harmless and even good to burn excess energy, but he was too keyed up to put up with it. "Knock it off, you two. Japs might come up the hill any second now."

"I hope they do, Coop. I want payback for Spaulding," Oliver said grimly.

The air suddenly hissed, and everyone froze. "Down!" Clyde barked and he dove into the bottom of his hole.

Mortar rounds slammed into their positions. The rounds impacted all around them. Clyde curled into the bottom of his hole and covered his head with his hands the best he could. The barrage continued, and his teeth shook in his gums with each impact. He felt the thumps deep in his chest. That's when he knew they were close.

They had their positions zeroed perfectly. He waited to die or be buried. He'd rather die from a direct hit than be buried alive and suffocate. The thought made him almost giddy. This crazy war made him choose between two grisly fates. Surviving barely made the list. It seemed impossible to survive out here.

The world shook and exploded all around him. He curled into as tight a ball as he could. It seemed to last an eternity, and he felt his sanity slipping away.

Finally, the barrage stopped. The relief of survival filled him. He stayed in his hole for a minute longer. Sometimes the sadistic bastards waited, hoping someone left their hole early and was hit by one final round. But that round never came. Perhaps they were scrambling up the hill right now.

He stood and an inch thick layer of dirt cascaded off him. Smoke curled up from fresh holes all around. He waited to see heads popping up from fighting holes. He saw a few, but not all. Huss would want to know the headcount. "Sound off, Third Squad!" he bellowed. His voice cracked and his throat felt as though he'd swallowed glass. He listened as stunned men called out. He did a silent count, picturing each man with each voice. He went through a mental checklist and momentary panic gripped him.

"Hicks! Gil!" he called.

He heard Gutiérrez's cracking voice. "He's hit! Oh God, he's hit bad!"

Clyde leaped from his hole and ran to Gil's hole. He slid in and saw a smoking crater had widened Gil's hole obscenely. Gil sprawled against the far wall with his arms splayed and his face a bloody mess. With his one undamaged eye, Gil looked around in dazed wonder.

"Medic!" Clyde bellowed, but his voice cracked. His best friend lay shattered in front of him. He was alive, but in bad shape. He didn't know where to begin. Should he push his dangling eye back into place?

"Coop?" Gil gurgled and his spit was tinged with blood.

Clyde snapped from his indecision. He pressed his hand against a chest wound that seeped dark blood through his shirt. "You're okay. You're looking good, buddy. You're okay."

Gil's eyes went to the dark sky overhead. Flares still lit up the night and he focused on them. "I'm alright," he said groggily. "Tired though."

Corporal Gaines, the medic, slid in beside him. "Stay awake, you stupid Wop. Stay with me, Hicks."

Gil smiled, but winced when Gaines tore his shirt open and applied pressure to the worst of the wounds. He splashed copious amounts of sulfa onto the wounds before wrapping them with strips of bandages. His hands worked fast and he stopped a good portion of the bleeding in seconds.

"What about his eye?" Clyde asked.

"Push it back in," Gaines said as though telling him about the weather. When Clyde hesitated, he barked, "Do it, Cooper!"

Clyde gulped back bile, cupped the eyeball, and popped it back into Gil's skull. He held his hand there to keep it in place. Gil's good eye stared at him. "Thanks, buddy," he said dreamily.

"Wrap it in place. Someone give him a bandage. I've got my hands full here."

Distantly, Clyde heard machine gun fire and the thumping of outgoing mortar shells. That could only mean one thing, but he couldn't pull himself away from his best friend.

Oliver held up a syrette of morphine for Gaines. Gaines nodded emphatically. "Yes, give it to him."

Oliver leaned in and his eyes locked on Gil's one good eye. "Here you go, buddy. Here you go." He sank the shot of morphine into Gil's quivering leg. Gil's eyes turned glassy, and he smiled, then passed out.

"Gil! Gil!" Clyde yelled.

"It's okay. He just passed out. He's okay," Gaines barked. "He's better off that way right now."

"You told him not to fall asleep, dammit!"

"It's the morphine. He's fine. Help me get him outta here. There's no stretcher bearers, we'll have to use rifles," Gaines said. The others looked at him with blank stares. "For crying out loud. Eject your mags and string the rifles through his pants legs and his shirt sleeves. It works better with Garands but carbines'll have to do."

They quickly went to work, being sure to clear the breeches first. The carbines were short, making it awkward, but they could use the stiff carbines to heft and carry the unconscious Gil off the hill.

Sergeant Huss bellowed at Clyde as he waddled past, helping Gaines carry him. "Need you on the line, Cooper."

Clyde just stared at the surly sergeant. Huss saw who he carried and his hard eyes softened. He pursed his lips into a straight line, then said, "Get back here as quick as you can." He raised his voice, "Rest of you to the line!" Oliver, Gutiérrez, and Hallon broke off with final words of encouragement for their fallen friend. They trotted to join Huss and the rest of Able Company.

Clyde entered a fog. He couldn't focus his eyes, and his entire body felt numb. He tore his eyes from Gil's bandaged face and chest and suddenly didn't recognize anything. He stumbled and nearly fell.

Gaines seethed at him. "Stay with me, Cooper. Pull yourself together."

The words cut into him, and reality smacked him in the face, hard. "I'm —I'm fine," he said.

"There's a jeep just ahead with a driver standing by. They'll have him to the surgeon in less than an hour. He's gonna make it."

Clyde felt his shoulders might pull from the sockets, but he didn't stop. He had to do this for his friend. A little pain was a small price to pay. He only wished he could swap places with him. Gil didn't deserve this.

The driver ran up the slope and took one side of the load. They marched him to the jeep and strapped him onto makeshift boards strapped to the back for that very reason.

Clyde moved to enter the jeep and hold Gil in place, but Gaines shoved him away. "I'll stay with him all the way. You'll just get in the way. Your platoon needs you up there." Clyde stepped back, stunned. Gaines handed him the two carbines. "Here, you might need these up there."

Clyde took them automatically. He stood there gaping as the jeep peeled out and fishtailed onto the muddy road leading to the rear. True to his word, Gaines hovered over Gil like a mother goose protecting a gosling.

The harsh sound of combat floated down to him from atop the hill. He still stood holding the carbines, one in each hand. He saw the flashes of explosions. He took one last look toward the streaking jeep, then took halting steps up the hill. His lumbering walk turned into a trot, then a run. He sprinted as fast as his legs would carry him. His lungs burned for oxygen and his legs felt they might simply drop off, but he kept pushing. The pain felt good—it kept his mind off Gil.

~

Clyde rejoined Third Squad. They'd moved forward from their foxholes and filled the zigzagging trench line overlooking the denuded slope. A constant stream of flares lit the area with incandescent light, and the sound of small arms fire and mortar thumps came from where he knew Third Platoon held.

He found Sergeant Huss. “I’m back,” Clyde grunted.

“How is he?”

Clyde only shrugged. He hadn’t had time to really process Gil’s injuries.

Huss added, “He’s a fighter. He’ll be okay.” Clyde simply stared down the slope, unable to form words on the subject.

Huss pointed right. “Here’s the situation. The Nips are pushing our right flank hard. So far, Third Platoon is holding. Stallsworthy thinks it’s a feint. He thinks the main event will come straight at us again. That mortar strike hit all across the line, but they concentrated more fire on us, but so far, we haven’t seen much.”

Clyde heard and understood the information, but his mind still felt foggy and dull. The sound of battle from the right flank barely registered. It sounded more like background chatter.

“Hey! You still with me, Clyde?”

Clyde tore his eyes from downslope and focused on Huss’s mud-streaked face. “Yeah, yeah, I’m with you.” Anger filled the void left by the uncertainty surrounding Gil’s fate. “Let them come,” he seethed.

Huss nodded grimly. “Make sure your team’s ready. I gave you Raley to fill in for Gil. His BAR can make the difference if it comes to it. Make sure Wallace is ready to use his rifle grenade. With the steep slope, he should be able to reach out and touch them early. And remember, try to kill the bastards near the back first. That worked well the last time.”

Clyde flushed at the way Huss seemed to be spoon-feeding him, but he realized he was making sure his head was in the right space. Clyde looked him straight in the eye. “I got it, Morgan. No problem.”

Huss clapped him on the back. “I know you do. I’ll let you know if we need to shift to the right flank.” He lowered his voice conspiratorially. “Oh, and Butler’s with you, too.”

Clyde nodded. Butler had more than proven his worth already. He asked, “Where’s Palinsky?”

Huss pointed behind their position. “He’s back with the radio, just in front of the mortar team.” Clyde raised an eyebrow. Huss put him at ease.

"He's doing fine so far." The sound of small arms fire increased and flashes from small explosions added to the light from the flares drifting beneath their mini-parachutes.

Clyde made his way along the trench until he found the first man in his team, Gutiérrez. They exchanged a hard look. Clyde could see the anger and hurt in his eyes. Clyde said, "Let's give these sons of bitches some payback tonight."

Oliver stood nearby with his carbine aimed down the hill. "Damn right."

"When they come, Huss wants us to hit the back line as much as possible, but I don't care what you do as long as you're killing the bastards." They nodded grimly. They'd stacked extra magazines and rows of grenades along carved dirt ledges in the walls of the trench.

He continued his inspection, making sure each man had enough ammunition and knew what to do when the enemy showed themselves. He came to Private Wallace, his grenadier. He already had a grenade screwed onto the top of his M1 Garand.

Clyde said, "When they come, don't be stingy with those things. Look for machine-gun nests."

"I'll put this thing right down their throat, Cooper. It'll be like the county fair back home."

"Just make sure you kill as many as possible, cowboy."

"Yep, they earned it tonight," he murmured bitterly. "We'll make 'em pay for Hicks and Spaulding."

The next man was Raley, the BAR man. "You got what you need, Raley?"

Raley tapped the line of heavy magazines he'd carefully placed. "Sure thing, Corporal. Bessie and I are ready to lay down the hurt on these assholes."

"Good man." He stepped past him and found Butler at the end of the line. He had swapped his carbine for the heavier-hitting Garand. He had his bayonet attached. "You ready?"

Butler still had streaks of blood on his face from knifing the enemy soldier. "Hell yes," he said.

Clyde pushed into the wall and propped his carbine on the dirt. He pulled grenades from a nearby box and stacked them. "I want to thank you for saving my ass down there."

Butler came off his sights and glanced at Clyde. "Anyone woulda done the same."

"It took guts. I'd be dead if not for you."

Butler looked back down the hill. "I know I messed up back in Australia. Thanks for letting me stay here tonight."

"You've done more than enough. You don't have to stay."

"I know, but I'd like to all the same. I still feel I owe you guys a lot."

"I owe you my life."

"Call it even then?"

"Deal." Clyde extended his hand and they shook. He pointed at the bayonet. "You think they'll get that close?"

"I hope not, but I wanna be prepared this time." Butler still had flakes of dried blood on his hands. He looked like he'd field dressed a deer recently and forgotten to wash.

"You okay? I mean up here?" Clyde tapped the side of his own head.

"Yeah. I haven't had time to process everything, though."

"Well, you did the right thing. You didn't have a choice."

"I know. I—I just can't stop thinking how it felt. Is that normal?"

Stabbing a man wasn't a normal, everyday occurrence. There wasn't an answer. Butler would have to deal with his own demons in his own way. Clyde remembered how bothered he'd been after killing the Japanese soldier at close range way back in Finschhafen. It had taken weeks to push past the incident and carry on. The man's face still haunted his dreams.

Butler turned back to the slope. "I'm real sorry about Gil. Is he gonna make it?"

It took a moment for Clyde to trust himself to answer. "The medic seems to think so," he managed.

"They said he was busted up pretty good."

The image of him sprawled with his arms wide open and his left eyeball hanging down to his cheek assaulted him like a physical blow. He said, "Yeah."

"Well, at least he's getting out of here."

The realization that the war was likely over for Gil slapped Clyde in the face. If he survived, he most likely wouldn't return to the front. They'd cycle him back to the States. He might never see him again.

The thought gut-punched him. He always thought they'd fight the good fight, side by side, until they both died or the war ended. He suddenly felt very alone.

His thoughts flashed to Abby. Her image brightened the darkness in his mind like a lighthouse beacon on a stormy night. He lost himself for a glorious moment as she filled him completely. He could almost smell her and touch her. The image soon passed, but it left him breathless. It felt like a mini-miracle. How did she do that?

The night came crashing back into focus when he heard the grinding of engines and gears down the slope. He concentrated on the sound and strained to hear and see what it was. He'd never heard anything like it before, and a sense of foreboding replaced the space Abby had so recently filled.

Somebody yelled, "Tanks! Jap tanks!"

Clyde could hardly believe it. How had the enemy snuck tanks past the 158th? Where were the Shermans? The heavy weapons squads had a few bazookas, but not much ammo for them. It wasn't something they thought they'd need here on little old Noemfoor. If they ran into enemy armor, the Shermans would engage them, not the infantry, but the Shermans were far forward supporting the 158th.

The clanking grew louder and the engines roared. Past where the slope met the jungle, trees swayed and bent. Loud snaps as smaller trees succumbed to the tank's treads and steel reverberated over the sound of the small arms fire from Third Platoon. It seemed like some massive predator snarled its way toward them. It was disconcerting as hell.

Orders bellowed up and down the line, calling for bazookas. Would mortars and grenades be enough to stop them? Could tanks scale the steep slope? He didn't think so, but he didn't really know and he didn't like unknowns.

He yelled down the line, "Be ready, Wallace."

"Yeehaw!" he shouted back, but his exuberance seemed forced.

A moment later, Clyde saw the dim outline of a boxy shape at the edge of the jungle. The flares overhead glinted light off a dull barrel, slowly elevating.

"Incoming!" he yelled. He pulled Butler back from the edge. A puff of white smoke and the hellish shriek of a tank round passing overhead made them all drop. The shell slammed into the top of the hill behind and exploded in shrapnel, flame, and smoke.

"The next one will be on us. Wish those Shermans were around."

The welcome sounds of mortars thumping from the rear made Clyde lift his head over the lip to mark their impact. He could still see the smoke wafting from where the tank had fired. It pinpointed it nicely. Was there another one? He'd thought so, but he couldn't see it at the moment.

A body suddenly slammed into the wall to Clyde's left. He startled, but saw Lieutenant Palinsky beside him. He had his binoculars up and directed down the hill. He hardly needed them. His radio man hunkered just behind him. He gave Clyde a sideways grin, as though apologizing for the intrusion.

The first mortar rounds landed in front of the tank. Palinsky spoke quickly to Erickson, his radioman. "Three degrees left. Add forty." Erickson relayed the correction. A minute later, Erickson said, "On the way."

Clyde saw the tank's barrel lower slightly. He clutched Palinsky's shirt and pulled him down. "Take cover!"

Palinsky scowled and tried to stay up, but Clyde kept him down. The tank barked and there was a quick shriek followed immediately by an explosion right outside the trench-line. Dirt erupted and dumped onto their heads like a crashing wave.

Palinsky spit and shook the dirt off. Clyde released his shirt and Palinsky gave him a thankful glance. He popped up and tried the binoculars, but the lenses were caked with dirt and he only succeeded in temporarily blinding himself. "Ah, shit, my eyes."

Clyde thought he might be hit, but then he saw him scraping hunks of dirt out of his eyes. Clyde took his place and watched for the mortar impacts. He saw smaller puffs of smoke stutter from lower on the tank's front end as the coaxial machine guns opened fire. The bullets laced the ground to his left. Two mortar rounds landed on either side of the tank.

The eruptions looked pathetically inadequate, but it might help keep the tank crew from focusing and aiming.

"Mortars are right on target. Keep 'em coming."

Erickson looked at Palinsky. Palinsky kept scraping at his eyes, but he could see well enough to see Erickson's hesitation. "Well, what are you waiting for? Send it." Erickson quickly sent the information.

The tank turret rotated a few degrees and centered. "Incoming!" Clyde yelled again. He ducked and gritted his teeth. The blast ripped at the dirt berm in front of the trench works to his right.

He popped up just as a flurry of mortar shells exploded all around the tank. He heard a clang as one landed directly on top, but it only caused it to smoke and probably gave the enemy inside headaches.

"They got anything more lethal? The rounds are just bouncing off."

Palinsky joined him at the lip. His eye sockets were still surrounded by dirt and his eyes watered copiously. He struggled to keep them open.

Clyde pulled his canteen. "Here you go, sir. Lean your head back." Clyde poured the contents of his canteen onto his face. He spluttered, but it worked. He squinted into the flare-lit landscape, confirming what Clyde told him.

He barked at Erickson. "Tell them to use Willy Pete on 'em."

Clyde couldn't keep the smile off his face. White phosphorous rounds wouldn't only set metal on fire, but they would also create copious amounts of smoke and hopefully burn the infantrymen lurking nearby. He hated the thought of being on the receiving end of such a brutal weapon, but he relished what the Japanese had coming.

Another plume of whitish-gray smoke spewed about fifty yards from the first tank and another tank round smashed into the top of the hill.

"There's the other tank," Clyde yelled.

Palinsky took a lesson from Clyde and poured the contents of his own canteen over the binoculars, clearing the dirt from the eye slots. "Where's Huss?"

Clyde pointed left. "Up that way, about forty yards."

Palinsky smacked Erickson on the helmet. "Let's go." They both hustled off, keeping their heads down. Palinsky offered encouragement to the men he passed.

Butler said, "He seems like a decent officer."

Clyde remembered what had happened to Palinsky's predecessor and who'd been responsible, but he didn't respond. Butler had earned his respect. He looked down the hill when the first white phosphorous mortar shell landed near the tank. White-hot tendrils reached out like a million spider legs, setting fire to every surface they touched. Three more shells burst and soon the tank disappeared behind a thick, white cloud.

Clyde saw flickers of flame through the cloud, but he couldn't tell if the fire had consumed the tank or not. He suspected they were reversing the hell out of there if they were smart.

The ground erupted slightly behind the trench-line, as the Japanese hurled mortar shells at their position. Clyde ducked automatically and curled himself into the dirt at the bottom. He wished he could tuck into a bunker, but they hadn't felt the need to go to such lengths since they were so far behind the main line of defense.

He cursed himself for not being more careful. He couldn't help thinking about what had happened to Gil only hours before in a similar situation. He loathed having to sit there and take it. He'd suffered through far too many enemy barrages. His brain felt like it shook inside his skull and his teeth rattled.

The only consolation came from knowing that this wasn't the heavy stuff and the enemy couldn't have stockpiled too much more ammunition. This felt like a last-ditch effort—a Hail Mary. If the paratroopers could hold out until morning, the Japanese wouldn't have any more capacity for offense, but they were certainly giving it their all tonight. He hated the sons of bitches, but he couldn't fault their tenacity and bravery.

The mortar barrage lifted. He checked Butler. He jolted when he touched him. "Aren't you glad you stayed?" Clyde asked ironically. Butler grunted and got to his feet, brushing the dirt and debris off.

Clyde moved down the trench, checking on each man from his squad. He finally sidled up to Huss. "All present and accounted for."

"Good. They're gonna push any second now." They both poked their heads up and peered downslope. The white phosphorous rounds had started countless mini-fires, but the constant jungle wetness didn't allow it to burn out of control.

Clyde pointed toward a burning pyre further back in the trees. "You think that might be one of the tanks?"

"Looks that way. The willy pete really ate 'em up." He focused his attention on where the second tank had been. "I don't see the other one."

Four Nambu machine guns suddenly opened fire. Their tracers looked like beams of light, and they crisscrossed and converged on the trench lines. Everyone ducked as bullets whizzed and zinged with bizarre ricochets.

Huss yelled over the din, "Get back to your team."

Clyde kept his head down as he crouch-ran back toward his position. He stopped between Gutiérrez and Oliver. "Looks like we'll be getting our payback any second now."

Gutiérrez gave him a thumbs up and a mirthless smile. Oliver crossed himself, then checked to make sure he had a round chambered in his carbine. He lifted his chin toward a rifle leaning on the back trench wall. "I might fire some of their own ammo back at 'em."

Clyde saw the Arisaka with the bayonet still attached. He wondered if it was the same one he'd used to slice the soldier a few hours ago or if Oliver had picked it up somewhere else. He cringed at the memory. Just another layer to add to his growing library of nightmares.

"Shoot straight. See you soon."

He encouraged Wallace and Raley as he passed, then stopped at the open slot near Butler. The hammering machine guns continued and it sliced the sky overhead with light from the tracer rounds. The night air suddenly quieted and Clyde's ears popped as though unable to process the sudden lack of sound.

Huss yelled, "Get ready!"

Clyde raised his head and propped his carbine on the lip of the trench. He saw a mass of soldiers dart from the jungle shadows made deeper by the flares burning overhead. Like before, they wore foliage in their uniforms and pith helmets, making it appear the bushes and trees of the jungle attacked them. But beneath the foliage, blood and bone would soon shatter.

The outgoing mortars stopped once they'd driven off the tanks, but now they resumed. The enemy soldiers made good progress. They didn't yell and scream, but darted from cover to cover without firing a shot. Clyde found a likely target and did his best to follow his progress up the hill.

The irritating sound of clanking treads momentarily drew his attention. The surviving tank must be pushing back into position. Mortar rounds landed among the advancing troops in flashes of fire and smoke. A few soldiers fell, or were momentarily lit up in the explosions, only to disappear, but it didn't seem like enough.

Out of the corner of his eye, the grenadier, Private Wallace, adjusted the angle of his rifle grenade, waiting for the order to fire.

Two of the four Nambu machine guns opened fire from the edges of the advancing troops. Clyde cringed and lowered his head slightly, but the Nambus fired in short bursts this time, obviously conserving ammunition.

Finally he heard Palinsky bark, "Open fire! Fire at will!"

Wallace launched his grenade with a loud crack. Clyde readjusted his aim and silently mouthed, "This is for Gil." He pulled the trigger and the enemy soldier in his sights faltered but didn't drop. He fired three more careful shots and he saw each one find the mark. The soldier finally tripped into the underbrush.

Butler fired through the eight rounds of his Garand. The clip pinged loudly. He quickly shoved another clip in, but forgot to hold back the bolt, which slammed forward, catching his thumb in the breech. "Ah, shit!" he cursed, and briefly sucked his thumb.

Clyde wished he'd thought to swap the carbine for the Garand. It made sense to start with the Garand and switch to the carbine as the enemy closed, but it was too late now. He swept side to side, choosing his targets at random and firing until they fell or dove to cover.

He dropped and pressed his back to the wall. "Reloading!" He ejected the empty magazine and inserted a fresh one. He rose and found a new target immediately, but he had to duck as a flurry of well-aimed machine gun fire swept the front of the trench.

He yelled to his left. "Take out that machine gun, cowboy!"

"I'm on it!" Wallace barked back.

The slowly descending flare dropped into the jungle beyond the enemy soldiers and extinguished. There wasn't one to replace it this time. Besides the bursting mortar shells and muzzle flashes, the darkness once again reigned supreme. Clyde could only see the outline of enemy soldiers. They took advantage of the darkness and surged forward all at once.

The enemy machine gun's sporadic bursts in the darkness were much easier to pinpoint without the flare. Wallace launched his grenade and it arced through the air, then slammed into the berm the machine gun nestled behind. The woodpecker sound stopped abruptly.

"Great shot!" Clyde exulted.

The heavy .30-caliber machine guns finally opened fire. Clyde hadn't noticed their absence, but was glad for them now. They walked lines of tracer fire into the advancing enemy soldiers. Flashes of light lit up the stunned faces and ricochets burned into the sky. It would be beautiful if it weren't so terrifying.

Clyde picked his targets carefully. He fired at shapes and didn't know if he hit his targets. He burned through three more magazines. The floor of the trench was littered with small brass casings. Butler's Garand pinged empty so often, he lost count, but the Japanese kept coming and they were getting dangerously close.

The remaining tank continued pouring machine gun and cannon fire into the line, but it didn't make an attempt to climb the hill. Wallace shot grenade rounds at it randomly and did little more than slightly dent the armor. It must be awfully loud inside.

"They're close enough for grenades!" Clyde yelled.

He clutched the first grenade, pulled the pin, and threw it as far as he could downslope. He threw two more in quick succession, then went back to his carbine. Flashes erupted among the enemy soldiers as the grenades cooked off. Clyde noted unhappily that Butler's grenades flew much farther than his own. The kid had an arm, after all.

He heard Huss yell over the din of destruction. "More tanks!"

Clyde felt his insides turn cold. If the Japanese tanks climbed the hill, they had no way to stop them. They'd roll right over their position and they'd have no choice but to give up the hill.

He heard the tanks, too. It sounded like every tank in the world had shown up. The firing from both sides eased up as everyone seemed to pause and tremble or exult at this new addition.

The tank that Wallace had been firing grenades at suddenly erupted in flames. The turret shot off the top and spun as though it weighed nothing.

Clyde yelled, "Good shot, Cowboy!"

"That wasn't me." His voice went up an octave. "Those are friendly tanks! They're ours!"

A flare erupted overhead finally and bathed the slope in light again. Sure enough, at least four massive Sherman tanks lumbered from the right side. The coaxial machine guns spit a constant flow of bullets into the Japanese and the 75mm cannons spewed high explosive rounds into their rear. Bodies flew twenty feet into the air, most having lost body parts.

A roar went up all along the trench line as soldiers exulted in the carnage. Clyde forgot to fire as he watched in stunned fascination. Japanese soldiers scattered and the few survivors darted into the shadows. A few paratroopers fired parting shots, but most hooted and hollered, taunting and cursing the retreating soldiers.

The flare finally drifted into the jungle and the only light came from the burning tank hulks and a few small fires on the slope itself. Black blobs he knew to be dead or wounded men dotted the slope. The celebration continued all along the line. He shook his head at the sheer violence they'd unleashed on the enemy.

The sky lightened in the east, promising another breathtaking sunrise. He looked at the sky. The clouds still lingered, but they took on a pink and yellowish hue that grew deeper with every second. Without him noticing, the moon had dropped below the horizon at some point during the night.

A few stars still twinkled, and Clyde fixated on one. "That was for you, Gil." He prayed his friend was still alive, but his wounds seemed too grievous. He'd seen far less severely wounded men die.

"How will I make it through the rest of this mess without you, brother?" he asked the fading stars.

22

Malawbum, Burma
March 5, 1944

Shawn Cooper felt every knot in the tree pressing into his back. His legs ached from being in the same bent position for hours upon end. He ignored the discomfort as best he could, trying to set an example for the platoon of American soldiers surrounding him. Bugs and creepers wiggled over and around him as though he were a natural part of the jungle.

The Americans from the 5037th Combined Forces Unit wriggled and itched at the discomfort, making far too much noise for Shawn's liking. This was the third day since they'd parted from the main force of Merrill's Marauders and pushed around and now behind the Japanese forces who now pushed from the west. They'd avoided patrols and now it was their turn to strike, but so far, nothing had come down the road. He knew that would change, but for now, they had to be patient.

As though speaking to this point, Lieutenant Natherton, a tall glass of water from the Nebraska plains, whispered in his ear. "Maybe they're not coming."

Shawn opened his eyes. He hadn't been sleeping, he'd been listening and concentrating on not feeling the discomforts of the jungle. He leveled his gaze at Natherton. He didn't think he glared, but Natherton looked abashed.

"They'll be along," he said simply.

"How long do we wait?" Natherton asked with an edge to his voice. "The men are eager to get back for the main defense. The Japs are pushing hard." To his point, they heard artillery and mortar rounds exploding in the hills around Walawbum.

"We wait for as long as it takes."

Natherton had learned not to expect a 'sir' from Shawn. He'd made a stink about it once and his commanders, after bringing it up to OSS Captain Burbank, were told in no uncertain terms not to worry about it. So far, it hadn't been a problem, but Shawn knew Natherton still expected it. As unconventional a unit as the marauders were, they were still a leg unit.

Natherton obviously didn't like the cryptic answer. His jaw rippled as he gnashed his teeth, but he didn't push the issue.

Shawn closed his eyes again. The monsoons would start any day now. They'd seen all sorts of weather over the past two days, from cold as they passed over tall ridges to sweltering heat in the valleys to torrential rainstorms. Now, it just felt muggy and wet.

The two squads of Kachin rangers tagging along with them showed the American troops what plants to eat and what critters to avoid. The lessons were endless out here. Surviving the jungle was often much harder than surviving the Japanese.

The marauders knew that better than most by now. They'd suffered bitterly from their journey from Ledo, India, to the outskirts of Malawbum. Even though they'd been living in Burma for months now, they still seemed raw and untested. If General Merrill had listened to reason and used vehicles instead of mules, they'd be much better off.

The past few days they'd fought mostly conventional-style battles. More and more Japanese filtered into the area, trying to dislodge them and open their resupply road back up. They'd clashed with the marauders' fixed positions and the Japanese suffered mightily.

Now Bellevue, along with a marauder squad and a few Kachin rangers, had pushed beyond the front line and waited to ambush whoever came along. He felt supremely confident in his and the Kachin's skills, but the marauders could easily get them into hot water if they didn't follow instructions. He hoped the Japanese came soon, or the antsy lieutenant would pull rank and insist on moving back to the main line of defense.

Long minutes passed. His eyes snapped open when he finally heard what he'd been listening for, the sound of distant engines. All the Kachin had heard it too, but the marauders obviously hadn't.

Natherton saw or felt Shawn's heightened awareness. "What? What is it?"

Shawn held his finger first to his lips for quiet, then his ear for listening. Natherton scowled at him as though he'd been disrespected again. But recognition finally dawned on him, as he couldn't help but hear the engines as they approached.

Shawn leaned forward slightly until his back peeled away from the tree trunk. He clutched his carbine, which had been leaning on his shoulder the whole time. He flicked the safety off and stared into the jungle and the overgrown road beyond.

They'd set the ambush in the early light of morning, having crossed a river first. Most of the day had passed, but now their patience would pay off. He could hear Natherton's breathing beside him. His eyes were wide and he looked like he needed to be doing something, but everything had already been done. His men were placed in optimum ambush positions. The Kachin and the OSS men from Bellevue made certain of that. Now all they had to do was to execute the plan.

Sergeant Boyd slowly turned to look at Shawn. They gave each other expectant nods. Neither knew the Japanese would come for sure, but this was one of the few roads leading from the Chinese front back to Walawbum. It might be the advance unit of the main force everyone expected to arrive to push the marauders out.

Shawn broke from Boyd's gaze and scanned the distant hillock. That's where he'd see whatever was coming. He hoped it was only the advanced section and not the entire Japanese force.

His pulse quickened as the first vehicle came over the hill. An armored car with a mounted machine gun facing forward and a soldier manning it careened down the hill. A few yards behind it, there was an identical armored car, but the gunner had his muzzle aimed to the side. Four transports trundled close behind the armored cars. He couldn't tell if they held troops or supplies, and it didn't really matter. His job would be the same: attack, kill, maim, and get the hell out of there before they knew what hit them. Speed and ferocity—the key to success.

Natherton licked his lips and sweat beaded on his forehead and dripped from his long, thin nose. He looked as though he might either throw up or dance a quick jig.

Natherton had the walkie-talkie in his right hand now. His hand shook slightly, and Shawn reached out and touched him. He gave him what he hoped was a reassuring smile. "Wait till I tell you to give the order."

Natherton looked like he wanted to curse him, but he reluctantly nodded.

Another armored car took up the rear of the column. Shawn hadn't seen such a heavily armed column yet and he figured it was a sign that the main force would come soon. They had enough weapons to annihilate a force twice the size.

The lead armored car was just about to enter the tighter confines of the jungle. Shawn watched carefully as the trucks slowed to maneuver the sharp turn he knew to be there.

He held up his hand for Natherton to see. Natherton watched it as though it might spit fire. He held the walkie-talkie and his finger hovered over the transmit button. Sweat poured off his hand and he had to grip tighter to keep the transmitter from slipping. When the last vehicle entered the jungle, Shawn closed his hand, forming a fist.

Natherton nearly dropped the walkie-talkie, but resorted to using both hands. He transmitted rather dramatically, "Attack, attack, attack!"

Before he'd finished transmitting, there was a loud boom, followed immediately by machine gun fire. For half a minute, the entire jungle came alive with violence. A whoosh near the back of the column grabbed Shawn's attention. A small projectile raced out and struck the tailing armored car in the butt. An explosion of shrapnel and fire sliced through the jungle canopy. The armored car's back end rose nearly vertically, dumping the occupants into the road. It came down with an astonishingly loud crash.

Shawn hadn't seen the deadly Piat antiarmor launchers in use yet.

Merrill and his men had packed them all the way from India. It was a deadly and welcome weapon that he was pleased to see worked as advertised.

The Japanese soldiers who survived the initial onslaught launched from the transports and ran into the jungle on the other side, away from the fire. Machine gun fire and grenade blasts continued pouring into the now stalled and burning vehicles.

Natherton watched in stunned fascination. His mouth hung open at the carnage he'd unleashed with a word.

Shawn yelled, "That's it! Tell 'em to get the hell outta there. . . . Now!" he added when he hesitated.

Natherton finally complied. "Cease fire! Break contact!" he yelled into the transmitter.

This was the dangerous part. If the Americans became too enthralled with the attack, if their blood lust burned too hot and they didn't disengage, they'd start losing men. This was the magic of the Kachin ambush theory: never let them see you unless they die a moment later.

A few shots rang out and Shawn even heard an overzealous soldier empty his entire magazine in one long burst from his Thompson. There was yelling and screaming from the Japanese, but the Americans made very little noise as they sprinted away from the road. A few desultory shots rang out from Japanese rifles, but the mounted machine guns on the armored cars remained silent.

Men streaked past Shawn's position. All of them had broad grins and a few were even chuckling to themselves.

He hadn't fired a shot and had no intention of doing so unless the Japanese rushed them, but he knew they were too shaken to mount an effective offense. When the last American passed, he waited for the Kachin. They came through the jungle like apparitions and he was struck by the difference. The big Americans seemed like blundering idiots in comparison. Was that how he'd first appeared to them? Probably. Maybe he still did.

Muffled explosions split the evening air occasionally as they hustled away from the ambush sight. Natherton raised a questioning eyebrow. Even the uptight officer had a smile on his face.

"Booby traps," Shawn said. "They're also finding lots of punji stakes in the jungle, particularly if they push into our old positions."

Natherton shook his head. "Brutal," was all he said.

"That's how you fight these bastards—meet their brutality with even more.

"Speed and viciousness," Natherton murmured.

"Exactly," Shawn said.

"We could've destroyed that entire column if we'd stayed and mopped up."

"Maybe yes, maybe no, but as it was, we didn't lose a single man, and the Japs lost plenty. They never even saw us. Think how that must be for them. Think how demoralizing and downright scary that is. You'd start believing you were fighting real ghosts."

"I don't have to imagine it. The Japs did that to us on the Canal."

"Feels good doing it back—doesn't it?"

"Yeah, it does. I'm beginning to think we might really make a difference out here," Natherton said.

"I'll bet those were troops from the front with the Chinese. Now half those troops won't arrive and the ones that do won't be worth much for a while. They've got wounded, which takes up a ton of resources, both men and material. Think of each engagement like a math equation." He pointed his thumb back the way they'd come. "That equation started out okay for them, but we interjected a big negative number and the gain has changed to a loss. They can't sustain that kind of math forever. Eventually, they'll lose too much."

Natherton gave him a bemused look. "Math, huh? You OSS guys aren't like anyone else I've ever come across."

Shawn thought of all the other characters he'd met out here. Calligan, one of the original OSS men, came to mind. Natherton's eyes would really bug out of his head if he saw that crazy son of a bitch step out of the jungle. Despite his size, he looked more like a Kachin warrior than the Kachin did.

He'd heard through the grapevine that Calligan and his intricate Kachin network of spies continued feeding invaluable intelligence from in and around Myitkyina.

He distantly hoped he might run into him on one of these forays into the Japanese rear areas. It would be good to see him again. He felt as though he was becoming more and more like him every day. He realized with a shock that the realization no longer frightened him.

East bank of the Nambyu River
March 6, 1944

After the successful ambush west of the river, they withdrew and crossed the river under the cover of darkness. Shawn's respect for the marauders grew as they moved expertly back into friendly positions. Lieutenant Natherton reported the successful ambush and that he thought it was the tip of a larger force.

It was past midnight when Shawn and the other OSS men found holes in the line overlooking the Nambyu River. A team from the marauders' Second Battalion held the area. They'd dug and reinforced foxholes with overhead cover, since mortars had harassed them and even heavy artillery that day.

They were told to sleep the rest of the night away and not to worry about taking sentry duty. They didn't hesitate and fell asleep within moments. It had been a long day.

The unholy sound of artillery shells shrieking overhead woke Shawn from a dreamless sleep. He'd heard artillery barrages, but he'd never been on the receiving end of one. He cringed in the hole along with the others as shells rained down all along the eastern edge of the river. The ground shook violently and he watched the overhead cover, hoping the marauders had built it well. It looked sturdy, but would it hold up to a direct hit? He doubted anything but steel would.

Time seemed to creep by. The heavy shells gave way to mortar shells. Shawn took the relative respite to peek out through the wood slats. Their hole looked west, out over the river. The far bank was only one hundred yards away and he had a clear line of sight all the way across to the jungle beyond. The mortars must be out there somewhere, but he didn't see any smoke, just early morning fog.

The mortars finally stopped. Smoking holes dotted the once pristine field. He heard soldiers calling to one another but he didn't hear any screams for medics, which he took as a good sign. Could all of that steel and fire have missed?

Despite the heavy barrage, the Japanese didn't appear from across the way. He heard the smattering of small arms fire and more mortars and even a few artillery barrages further north, toward the airfield, but nothing fell here again.

They ate K-rations, which the marauders had given them. It wasn't the best food, but they appreciated the calories.

"Well, I guess this is what it's like to be a regular line unit," JoJo said.

O'Keefe slurped food and wiped his mouth with the back of his hand. "Besides the shelling, it's not too bad. Whaddya say, Coop?"

"Feels weird. I guess this is probably what our airborne brothers are doing most of the time."

"Do you wish things had turned out that way?" JoJo asked.

"Not really. I'm sure those guys are holding their own, but they're nothing compared to Bellevue guys."

Boots appeared beside their hole. "You guys okay in there?"

Shawn recognized Lieutenant Natherton's voice. "Yep. Buttoned up nice and tight. Everyone else okay?"

"Yeah, they didn't hit nothing but dirt."

They moved around the corner and emerged from beneath the cover. Natherton grinned down at them. It made Shawn nervous. "Why don't you come on in here?"

Natherton shrugged and dropped into the hole. "That better?"

"Yeah, thanks. So what's the situation here? What d'you hear?" Shawn asked.

"The Japs are pushing hard up at Wesu Ga. Third Battalion and most of Second Battalion—except us, have moved up there to defend. We gotta stay here in case they try to cross here."

"Think they will?" O'Keefe asked.

"I dunno. Maybe, but it'd be a tough crossing in daylight. We got it covered pretty damned well." He pointed to two different areas. "We have machine guns there and there. Also, our mortars are ready to hit the open ground on the far side. It'd be a meat grinder if they come. But they're desperate to push us out of here, so who knows? General Merrill says we should expect a push today."

"Any idea where the Chinese are?" Shawn asked.

"They've broken out of the Maingkwan area and are heading our way. If we can link up, that'll be it for the Japs. They'll have to withdraw or risk being surrounded."

The buzzing of an aircraft overhead drew their attention. A C-47 flew slowly and dumped supplies out the back as they flew by the airstrip a few miles away. Tracer rounds reached up from the jungle, but the rounds seemed to fall short.

"That's the Lagang Ga Airstrip. I didn't think they were that close," Natherton said.

"Hey," JoJo said, "this isn't really our thing, fighting from foxholes and whatnot."

Natherton said with an edge to his voice, "You wanna leave?"

"No, no, not at all. I was just wondering if you guys have any more ammunition you can spare. I've only got two magazines and if they try to push the river, I'll need more."

Natherton smiled and slapped him on the back. "Hell yes, we got plenty more ammo. I'll have a runner bring some for you."

"You got any more of those Garands sitting around?" Natherton nodded and JoJo added, "Just in case."

As the day crept by, the tension grew. The sounds to the north rattled them. Great plumes from artillery strikes blasted the area and small arms fire crackled almost nonstop.

Shawn hunkered beneath the wooden roof and peered through the firing slit at the far bank, expecting to see a flood of Japanese at any moment. They seemed to be the only area that hadn't been assaulted yet. The occasional reports from Lt. Natherton told them the other battalions were holding off the attackers and inflicting heavy casualties. They were told to remain in place.

Five o'clock rolled around and he thought he should try to find more K-rations. He suspected the Japanese might try to cross at night, so he wanted to eat before that.

O'Keefe and JoJo shared his hole. Throughout the day, a few other Bellevue men had visited, but now they were all back in their own holes, waiting for darkness to descend.

A shriek overhead made him cringe back down. "Shit, more artillery." He sunk to the bottom of the hole and held on. High explosive rounds exploded all around the field, sending up great plumes of black soil.

The barrage stopped after only five interminable minutes passed. Shawn turned his baseball cap backward, hefted himself to the firing slot, and at first he thought his eyes played tricks on him. He quickly found the Garand. "Here they come," he said to the others, still cringing at the bottom of the hole.

JoJo and O'Keefe sprang up, bringing the Garands to the firing slots. JoJo gave a low whistle. "I'll be damned. Look at 'em all."

O'Keefe primed his Garand, "Must be hundreds of them."

"It'll be a slaughter," JoJo said with relish.

"Why didn't they wait for darkness?" Shawn wondered.

"Chinese are probably right on their tails," O'Keefe ventured.

Mortar rounds arced overhead and erupted on the far side of the river near the tree line. Small spouts of dirt and fire sent the enemy scurrying for cover. They moved faster as the rounds impacted. They pushed toward the river.

"It's like kicking an anthill," JoJo exclaimed.

Mortar rounds impacted in front of their hole, but they stayed up at the firing ports, waiting for the order to fire. A couple of the hated Nambu machine guns opened fire and geysers stitched up the field, walking back and forth across the line. No one returned fire yet.

The mortars continued wreaking havoc on the enemy, but it wouldn't be enough to keep them from crossing. More and more men clustered at the water's edge and a few had ventured in and waded up to their chests.

Shawn had one of those in his sights. His finger hovered on the trigger, but he held fire, waiting for the word. He wondered if everyone had left and they hadn't gotten the word.

Finally, he heard the yell. "Open fire!"

He pulled the trigger, but his target and the area all around disappeared in a torrent of splashes as hundreds of bullets impacted all at once. The heavy chatter of the machine-gun nests that Natherton had pointed out swept across the tight group of soldiers near the river bank, sending them sprawling and spinning like rag dolls.

The intensity and deadly accuracy of the fire made him stop and watch in morbid fascination. JoJo fired until his clip pinged. He quickly reloaded and whooped, "Yeehaw!" He noticed Shawn just watching. He slapped Shawn's ball cap. "Remember what they did to Clem!"

Shawn snapped from his revelry. He found a swimming target and fired until his man dropped beneath the surface. The water streamed red and scores of bodies floated downstream in clumps.

Enemy soldiers crumpled at the water's edge as the machine guns continued sweeping them. He concentrated his fire on the field beyond where more men rushed toward their deaths. They seemed so eager to die.

He blazed through scores of clips before switching back to his carbine. The flow of bodies lessened finally. He had to pick and choose his targets now. He did so methodically and efficiently. He had no idea how many men he'd personally shot that day, but it had to be more than twenty and it wasn't over yet. But the real harvesters had been the machine gun crews. They only stopped to reload. He thought they must've burned through several barrels, but he'd never heard them stop for long to change them out.

Finally, the order to cease fire came. Shawn's entire body quivered from the adrenaline and the vibrations from so much concentrated sound. His hands tingled. He coughed as the gunpowder filling the hole filled his lungs. Smoke wafted across the hole, obscuring the carnage for a moment.

When the smoke cleared, he saw the carnage with a fresh eye and he could barely speak. He'd never seen such devastation. He uttered, "My God. It's a massacre. Look at 'em all."

"Hundreds," O'Keefe marveled.

"If this is what regular army pukes get to do all the time, sign me up," JoJo said.

Shawn wanted to feel disgust at what had just happened and the role he played, but he couldn't. He felt only exuberance. He took Clem's hat off and spun it in his hands. "We paid them back in spades."

No more Japanese came and when night finally descended, hiding the terrible scene across the river, they were called to meet with Captain Burbank.

Captain Burbank gathered them in a building a few hundred yards back from the action. The men talked excitedly about the incredibly lopsided battle until Burbank cleared his throat. "The Chinese linked up with Third Battalion an hour ago. They say the Japs have had it and are in full retreat."

A whoop went up and the men hugged and congratulated one another. They hadn't been there long, but it felt like an eternity.

After the congratulations and backslapping, Shawn went outside and looked up at the stars, darting between heavy clouds. Even though the incredible burst of adrenaline had come and gone, he still didn't feel any remorse. Somewhere, in the far reaches of his mind, he knew he should be worried, but he ignored that part and concentrated on the part that yearned for more.

23

Shawn settled into the depths of his chair and enjoyed a hot drink of tea in the Kachin village on the hill. After Malawbum, they'd gone to the village and been greeted by the locals who brought them food and drink. Many of the Kachin rangers in their group called the village home. It was a frequent resting stop for the OSS men, and they planned to spend the night there, then head back toward the Hukwang Valley.

They'd parted ways with the marauders. Not much was said, but the OSS men had gained respect for them and Shawn hoped the reverse was also true.

JoJo blew cigarette smoke out the side of his mouth. The marauders seemed to have an endless supply of American cigarettes and shared with the OSS men before they left.

JoJo said under his breath, "I guess we're back to the easy life."

Boyd said, "You coulda stayed with them if you wanted to, JoJo. We wouldn't miss you."

Shawn said, "I'd miss you."

"Long as I live, I'll never forget that magnificent shooting gallery."

They each held a cup of Kachin hooch. JoJo took a big gulp and scowled, then his entire body convulsed as the foul alcohol burned its way down his throat. "I don't know if I'll ever get used to this stuff." He had the beginning of a slight slur.

"I'd be careful if I were you. A little goes a long way," Boyd warned.

JoJo pshawed and took another sip. His cheeks had a noticeable pinkness and his eyes sparkled in the light from the centrally located fire.

A memory of a hunting trip with his cousins flashed into Shawn's mind. This felt a lot like that, only that had been half a world away and a lifetime ago and the hooch had been much more palatable.

A ruckus from the darkness, out of sight of the light from the fire, made them all turn. Voices rose in greeting, not alarm, and Shawn relaxed and stopped reaching for his carbine. He strained to see into the darkness, but decided it wasn't important enough to actually get up. He was comfortable and he might make the chair his sleeping spot for the night.

The boisterous voice he heard changed his mind. He exchanged glances with the others. They'd all heard the same familiar voice, and they perked up.

Shawn sprang to his feet and waited for the person to appear from the darkness. But what he saw first wasn't what he expected. A Japanese officer, dressed in a one-piece flight suit with his hands bound behind his back, stepped into the circle of light. Every man there glared at him and a few even spit in his direction, but the officer remained stoic and completely unfazed.

Behind the prisoner, he saw the man he expected, Henry Calligan. He looked the same as he ever did, but his beard had grown and nearly touched mid-chest. He perused the men around the fire. His scowl grew when he saw Shawn and the other OSS men. He smiled at them and opened his arms as though in greeting. "Hello, hello, my furry friends."

Shawn could barely believe his eyes. He'd just been thinking about the old son of a bitch and now here he stood and with a Japanese officer, no less.

He avoided the enemy officer and extended his hand. "How the hell are you, Calligan? Been a long time."

"Yes, it has." He took Shawn's hand and shook vigorously while looking at the other OSS men. "It's good to see you all." He squinted at them in the firelight. "You a part of that dust-up at Malawbum?"

Umberland stepped forward and they shook hands. He answered him, "Yes, we just left there. We were just discussing it."

"Japs are on the run, that's for sure. I had to dodge 'em all the way here." Calligan said with a dismissive wave of his hand. Without looking at what he was doing, he jammed his knees into the back of the Japanese officer's knees. The pilot's face contorted in pain and he dropped to the hard ground. He glared back at Calligan. If those eyes could kill, Calligan would be a smoking heap of ash. He smacked the officer in the back of the head. "Relax," he said. It did nothing to simmer the prisoner's hatred.

"Who the hell is this?" Umberland asked.

"A Jap pilot who bailed out too damned close to us for his own good. We saw the whole thing. The little bastard jumped some heavies, but got more than he bargained for. They shot him up pretty good. He thought he was home-free bailing so close to his home base, but he didn't account for us." He smacked him in the back of the head again. "Me and Didi wanted to gut him, but someone radioed command and they want him, so I'm bringing him back for them."

The pilot glared at all of them. He seemed to know he was the center of the conversation. He raised his chin, telling them he wasn't defeated or demoralized.

"A major?" Shawn asked.

"Yeah, far as I can tell."

JoJo said, "Might as well kill him now and save yourself the trouble. A Jap major won't talk to our people. He'd rather die. You want us to arrange an accident?"

Calligan looked at JoJo with renewed respect. "Last I saw you guys, you were all bleeding hearts—now look at you." He looked around at the Bellevue men as though he were a proud father. "You're cold stone killers. Even you!" he pointed at Shawn, who inwardly cringed. Calligan laughed. "I knew this place would get under your skin. There's no avoiding it."

Compared to the Bellevue boys, Calligan looked like an old man of the jungle. His eyes had a craziness to them, which was hard to describe or look away from.

"Much as I'd love to bury him alive in an anthill, I gave command my word that he'd make it back in one piece."

Shawn raised an eyebrow. Calligan followed orders, but he liked to bend them, too. That didn't sound like him. Maybe he had some other plan for the arrogant pilot.

"You heading to Knothead?" Shawn asked.

"That's right. They wanna fly him out instead of walking him out."

Umberland said, "There's an airstrip where we just left. They could take him outta there no sweat."

"Is that so? Well, that'd save us a long trek."

Umberland studied the Japanese officer. "He's pretty full of himself, isn't he?"

JoJo, feeling his alcohol, blurted, "Aw, come on, let's gut him."

Calligan's voice turned icy. "Leave him alone." For a fraction of a second, he looked as though he may gut JoJo instead.

The dark and dangerous Henry Calligan changed to the happy-go-lucky Henry Calligan in a flash. It always amazed Shawn how quickly he could change his entire attitude so quickly and seamlessly. Was it a sign of brilliance or insanity?

Calligan said, "It looks like you're having a bit of a party." He rubbed his hands together in anticipation.

Shawn handed him his own, mostly untouched, cup of jungle juice. He couldn't stand the stuff. "Here you go."

Calligan took it and quaffed it down in one gulp, as though the vile stuff was water. "Ah, good batch!"

A Kachin woman refilled his cup. Calligan glanced at the Japanese officer, still on his knees. He offered the cup to him. The officer leveled a hate-filled gaze at him, then stared straight ahead. Calligan kneeled and held the drink to his mouth. The officer didn't open his mouth and he kept his eyes focused on a distant point.

O'Keefe said, "Don't waste it on him."

Calligan smiled. "I'm not doing him any favors. The vile stuff'll probably bore out our insides." He shrugged when it was obvious the prisoner wouldn't drink. He held the cup up as though toasting his captive. "Cheers!" he said as he tilted the cup back and drank. "If it's alright with you lot, I'll join you in the morning. I could use the company and I don't really know where this airfield is."

Shawn didn't know why, but he felt buoyed knowing Calligan would be joining them. He'd done everything in his power to avoid the brutal son of a bitch, but now he felt a fundamental shift in how he felt about him.

Umberland said, "Of course."

SHAWN PACED JUST outside General Merrill's HQ area. The other OSS men had faded into the woodwork, but Shawn worried about how long Calligan had been inside. Despite a slight headache from the festivities the night before, Shawn felt ready for another mission. He didn't return to the river to see the carnage, but the wind carried a slight scent of rotting flesh.

"What's gotten into you?" JoJo asked. "You're pacing. Why're you so eager for another mission?"

Shawn kept pacing. "I dunno. I just feel like now's the time for something definitive—something big. The Marauders are confident and will continue harassing the Japs, and the Chinese are finally making gains, too. The Japs are on the run."

"Yeah, but so what? I mean, what's changed for you? You seem more keyed up than normal."

Shawn thought for a moment, trying to explain it to himself first. "Seeing Calligan again—it just reignited something in me. Don't you feel it?"

"We're in the middle of Burma at the tip of an attack on the Japanese. Of course I feel it, but I'm not the one pacing like a nervous father in the delivery waiting room."

Shawn finally stopped pacing when he saw Calligan moseying toward them. He'd cleaned himself up for his meeting with General Merrill. He wore a crisp new uniform. He'd combed his hair, and even brushed out his beard. Shawn almost didn't recognize him.

"Where's your prisoner?" Shawn asked.

"Merrill promised to have him delivered to OSS intelligence back in Nasira. They think he's a big deal, but I doubt he'll talk to them. From my short time with him, he's stubborn as hell, but we took a few letters and pictures off of him before he could destroy them. I already sent those ahead over a week ago. Based on those, they think he flies out of the airfield responsible for giving our transports so much hell as they fly the hump. That's why they're so interested in talking with him." He looked around conspiratorially. "But I'm probably not supposed to discuss any of that."

Shawn smirked, "Yeah, no shit."

"You won't tell anyone, though. That's for sure."

"And what makes you so sure?" Shawn asked playfully.

JoJo and O'Keefe pretended not to be interested, but Shawn could tell they were listening just as intently as himself.

Calligan's gaze turned icy. He finally said, "'Cause you boys are coming with me and you'll be too busy to pass on sensitive intelligence to anyone."

O'Keefe and JoJo dropped their aloof act and both sat up straighter and stared at Calligan.

"Bellevue's been assigned to you? I didn't hear anything about that," Shawn said.

"Not all of you, just a select few," he grinned evilly. "You three, plus Killigrew. We'll head back toward Myitkyina. We'll meet up with Guthrie and O'Donnelly. You remember them? From the airdrop?"

Shawn remembered meeting the OSS pair briefly just before they left the Myitkyina area a few months before. He hadn't heard their names since. "The Texan and Irishman, right?"

"That's right. Up till now, we've just been spying on the Nips, but command wants us to activate our resistance cells and really start hitting the Nips hard."

"Resistance cells?"

"Yeah, we've got informants all over the base and the town. They've just been waiting for the word." He lowered his voice and continued. "And now that these jokers are here," he swung his hand to indicate General Merrill's Marauders, "Putting even more pressure on the Japs, it's time to activate those cells into something a bit more lethal. You men are gonna help us with that."

A strained silence extended for half a minute. Shawn remembered their last assignment with Calligan. Back then, he couldn't wait to be finished, but now he felt a surge of excitement. He could feel the other's trepidation, however.

He finally nodded and stepped up to face Calligan. He extended his hand. "Well, I'm thrilled. We'll have a chance to get more payback," he said simply.

Calligan shook his hand and looked at the other two. They exchanged glances, nodded to one another, and joined them.

"It'll be good to work with you again, Calligan," JoJo said and extended his hand.

O'Keefe said, "Two Irishmen on the team might not be the best idea, but I'm in, too."

"Where's Killigrew?" Calligan asked.

"I'll tell him the good news," JoJo said and sauntered off to find him.

"I'll join you," O'Keefe said.

Shawn watched them go. Calligan said, "I see a difference in you four. It's why I chose you."

Shawn thought he knew what he meant, but he still asked, "Yeah, what's that?"

"Like I said before, you're killers now."

"A year ago, I would've disagreed with you, but now . . . well like you said, this place gets under your skin."

24

Seattle, Washington
May 1944

Abby tried to process what had happened, but she could barely stay focused long enough to answer the police officer's questions. They wanted to know the answers to all sorts of questions, but she couldn't keep the image of her friend Trish's body sprawled on the apartment floor with an ever-expanding pool of blood from forming.

The bullet from Private Lou Connor's service pistol had torn through Trish's chest and exploded her heart. She remembered hearing the medics discussing it in their macabre, distant way. It was the first time she realized Trish was actually dead.

Time seemed to stand still after the shooting and she sat staring at the immobile body, even eschewing the frantic yells and anguished calls from Private Connor. She distantly recalled him bolting out the door and up the stairs, calling for help. What only seemed like seconds later, the room was filled with police officers and elderly medics.

She didn't remember being carted out of the room or being transported in the back of a police car to the station. She only remembered the questions—the pointed and harsh questions. They smashed her back to reality.

She clammed up mostly, not giving the police answers to their probing questions.

When they became frustrated, they put her in a room with two chairs around a simple table and a harsh lightbulb burning overhead. The only sound came from the light bulb's annoyingly consistent buzz. She had no idea how long she stayed there before the door opened and a vaguely familiar man she guessed to be in his late sixties entered with a flourish with a few officers in tow.

He explained his name was Mr. Lattimore and he was the Brooks family's long-standing lawyer. Abby remembered him, but only from dinner parties. She'd never needed his services before. He espoused that the thugs at the station had grossly overstepped their boundaries and could expect Mr. Brooks to file a formal complaint, possibly even a lawsuit.

Abby had responded to that threat with a question. "Is Father here?"

Mr. Lattimore shuttled her out of the station to a waiting car before he finally answered her, "No, your father is in Spokane on business. He sends his regards and is excited to see you."

Abby nearly threw up at the thought. The last person she wanted to see was her father. In a bizarre and twisted way, he was responsible for Trish's death. How much blood did her father have on his hands?

How could Trish be dead? How had that happened? It seemed impossible. She asked, "What happened to Lou?" When she saw his blank stare, she added, "Private Connor, the boy that . . ." she couldn't finish the thought.

"The police released him to the military police, but I don't think he'll be charged with anything. From what I understand, she was going for a gun when he tried to break up the fight. He had to shoot her or risk being shot himself."

Abby recalled the scene. It played out in slow motion for her. She could barely make herself speak. "Am I being charged with something?"

He shook his head as he opened the back door of his sedan. "No. Your father had a word with the police chief. You won't be questioned again, although they might want a written statement from you. The military police certainly will. I can help you with that."

She remembered what Sal had said about her father and the Seattle police department. He'd said not to trust them with the journal, that it would be like handing it over to Victor himself. Now she knew that to be true and it nauseated her.

He shut her door, went to driver's side, and slid in. His perfectly oiled gray hair swept across his head, obviously covering a growing bald spot. She wondered how much money her father paid him. Did he know about the arson? He'd undoubtedly be the one helping to defend him if it ever came to light.

He looked in the rear-view mirror. "I'll take you home now. You need to rest. You've had quite a shock."

Quite a shock? She nearly laughed at the absurdity. She'd just witnessed her friend being gunned down in front of her. But was she really her friend? It sure didn't seem that way. Trish had been openly hostile, even dangerous. She wasn't the person she remembered when she'd first met her. She seemed hard, jaded, and infinitely cruel, but she didn't deserve to die. *Would've she killed me if she could've?* She doubted that. Trish thought the man at the door was there to kill her—*he did kill her*, she thought ironically, but that had not been the young private's intention when he opened the door. Trish had left him with little choice.

Her thoughts suddenly became crystal clear. "Take me to the airport."

"What? Why?"

"I need to go there immediately."

"But what about your father? He expects you to be home when he arrives."

"Please do as I ask," she said, with some venom in her voice.

"Yes, ma'am," he answered and made the turn.

They didn't speak another word to one another. He kept glancing into the rear-view mirror, obviously trying to come up with some argument to dissuade her from the airport, but she earnestly ignored him.

She directed him to the proper area, then hopped out, grateful the police had thought to return her pack full of clothes and toiletries. She'd left her flight maps and other flying gear at the airport, knowing she'd be using it soon.

Mr. Lattimore rolled down the window and asked in an exasperated voice, "Do you want me to wait for you?"

She turned to him. "No, you'd be waiting a very long time. Tell my mother I won't be coming to dinner. Thanks for your help."

She turned abruptly and slung her backpack straps over her shoulders. In desperation, he called, "But what about the police statement? You'll need to sign it."

She waved her hand as though it were a trivial matter. "I'm sure you'll think of something."

"But what'll I tell your mother and father?"

She stopped and turned back to him. "Mother will understand." She rubbed her chin, considering her father. "Let Father know. He might want to get his affairs in order."

Lattimore's jowls sagged, making him resemble a Bassett hound. He grumbled under his breath and rolled the window back up.

Abby strode into the special zone of the airport. She flashed her badge with her picture and the bored guard let her inside.

No one at the airport expected to see Abby until the following day. No one seemed to know what had happened in the city. Private Connor was on loan from the army and wasn't affiliated with the ferry service, so they didn't know he'd been detained by the military police.

She still felt her heart rate was fast, even though the adrenaline from the incident had passed long ago. She chatted with the mechanics and airport personnel as though nothing had happened. It felt surreal and made her want to scream. Trish was gone and it didn't seem to make even a ripple in the world.

She found the ferry flight scheduler, an aging woman named Gretchen. She asked her if the aircraft she was scheduled to fly out of here the next day was ready today.

"We received word from the pilot, she's coming in late tonight, deary."

That surprised her. "Tonight? Where's she coming from?"

"California."

"Isn't it unusual to fly at night? I mean, we're IFR rated, but it's not encouraged."

"Yes, you're right, but this is one of our highest-hour pilots. She insisted that it's no problem for her."

Abby had goosebumps. Did she know her? "Can you tell me who it is?"

Gretchen adjusted her glasses and read the scrawled name. "Amanda Flannigan," she said in her raspy voice.

Abby could hardly contain herself. She hadn't seen Mandy since training. They hadn't been friends at first. In fact, they nearly came to fisticuffs, but by the time they graduated, they were fast friends—and she was indeed an incredibly skilled pilot.

Mandy had gone off to ferry airplanes almost immediately after graduation and she hadn't answered any of the letters Abby sent. It wasn't surprising. She probably didn't sit still for more than a day or two and the letters probably weren't even at the correct address—the harried life of a ferry pilot.

"Do you know her?"

"Yes, I do. We were in the same class in Sweetwater."

"Oh, wonderful." She checked the notes written in impossibly small handwriting. "You're both scheduled to fly together tomorrow. It'll be like a grand reunion."

"Together? Whatever do you mean?"

"I mean, you're both taking P-40s and you're both going to the same place—Virginia."

Abby could hardly contain herself. She'd never heard of such a thing, but it couldn't have happened at a better time. She still felt uncentered after the shooting. Flying with Mandy would take a lot of the strain off her. *Should I tell her about Trish?* She decided it would be best for both of them if she kept it to herself, at least initially. Mandy might not want to fly with a pilot who wasn't in the proper headspace. She didn't want to put her in an uncomfortable position.

"Do you have somewhere I can sleep tonight? And maybe take a shower, too?"

"Of course, right through here." She opened the door and led her through a labyrinthine maze of hallways. The place seemed mostly empty. Gretchen took her to a short hallway with a few doors leading into bedrooms. She stepped inside and took in the sparse accommodations. A single bed and a single desk with a lamp, and a well-used love seat in a small greenish-hued room.

"Here you go. The bathroom and shower are down the hall. There are towels in the bathroom. Just leave them on the bed when you leave. The cafeteria is open until eight tonight, but I'd get there earlier if you want anything good. The mechanics have enormous appetites."

Abby thanked her, and the matronly woman left her. The thought of food still nauseated her. The walls were bare save for one poster depicting a woman in a red scarf showing off her muscles. It instantly reminded her of Trish. She couldn't keep the flood of emotions in check any longer. She buried her head in the lumpy pillow and cried until the pillow nearly dripped with her tears.

~

ABBY TRIED to stay awake to wait for Mandy to arrive, but after food and a shower, the events of the day caught up with her and she fell asleep.

She startled awake and took in her unfamiliar surroundings. She'd fallen asleep with the light on and without windows to peer through, she didn't know the time.

She cursed herself for falling asleep. Her level of grogginess told her she'd been asleep for quite a while, but perhaps she was mistaken. Perhaps it was still early and Mandy hadn't arrived yet.

She squinted at her watch face. "Oh no," she lamented. "It's five AM, for crying out loud." The last she'd checked, the time had been ten PM. She'd fallen asleep in her clothes and, despite the shower, she felt grubby.

She wished the place had a mirror at least, but the community bathroom down the hall would have to do. She must look a mess.

She gingerly opened the door and peered into the hallway. It reminded her of a hospital hallway but without the nurses, doctors, and patients. Her thoughts turned to Trish and a heavy cloud set on her. She'd cried for hours yesterday. It felt good to let it out, but her grieving had only just begun. Even though she didn't pull the trigger, she couldn't help feeling responsible. If she hadn't visited, Trish would still be alive. But she knew that was rubbish—she'd simply wanted to visit an old friend. She couldn't know the tragic outcome.

The hallway was empty. She wondered if Mandy was behind one of the doors. If she'd arrived late, she'd need her sleep. Her mood lifted, thinking of the upcoming reunion and the joint cross-country flight.

She crept down the hallway. She checked each door, looking for some sign that someone was inside, but they gave nothing away. She was nearly to the bathroom when the final door burst open and out stepped Mandy Flannigan. Her hair was a disheveled mess and her PJs had seen too many nights between washings.

Abby gasped and put her hand to her mouth, "Mandy!" she said.

Mandy spun and stared at Abby for a stunned moment, then she flung her towel and toiletry bag into the air and ran to her with open arms. "Abby Cooper!"

They came together and hugged. Abby thought Mandy might break her ribs, but she squeezed Mandy back just as hard.

They finally parted and took a step away from one another. "How long has it been?" Mandy asked.

"Six months at least," Abby said. "You look great."

"Ha, liar. I just woke up."

"*You* look . . ." she hesitated and concern crossed her face. "Like you've been crying," she finished.

Abby waved her hand. "I always look like this in the morning."

But Mandy wouldn't have it. "No, no. Back at Bay 7, you always looked as fresh as a spring daffodil in the morning. Everyone was always jealous. What's the matter?"

Abby did her best to keep her composure, but the shooting was still too fresh in her mind. In an attempt to keep from crying all over again, she stared at the floor and shook her head, but she couldn't make herself deny it anymore. She finally looked into Mandy's eyes and saw the compassion and concern there—exactly what she hadn't seen in Trish's eyes. This is what genuine friendship looked like.

She felt the despair coming on again. She couldn't stop it. Her shoulders shook and she sobbed quietly.

Mandy took her in her arms and rocked her side to side. Abby hung there, unable to hug her back. They stayed like that for long minutes. No one came down the corridor, but the sound of doors opening and closing told them the place was waking up. The smell of breakfast wafted down the hallway.

Finally, Mandy said, "You feel up to sitting with me at breakfast? If not, I'll make you a plate and we can eat in my room."

Abby wiped her tears and nose. She felt awful allowing her emotions to get the best of her, but she'd lost control. She'd never felt so out of control in her entire life. "I don't think I can handle being around other people. Would you mind?"

"Not a bit." She held the door open and Abby went inside and sat at the little table. "I know how you like your coffee, too. Be right back."

Abby sat down heavily at the little table. She suddenly felt trapped. How much could she tell her? Would telling her put her in danger? She didn't think so. Mandy Flannigan was as far removed from the whole sordid affair as she could get. It would be nice to talk to someone about all of it. Get it out in the open and see what she thought. Perhaps she had some good ideas. She was one of the smartest pilots in class 43-6. But was it fair to bring her into this?

Mandy came in ten minutes later, balancing two trays. Despite Abby's sorrow, her stomach rumbled. Mandy placed the food down and they both ate heartily, without speaking a word.

Finally satiated, they both pushed back from the table and sat side by side on the little couch, where Abby told her friend everything. She started with the poker club and ended with Trish's death. To her credit, Mandy let her talk, never once stopping her to ask a question or espouse her disgust and, finally, shock.

Exhausted from telling the tale, Abby's shoulders slumped and her whole body ached, but her mind felt lighter and clearer than it had since arriving back in her hometown.

Mandy finally said, "You've been through a lot, Abby. This has been going on for years and you never let on to any of us at Avenger."

"I thought I put it all behind me. I—I can't believe she's dead." Mandy placed her hand on her shoulder and gently squeezed. Abby looked her in the eye and said, "What do you think I should do?"

"I don't think you can do anything. I mean, it's in Sal's court now. The only question I have for you is this . . ." Abby held her gaze for long seconds. Mandy finally asked, "Are you fit to fly?"

Abby didn't answer right away. She nodded and said, "I don't know if I can concentrate well enough to plan the trip, but yes, as long as I can follow your lead, I can fly."

Mandy beamed her a bright smile. "Leave the planning to me. I'll do everything. The only thing you have to do is follow my tail. Can you do that?"

"Yes, absolutely."

"Good. I think you have the right idea. The quicker we get out of here, the better. Eventually this'll get back to flight ops and who knows what they'll do."

"Oh Mandy, I'm so happy you're here. I don't know what I would've done otherwise."

"Yeah, me neither, but I have a feeling you would've sucked it up like you normally do and pressed onward."

A few hours later, Abby and Mandy took off in tandem from the Seattle airport. The stick felt solid in her hand and the P-40 Warhawk responded to the slightest adjustments like a true thoroughbred racehorse.

They took one turn over the city as they gained altitude. She recognized landmarks and even thought she saw the Brooks Estate. Despite her melancholy heart, the city sights and the powerful aircraft she controlled couldn't help but boost her mood. It was exactly what she needed.

They gave each other plenty of room and soon they pushed into the thick layer of clouds, which seemed to perpetually hang over the city no matter the time of year. She climbed through the gray clouds, and some of the despair and sadness tried to take hold again, but she pushed ever upward. The solid white and gray felt constraining and disorienting. She kept her eyes glued to the instruments, relying on them to keep her level and at a constant rate of climb.

She suddenly burst out of the gray world and into the bright blue sky. The brilliant sunlight blinded her momentarily, but she couldn't keep from smiling. No matter how thick and gloomy the clouds were, there was always blue sky and sunshine above. You just had to climb high enough.

25

Sal Sarducci decided it was finally time to deal with the Miles Burr journal once and for all. Abby had given it to him a week before. He'd kidded himself that he hadn't dealt with it because they'd been too busy. It was true, but not entirely true. He could've made time, but he was enjoying his time with Beatrice and Cora and they really needed his help.

Deep down, he knew the real reason had something to do with delaying the inevitable. Perhaps if he held onto it long enough, he'd have an epiphany that would solve the problem to everyone's satisfaction, but he knew that was fantasy.

The easiest thing to do would be to simply destroy the damned thing, but he knew he'd never earn back Abby's trust if he did that. He may even lose Beatrice and Cora.

He remembered Beatrice's face when he finally told her about the journal and why it was important. She'd stared at him with a stunned look on her face. He didn't plead, didn't simper, just told her the truth and didn't make any excuses for himself. He remembered how she pulled Cora close and rocked her as though protecting her from him. It had broken his heart.

She'd asked for some space and he'd given it to her. He hadn't had an urge to drink in quite some time, but he craved one then. He found the bar, but before he could order one, she'd found him and called him back to their room.

At first he thought she'd tell him to leave—that their relationship was over—but then she touched his arm whilst holding Cora in the other, and she smiled. Her eyes sparkled, and he'd never forget what she said. "I don't know that man from the journal. He died when he chose the high road and quit working for that horrible man. I love *this* Sal Sarducci. The old one can just go to hell."

Every time he thought of it, he smiled. He didn't think his love for Beatrice could grow, but she constantly proved him wrong.

But now it was time to tackle the problem head-on. He found a telephone exchange and went in with the phone number written down on a scrap of paper. He hoped the numbers hadn't changed.

It took a few minutes for the operator exchange connected him. He listened to the tinny buzz of the phone nearly all the way across the country. The technology still amazed him. He supposed telecommunications might be a good industry to invest in. The war, like all wars, tended to improve technology, and he supposed telephones wouldn't be an exception. His thoughts were interrupted when he heard a distant female voice. "Victor Brooks's office, this is Camilla."

The operator told him he had ten minutes for the call and then signed off. He hoped it didn't take that long.

"Hello Camilla, this is Sal Sarducci, calling for Mr. Brooks. Is he in?"

The long distance made a pause as his words traveled across thousands of miles of telephone lines. Camilla's voice finally came back. "I'll connect you, please hold a moment."

Sal didn't know why he felt nervous. He would much rather do this in person. He doubted his nerves would be a problem at all, but the phone call made him nervous.

He heard hissing and a few clicks, then Victor Brooks's unmistakable voice. "Sal, is that really you?"

"Yes, sir. It's really me. I'm calling from across the country."

A pause before the reply came back. "Yes, I can tell. Are you calling to get your job back? I hope not, because I've already replaced you."

"No, sir. That's not why I'm calling." He heaved a heavy breath, then pressed on. "I have some news you'll want to pay attention to."

He allowed him to respond. "I'm listening."

"I'm in possession of Miles Burr's journal. I've read it many times. It's very detailed and it implicates you in the Trask factory fire."

The pause was even longer, no doubt, as Victor digested the news. His voice finally came back, although not so exuberant as before. "I'm assuming you're calling to tell me you destroyed it, then. After all, you must be mentioned as well."

"I haven't destroyed it yet. I wanted to bring it to you, but only if you agree to hand it over to the people who will act upon it. The proper authorities."

He heard a bitter chuckle before the words, "You must be joking. Why would I implicate myself in such a way? That's a ridiculous notion."

"Because if you do, you'll get your daughter's respect and possibly even forgiveness."

"What does Abigail have to do with this? She's my daughter, of course she loves me."

"She hates you for what you did. She hates me, too, for the same reason, but I told her I'd do the right thing with the journal. That's why she gave it to me and that's what I'm trying to do now."

"By handing it over to me?"

"That's correct. We'll go to the authorities together."

"Let me get this straight. You're coming here with the journal so we can both turn ourselves in to the authorities. Is that correct?"

"That's correct. It's the only way out for both of us. I'm ready to face the consequences of my actions. I can't move on with my life until I've done that . . . and neither can you, whether or not you can admit that to yourself."

"I'm a successful businessman, Sal. I didn't get here by being Mr. Nice Guy. I did what I had to do. I don't need to move on from anything."

"Then I'll simply hand it over to the authorities myself and let whatever happens happen."

"For crying out loud, Sal. Don't do anything stupid. If you're so bent on bringing it to me, go ahead. Are you taking a train?"

"Yes, but I'll want your assurance that you'll do the right thing. If we turn ourselves in, I think the courts would go easier on us. Since you're the head of a vital war industry, they might do nothing at all, or perhaps a slap on the wrist. Perhaps a fine."

"Well, I suppose I see your point. It would be nice not to have it hanging over my head all the time. It does bother me sometimes."

Sal nearly laughed out loud. Even over the tinny phone line, he could hear the mock sincerity in Victor's voice. "So you agree to my terms? When I get there, we go straight to the police?"

A longer pause ensued, no doubt trying to make it appear as if he were in deep contemplation. He finally sighed and said, "Yes, you have my word, Sal. It will be good to see you again."

"I will leave tomorrow. If all goes well, I'll be in Seattle by the end of the week."

"Fine, fine. I'll have my new man pick you up. His name is Hastings, Guy Hastings."

~

THE TRIP across the country took nearly all week. In that time, he went through every possible scenario that might occur once he arrived in Seattle. The least likely scenario was the one he'd laid out for Victor. The odds of Victor turning himself in were one in a million at best. If he surprised him, it would be the greatest surprise in history.

At the last stop before arriving at the main Seattle train station, he'd called the number Victor had given him. It went directly to his office and after the operator connected them, he'd picked up on the first ring. He sounded positively giddy to see him. He assured him his man would be there to pick him up promptly on time.

Sal adjusted the briefcase he had chained and locked to his wrist. He hated having to resort to such drastic measures, but he didn't want this Hastings fellow to simply take it off him. If Hastings shot him, then none of this would matter anymore—but he didn't think Victor would go to such lengths. After all, they'd been best friends most of their lives. And even if their friendship had faded, it wasn't Victor's style. He liked to vanquish his enemies, not kill them outright.

If Victor had slipped that far, then it would be better for everyone if the journal disappeared forever. It would keep Abby out of the whole sordid affair and even Meredith could go on as though nothing had happened. She'd mourn his death, as would Beatrice, and hopefully Abby, but he'd be beyond caring. Eventually, Victor's crimes would catch up with him, one way or the other.

He retrieved his suitcase. It was light, since he didn't plan on staying long. He left the train with the briefcase in one hand and the suitcase in the other. He shuddered to feel the cold wet. Even in summer, Seattle could be cold, certainly colder than Texas.

He spotted Guy Hastings instantly. Even if he hadn't been holding a sign with his name neatly printed, he would have spotted him and marked him as a security man. He wasn't big and burly like Sal, but he had the look of a professional—someone who could handle himself in a fight—a dangerous man.

Sal smiled as though he were an old friend. Best not to give away too much too soon. Victor would've filled Hastings in on his own skill sets, so Sal was definitely at a disadvantage, but hopefully it wouldn't matter. Hopefully, Hastings would simply deliver him to Brooks Industries with no trouble.

"Hello," he dropped the suitcase and extended his hand. Hastings didn't take it. Sal brought it back hastily. "I'm the man on your sign there."

"Cut the crap, Mr. Sarducci. I know it's all an act. I know all about you and smiling and carrying on is beneath you, really."

Sal cut his smile and let his natural scowl return. He'd found it quite easy to slip back into his old self. He'd practiced in the mirror in the train cabin. He found he simply had to push Beatrice and Cora into the recesses of his mind and concentrate on the task at hand. It made the transition seamless.

Hastings pointed at the briefcase and the handcuff-style lock. "That's a bit much, now isn't it?"

"Like you said, cut the crap, Mr. Hastings. You'll have to saw my hand off to get the journal and I don't think Victor has sunk that far yet."

"Pity, really. I'd rather enjoy that."

Sal eyeballed him and suppressed a shiver. He'd seen his kind occasionally in the trenches. Most men desperately tried to maintain their hold on their morals and virtue while doing whatever they had to do to stay alive, but there were a few who thrived on all of it—men who relished the pain and suffering and it didn't matter if it was the enemy or not. Their eyes were vacant—it's what he saw in Hasting's eyes.

Sal didn't respond, but updated the possible scenarios to include a few he sincerely hoped wouldn't come true, but quite possibly might now that a sociopath had been added to the mix.

He stepped into the back of the Rolls Royce. He relished the feel and smell of the old leather. It wasn't as well maintained. He never would have allowed the dust or the grime he saw on the dashboard. He bit his tongue, not wanting to provoke him.

Hastings eyed him through the rear-view mirror. He said, "If it was up to me, you'd already be dead and I'd have the journal."

"Was that the professional advice you gave Victor?"

"Of course. What else?"

"He has no intention of going through with it? With my suggestion?"

"I'm not supposed to talk about it."

"I'm sure you're against it, even though it would be better to do it now while the government needs him and his factories the most."

"If I killed you and took the case, it wouldn't come up at all."

"What makes you think I don't have safety checks in place? If I end up dead, it will set things in motion and then heaven help him."

"Copies?"

Sal stared straight ahead, not deigning to answer. He finally said glibly, "Just do your job, Mr. Hastings." He could see the fire flare in his eyes.

He wondered if Victor knew how dangerous this man was. He doubted it. He'd never seen what these types of people were capable of. It worried him. He might already be conniving behind Victor's back. Did he owe it to him to warn him? It all depended on what happened over the next few hours.

Hastings took him down to the industrial district. Not much had changed in Seattle, although most people looked happier than when he left there months before—and it wasn't just because the weather was slightly better. He suspected it had to do with the improving news from the front lines. Germany continued suffering defeats on the eastern front and the successful landings on the Normandy Coast put them in a deadly pincer between two massively overpowered forces. In the Pacific, the Japanese kept having to retreat as the island-hopping campaign wreaked havoc on their supply lines. *But more victories bring more fallen soldiers,* he thought bitterly, thinking of Clyde.

He pushed it out of his mind as they pulled up to a new building tucked between two factories. Sal didn't wait for Hastings to open his door—he stepped out quickly. The weight of his pistol in his shoulder holster felt reassuring. He almost didn't wear it—it might cause more problems than it solved, but old habits die hard.

Hastings motioned for him to lead. He didn't like him behind him at all, but he doubted the crazy bastard would jump him where all the factory workers could see. Not good for morale, but once he was inside, all bets were off.

Someone he didn't recognize stood just inside the door leading into the new building. He pushed the door open and Sal glimpsed a pistol beneath his unbuttoned light coat. Had Victor upped security in general, or was he here because of his visit?

He eyeballed Hastings as he passed by the doorman. "One of yours?"

Hastings didn't respond. Once they were both inside, the doorman closed the door and Sal heard the ominous sound of a lock bolting into place. The lobby was empty save for four other security men, all wearing light coats concealing firearms. He thought about reaching for his pistol, but thought better of it. It might be what they wanted to happen. It would give them an excuse to kill him.

Fear crept into his belly, but quickly subsided when Victor pushed into the room from a door behind the lobby desk.

"Sal," he said with raised hands. "So good to see you."

The thugs glared at him, daring him to try anything. "Is this how you greet an old friend with goons and guns?"

"A precaution. I know what you're capable of." That elicited a derisive grunt from Hastings, who stood directly behind Sal.

Sal held up the briefcase. "Are you ready to go to the police station?"

Victor sucked air into his sallow cheeks and made a hissing sound. "Unfortunately, I've reconsidered our arrangement. I think you're probably right about the authorities letting us off easy. I truly believe that, but now's not the right time. You see, I'm expanding and a trial will scare off the investors I have on the line. You can understand that."

"What about Abby? Don't you care that your own daughter hates you?"

"My own daughter? You know as well as I do that . . ." he waved his hands as though shooing away a pesky fly, "well, let's just say, I'm not worried about her. She'll come around or she won't. This is just business, Sal. You do understand that, don't you?"

The men closed in around him. They sneered and a few produced wooden dowels and police sticks. He sensed Hastings closing on him from behind. He knew a beating was coming, but he wouldn't allow that son of a bitch the pleasure—not without some pain first.

He spun fast, bringing the briefcase around in a wide arc. Hasting's eyes widened just before the edge caught him in the jaw. Teeth and blood streamed from his shattered mouth, and his eyes rolled into the back of his head. His knees collapsed, and he melted into the floor. Sal only had an instant of satisfaction before blows descended on his back and head.

He collapsed, doing his best to keep the damage to a minimum, but knowing this part had always been inevitable. The thugs worked him over and pain wracked through his body with each baton strike. His vision blurred at the edges. He hoped to pass out, but knew his will was too strong to allow it. He did his best to absorb the beating. If he didn't fight back, they might stop sooner.

A long time later, they finally did.

He felt the briefcase pulled, and his cuffed hand went with it. He kept his eyes shut, feigning unconsciousness, but Hasting's bitter voice made him nervous. "I'm gonna cut his fucking hand off," he slurred through broken teeth and a lacerated tongue.

"The hell you are," Victor barked. "Just cut the chain and give me the journal. And for crying out loud, stop bleeding on the new carpet!"

Sal heard wire cutters making quick work of the heavy chain. "It's locked," a thug said.

"No shit," Hastings spat. "He'll have the key on him, you dolt."

Sal had left the key dangling on the chain near his wrist. He hoped they found it before rifling through his pockets. Hands descended on him, and one of them found his pistol and disarmed him. Another found the small key. "Found it!"

Where had they found these jokers? With the war on, he supposed most of the good help had all gone overseas—yet another trade affected by the war—thuggery.

He heard the key being inserted into the briefcase. The man muttered, "Why's it so damned heavy?"

Sal chose that moment to cough and pretend to come to his senses. He spit blood onto the white carpet and looked around the room. Hastings glared at him with pure hatred. If Victor left, he had no doubt the man would kill him and ask for forgiveness later. He couldn't let that happen. He pushed himself to a sitting position. He clutched his head as though fighting dizziness.

He staggered to his feet at the same moment the thug finally opened the briefcase. Three bricks fell onto the carpet with thuds. Hastings held a handkerchief to his mouth, but reached in and grabbed the leather-bound journal. He glared at Sal with fresh hatred, then handed the journal to his boss.

Victor held it and patted the leather. He addressed Sal, his oldest friend, "I'm sorry this had to happen, Sal, I really am. It's just a deceased man's stupid diary, probably wouldn't even hold up in court, but I couldn't take that chance. I'll destroy it for both our sakes."

Through the bloody handkerchief, Hastings said, "He said on the way in that he had precautions in place. He might've had it transcribed —copied it."

"Copied a diary? Come on, Hastings, use your head. It would be worse than useless."

Sal saw the anger mounting inside Hastings like pressure building inside a volcano. He looked ready to kill and he'd be the likely candidate.

Almost as an afterthought, Victor thumbed the journal open. His spine went rigid and the corners of his silver mustache drooped farther than he'd ever seen before. He flung it at Sal and it bounced off his chest. "You bastard! It's blank! What did you do with it?"

Sal couldn't keep the smugness off his face. "I wasn't kidding when I said I had taken precautions. It's somewhere safe." Hastings dropped the bloody rag and went for his pistol, drawing quicker than Sal thought possible.

He leveled the muzzle at Sal's forehead. His finger went to the trigger and Sal knew his life hung by an ounce of finger pressure.

"If you kill me, the journal gets sent to the *New York Times*. It's all set up and there's nothing you can do to stop it, unless I show up back home, all safe and sound."

Victor's face turned a bright shade of red and the vein on his head popped out like a tiny snake. "You son of a bitch! This is all just a colossal waste of time, Sal. Nothing will come of it."

"Maybe not now, but this war won't last forever, Vic. Once things are back to normal, the government will take more interest in these sorts of scandals. A suspicious fire that benefited one company. One rival company. I'm sure Mr. Trask will also be interested in getting a little payback. Their company and family have suffered the most. They deserve the most."

"So, you're blackmailing me? Is that it?"

Sal shrugged and stretched his neck from side to side. The soreness from the beating was already setting into his muscles. He might not be able to move by morning.

"What do you want from me, Sal? Money? We can work something out, no problem."

"I want you to turn yourself in, just the way we talked about it."

Victor looked at a loss. His face changed colors as he went through scenarios and came up empty.

But the unlikeliest man stepped forward. Hasting sneered at Sal. His mouth dripped blood and his cut cheek added to the mess. He spoke around the blood and the spit, giving his voice a wet sound. "Your little plan might've worked—in fact, it would've worked—but I outsmarted you."

Sal had no idea what he meant, but he took the threat seriously. There was no reason to make anything up. What could it possibly be? He noticed

Victor also looking at him expectantly, as though he didn't know either. What the hell was going on?

He spoke directly to Victor, but cut his gaze back to Sal often. "You remember when Abigail came a couple of weeks ago?"

"How could I forget? A young woman died."

Sal couldn't keep from interrupting. "What? Who died?"

Victor quickly said, "That awful woman Abigail met from the inner city."

"Trish? Trish Watkins?"

"Yes, yes, now shut up or I'll have my men beat you again. Continue, Hastings."

Sal could hardly believe his ears, but judging by everyone else's reactions, it was the truth. His mind reeled, but he pushed it to the back of his head and concentrated on understanding the sloshy words coming out of Hasting's mouth.

"Just before that, your daughter and your wife sat down in the living room and had an interesting chat." Both Victor and Sal flared at the breech of privacy, but neither interrupted him. "I overheard them talking about a journal. How she'd given it to Sal and thought he'd do the right thing."

Victor looked ready to explode. "You—you knew this and didn't tell me?"

"I thought I'd take care of it myself. You were out of town and it wasn't a problem yet." Sal's keen eye could tell the man was lying about that part, but he let it pass.

Hastings leveled his gaze directly at Sal and he saw pure evil and hatred, but also a glimmer of joy. It made him cringe.

"I sent men to retrieve the journal. I suppose you must've passed each other as you traveled here. I should hear from them any time now."

Sal dropped to one knee and kept his eyes on the ground. His mind raced, but what could he do? These men wouldn't allow him to leave and it might already be too late, but should he try? No, he'd just be beaten again and perhaps this time, Victor would allow his man to kill him. He tried to keep his breathing steady. He thought of Trish. What had happened to her—and how was Abby involved? Too many questions circulated in his mind. His head hurt.

26

Sweetwater, Texas
May 1944

Gregory Trambolini and his cousin Horace Trambolini stepped off the bus, which had taken them from the train station into the town of Sweetwater, Texas. Gregory took off his hat and waved it like a fan. "This place stinks to high heaven. Why the hell would anyone live in a place like this?"

Horace breathed in deep and spread his arms wide. "What d'you mean? It's warmer than Seattle. I could live here easily."

"You're not hot?"

"Course I'm hot, but you have to acclimate. Look at the locals. They're not sweating."

Gregory smacked his arm, then pointed. "Bullshit. That guy with the cowboy hat's sweating his balls off. He must be a local."

"Yeah, maybe you're right." He looked at the name written in his notebook. "Let's get this over with. We're looking for a big guy and a gal with a six-month-old baby."

"That's all we got to go on? We'll never find 'em."

"We got their names too, but a small town like this? We'll find 'em easy enough." He pointed at the local eatery, which looked like it doubled as a bar when the sun set. "We'll ask over there while we get something to eat."

"What'll you suppose they eat out here?"

"It's not gonna be Italian food, so don't get your hopes up."

"You don't know that. Maybe there's a contingent of Italian immigrants here."

They pushed into the tavern and let their eyes adjust to the dark interior. The place was mostly deserted. Two customers sat in the corner and they stared as though they'd stepped off a spaceship. The woman behind the bar shook her head at them. "Can I help you two?"

"Yeah, we'd like some lunch . . . and maybe a little information."

~

Beatrice pushed Cora along the sidewalk in the stroller. She wondered how much longer Cora would allow her to do so. She was only six months old and an avid crawler. More and more, she wanted to do everything by herself. She had to coerce her into the stroller with toys and treats, but those only lasted so long. When she got bored, she'd arch her back and squeal, wanting to be released into the world.

Beatrice stopped at a park and took in the sights. It was a beautiful summer day. It was hot, but that was certainly expected in these parts. She bent down and released Cora from her makeshift restraints. Cora launched from the stroller, but Beatrice was ready. She lowered her to the grass and let her go. Cora gurgled in delight at the feel of the lush grass.

Cora crawled a few feet, the grass staining her hands and knees green. Predictably, she yanked a full clump of grass and shoved it into her mouth. A moment later, her tongue pushed most of it out, and a torrent of drool got rid of the rest. Beatrice shook her head. She turned to relish the moment with Sal, but he wasn't there.

She desperately wanted to hear from him, but knew it might be quite a while until she did. She hoped and prayed she wouldn't read about his murder in the paper. She didn't know if such things would even make the paper. It was a big country and, after all, there was a war on. He'd told her not to worry until a month had passed. *A month!* Only a man would say something so outlandish. She'd start inquiring if she didn't hear from him in a week, not a month.

Cora's fat, little legs pumped as she did her best imitation of an older boy she saw running. She hadn't walked yet, but she already wanted to run. Her knees scraped something and she rolled onto her face and came up crying.

Beatrice sprang into action. She hadn't fallen hard, but she didn't normally cry unless she was truly hurt, or just wanted something she couldn't have.

Beatrice picked her up and saw that she'd scraped across a rock hidden in the grass. She checked her tiny knees and saw blood on one. "Oh, you poor dear," she said. "Looks like we'll have to explore the park some other time." She pushed the stroller with one hand while holding Cora with the other. Sweat poured off her and she thought she must look quite the sight. Oh well, Sal wasn't around to impress.

She thanked her lucky stars that the park wasn't far from the little house. She left the stroller outside and pushed the door, but forgot that she'd locked it. She set Cora down. She'd recovered from her booboo, but she liked to be held for a while after such things, and she reached out for Beatrice. "Just a moment, sweetie. I know, I know," she cooed as she finally found the key and opened the door.

She scooped up Cora and shut the door behind her with her foot. It slammed and she hoped the glass didn't break. She'd have to be careful about that next time. She took Cora to the kitchen and set her into her high chair. "Would a snack make you feel better?"

Cora blew saliva bubbles and pushed her back against the highchair while grunting—a sure sign of hunger. "Okay, okay. Hold your horses," she said as she searched the cupboards for something quick and easy. She finally found a few crackers. She crumbled them up on her high chair platter and Cora dug in with abandon. A few found her mouth, but half found the floor. Perhaps a dog would be a good idea. Something to pick up the crumbs, but she scoffed at the idea. She was busy enough without adding a dog to the mix.

She went to the bathroom and kept the door open so she could keep her eye on Cora. She really missed Sal.

She'd just flushed when there was a knock at the door. She startled. Who could it be? A neighbor, perhaps? She quickly washed her hands. Cora reached for her and looked ready to cry, so she veered her way and scooped her up first. Another, more insistent knock at the door made her furrow her brow. "Just a moment," she called out.

GREGORY AND HORACE stood at the head of the paving stones leading through the front yard to the address they'd been given. A few toys were strewn along the well-kept lawn, proof that a child lived here.

"So what's the deal?" Gregory asked the older Horace.

"We go in and get the journal. If they resist, we rough 'em up until they spill it."

"I'm not roughing up a kid."

"You don't have to, you just threaten to. Nothing makes people cooperate better than threatening their kids."

"What if that guy, Sal's home? He sounds like he might be a problem."

"He popped our boys at that poker club. If he gives us trouble, I say we pop him. That'll make the woman talk even quicker. Even if he don't give us trouble, we owe him some payback for our cousin. At the very least, I'm gonna bust him up some." He pulled his right hand out of his pocket, revealing a set of brass knuckles. "I hope the bastard's here."

"Yeah, I guess he earned that much, at least," Gregory said.

"I'll take the lead. You cover me, but don't pull your heat until we're inside." He glanced around the neighborhood. "It's the middle of the day. Sal's probably at work. If no one's home, we'll trash the place and wait for 'em. Capisce?"

Gregory nodded and put his hand on the butt of his pistol hanging from his shoulder holster. Sweat poured off him, but he wasn't willing to expose his firearm by taking off the light cover he wore. They didn't want to attract the wrong attention in a town where most of the public likely carried a firearm or had quick access.

They strolled to the front door. The glass had a curtain blocking their view inside. Horace knocked softly at first. He put his ear close and listened.

He nodded to Gregory. Someone was inside. He waited a few seconds, then knocked harder. He heard a woman's voice. "Just a moment."

He stepped back and grinned at his cousin. "Now for the fun part," he said and he licked his lips.

The woman came to the door and Horace could make out her shape through the lacy curtain. He didn't notice anyone else's shadowy form behind her. He heard a baby squawk as the curtain parted and the woman looked out.

The men exchanged worried glances.

~

BEATRICE SLOWED as she approached the door. Should she be worried? Should she be careful? What if it had something to do with Sal? What if it was news of his death? She nearly stopped in her tracks at the thought, but no, no one would come to her door if the worst happened. It must be a neighbor.

She propped Cora on her hip and went to the door. The curtains blocked her view, but she could see the outline of two people standing there. It must be neighbors. Perhaps they came to invite her and Cora to a play party. She'd be thrilled to finally make a few friends. She parted the curtains and looked out at her two visitors.

She thrust the door open and nearly dropped Cora. "Abby! Mandy!" She jumped up and down and yelled their names over and over like a crazy person.

Cora held on for dear life and Abby reached out and took her from Beatrice's arms. "There's my little beautiful girl," she cooed.

Cora's eyes were wide as saucers, but she took it all in stride. Beatrice hugged Abby and they rocked from side to side. She released her and went for Mandy next.

"What in the world are you doing here?" She directed the question at Mandy.

"We flew back from Seattle together. Well, in separate aircraft, but together. It was wonderful. I'm so happy you and Sal moved here. I'll see so much more of you."

"Me, too. The move was tough, but Sal and I are thrilled to be here. We're still not all moved in yet." She turned to Abby. "But enough of that, I didn't expect you back yet. How was the flight? I want to hear all about it."

Abby exchanged an unreadable look with Mandy. "There's a lot to tell," she said. "But first I want to keep holding little Cora for hours and hours."

Mandy shook her head and said, "Uh, uh, not before I get a turn." She reached out and Cora reached out too and willingly went to Mandy. She took her and placed her on her hip and glanced at Beatrice with an impressed look, then back at Cora. "What a brave girl. Just like your momma," she said.

"And her daddy," Beatrice said wistfully.

Abby didn't know if she meant her paternal father, the deceased British fighter pilot, Standish Hercules, or Sal, but it was true of all those men.

The Light After the Storm
A Time to Serve Series, Book 5

In the darkest hours of World War II, courage flares brightest.

As the storm of war intensifies, Clyde finds himself in the thrumming heart of the action. While his valor is tested on the battlefields of Leyte Gulf, Mindoro, and Corregidor, an unacknowledged yearning for the normalcy of civilian life gnaws at him.

At the same time, Shawn battles his inner demons in the unforgiving Burmese jungle, his spirit strained by the brutal realities of guerrilla warfare against the Japanese. The line between duty and darkness blurs, threatening to consume him.

Back on the home front, Abby, scarred by a personal loss and burdened by guilt, seeks solace in the adrenaline-fueled flights of the Women's Auxiliary Ferry Squadron. Her reckless escapades in the sky mirror her turbulent emotions, but a fateful encounter forces her to confront her trauma.

Across the Pacific, Frank navigates treacherous waters of passion and retribution, his mission complicated by his fervor to protect a Filipino woman whose life hangs in the balance. Meanwhile, Sal finds himself in a dangerous game of cat and mouse, his quest for justice pitting him against ruthless adversaries.

The lives of the Cooper family intertwine within the epic tapestry of WWII. In the tradition of Jeff Shaara and Ken Follett, *The Light After the Storm* delivers an epic tale of heroism and sacrifice that will captivate readers from beginning to end.

ABOUT THE AUTHOR

Chris Glatte graduated from the University of Oregon with a BA in English Literature and worked as a river guide/kayak instructor for a decade before training as an Echocardiographer. He worked in the medical field for over 20 years, and now writes full time. Chris is the author of multiple historical fiction thriller series, including A Time to Serve and Tark's Ticks, a set of popular WWII novels. He lives in Southern Oregon with his wife, two boys, and ever-present Labrador, Hoover. When he's not writing or reading, Chris can be found playing in the outdoors—usually on a river or mountain.

From Chris:

I respond to all email correspondence.
Drop me a line, I'd love to hear from you!
chrisglatte@severnriverbooks.com

Sign up for Chris Glatte's reader list at severnriverbooks.com/authors/chris-glatte